Praise for EYES OF THE SEER

"This isn't Twilight folks, Peter is now a Vampire. He has enhanced senses, increased stamina, intense bloodlust, and a fondness for swords. He has disassociated from his humanity even further by taking on the new name Flynn. The ensuing story isn't puppies and lollipops. In a sophisticated and eloquent manner very reminiscent of early Anne Rice, we are taken through Peter/Flynn's journey from healer, to Vampire, to Assassin."
Author Jessica Fortunato
THE SIN COLLECTOR

"*Eyes of the Seer* is a vampire story at its core, but you can throw out all cliches. Flynn is a complex character, a man who's both gritty and sleek, who's been delivered into his new life by a delicious coven of classy, sophisticated, sharp-dressing blood drinkers in the city of Philadelphia."
Author Jodi McClure from Grit City Fiction
SWING ZONE

"I've been lucky enough to see this story evolve from a rough to the form it's in now. And man, it has grown into a polished, decadent tale of evil plots, warring supernatural forces, and zee power o' love. I recommend this to anyone tired of the modern 'vampire fad,' for these vampires are traditional, bloodthirsty gods in the night. But in each of them, a streak of humanity runs, and how that influences their 'dominant nature' makes a great mess of things, but a great treat to the reader. The ensuing drama is a tale worthy of being told, and the author tells it with skill and excitement. Plus you know you've always wanted to read about an angry vampire slicing other vampires in half with a katana. Don't deny it."
Author Heather Watson
THE DROWNED

"This book really explores humanity, and the struggle of one's self. Peter struggles reconciling the man and the monster throughout most of the book. Also, on a more subtle level is the question of freedom. Are you responsible for the deeds you have done if you were manipulated? The author presents both themes beautifully."
Author Noree Cosper
TRIP THE ECLIPSE

The Vampire Flynn

Eyes of the Seer
Rebirth of the Seer
Fate of the Seer

⁌⁗

Short Stories by Peter Dawes
Featuring The Vampire Flynn

Hunting on Halloween

A Vampire's Game

Short Stories Published by Crimson Melodies

Karyn Mitchell - To Sir, With Love

Victor Mason - Urchin of Atoranon

October 2011

EYES OF THE SEER

BOOK ONE OF THE VAMPIRE FLYNN

PETER DAWES

CRIMSON MELODIES PUBLISHING

A Crimson Melodies Book

Copyright © 2007-2011 by Peter Dawes
Edited by J.R. Wesley
All rights reserved, including the right to reproduce this book or portions thereof in any form whatsoever, without permission in writing from the publisher.

www.crimsonmelodies.com
www.vampireflynn.com

Front Cover Design © 2011 by Crimson Melodies
Front Cover Illustration by Christine Griffin
http://quickreaver.deviantart.com
Swirl Parts Brush by Obsidian Dawn
http://obsidiandawn.com

ISBN: 978-0-615-55893-6

"He who fights monsters should look into it
that he himself does not become a monster.
When you gaze long into the Abyss,
the Abyss also gazes into you."

Friedrich Nietzsche

PROLOGUE

I spent the final days of my life alone, even though I did not know I was dying. Around me, the world seemed to be shifting. A cloud of darkness shrouded what had once been an ordinary existence and ripped from me everything I had known. For long hours, I would stand at work and stare at the people who passed me by as though attempting to figure out what changed and when. Little did I know what waited for me around the corner.

Granted, the final days leading up to the earliest hours of January 20, 1983 are somewhat of a blur to me. It might have been the enchantment I was under, or the haze of realizing I lived on borrowed time without knowing how I could be certain of such a thing. I could not tell you what those final nights were like, or if anybody could sense the fact that I was fading in the background, about to cross paths with destiny. About to slip from one skin to another. I only know that night, it all reached a crescendo and set me on the path I find myself today.

I have lived many lives by now. I have held many titles and been several people and several things already. There were years when I gazed at others with compassion latent in my stare, and years when I beheld each victim I have claimed with coldness before sending them to meet their maker. Saint and sinner; bastard, friend, and foe. So many deaths and so many rebirths. So many layers to this creature I am. This being I became.

I am a vampire, but I have not always been. I can yet recall the days when I bore a pulse. Some memories stick out much more potently than others, but the first quarter century of my immortal existence frames the lot of them in a panorama of cause and effect. Through everything I face and have faced, I can look back upon the events which preceded me and see where I have arrived and how I have arrived there. I can see the hand of fate.

Oh, if only I would have known.

Back when this all began, if I could have seen the clear path to the present, I often wonder if I would have walked gracefully into the trials which followed. I would like to think so, but I know the experiences which have filled the years. The highs and lows; the moments of despair and the moments of triumph, they have made me what I am. I am vampire, yes, but I am no ordinary immortal. I still feed as one. I possess the fangs, the will, and the consuming instincts of one. The casual observer misses something very important when it comes to me, though; a very crucial feature beneath the unruly brown hair and above the crooked smile.

Most people do not know what they should be looking for when they see me. Not many humans recognize the emerald green eyes or know of their relevance for very good reason - because unique creatures such as I do not wish for them to know. There exists an entire world underneath their noses they overlook every day and only when the supernatural falls onto their laps do they learn of its presence. I was much the same as them a few decades ago, an unsuspecting, unknowing mortal with pale blue eyes instead of the ethereal irises I now possess.

I shall not linger any longer on riddles. Suffice to say there are many layers to this creature who inhabits this mortal coil, and yet the world around me rarely casts a second glance my way. When the Fates fashioned what would be my existence, they created a paradox; an eternal enigma.

My name is Peter Dawes and this is my story.

It all started with a murder.

PART ONE

⁓

THE BLIND

"If man were immortal he could be perfectly
sure of seeing the day when everything
in which he had trusted should betray his trust."

Charles Sanders Peirce

CHAPTER ONE

I cannot recall what caused the clarion bell to sound an alarm through my psyche, but all at once the haze shrouding my world began to lift. Time froze and an epiphany struck in all its horrible glory.

I had completely and utterly screwed up.

Blood covered my hands. I gazed down at the knife I held, both fixated on the sight and yet failing to see it. A thought echoed over and over that this was some twisted nightmare I would wake from, but I could not help trying to piece together facts until reality could finally set in. Recollections jumbled into a mosaic I focused hard on deciphering with wide eyes and furrowed brow. It left me naked before my own scrutiny, lost with the unpleasant reminder that my life thus far had been filled with more than a fair amount of calamity. Except this event trumped any which preceded it.

Lifting my gaze from the weapon poised in my palm, I spied them lying there. Two people, a man and a woman. And both of them were dead.

My knees gave out. I slid down the bedroom wall. Settling on the floor as the knife dropped from my slackened grip, I brought both hands to my head and rocked back and forth. I had walked in on her, this was true. She looked at me and screamed; yes, yes, I recalled this as well. It was when the other person shot out of bed that my memories seemed to shatter like a pane of glass. I struggled to replay the events, my head throbbing and the sensation of the knife's hilt lingering on my skin.

The knife. I fetched it from the kitchen. Oh God, what had I done?

Curling up with my back to the wall, I hugged my knees and winced. The dam of shock buckled under the weight of too many images crowding in at once. Too many images, such as her calling out, "*No, Peter! This isn't what you think!*" and me spitting out the words, "*You selfish whore, what did you do? What did you do?!*" An involuntary laugh suddenly broke the silence when I remembered the bastard she had been fondling. He fell to the floor, tripping over his own jeans, and barely came to a stand by the time I rushed upon him.

Tears clouded my eyes. Hysterics burst forth from my lips. Neither convinced me I yet possessed my right mind, but did nothing to make me feel justified in what I did next either. Rather, I plunged deeper into the abyss while crimson tainted the black and white movie playing in my mind.

He was my first victim. I did not pause to ask his name. I gave no warning of what I meant to do. Instead, I charged forward with the kitchen knife and sank it deep into his stomach. His face contorted in pain, but as he looked up at me he revealed a sight I found strangely delicious. My gaze focused on his neck. I licked my lips and slashed the blade across his throat. Whatever he had been struggling to say, the gash ensured he would speak no longer.

My senses should have come screaming back when he hit the ground, but my lover of two years looked at me with glassy eyes and her tears were not for me. Enraged, I closed the distance between us and tore her gold chain away from her neck. The knife plunged through her chest with sickening ease and I held it there while staring her in the eyes. Moments ticked by as hers dimmed and became vacant. The instrument of her death slipped from her body when she crumpled to the floor.

"I have to get out of here," I whispered, swiping at my cheeks as recent memory converged with the present. Two dead bodies lay before me. A lifetime of remorse loomed on the horizon. My fingers left bloody tribal war paint smudges where I had touched my face, but I did not care. In fact, I was amazed when my weak knees supported my weight and allowed me to pick myself up.

I stumbled down the hallway to her front door. The thought occurred to me that her neighbors may have heard the screams emanating from the apartment. They might be gathered outside, a lynch mob with pitchforks and torches to carry off the monster I had become. When I swung open the door, however, I saw nothing more than an empty corridor. So I trudged forward, not knowing where I intended to go yet realizing I could not stay there.

Images assailed me again.

I saw the look in her eyes as our gazes locked, her brain not yet dead from the lack of life-giving oxygen. "*Peter... I'm sorry.*" That miserable bitch. Why did she say she was sorry? Why did she rob me of a pure lover's vengeance by staining my actions with her repentance?

My walk became a run.

I remembered the scowl of hate I shot her in return. "*Burn in hell,*" I muttered. How could I say that? Did I not realize what I had just done? Even if her love for me was cast aside with such callousness, mine for her still held strong.

Hysteria threatened to claim me. I dashed for the door to the outside and slammed through it, only to recoil when the cold of January rushed headlong into me. Once again, the idea of being lost – vulnerable – struck me.

I ran toward the street, trying to escape the guilt pounding through my head. The angry mob might not have been following me, but my conscience was and its feet moved swifter than mine. I passed beneath awnings of upscale apartment buildings, raced across a dimly-lit park, and when a patch of Philadelphia asphalt suddenly stretched before me, I darted across it without caring one iota for the traffic.

One car swerved, then another, but I did not remain on the street for long. The urge to disappear from view became too overwhelming for me to ignore, so I dodged down an alleyway, still running from the pain threatening to tear me limb from limb. I heard footsteps closing in. I felt breath against my neck that prickled my skin. I sensed a presence enveloping me. None of which prepared me for the abrupt way my sprint came to a halt.

It was as though my conscience obtained corporeal form; or so I thought at the time. Ignorance converged with my own frenzied panicking and prevented me from understanding when one hand grabbed me, followed by another. I struggled wildly against the grip, screaming, "I was going to marry her! It isn't my fault! Oh God, why did she do this to me? Why did she make me kill her?!" The pair of hands kept firm grasp of me through my manic attempts to break away, and I continued shouting pleas for understanding until my attackers silenced my rant with a swift smack against my throat. Suddenly, I began to realize I was not being held back by my conscience at all.

The second clue was even more painful.

I felt a tongue slide along my neck milliseconds before a set of sharp teeth pierced my skin. Hollering as an afterthought, I gasped while blood ran down to my chest and mingled with the sweat already present. The lips pressed against my flesh pursed and drew inward. A sickening sucking noise resonated in my ears and the hands around me tightened.

My eyes fluttered shut. My head bobbed. I could not see the face of my attacker, but had little desire to as my pulse became faint and my knees threatened to buckle a second time that night. Whoever held me prevented me from falling over while my brain commenced the same shut down I had witnessed when Lydia had collapsed at my feet.

"... Lydia." I whispered her name as though remembering it for the first time through all the chaos. It formed all the apology my dying breaths could manage before I was robbed of the chance to add any further words of remorse.

Instead, the cool flesh of somebody's wrist touched my lips. It silenced even my thoughts and focused my fleeting attention toward a viscous liquid which ran into my mouth. The moment I tasted blood, a foreign notion stirred my senses the same way seeing the exposed throat of Lydia's lover had. A feminine voice spoke in a soothing manner. "Drink," she said. "Take it in, Peter. Because tonight, we will fulfill your destiny."

I drew inward once, compelled by the woman's command. It restored enough of my strength for me to drink again, leaving me wanting more without knowing why. In fact, I became more and more ravenous with each mouthful of blood and did not realize I'd grabbed hold of her arm until a violent pulse of pain caused my fingers to tighten. My mouth lifted from her wrist so I could cry out in agony. Before I figured out what was happening, another wave of fatigue struck.

My body slumped into a set of arms. The world drifted from my consciousness while voices spoke around me in a dissonant manner. My breaths became shallow, then ceased altogether, and I drifted to sleep.

Little did I know, as my heart stopped its rhythmic beating, the blood I had been given belonged to a vampire.

I had just lived my final night as a mortal.

CHAPTER TWO

A voice resonated through the blackness, stretching toward me as though echoing down a long corridor. At first I could not understand what it said. Its cadence was far too dream-like and my thoughts were too fragmented to assemble the pieces. It took several moments, but eventually the voice gained volume and purpose.

"Peter, dear," she said. "It's time for you to wake."

I struggled to ignore her as she continued trying to draw me out from void. Already, I knew something was different and there seemed to be too many alterations for my rational brain to take in all at once. Even the air about me felt changed. So, I twisted my consciousness away from the woman calling me, but her voice persisted. "Come now, young one. Rise and embrace your destiny."

It pushed me another step closer to the surface. As I stumbled forward, a host of strange sensations began overwhelming me, contradicting the romanticism of her words. Rather than being some pleasurable entanglement with 'destiny', waking brought with it nothing more than excruciating pain that threatened to strangle me. I gasped for breath, but the act of breathing stung and the air sat useless in my lungs before being exhaled noisily. Every sense and synapse in my body fired simultaneously. The initial pangs of awareness were not to be the worst of it, though. They built to a crescendo when I opened my eyes.

The burning intensified and localized. I screamed, struggling to keep my eyes open while the light filling the room waged an assault against them. Turning my head to the side, I discovered I lay on a bed, and found myself being subjected to the scrutiny of three strangers - two men and one woman. Their piercing eyes regarded me in silence, watching me tremble, and apparently unmoved by the sight. In turn, I studied them, knowing something about my sight had changed, but unable to place it before the agony became too much for me to bear.

I clenched my eyes shut and flipped onto my stomach.

"Peter, calm down."

My fingers clawed at the sheets. I buried my head into a pillow to block out more of the light. "Make it stop," I said. "Fucking kill me if you have to, just make it stop."

"We can't kill you, Peter." Her voice stayed eerily calm while issuing the response. The woman who brought me into this hell in the first place walked closer and sat on the edge of the bed. "What is it that hurts, dear child?"

"My eyes." I moaned. "My fucking eyes are burning."

"Michael, turn off the lights." The sound of fabric rustling preceded a series of footsteps pacing to the other side of the room. Tempted to furrow my brow at how distinctly I heard each action, I instead lost myself inside a flood of relief once darkness crashed over me. Still, the rest of my body continued to tremble.

"What..." A pained breath punctuated the one word I managed. I swallowed more air and waited for something - anything - to feel familiar, but even inhaling could not provide me that comfort. I coughed out the wasted oxygen and regrouped. "What... did you do to me?"

A hand reached forward, attempting to settle atop my head, but I flinched away. It retreated at once. "Peter, the woman said. The calm in her voice felt contagious, threatening to soothe me regardless of how little I wished to be soothed at the moment. "Don't you remember our discussions? Do you know who I am?"

"I don't know who the hell I am right now."

"Look at me, dear. It's alright. The lights are out now."

I wanted to look at her about as much as I wished to be calmed by her, but something told me I would have to face her at some point. Slowly, carefully, I pushed off the mattress and lifted my gaze toward the woman talking to me. The sight of her started an immediate debate, one I indulged while taking a moment to evaluate her.

Did I recall her? Yes, there was something familiar about her. Her flowing red hair fell over strong shoulders and her suit accentuated a curvy, slim body. Middle-aged in appearance yet still quite attractive, her face stirred the recesses of memory but left me with nothing more than a fleeting sense of déjà vu. She gazed at me like a mother and I found myself regarding her as a son. "Who are you?" I asked, my voice reduced to a whisper.

She smiled. "You know who I am and yet, you have no idea." She reached forward, her fingers grazing past my cheek. This time, I did not flinch. "My name is Sabrina. I'm sorry, this part is never easy, dear. It will take you some time to adjust."

"Adjust," I said, trying to decipher the word and its relationship to me. The riddle too much for me to unravel, I allowed my eyes to wander toward the others. I sensed no sort of recognition; nothing like what I experienced when I first laid eyes on Sabrina. Instead, I was left to clinically observe what I kept thinking of as a silent jury.

A woman in sensual, Gothic dress remained seated next to a dark-haired man in a finely-tailored suit. Her hair blonde, it flowed down her shoulders and framed a face with pale, green eyes which looked terminally bored. The man sighed, his blue eyes shifting from me to anywhere else as though avoiding my gaze. The third onlooker, however, stood against the wall, close to where the light switch was. He scrutinized me with the most disdain, his long hair tied back in a ponytail and a three-piece suit hanging from a wiry frame. The corner of his mouth was curled in a condescending grin, and I vaguely recalled Sabrina calling him Michael a few minutes beforehand. Without one word exchanged between us, I knew he loathed me. The sentiment was rapidly becoming mutual.

My gaze returned to Sabrina. "Why does it hurt?" I asked, with the pitiful frailty of a child.

Sabrina smiled. "Young one, you have just risen from the crossing," she said. "You are facing this harsh world as a newborn again."

"What's that supposed to mean?" I brought my hands to my head. Crossing? Sabrina's words looped in a nonsensical manner. I did not have the foggiest idea what a 'crossing' was. "How long have I been asleep?" I asked. "A few hours? A day?"

"A bit longer than that." Sabrina paused. "Do you remember what happened before you fell asleep?"

I blinked, trying to recall anything prior to the pain of waking. That was when one memory came crashing through the haze. "I remember a knife," I said, my eyes gazing into the distance. "I had been holding a knife and then I ran. I stabbed her. I stabbed Lydia."

She frowned. "Yes, I've never seen one so covered in blood prior to the conversion. Such violence doesn't make this transition any easier, but you have been given the gift you asked for..." The next words caused me a start, as though Sabrina read my previous thoughts. "... my new son."

I perked an eyebrow. "Gift?"

"Yes, gift." Sabrina's frown settled into a more even expression and her eyes drifted away. I shifted into a seated position, forced to spend a few additional seconds to get my wits about me when a slight wave of dizziness followed the effort. Glancing down at my body, I regarded the simple pair of khaki slacks and black, button-down shirt which hung from my frame. It occurred to me for the first time that I was feeling weak.

My gaze shifted back to Sabrina as she continued speaking. "You told me about your parents," she said. "About being a doctor. Do you remember? How everything in life seems so transient and how you wished to be part of something more permanent?"

I struggled to recall the conversation. Familiar though it was, the words echoed at me from the other side of an impenetrable wall. I closed my eyes and shook my head. "I want to remember, but I can't."

"No reason to be concerned," Sabrina said. "It's all part of the process. Some vampires have a hard time recalling much from their past lives, I'm afraid, until the initial shock wears off."

The word forced my eyes open. "Vampires?"

Sabrina smiled wide, baring a set of pointed fangs. "Yes, my dear. You have become one of us. Just as you asked to be."

The sight of her ungodly daggers frightened a shout past my lips. I backed away with such sudden force, I fell off the other side of the bed. Struggling to my feet, I fought past another bout of dizziness while finding the wherewithal to retreat. Sabrina came to her feet and walked toward me as I backed away, her steps slow and cautious. "Peter, don't be afraid..."

My back hit a wall. "I don't believe you," I said, frenzied, "I don't believe any of this." My eyes shifted toward the others as they peered at me with upturned eyebrows. "Who are you people?!"

Sabrina did not allow them to respond. "Those are your brethren."

I shook my head once more and edged along the wall until I stopped by the corner of the room. This beast of a woman I initially found captivating came closer to where I stood and I, in turn, pressed against the wall. "No," I said. "I don't know you. I've never met any of you. This is a nightmare I'm going to wake up from when I..."

"Peter," Sabrina interrupted. "This isn't a dream. You've been asleep for almost a week..."

"No I haven't..."

"... and during the course of that week..."

"No. Stop. I'm not listening to you."

"... you've died and been reborn again."

"*Stop saying that!*" I shouted with a hiss, but the death knell to my denial sounded its toll when I felt something cut into my lower lip. Although I had closed my eyes to holler, they shot open when I realized that whatever the 'something' was, it was coming from my mouth. One shaky hand relinquished its hold on the wall and lifted, hesitating at first before tracing the contours of a sharp, pointed incisor akin to Sabrina's. My hand recoiled in shock, but the wall of truth had been broken. Curiosity took the reins away.

I raised my other hand, touching a complementary dagger on the other side of my mouth. Inhaling another breath amplified the silence in my chest. My fingers lowered to my neck, searching for a pulse, and met with nothing but cool flesh without the normal rhythm of a heartbeat. I was dead and yet, there I stood with fangs exposed. "It's true," I said, my voice just above a whisper. My eyes found Sabrina again. "I've become a vampire."

She smiled with relish. "Welcome to the coven," she said. "Don't worry, all of the answers will come in time."

At first, I nodded in semi-acceptance, but an unfamiliar shiver crawled up my spine that no amount of disbelief could stand against. A litany of symptoms blossomed with greater intensity the longer my fangs remained exposed. I felt dizzy; my throat felt dry and an infantile thought brought me face-to-face with my first entanglement with bloodlust.

I was hungry. So very hungry.

Sabrina's voice broke through my senses. "Are you alright, my new son?" she asked. When our eyes connected, however, her look of anxiety morphed into a wicked smile. "You're hungry."

I leaned my head back and stared toward the ceiling. "Yes, I am," I said, although the term 'hunger' did little to capture the all-consuming thirst overwhelming me. "I need something to eat. I don't think I've eaten in a while."

The grin on her face broadened. She turned toward the man standing on the opposite side of the room. "Michael, bring in the girl," she said. "It's time we taught your brother how to feed."

"As you wish, Mistress," Michael said, emphasizing the term of address in what struck me as a disdainful manner. He flashed another condescending smirk at me before departing, and I fought the urge to sneer back at him. If he was to be the solution to the problem I faced, I did not wish to raise his ire. Still, I choked back a sizable amount of contempt as I shut my eyes and waited for his return.

A few moments later, the door opened. An intoxicating aroma emanated from the doorway and my eyelids lifted to behold a woman, hands bound and mouth gagged. She regarded me with panic-stricken eyes as Michael forced her further into the room. The sight of her fear intrigued me and the steady pulse I heard summoned a craving unlike any I had ever experienced before. Where once I would have looked at her and seen a human being, hunger reduced her down to little more than the means to sate my need.

Michael held her steady. "Come here and observe me," he said.

I nodded and stepped closer, my gaze shifting to my new immortal sibling. Michael's fangs slid down, forcing me to shiver while he pressed his nose against the girl's neck and drew in a deep breath. She squeaked pitifully.

He ignored it, as did I.

"You can always tell where it is the sweetest by their scent," he said. Michael closed his eyes and ceased his pursuit at a certain spot. "Those sharp teeth you possess cut deep enough to reach it. I will demonstrate."

I watched the girl jump when Michael's fangs pierced her skin. Blood ran down in rivulets, staining her shirt and producing a sight which unnerved and excited me all at once. Her eyes brimmed with tears, but again I found myself strangely apathetic to her plight. Instead, the viscous, red liquid running from her veins held my interest captive.

Michael pulled away and lifted his eyes to regard me. "Now, your turn. Don't think about it, merely do it."

Nodding, I approached the woman, her potent scent tangling me inside an enchanting web. I wrestled with the notion of ripping her apart and imbibing whatever did not spill to the ground, but images of Michael's fangs driving into her flesh lulled me into a fledgling form of temptation. I rather liked the way that bite looked. So sensual – intimate, even. A communion with this frail being for fleeting seconds before she had nothing left to offer.

Without further thought, I allowed my senses to become saturated with her and ran my nose along her neck until that golden spot gripped me and forced me to pause. With that, I drove my teeth into her neck and spilled forth the first drops of human blood I ever consumed.

The taste was exceptional, slipping past my tongue in rivers of ecstasy which stirred to life the most primeval of urges. It was reminiscent of the pleasure I had experienced while drinking from Sabrina's wrist, but this time the fire of human blood filled my veins and lit an inferno of all-consuming need. I drew inward with dire urgency, swallowing mouthfuls in a lusty manner, taking her in until she had to be held upright.

Her pulse wavered before ceasing altogether. My fangs retracted and the heat of blood warmed the chill of my body, filling me with sated contentedness. I pulled away, my eyes closed, and allowed my victim's depleted body to crumple to my feet.

"Very good, my son," Sabrina said, her voice ebbing toward me through the haze of afterglow. "It's like you were born to be a killer."

I turned my head to look at her, still ignorant of so many things. I could not remember who I was beyond the vision of a knife and flashes of imagery centered on confessing the death of a girl named Lydia, but the lack of memories from my past life failed to bother me at that moment. I could only think of how it felt to drain that girl dry.

"I could get used to being a vampire," I said, allowing my gaze to shift away from Sabrina and the others. A sinister grin overtook me and my own voice rang peculiar in my ears. The being speaking now was a different man than the one who had died; I had no need of remembering my mortality to be certain of that much. With one mere feed I had transcended even the frightened being that woke with his eyes blinded by pain. Something squeezed away that fear and dread, replacing it with an enamored state of euphoria.

I smiled as it left a mark on my psyche. Its caress was cold and calculating; sadistic and enchanting. "Yes, I enjoyed that very much," I said with a nod. "In fact, I'd like to do it again."

CHAPTER THREE

The taste of blood far sweeter than I could have ever imagined, it remained on the tip of my tongue as though taking up residence. The lingering memory of the woman from whom I drank burned upon my soul as an everlasting tribute, the experience without parallel even if I did not have much with which I could compare it.

Regardless of how hard I tried, I still did not recall who this man named Peter had been prior to waking. A fleeting recollection of Lydia remained the sole concept I possessed of who I was, and even that painted a grim picture. I saw myself crying toward the night sky, expressing remorse over the fatal wounds I had inflicted, but another piece to the puzzle provided a sharp contrast to my tear-stained repentance. The sight of blood; I remembered slitting the throat of the man in Lydia's bed and knew I had enjoyed it. My vampire instincts reveled in it, taking hold of it as proof Sabrina was right. I was born to be a killer.

That moment marked the genesis of a dichotomy.

The seed planted did not bear fruit immediately. At first, the gaping, black holes forming my past life were a wide enough berth for the fledgling vampire to roam free. My new condition had me far too enamored to lament the absence of my past recollections and as such, I merely lived within the moment, with no thought or reservation given over to what I did. Blood seared my conscience, cauterizing it from the start.

The morning following my awakening, I returned to my new quarters after a night spent becoming acquainted with the other immortals in the coven. More crimson was spilled, and wine and decadence teased me with a hint of nights to come.

It should be noted none of this would have been possible without a pair of sunglasses. Before Sabrina presented me to the others, we had tested the lights only to discover they continued to burn my eyes, something which both surprised and yet did not surprise my mistress all at once. When asked about it, she said, "This just makes you unique," before turning to Rose – the female member of the silent jury – and asking her to fetch the darkest lenses she could find.

She received no help from Michael in the venture, which started to become a trend. The next evening, it was Sabrina who entered my room after the siren call of night threw my eyes open and woke the thirst within me. By the time she arrived, my fangs ached and I could not retract them. My eyes immediately gravitated toward what she held as the scent of blood became pervasive throughout the room.

"My young one hungers," Sabrina said fondly the moment she saw my condition. She sat beside me and handed over a goblet filled to the brim with that thick, scarlet liquid I now worshipped. I consumed it with vigor, drinking each drop as though starved. She watched with barely bridled enthusiasm.

Lowering the empty cup, I wiped the remnant from my mouth and asked, "Why didn't you have me feed from a mortal?"

Her brown eyes danced. In that moment, the sensuality she wore so effortlessly spoke to every baser part of me, dispelling any doubt of why she caught my eye as a human. A simple response drifted past her luscious, ruby lips. "We are going to teach you how to hunt." Little did I realize the concept would captivate me as much as it did. She led me from the room, entrusting the short-haired vampire present for my awakening – Timothy – with the task of assisting me.

On our way outside, though, we passed Michael in the foyer. His conversation with a younger-looking vampire named Charles paused just long enough for him to watch me pass. We exchanged a look of mutual disdain, and then severed the gaze. I dismissed it, but only for the time being, in favor of focusing on the task at hand.

Though the lesson itself was as rudimentary as biting a mortal, the hunt enchanted me far more so. My predatory instincts took hold of it naturally; my ears only distantly hearing Timothy speak of the harmony of a pulse and the allure of a human's scent. The first mortal to cross our path became my next victim and their death was just as insignificant to me as the one from the previous evening. I discovered stalking them was a game of unparalleled thrill.

Successive nights were spent lavished in blood and lessons. Sabrina summoned me to the common area one night the next week and left me in Michael's care, saying, "Teach your brother the things he needs to know." Her instructions seemed to leave a poor taste in both our mouths. I thanked heaven for my visual infirmity at that moment, as my sunglasses blocked the annoyed look in my eyes while Sabrina walked away.

Michael huffed and motioned for me to follow him toward the opposite end of the room. "Well, now that you're a vampire, we must keep you from destroying yourself in neophyte stupidity," he said as we passed several of the others. His manner of speech struck me as odd for the first time; a distinctive brogue laced his words with what I thought might be British or Irish, or both. It bore a formality also present in Timothy's more American accent, and inspired me to glance around the room and take stock of the well-tailored suits and handmade dresses surrounding me. It made my hand-me-down shirts and slacks pale in comparison.

In that instant, I realized I had been born into a haven for bloodthirsty sophisticates.

"Are you listening to a word I'm saying?"

My gaze shifted back to Michael, a sarcastic grin accompanying my response. "Loud and clear," I said. "Keep the idiot from killing himself."

"So long as you recognize your station." Michael lifted an eyebrow, regarding me in silence for a moment before looking away. He did not bother to sit when I did, merely paced around avoiding eye contact as he laid out before me the first of several instructions.

It did not take long for me to discover that most of what mortals know about vampires is absolute nonsense. Certainly, the rumor about feeding on blood revealed itself in all its naked honesty as did another vital tenet which Michael laid out in the very first lesson. "When you see the sky lighten, you must seek refuge at once," he said while leaning against the wall. "Do not question how many minutes you may have. Get inside before the sun has chance to rise."

"What will happen if I'm caught outside at daytime?" I asked.

Michael huffed. "Well, we will be certain to sweep up your remnant when the sun sets."

"What do you mean by 'remnant'?"

"Dust, dear brother." Impatience dripped from the term of endearment. "You will be dust and nothing more. There's a good reason why it's called a curse."

I perked an eyebrow, but did not ask him to elaborate any further. Although the word curse manifested itself multiple times, the picture he painted hardly seemed like a curse to me. Yes, stakes through the heart would kill us, as would decapitation. Starvation would weaken us and possibly push us to the brink of insanity. The young ones must feed, he said, and I certainly had no qualms with that. I was well on my way to indulging the hunt like an art form.

From there, the dismissal of superstitions surfaced; holy water was nothing more than water, crosses were religious iconography, and garlic merely a mortal delicacy. Michael barely touched on the sensual aspects of being immortal, but he had no need of doing so. I discovered those well enough on my own.

The night whispered tempting prospects in my ear each evening as though it had become a tender lover. Dark, warm, and satisfying, blood ran from mortal veins into my throat for three blissful weeks of ignorance. I became more attuned to my amplified senses each time I stalked and fed. My new eyes, sensitive though they were, possessed a level of awareness I was certain they did not have when I had been mortal. Tools of a hunter, they could track any moving creature within the darkness in detail. My sunglasses did nothing to hinder them. My hearing had become amplified as well, quite literally allowing me to hear a pin drop in a quiet room.

Neither my eyes, nor ears, were what held me hostage the most, though. The chase was thrilling, yes, and my limbs moved with strength and agility mortals could only dream of possessing. But nothing could surmount the scent of fear and the taste of unadulterated terror I was able to inspire in the hearts of my victims.

Sustaining the disconnect between what I once was and that which I had become gave me no problem at first, but as I stalked a mortal one evening – alone, having proven myself able to hunt without detection – the cadence of a whisper grew in volume and jarred me straight from my feed. I heard a voice speak in my head and a name resurfaced along with an unwelcome visitor from the grave.

Lydia.

Something other than the memory of her dropping dead at my feet rushed through my newborn vampire haze and brought me face to face with a creature that looked strangely familiar. In my mind, I saw a reflection of the person whose identity she called outward, a tall man with sympathetic blue eyes. That man had been me.

'Peter Dawes, I love you.'

The first time my full mortal name surfaced and it occurred with a woman clinging to the final spark of life, my arms wrapped around her and my fangs still deep inside her neck. I pulled away and took several deep breaths, having no need of the air but plenty of need for steadying myself. The dam of recollection had yet to burst, but it buckled just the same.

Who was Peter Dawes?

This proved to be the most dangerous question I could possibly ask. I finished the woman and discarded her lifeless body, but my steps back to the coven house were uncertain, my mind tracing over the question again and again. Images of me screaming toward the sky, accompanied by the guilt – the horrible, wracking guilt – which held me in its unrelenting throes the night I died resurfaced as though I had lost all control of my mental faculties. Who was Peter Dawes? Whoever he had been, he did not revel in death nearly as much as I did.

In fact, he seemed to loathe it to the point of inconsolable madness.

My rest that morning was unsettled for the first time in my short, immortal life. I tossed and turned, seeing dualistic pictures play out of my mortal self murdering two people and subsequently losing his mind. This Peter seemed closer to the Peter who first woke, petrified over the change that had taken place within him. He cowered in the corner of my mind, until I woke and the instincts of a vampire silenced his voice by bringing temptation back to my doorstep.

That following evening, my brethren knew something was the matter with me. I became short with each one, especially Michael when his attitude flared once more. "What is it, Peter? Having a difficult evening?" he asked with mocking sarcasm. I ignored it, but the taunts only worsened as my recollections mounted.

Searching for my identity wound the clock backward, and the more I sought myself, the more I realized what I found buried deep inside was no vampire. Peter Dawes not only loved the woman he conscripted to death, he protected life itself with determination. A cast of characters manifested themselves within my psyche, searching for something other than this pale-faced creature when they dove into the recesses of my soul.

They sought someone benevolent, someone with a passion for life and vitality for what he did. Sitting alone in my room with bloody sweat running down my forehead, words flew from my lips as though I was possessed. "Dr. Peter Dawes. Resident. Emergency room physician. Temple University Hospital." I shook and shivered, staring at my hands and seeing the pallor of death, imagining the red which stained them after I had murdered Lydia. In my mind's eye, the crimson thickened and pooled, beginning to drip from my fingertips as the blood of my other nameless victims joined hers.

Death, death; all around me was death. "What have I become?" I muttered to myself, clutching onto my body as a frightful cold descended into my bones. I scoured memory after memory, trying to determine how I started down this path in the first place, but my initial attempts were all in vain.

It was not until I remembered Sabrina that I found the answer.

⟡

The man who would become a killer found immortality in the most unlikely of places.

As my human memories resurfaced, I began to recall a coffee shop. The mental image gradually filled with day-to-day nuances and idle details. Things such as the crowds I used to see – when human beings were more than prey – materialized, as well as the thoughts I entertained when I found myself enjoying the house beverage and contemplating the state of my life. This is how she found me, my eyes distant while I mused with sadness over my relationship with Lydia.

It was the perfect timing for a vampiress to lure her latest conquest.

Lydia and I had been together for more than two years and although I could not yet recall everything about our time together, I distinctly knew that things had changed by the time my dark dance with immortality began. Where we once knew such closeness, it all seemed to be slipping away, given over to the distance of busy lives spent immersed in differing pursuits. I brooded over the sands of time, noting their pace outran my quest for happiness.

Sabrina sat across from me and startled me away from my thoughts.

I looked at her, jumping from the sudden appearance of the woman who would become my coven mistress. Her lips pursed together, hands knitted on her lap. She crossed her legs and regarded me with interest.

I raised an inquisitive eyebrow at her. "Can I help you?"

Sabrina lifted a hand and used it to cradle her chin as her elbow settled on the arm of the chair. She was vivacious, yet distinguished at the same time. I noticed the long, pristine nails that adorned her fingers as an afterthought. "I've never seen such a young man appear as though he was holding the weight of the world on his shoulders," she said. "You have me curious."

I shook my head. "Life," I said, spitting out the best summary of my thoughts I could fashion. "I'm just thinking about life, that's all."

"That's a pretty weighty subject, Mr. ..."

"Dawes, but please call me Peter."

"Peter," she said, allowing my name to roll off of her tongue as if tasting it. She nodded. "My name is Sabrina, Peter. A pleasure to meet you."

I nodded in return and reached forward. "Likewise." We exchanged a handshake over the table before sitting back in our seats once more. "I don't think I've ever seen you around here before," I said in the effort to make conversation.

"I take it that means you're a regular," she said, an amused glint emanating from her eyes as they plunged deeply into mine.

I did not mind the scrutiny, although I am certain I should have. "I'm a doctor at the hospital just up the street. I come here often."

"Ah, a doctor." Sabrina looked at my hands, studying them as she spoke. "Steady, strong hands." Her eyes lifted back toward mine. "And eyes that see a bit of death, I'm sure."

I winced at the reminder. "More than you can begin to imagine."

She raised an eyebrow. "Beyond the operating table?"

I met her eyes directly, and then looked away. "Mostly at the hospital, though I've seen it elsewhere. My parents were killed in a car accident." I paused, reliving the traumatic experience without knowing why I was disclosing this to a complete

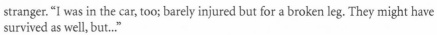

stranger. "I was in the car, too; barely injured but for a broken leg. They might have survived as well, but..."

When I trailed off, I detected the slightest hint of excitement radiating from Sabrina. She spoke before I could acknowledge it. "What happened?"

I looked back at her. "I didn't know how to help them. It took an hour for the police to arrive and I was too young to be able to do anything for them. That's why I became a doctor. I wanted to help people."

"Have you succeeded, Peter?"

"I don't know how to answer that question."

"Have you helped others avoid death?"

I frowned, my gaze drifting toward my hands. "That's the one thing about death, I've discovered. Even when you try to avoid it, it comes looking for you anyway."

"That it does, dear. The question is hardly whether it comes, but what it finds when it reaches you."

"What do you mean by that?"

She chuckled. "Some cower in fear at its presence and buckle when it looks for them, but others overcome it. They scoff at it and subjugate it, rather than allowing it to take possession of them. I rather prefer that attitude, don't you?"

"No one can subjugate death, Sabrina. It happens to all of us." I paused as a peculiar thought entered my mind. "Now, if only there was some way to avoid it altogether. I think I like that option much better."

Sabrina grinned and allowed my comment to linger, savoring it before offering her thoughts in return. With that simple confession, I had sealed my fate.

We had several discussions after the fact, whenever we chanced upon one another in the coffee shop, which always came back around to the macabre. What sorts of things I witnessed in the emergency room; the people who arrived beyond help, the people who were brought back from the brink. The constant stream of death and near misses I was forced to gaze upon each and every day. Her words poisoned my thoughts the more I spoke with her, until the evening she came right out and asked if I had ever treated puncture wounds.

I laughed and took a sip of my coffee. "Like knife wounds?"

"No, no, my dear," she said. She raised a daring eyebrow at me. "I mean something like vampire bites."

The statement nearly caused me to choke on my beverage. "Vampire bites? You have got to be joking."

Sabrina laughed, cupping her hand over her mouth in the process. "Oh Peter, let's say for the sake of argument that I'm not." Composing herself, she cleared her throat and challenged me with her gaze, the corner of her mouth still curled upward in amusement. "Have you ever treated anything like that?"

"No, Sabrina. I've never treated vampire bites."

Her smirk only solidified. "You find the idea incredulous, don't you?"

"Of course I do." I scoffed. "Vampires are monsters in horror movies. They don't exist."

"You're certain of this?"

"Oh please." I nearly punctuated the statement by rolling my eyes, but something caused me to stop. A strange premonition had been asserting its presence in recent days. For as long as I could remember, there had always been a melancholy darkness shrouding my demeanor, but I never sensed it nearly as much as I did when Sabrina was around. It had begun affecting the way I looked at everything.

My temper had started to surface a bit more readily. I was more distracted. My normally-keen focus at work was given over to strange daydreams and notions, many of them chillingly horrific. Just as soon as they would surface I would shake them away, but in that moment, sitting in the coffee shop, I sensed the chill in my soul attempt to wrap its bony fingers around me once more.

"Think of it, dear Peter." Sabrina's voice drifted to me as though through a dream. "A being elevated beyond death. Fanciful or not, you have to admit it's a tempting prospect."

I perked an eyebrow at the notion. Was it a tempting prospect? My thoughts returned to what I had been mulling on earlier and painted a frown on my face. "Yes, you're right," I said. "Perhaps being a vampire wouldn't be such a terrible thing."

Sabrina studied me intently. "What troubles you, Peter? Once again, I see the weight of the world on those shoulders of yours."

"Immortality," I said, my gaze distant as I stared across the room. Thoughts of Lydia wove with whatever strange revelation had me in its throes. All at once, it caved in on me; her distance and our periods of separation. The surety I thought I had, being replaced by two busy schedules and two ships passing in the night. Lydia's own strange behavior with me, her absence, and the suspicious nature of it all. I shook my head. "Just when you feel as though you have something reliable – something permanent – it starts slipping away from you. I wish I could be immortal and not have to worry about..." I trailed off, struggling for the right word to encompass everything.

"Immortality can be as much of a curse as it is a blessing."

I scoffed, my eyes drawn toward her again. "I don't see how that could be a curse, Sabrina. Everybody wants to live forever."

"Not many people are able to handle the responsibility of being something more than human, though." She leaned forward in her chair, her eyes grabbing hold of mine in an unrelenting grip. "Mortals long for death without realizing it. Could you handle eternity, dear Peter? Would you accept it if it was handed to you?"

My voice sounded queerly subdued as I spoke again. "I only want the things in my life to stop changing with the wind."

Sabrina's voice lowered as well. "Things like your girl?"

"Yes. Lydia." I closed my eyes. "We used to be inseparable, but she hasn't felt close to me lately. It seems as though we're drifting apart and..." I fell silent, unwilling to give voice to my fears.

I opened my eyes in time to see Sabrina perk an eyebrow at me. "And what, Peter? Wanting different things, as often happens between two people? She in search of her own pursuits and you in search of permanence?"

I was unable to respond, but Sabrina continued as she turned her head askew to size me up. I felt her drift closer to me without moving at all. A shiver ran down my spine. "What do you desire, dear confused one? Permanence? Or the fickle love of someone who could cast you away at a moment's notice? Which would you seek more if the option to be immortal were valid?"

"I don't know," I murmured, slack-jawed, as if in a trance.

"What if I could grant it to you? Here and now, on a silver platter. What would you ask for?"

"Immortality. I want to be sure about something for once."

Sabrina's voice descended into whisper. "Then ask me for it."

My eyes drifted shut. "Give me immortality, Sabrina."

"Open your eyes and claim it, dear child. Find your surety."

My lids shot open. I stood and excused myself, mind swimming, compelled to do something other than sit there. I had attempted to call Lydia on the phone earlier, but somehow the discussion of what was lasting and what was transient gave me the inclination to head for her apartment and clear the air once and for all.

I would never look upon the world with mortal eyes again after that night. For, as Sabrina watched me walk away, she had her own set of plans and was poised and ready to exact them. She found a searching, lost young man and rescued a murderer.

Now, Sabrina would train a killer out of me.

Chapter Four

Suspicious eyes seemed all about me, following me wherever I went. Paranoia infected the inner recesses of my psyche, not merely from the gaze of my brethren, but from the very cosmos. I felt as though the world watched each step I took, scrutinized me, weighed me and found this new manifestation of myself wanting. It disquieted me down to the pit of my soul.

I became a belligerent bastard.

Hunting lost its intrigue. Snapshots of my mortal life ebbed into my consciousness with maddening slowness and tainted the thrill. I would see manifestations of Lydia while feeding, and when the lifeless bodies of my victims dropped to my feet, I saw her face on them. Blinking past the sight did nothing to eliminate the shivers which ran up my spine. A week of flirting with the threshold of insanity brought me face-to-face with the truth. I was a conflicted man with half his memories.

Although the prospect of recalling anything else should have scared me away from exploration I pursued it nonetheless, as much teased as haunted by the gaps in my memory. I spent several nights pondering Lydia's murder until the distorted memory of the knife sunk deep into her chest caused me to remember ripping her necklace from her throat. I furrowed my brow at the thought. Had I dropped the chain or carried it with me? Through the haze of trauma, I could not remember either way.

It led me to Sabrina one evening. She and I strolled down the corridor, Sabrina tapping her long nails against her chin as she spoke. "What happened to your personal effects?" she intoned, repeating the question I had cautiously posited to her. "Honestly, I have no idea. Your clothing was covered in blood and the rest were just mortal trivialities."

We passed another immortal as we walked down the corridor. Sabrina waved to him while I frowned. "Does that mean you threw them away?" I asked.

"The clothing, I'm certain, but Timothy might've stored away your other items." Sabrina stopped and turned to face me. "Why do you want them anyway? Is something the matter?"

I thanked heaven for my sunglasses as my eyes shifted away from her scrutiny. Shrugging, I buried my hands in my pockets. "Not exactly, no. I'm just having some issues with my..." I tapped my head twice. "... Memories."

Sabrina raised an eyebrow. "What about them?"

"They're incomplete. I can remember a few bits and pieces, but there are gaps."

"Why do you need to know such things? That life is over." Sabrina stepped closer to me, far closer than she had since the days of my awakening. She reached up, her fingers brushing through my hair and tousling the locks. "You are not a mortal any longer, dear. Why trouble yourself with the recollection of being one of those inferior humans we consume? You are forming a new life. Let the past lie in the grave."

"I know, but it's important to me." I caught one of my useless breaths in my throat when her fingertips slid past my cheek, her razor nails dragging across the flesh in a deliberate manner. "I... need to fill these blank spaces in so I can move on. Otherwise, they'll keep nagging at me." I attempted a disarming smile. "And we don't want that, right?"

"You concern me, my son." One finger coasted past my lips, and then her hand abruptly dropped to her side. She sighed and raised her eyes to mine. "If it will help you put matters to rest, then I will look for your mortal possessions. Beyond the clothing, what were you carrying?"

I glanced away, indulging in a steadying sigh to calm my spirit past the lingering sensation of Sabrina's touch. Focusing on my blurry memories, I replayed the mental picture of stabbing Lydia. "A watch. I'm sure a wallet. Some keys and..."

I paused. The image of Lydia's necklace in my hand shot a tingle through me as I saw my former self slide his hand into his pocket.

"And what?" Sabrina asked.

Shaking off the recollection, I looked at Sabrina again. "And a necklace, I think." I tried to conceal my enthusiasm over that last object, not having the slightest notion why it held my interest. My nervous gaze met Sabrina's. "The necklace would at least be worth pawning."

Sabrina eyed me for a few tentative moments before nodding. "Very well. I will have Timothy look for your personal items." Without any further words given over to the matter, Sabrina turned and walked away. Two nights later, a small bag containing these items found their way to my doorstep. I took it into my private quarters and dumped its contents onto my unmade bed.

I saw the keys and wallet I expected. The driver's license verified my identity and my last place of residence, and there was a small amount of money. Other forms of identification and old receipts were tucked into various pockets in my billfold, but no necklace. Sitting on my bed in an exasperated huff, I threw the wallet across the room and shoved the other items onto the floor without any further thought. As my eyes drifted back to the bed, however, I caught sight of something shimmering atop my black sheets.

The thin chain attempted to disappear within the folds of bedding before my fingers pinched around it, allowing me to raise it level with my line of sight. Even through my sunglasses, I noticed dried blood streaked across the pendant, staining two hearts with a thorny rose atop. On an impulse, I licked the blood, but dropped the jewelry when the remnant burned my tongue. I hissed at it on instinct, and then left it with the other discarded items.

Shortly thereafter, the dreams commenced.

⋅◦⊰☙⊱◦⋅

These were no mere shadows slipping from behind the veil; full-fledged memories took flight through my mind, painting animated snapshots of my mortal existence in its entirety. I witnessed twisted metal and death. I felt an ancient, psychosomatic ache in my leg. I saw the youth I once was and bolted awake from a sound slumber on more than one occasion as the defining moment in my life played out in nightmares.

Not that it was the first moment I recalled my parents were killed in a car accident. I remembered telling Sabrina about it in the coffee shop, but it had lacked any depth of detail. Now it was vivid. John and Marjorie Dawes gained life and lost it just as quickly as reverie gifted it to them. I was a petrified thirteen year old when they died, and their death changed the entire course of the rest of my life.

My father, a service veteran, met my mother in England and they married within months. Home became a farm in the middle of Pennsylvania and together, my parents created an environment of discipline and faith, one that possessed the warmth found in television shows and wistful paperbacks. I was a headstrong only child, but never had cause to question my parents' love for me.

It all ended in a car accident, giving birth to the real Peter Dawes.

The ambulance carried me, the sole survivor, from the scene with a compound fracture in my right leg. It left an indelible mark on me, even after I was sent to live with my father's sister in the suburbs of Philadelphia. An uncertain future as an orphaned boy in the care of an aunt and uncle he barely knew left me petrified as it was, but lingering memories of the accident also haunted me. I found myself reliving the hell of watching two parents succumb to their injuries even after the first of two surgeries to repair my broken leg. Tears were shed at the funeral, but no more after that. The rest of the time was spent ruminating on a fledgling form of survivor's guilt.

Had I been a doctor, the possibility existed that I could have saved them. After a short while spent musing on this notion, my mouth opened with questions for my physician during my postoperative examinations. How did he come to practice medicine? What type of schooling did he receive? The singular motivation to become a doctor possessed me and the saint who emerged from the carnage of a mangled automobile held a near religious passion to save souls with a stethoscope and scalpel. Everyone I met from that point forth saw the would-be doctor and extolled my determination.

Now, I murdered the lot of them with my teeth.

The ghosts railed at me.

My mother joined Lydia in the chorus. A transplanted German, she lived in Great Britain for half her life and developed a strange accent in the process; a confluence of Bavarian and British which stretched across the years to accuse me of my sins. "You let the devil in, Peter," she said. "And now you've become a demon yourself."

My father regarded me through the sweat of his brow – the man who instilled in me the work ethic which pushed me through medical school. "Have you forgotten what you were?" he asked. "You used to care for people, Pete. Remember what I told you – if you lose your love for others, then you risk losing your humanity."

I held my head in both hands, screaming past the sound of all the people who knew Dr. Peter Dawes. "Who are you?" they asked. "Where is the Peter we loved?" I spent nights arguing with them, my wandering footsteps leading me throughout Philadelphia as the vampire sought to feed and the mortal died a little more with every human he consumed. Two months past my awakening, the dualism had me so at odds with myself, I agonized over every person I stalked.

When I fed, though, I reveled in the taste again. I wore a wicked smile and drank deep until the demise of one sated the needs of the other. The fledgling vampire did not wish to give his life and yet, mortal and immortal sides could not reconcile. The voices persisted in their mission to silence the blood thirst. They might have succeeded if not for one thing.

Their sainted doctor was a hypocrite. The immortal gritted his teeth and issued a response. "An impostor," I said. "No benevolent doctor kills two people in cold blood, one the woman he was going to marry. He had all of you fooled. The man was as much a murderer as the vampire he begged to become." When the ghosts could not issue a response, my new nature planted its roots deep.

My erratic behavior did not go unnoticed, though. The coven watched me lose my grip and listened as I carried on inside the confines of my private quarters. I railed and ranted until the walls shook. I fought immortal thirst during nights when the chilling memories kept me indoors, though it drove me mad with hunger in the process. My outbursts sent my housemates clamoring to Sabrina for relief when it got to be too much.

Peter the vampire was going insane. Something needed to be done.

◦◦◦

Ten weeks after my awakening, sunset heralded another night in the battle of a tortured immortal faced with shaking off the relics of his past. I sat on my bed, fingers tangled in my hair as I shuddered through an escalating craving for blood. The whole manic episode came to a head with a knock at my door. Shooting a quick look at the entryway, I furrowed my brow when a voice followed the gentle tapping. "Dear Peter," Sabrina said with a hint of annoyance in her voice. "Please open up, I wish to speak with you."

I stood and walked to the door, dizzy from the effort, but not about to have Sabrina enter and see the state of my quarters. When I opened the door, I stood behind the gap, holding it just barely ajar. Sabrina raised an eyebrow at me with her lips pursed in a frown. "How long will you do this to yourself?" she asked. "I've been told you continue to torture yourself, and the people around you, and have grown quite irritable in the process. This is becoming taxing, Peter. It must stop."

I was forced to look downward. "I don't know what to do about it," I said, my voice a hoarse whisper.

"About what, dear son?"

I shook my head.

Sabrina grabbed my chin, forcing me to look her in the eyes. "Tell me why you have been in such a foul mood lately or I shall take those glasses away and leave you to writhe in pain in a well-lit room. First, Michael tells me you have been acting snippy with him. Then, you ask for your old personal effects. And now, you have become insufferable – locking yourself within your quarters. Carrying on, being a nuisance to your brethren, who all tell me you have gone insane." She paused expectantly, her eyes shooting flames at me. "I demand a response from you."

I could no longer hold back the words. "Ghosts, Sabrina. I keep... seeing people I knew when I was mortal. They've been torturing me and I can't shut them up."

"So, you become the coven terror." Sabrina forced the door open and grabbed my hand. "Come now, Peter. We will converse in the cómmon area. You have need of removing yourself from this room."

After weeks of wrestling, I had no resolve with which to fight her. I acquiesced to the coaxing, even when I spied a group of onlookers watching from the hallway, snickering at me. I sneered back as I closed the door to my room. Then I followed Sabrina to the staircase.

Neither of us spoke until we began to descend and Sabrina gently broke the stillness. "I told you at your awakening that this would not be easy and, in some regard, I think I took too much for granted when I saw you embrace this new life you were given. Your memories have not been kind. I had no idea they would cause this much pain."

"There are constant voices, Sabrina," I said, eyes focused straight ahead. "Every time I try to feed or sleep, I see those I used to know, reprimanding me for being a vampire. Sometimes I see their faces on my victims." I frowned, shaking my head. "I feel like it's going to rip me in two."

"Rip you in two?"

"Into this bleeding heart mortal that listens to the voices and the immortal that still enjoys the kill."

Sabrina nodded, but said no more. Reaching the bottom of the stairs, we turned toward the grand parlor where my brethren once received me with open arms. Now, the reception was lacking. They watched me with disdain, prompting me to avert my eyes while Sabrina received nods and bows of respect, which she reciprocated.

I indulged one glance upward, however, when I sensed someone studying me from across the room. My gaze countered Michael's dare, but only for a moment. Suppressing a hiss of rebuke, I looked back at Sabrina as she paused beside two empty chairs.

Sabrina sat and crossed her legs. "I fear you are on the path to self-destruction," she said sighing, her eyes shifting away. "And this would be a pity, not only to us, but for the vampire collective as a whole, if we were to lose a being such as you."

"What? A brooding, neophyte vampire?" I asked as I dropped, defeated, into the chair beside hers.

"You don't know all ends to this matter." Sabrina paused, as if turning a notion around in her mind before nodding to herself and folding her hands atop her lap. "I didn't plan on telling you this for some time, but you need a bit of motivation. Child, there is more to your identity than even you know."

I scoffed. "What the hell does that mean?"

"Your eyes. You've dealt with this handicap, but have not asked me why they are this way since the first night you woke."

"You mean you know the reason for this?"

"Yes, or, at least what I suspect is the case. You are a unique being. It is difficult to know for certain that one matter has caused the other."

"Sabrina I have no idea what you're..."

"You have the Second Sight," Sabrina said, interrupting me. "Gifts beneath the surface which have yet to emerge. Your infirmity is the sign of something greater."

"You call this a gift?" I pointed at my sunglasses. "All I see is a curse."

"Only because you choose to look at it that way."

"Is there any other way to see it? If it tortures us so much to be vampires then why don't we all just kill ourselves and be done with it?"

"You are the tortured one, child." Sabrina frowned at me. "You are the one who has allowed these visitors from your past to dictate what your life is worth and now, you see ill where you should find delight."

I sighed, studying the rug beneath my chair. "Delight in what?"

Sabrina inched forward in her seat, her body angling toward me. I looked into her eyes again. "Do you not recall it? The way it felt when you fed from your first victim? Have you not experienced it since then when you have killed? When you last relished the blood of the feed and allowed yourself to experience it as only immortals can?"

"I don't know. I can't even enjoy the kill anymore."

"Because you look at immortality like a mortal. You are not one any longer. You are something far better." Sabrina grinned. "A higher being, if you will. And you, with gifts precious few creatures possess. Bonded to immortal form, they could make you a formidable vampire someday if you allowed yourself to become what you are destined to be."

I shook my head. "I think you're telling me what you think I want to hear. I don't have any special talents."

"I speak the truth."

"Then explain this second sight bullshit."

Sabrina shrugged. "You will recognize it when you see it. It will never find you, though, if you continue to cower instead of evolving into the creature you were meant to become."

"Evolving?" I huffed, pointing about the room as I spoke. "I look at the others and don't see evolution. I see a group of lazy, decadent immortals. They hate me and I hate them, too."

She smirked. "You are part of a coven. Everything you fire at your brethren will be returned tenfold. They see your inability to assimilate and think you spiteful, Peter."

Cringing away, I all but spat, "I hate when you call me that." My words were laden with disgust.

Sabrina hesitated before replying. "When I call you what? Peter?"

"Yes, when you call me Peter. I don't know who the hell I am now, but every voice inside my head makes sure to tell me that I'm not Peter any longer. I get sick and tired of hearing it."

My brow knitted at the sight of Sabrina's eyes. Her impish orbs of brown danced with amusement, ruby lips curled in a smile. "Well then, dark son," she said,

"If you dislike the name and wish to distance yourself from this Peter who troubles you, why don't you change it?"

"Change my name?" A sardonic chuckle rose from my chest. "If I change it, then Michael won't be able to call me Peter the Blind anymore."

Sabrina laughed and I could not help but succumb to a quick grin. "You harbor such disdain for him," Sabrina said. "I have never seen two vampires in the same coven so at odds with each other. Again, you fail to take note of your attitude, though. What you dish to him will be returned."

"I don't dish anything to him."

"A proper amount of respect might be nice. He is my second-in-command, after all."

"Right, sure." I narrowed my eyes. "Maybe when he shows me a little respect, first."

Sabrina sighed. "There is much Michael could teach you. You could become fast friends."

"When hell freezes over." Looking away, I frowned, moving back to the point at hand. "So, what am I failing to do, then?"

Sabrina touched my face, directing my attention back to her. As our eyes met, she stared as though she could behold the bright, blue irises staring back at her through the lenses of my glasses. It unnerved and excited me all at once. She could have kissed me and I would have plunged into the embrace without a second thought. She kept her distance, however, while still maintaining that intimate closeness.

"You are not the same being you once were," she said. "You are the vampire who rose and sank his teeth into that mortal girl, regardless of what these shadows of your past try to tell you. You can feel him, can you not, my dark son? The creature you are within?"

I nodded in a daze. "I feel him every time I kill." Thoughts of feeding reawakened the thirst in me, causing a deep groan to ebb from my throat before I could stop it. "Oh, the taste of blood is incredible."

"Yes, it is, isn't it?" Sabrina leaned closer still, her cheek brushing against mine before her lips touched my ear. "That is the vampire, my dear. Stop stifling him with the artificial heartbeat of humanity. That siren call is your true self speaking. And when you embrace your nature, you will discover gifts that would make the lot of your brethren jealous." Sabrina backed away enough to wink at me. "Michael included."

My eyes met hers. "What do I do, then?"

Sabrina smiled. "Find a new identity, my unnamed one, and bid the mortal within to remain dead where we ended him. You found your escape from the mortal world covered in the blood of those who dared to trifle with the dark killer you were meant to be. Peter is dead and you thrive. Silence the voices with the blood you consume."

I felt her place a kiss on my cheek before she stood and patted me on my shoulder. As she walked away with a lithe, carefree air about her, I found myself likening Sabrina to an angel and felt a loyalty to her in that moment unlike any I had experienced before. With a sigh, I stared until she left the room, and then focused on the others milling around me.

I studied those bound to me as immortal brethren, attempting to connect with them. They spoke amongst themselves, drinking wine and blood while reclining about plush couches and pillowed chairs as though content to waste away eternity in slothful decadence. I frowned. Perhaps I did need a new identity, but I could not abide by the prospect of being such an utter waste of space.

I stood, but had to steady myself through a wave of dizziness. Yes, something had to change. I could not spend eternity scared of my own shadow, ignoring my base needs. Crossing to a pair of vampires engaged in conversation, the hallowed argument resurfaced in my mind while I snatched a glass of blood from a dark-haired vampiress named Rebecka. "Your doctor was a hypocrite," I said aloud, draining the contents of the glass in one drought before wiping the remnant from my mouth and throwing the empty goblet at its previous owner.

Rebecka gasped in horror. I ignored her. The eyes of my brethren shifted toward me, undoubtedly wondering 'what the devil Peter was doing' while I continued my argument. "You defend him and you tell me what to be, but none of you bastards can tell me why he killed his girlfriend. I don't give a shit if you think he was a saint, or not. Saints don't slash through two people." I continued walking until I stopped in front of a set of Japanese swords mounted to the wall beside Asian-themed tapestries. My hand lifted to caress one of the blades without breaking my train of thought. I smiled. "Argue all you want, but there's your real doctor. He's a killer, just like me."

"So, he speaks to himself like a madman. What the others say about you losing your mind is true."

I turned at the sound of Michael's voice, seeing him standing behind me with his hands tucked inside the pockets of his fine linen pants. The regal, pompous bane of my existence was clad in a suit, his hair tied back again as though the Victorian era came and departed while leaving him behind. "I'm sorry," I said. "Was that directed at me?"

Michael raised an eyebrow. "I don't see who else I would be talking to, unless you have imaginary people to accompany the voices in your head."

I shrugged and looked back toward the wall. "Doesn't matter either way. I plan on ignoring them now."

"You don't have the resolve to accomplish that."

Turning my head to regard him again, I furrowed my brow. "What's that supposed to mean?"

"You're weak." Michael narrowed his eyes at me. "I've known that from the start, when you were writhing on that bed like we'd set you on fire. And you have been utterly useless ever since."

"Oh, I see," I said, smirking. "So, I take it that you rose and immediately became the king of all vampires."

"I didn't scream like a stuck pig." He folded his arms behind his back and walked two, measured paces around to my side as if sizing me up. I shifted to face him fully and allowed him to continue. "Utterly useless," he repeated, eyes surveying me from head to foot. "Nothing more than a deathless mortal. And an insane one, at that. You will be nothing but a burden to this coven for all of your miserable existence."

"You have a lot of room to talk, you reject from an antique store." I shook off a wave of irritation as it surfaced. "You call me a madman? Well, what does speaking with a madman make you?"

Michael huffed. "As if your words could wound me. You are no better than our prey, *Peter the Blind*."

I felt my fangs start to peek from their hiding place, and clenched my jaw to hold them back. "I'm going to love having a new identity and telling you to shove that pet name up your ass."

"A new identity?"

I stepped closer to him. "Yes, I'm choosing another name. Going for a change of pace."

"So we can mock another moniker instead?" Michael smirked.

"No, so I can show you just how little you actually know about other people. You're nothing more than an arrogant prick."

He laughed and I saw his fangs slumbering inside a sea of porcelain. "Bold words for an ignorant neophyte afraid of his own shadow. Do you think me just weaned from my mother's breast? I have lived for many years while you have barely left a footprint on this mortal coil."

The corner of my mouth curled. I closed our distance with another stride. "How old does that make you, then?" I asked.

Michael's blue eyes steadily held mine behind the sunglasses. "One hundred and one years, with thirty-two mortal years prior to that."

An eyebrow rose in defiance. "And in all those years, you never checked the calendar?" Tension filled the space between us. "You look like you haven't left the last century."

"And you speak as though you were not educated in this one."

"You don't know anything about me," I spat.

"Allow me to enlighten you," Michael said, a smirk enveloping his countenance that possessed such smugness it made his words drip with malice. "I can tell you have no clue what you are now. That you have no notion of what it is to be an immortal despite what others have attempted to teach you, and as such, do not deserve that title." He paused. "I can tell one other thing, too."

"Oh?" I asked. I held his gaze and reciprocated it measure for measure. "What would that be?"

Michael's grin broadened. "That I have a coward of a being standing before me, not having the strength or the genitalia to keep his mortal girl happy. Little wonder she sought greener pastures. I would have as well."

The anger bubbling up inside me burst in a glorious spectacle of fist meeting face. I punched Michael across his jaw before he could dodge the blow. The impact sprawled him on the ground, blood running from a cut on his lip, but I had no chance to relish the moment. Michael swiftly came to his feet and hissed at me, fangs elongated.

He wished a fight?

I hissed in return, more than willing to oblige.

Michael swung for me. I moved out of the way prior to impact, but failed to dodge his other fist when it came for my face. He avoided breaking my sunglasses only by a hair's breadth and I determined not to give him a second chance. I grappled with him, attempting to pin one of his arms before resorting to throwing another punch that smashed him on the cheek.

A crowd was gathering around us as Michael threw me off him. The force sent me flying into the group of onlookers, knocking several off balance. They remained on the floor while I came unsteadily to my feet, woozy from hunger. Rage compensated for what I lacked in nourishment, though, and powered the violent swings I threw in Michael's direction when I charged back in. He dodged one and captured my hand with the next, crushing my fist with all the immortal strength he could summon. I gasped in pain, but was close enough to knee him in the stomach in instinctive retaliation. The blow doubled him over and freed my hand from his grip. I stepped back and followed it through by connecting my foot with his chest, taking him off his feet again.

Hate shot from Michael's eyes as he stood, hair half-hanging out of his ponytail, suit rumpled and askew. His hands balled into two weapons as he stalked me. The intimidating look should have been accompanied by venom dripping from his fangs, and caused me to take another step back. The full measure of a vampire pounced at me and before I had a chance to react, he hefted me by the fabric of my shirt and snarled into my face. "I care little for what she says you are," he hissed. "You were a mistake."

Michael threw me. The door which separated the adjoining room buckled and splintered as I crashed through it, and when I landed on tiled flooring on the other side the second impact completely knocked my glasses from my face.

The effect was instantaneous as light seared my retinas with exquisite pain. I wailed in agony while cupping one hand over my violated eyes.

A shiver ran up my spine. I rolled onto my stomach and groped with my free hand for my sunglasses. It took several frustrating seconds for my fingers to locate the frames and slip them where they belonged. No sooner did I come to my knees with glasses on, though, than a sharp point touched my throat just above my Adam's apple.

Opening my eyes, I swallowed hard and looked up to find Michael standing before me, a European-styled sword in hand. "Beg for your life," he said, "And I might allow you to retain it."

In the perfect position for doing just that, I strangely found myself smiling when my eyes finished adjusting. Knives and swords, some hanging on the walls and others situated on display shelves like prized jewels, were arranged around the room. Sabrina's armory surrounded me, whispering sweet temptation into my ears.

I looked back at my older, more regal brother, and sneered with more confidence than I had any right to exude. In one manner or another, I knew my salvation was in this room.

CHAPTER FIVE

Not even one year into life as an immortal and the end already seemed nigh. A blade to my throat and a vampire standing before me who eclipsed my years by over a century, I sneered in defiance of my peril.

But a foreign temptation was still whispering in my ear.

It happened when my eyes caught sight of the armory. Time itself seemed to pause, affording me the chance to study Sabrina's weapons. The same sentiment which tickled at me in the common area – when I admired the Japanese swords on display – came over me again. I did not have the foggiest idea how to wield anything besides a scalpel, but I knew I needed to get to the blades across the room.

If I could ever get off my knees.

Looking at Michael, I held a firm and steady gaze with him as time resumed its normal course. "What are you waiting for?" I asked, indulging in a dangerous smirk.

He pressed the sharpened tip against my larynx, causing me to wince. The sword did little more than create a superficial cut, but Michael's case was stated. "Beg me, neophyte," he spat. "What cause does a useless waste of space like you have to exist?"

"You can't do it." His weapon parted flesh, suggesting otherwise and causing a thin rivulet of blood to run downward.

Michael scowled, fangs elongated. "I'll make you suffer first if you continue taunting me."

"You can't do it," I continued, "Because if you could, then you would've already."

"Do *not* try my patience."

"What do you want from me?" I scoffed. "I'm not going to beg you for shit. You know why? Because you bark like the big dog trying to piss on his territory to mark it. You throw around your weight like you own the place without showing any respect in return."

"I have no cause to respect you." Michael's hands began to tremor, his voice descending even further into an enraged snarl. "You're nothing more than a nuisance. Her new little pet I am expected to coddle and train when he has been nothing but a disgrace to the word immortal." The fraction of a pause was just long enough for me to see deadly intent resolve itself in his eyes. "Now, I'll end you like I should have when you were just a pitiful human."

A voice cut through the crowd assembled by the broken door. "Michael!" Poised to drive the point of his sword through my throat, Michael hesitated when he heard Sabrina. My instincts seized the moment and both hands captured the blade. I threw it to the side, knocked Michael off-balance, and leaped to my feet.

Michael hissed, his feet planting on the ground to steady himself as mine took their first steps past him. Sabrina clamored to break through the crowd while I ran for the blades, feeling Michael pursue me all the way. While the weapons in the parlor were intended for show, these swords were more than display pieces. A Japanese-styled one found its way into my hands with sheath flying to the ground in an instant. I swung an untrained blow out of instinct as I whipped around to face Michael.

Our blades connected, saving my neck from a fatal strike.

My eyes widened, both hands wrapping around the katana's hilt. As Michael moved to attack again, I raised my blade and blocked another blow, but the edge of his sword came within a hair's breadth of cutting my cheek. It forced me back, and he took advantage of the opening to slash my arm as I attempted to dodge.

Fangs elongated, I hissed and responded with a strike.

He twisted his sword downward, deflecting my shot. Our blades caressed for a split second before he threw his weight into it and sent me to the ground. I hit the floor. He drove his weapon toward my stomach, but I rolled away from harm and raised my sword when he struck again. Michael gritted his teeth, hesitating only for a second as he paused to study me with his brow furrowed and our swords touching.

Now, I took the offensive. I pushed his blade away and came to my feet.

He and I swung at the same time. Together, we filled the room with the harsh sound of metal clanging. The awkward blows I threw somehow met his, which brought a look of confusion back to the forefront of Michael's eyes. Metal struck metal again. Michael whipped his sword upward and immortal reflexes saved me as I avoided the tip of his blade. I could not keep this up forever, though. The sight of blood staining my shirt invaded my periphery with the reminder I would not outlast my brother in my hunger.

"What do you want from me?" I asked. Our swords intersected again. "To die? To go away? Tell me what the hell you're really upset about, because you've had it out for me from day one."

"You aren't supposed to exist," Michael said through gritted teeth.

I stepped back. Michael stalked forward. We each poised our swords in anticipation of another strike, but neither of us moved. "What does that mean?"

"It means you are a mistake. You want a name? I'll give you one." Michael's eyes shifted to the side, glancing at someone standing nearby. I did not see who before his gaze returned to mine. "I think you should call yourself Flynn."

"Flynn, eh?" I smirked in defiance of the veiled insult. "I like that. But if I get you to your knees with my sword about to give you a tracheotomy, then I think I deserve the right to name you back."

"Name me what?"

"Robin." I paused to regard Michael. "Seems like a good name for such a pompous prick."

"So be it then," Michael said. I watched his rigid posture relax a bit, his mouth opening to issue more condescending banter. He began to say, "I'll not give you the chance," but his drop in guard worked to my favor.

I was already moving with the first word.

Ignoring it all – the dizziness, the hunger, the anger – I summoned a form of focus I had never experienced before. The movements played out in my mind before they even commenced. I leaped for Michael and swung my sword in a confluence of instinct and vampire prowess. No sooner had he spoken than I landed before him and knocked his weapon from his hands. The attack set Michael aback. Too stupefied to respond, he could not block the sweeping kick to his knee that sent him crashing to the ground.

He fell. The tip of my blade pressed against his throat, drawing blood. Michael's eyes widened as they met mine.

I held the sword steady. "You were saying?"

"Child!" Sabrina's voice cut through the heat of battle. I felt a hand touch my shoulder, but did not turn to look at my mistress. She persisted just the same. "Let him go. I will reprimand him in private."

Michael and I continued to regard one another, but there was a difference in the gaze he returned to me. I could not put my finger on it at the time. A small dose of fear, perhaps? A subtle awe? Maybe a fledgling form of respect rising to the surface? Whatever the matter, I withdrew my blade and allowed him to stand. Then, I looked at Sabrina.

She furrowed her brow at the expression on my face. "What is it?"

"I like the sword," I said, smirking in a manner that hinted at the dark side who wanted out again, who hungered for blood to make up for his weakened condition. He knew exactly what he held in his hands. He held fate. "I'd like to keep it, please."

Sabrina did not respond. I turned from the field of battle, walking past stunned bystanders and stepping over shards of wood with sword in hand. I made it to the threshold separating the two rooms before Sabrina ran for me and grabbed my arm, coaxing me to face her. She held the disregarded sheath out toward me. "You forgot this, dear," she said. As I reached for it, she leaned in and kissed my cheek, whispering, "Dark killer Flynn, go do what it is we immortals do."

The name resonated in my ears with decadent sweetness. Another identity. Another life. Someone other than the Peter stopping me from vampire fulfillment. I nodded at Sabrina and slid the sheath over the blade while I walked past my brethren.

Everything changed from that point forth.

Striding to the stairs, I passed a mortal familiar assigned with managing our affairs and shot him a hungry look. The short, wiry human scurried away like a petrified mouse. I grinned. The added sense of power draped about my shoulders like a cloak of arrogance and clothed me even as I entered my room.

I kicked displaced furniture aside and set the sword onto my dresser. Stripping off my violated shirt, I tossed it on my bed before walking into the bathroom to clean the blood from my mending wounds and freshen up. That accomplished, I opened my closet and picked through the woefully sparse collection of hand-me-downs gifted to me upon my awakening. It uncovered one item donated to me by Michael himself.

A black suit, perhaps the most contemporary piece of clothing my older brother owned before he passed it down to me. It was tailored to his lankier frame, but our overall similarities permitted me to experiment with a different style. The more formal attire with its inky, midnight hue contrasted against my pale skin in a curious, yet satisfying, manner.

I wore it onto the streets to sate my hunger with a proper feed.

⋅ͼ℘ ℘ͻ⋅

That night, I brushed past an unassuming mortal girl and followed her into a club. She lost several pints of blood and her life in the back of the establishment, with the suit-clad devil that lured her there gone long before anybody found her lying face down in the remnant spilled from her jugular. My feet possessed the stride of a killer entirely unlike my previous self when they touched Philadelphia asphalt again.

I returned to the coven. The smile I shot Rose as I passed caught her attention and halted her conversation with Rebecka. The latter still wore splatters of blood across her dress, but said nothing and parted company with Rose without one word of protest. Rose floated toward me with lithe footsteps and pressed her body against mine, a million intentions stated in that one action.

The sounds shaking the walls that night were of a much different nature than the ones in weeks prior. Claw marks and puncture wounds littered my body. The name called in the throes of passion reverberated in my ears, cementing my new identity in decadence. When I closed my eyes to rest, I slept much sounder that morning than I had since my earliest days as a vampire.

When I opened my eyes the next evening, it was as though I had experienced a second awakening. My tongue still tasted the woman I murdered the night before and my hand buzzed with the recollection of holding the sword. While I did not see Michael in the hallowed halls of the coven, I crossed paths with Sabrina in the main vestibule as I returned from another outing.

My mistress placed her hand on my shoulder, stopping me. I studied her, eyebrow raised, while her fingertips brushed across the fine linen of my suit. "Did your brother give this to you?" she asked.

I nodded. Sabrina shook her head and raised her eyes from my lapel to my glasses. "You need a few of your own, my dear. I will summon a tailor at once. For now, come to my quarters. I have something I'd like to discuss with you."

"As you wish, Sabrina," I said. She flashed a seductive smile and I followed her up the stairs, marveling over the change a day brought with it. The people who passed us all looked at me in a different manner, word having spread by then, no doubt, of the coven second-in-command being brought to his knees by an untrained neophyte. Where once their gazes were laden with disdain, now I saw the same expression on their faces I had seen on Michael's at the finale of our duel. The experience was intoxicating.

"What do you want to talk about?" I asked, as we approached the door to Sabrina's penthouse.

Sabrina nodded at the stocky bodyguard beside the door. Paul only offered me a quick glance. "We shall discuss this in more detail inside, but I believe I have an offer that will interest you." A deliberate pause followed while her eyes traced over me. "Flynn."

A wicked smile surfaced in response, one I could not have contained if my life depended on it. She chuckled in response. "You like this new identity?" she asked.

"Yes, I do, actually." My smile broadened.

She raised an eyebrow at me, her grin never wavering. "Well, I believe we can help you make some good use of it, child." Sabrina turned before I could answer and opened the door to her private quarters, pausing to allow me to step inside ahead of her.

I stopped, though, the moment I saw him standing in her living area.

Michael raised his head, his eyes studying me longer than they did Sabrina. Standing in front of a leather couch with a book in hand, he lowered it onto a table and then straightened again, slipping one hand into a pocket. He did not flash condescension or loathe, but gazed at me, neutral. I had not crushed the elder vampire's spirit, but he did not regard me as an inferior nuisance any longer, either.

Sabrina closed the door and preempted any exchange of greetings. "I believe we are on the dawn of an epiphany, my dears," she said, stepping past me into the room where Michael stood. "And while I should be reprimanding you both for that childish little fight you engaged in, I'm actually tickled that it happened."

My mistress sat in a matching leather chair and crossed her legs. Her eyes studied me. "Well, come. Sit." Sabrina pointed at another chair. "Robin and I have a proposition for you."

"Robin?" I stepped forward, remaining standing for the time being.

Michael looked away. "What's fair is fair. I accepted your wager and you bested me."

"I think it's splendid," Sabrina said, a chuckle in her voice. "Flynn and Robin. Suits both of you, if you ask me. You wish to act like a pair of brigands? Then you will wear their colors." Her amusement dissipated as quickly as it surfaced. "Now, sit."

I lowered my frame into the chair and watched as Michael – Robin – did the same. He settled onto the couch, his focus on Sabrina, which compelled me to regard her as well. Sabrina glanced between us. "As I said, I should be handing out punishments for the spectacle of last evening." Her eyes settled on me. "You, for insubordination to a second-in-command and the blatant lack of respect you have displayed toward him."

Sabrina looked next at Robin. "And you, for threatening the life of a member of this coven. You know what type of punishment I exact on those who threaten my offspring. You acted as though a mortal child, not a vampire of your years, and should count yourself fortunate I do not send you into exile."

Robin dropped his gaze toward his hands resting on his lap. "If exile is the punishment for..."

"Oh, stuff it. We have spoken of how you are going to pay your debts." The red-headed vixen turned her attention back to me. "Prior to that little debacle, I believe you and I were talking about gifts and talents. You only seeing a curse and me telling you the talents would emerge when you embraced what you are." Her grin resurfaced, in all its decadent wickedness. "And then I witnessed you with that blade and saw a prodigy in the making. Tell me, dear Flynn, have you ever wielded a sword before?"

I scoffed. "The only thing with a sharp edge I used before was a scalpel." I stifled adding the butcher knife assassination of my former paramour to my resume.

"Which makes this all the more of a wonder to me." She shook her head. "You creatures truly are born with that proclivity."

"Excuse me?"

She flicked her hand to the side in a dismissive manner. "Never mind, dear. The point is, what you did transcends astonishing. I think we need to cultivate this."

The way she suddenly regarded me caused a shiver to run up my spine. Sabrina opened her mouth wide enough to flash fangs at me "You liked that sword, yes?" she asked. I nodded without needing to consider the question. Sabrina nodded as well. "This is why you wanted to keep it. You have a pull toward it, don't you?"

"Yes, I do." I furrowed my brow. "Even before I stole that sword off the wall, I was looking at the display weapons in the parlor and felt something strange. Like something was –" I pointed to my ear. "– Whispering at me."

Sabrina's expression turned amused. "Child, you hear too many voices. You need to put that all behind. I need you to have your wits sure and steady. Robin is going to teach you how to properly use that blade. I am going to keep an eye on you to see how you progress. You might have great things in store for you."

"Robin's going to teach me?" I looked at him as his eyes shifted toward me. A smug grin enveloped my countenance. "Didn't I just beat him in a sword fight?"

"Don't get cocky, neophyte," Robin said, a dash of annoyance bubbling to the surface. "You barely won. Had I not been so incensed, I would have impaled you before you found the opportunity to play dirty."

"Sour grapes?" I asked.

"Hardly." Robin scoffed. "You swung the sword like a madman. No discipline to it whatsoever. There were only two things working to your advantage." He raised a hand, lifting fingers to enumerate his list. "Passion and instinct. One could have just as easily resulted in your demise and the other is what took over when you had no idea what the devil you were doing. If you want to do anything other than throw a piece of steel around and pray for impact, then you have need of instruction. A lot of instruction."

"Alright." I looked at Sabrina. "So, if I learn how to use the sword correctly, what's going to happen?"

"Oh, there is much more to it, my dear. Not only learning how to use the sword. Learning a love for the blade as a whole. I believe you have it in you to become a virtuoso." Sabrina uncrossed her legs and slid forward in her seat. "Robin will instruct you at first. If you do well with him, then I will summon the best instructors from the four corners of the world to train you. You fancy the Japanese blade? I will have somebody direct from Japan come to this coven to ensure you become a god with it. And Robin will teach my blade-wielding assassin how to become a shadow and a myth."

"An assassin?" I asked, a queer rush of excitement springing up from the depths of my soul, awakening the sadist inside that much more. My mind spun, dizzy with the prospects. "You think I can become an assassin?"

Sabrina flashed her decadent smile once more. "I think you were born for it, Flynn."

The rest of the conversation flew by like a blur, a matter of formalities and little more. Sabrina dismissed Robin and me, leaving us to depart together with a heavy silence hanging between us. His eyes remained fixed ahead of him, his mouth pursed in thought.

The change in tenor begged to be recognized.

"Why did you get in my face last night?" I asked as Robin closed the door to Sabrina's private quarters.

Robin paused, looking at me with a scowl. "'Get in your face?' For God's sake, speak English." He shook his head as he looked away. "You have need of learning more than sword skills."

"You're going to teach me how speak properly now, too?"

"Whatever it takes."

Robin fell silent, but did not walk away just yet. I sighed and rolled my eyes. "What provoked your outburst last evening?" I asked. A smirk punctuated my question. "Is that better?"

"It's a start." Robin's gaze shifted toward me again. "Personal matters which are none of your business."

"Then at least explain 'Flynn' to me."

"A child of red," he said smoothly. "The name comes from my native country. You are a vampire, brother." He looked me over from head to foot before staring me in the eyes. "Start behaving as such."

Robin turned and started for the stairs. I did not give pursuit, allowing him enough time to put distance between us before I followed his path to the second floor. It was just as well that we would not encounter each other again that evening; the bruises of a wounded ego were apparent in Robin's behavior and I was yet adjusting to my new way of life.

I slipped into my room and was reminded of the chaos of the past few weeks when I took stock of the mess that had accumulated. I began to sort through the wreckage, bent on finding the contentment and order I once possessed. The changes taking place by my hands and beneath my skin were relished equally, like a taste lingering sweet on my tongue.

The knife-wielding mortal, transforming into a bloody assassin.

Only fitting to see Peter off by the same razor edge which made him a killer as well.

PART TWO

❧ ❧

RISE OF THE ASSASSIN

"A sword is never a killer,
it is a tool in the killer's hands"

Seneca

CHAPTER SIX

My room became a different sort of refuge in the weeks which followed. What once was a cell for the conscience-laden became a haven for a sociopath, a proclivity creeping through my system like a slow poison releasing its toxin into my veins. The mortal inhibitions which kept my dark side at bay were gone; I rose each evening to find temptation crawling up my spine, something which worsened the more I used the blade. It was a good thing Robin kept me too busy to indulge.

The inevitable might have come to pass much sooner otherwise.

Oh, I still hunted. Robin demanded it, but he refused to leave me to my own recognizances. His constant presence irritated me a great deal at first – where my brother had once been the mocker in the corner, he now became a demanding taskmaster. And his instruction did not end with sword skills and weapon handling.

Robin became determined to reinvent me altogether. My speech, my stalking, the art of luring and seduction – the Victorian vampire held nothing back and I, in turn, could not so much as spit without evoking commentary. "Who the devil taught you how to hunt?" Robin asked one evening, his arms folded across his chest with his blue eyes observing me as I held a mortal in my arms. Her head tipped back, vacant eyes beheld the heavens while I drank from her violated jugular.

I raised my head, fangs still elongated and stained with red. "Are you going to critique the way I hunt now?" I asked.

"You kill like an animal. This isn't what I taught you."

"Your way takes too damn..."

"Language, Flynn."

I grumbled. "Fucking prude."

It happened too fast for me to react. Robin closed the short distance between us and smacked the glasses off my face. Dropping the mortal, I raised my hands to cover my eyes and yelled as my victim's body hit the ground. "Why the hell did you do that?!"

"First of all, your reactions are too slow. You should have been able to move out of the way before I reached you. If you have a weakness, then you must be on guard at all times for those who would exploit it be they friend or foe."

Doubled over, I pressed my palms against my eyes while turning in the direction I heard the hard plastic land. Robin stepped forward, though, and pulled one of my hands from my face to slap the frames into my grip. I thrust the glasses over my eyes and grumbled at Robin again. "You have a lot of fucking..."

"And two... Watch. Your. Language." He scowled at me when I met his gaze. "You sound uneducated and ignorant when you indulge this habit of yours. Now..." He glanced at the body lying on the ground before looking up at me again. "... Are you an animal or a vampire?"

I raised a hand to rub my eyes. "Your method takes too long."

"Takes too long? Did you learn nothing from that first day? You grow lazy and stupid and apt to produce bodies which look like animals were set loose, instead of learning to do it correctly."

"Does it matter either way?"

Robin paced around me. "Yes, it does, in fact, for several reasons. Cleanliness, for one. Finesse, for another. It is much like your sword skills; you can raise the sword, but your blows lack discipline. This is what I am trying to teach you." As I looked at him, I beheld the upturned eyebrow directed at me, a hint of the old Michael surfacing in his gaze. "Besides," he said, "You were a doctor and have not heard of the carotid artery?"

"Of course I've heard of the fu..."

"Language, Flynn."

"... carotid artery."

Robin nodded. "Then you should know what to do with those teeth of yours. I showed you, for the love of all things." He huffed and leaned against a building in the side street where we stood. The breeze of an early spring evening blew past Robin, as though bent to tousle his hair while unable to ruffle even a strand. "Timothy taught you ill. He has a taste for the jugular. The man never possessed a drop of aristocracy in his veins that he did not drink from a victim. Your teeth are long enough to nick the artery and drawing from it will force the blood flow through the wound."

"Why does it matter, Robin?" I asked. "We are predators. Who cares how we do it?"

Robin looked at me, an even expression on his face. "I am teaching you the difference between a butcher and an assassin. If you wish to be an animal, suit yourself."

I furrowed my brow while he walked away, giving chase the moment I saw he was being more than a scornful twit with me. He did not look at me, but continued speaking as though repeating a mantra. "An assassin has finesse. He leaves nothing in his wake but death. Everything is clean and done with precision. Patience should be demonstrated when patience is called for and expediency at the ready when that is in order. It translates into everything, Flynn. From the way you stalk, to the way you kill."

I smirked, my eyes fixed on the city. "When do we get to the swords?"

Robin rolled his eyes. "You are still an impossible nuisance, Flynn. Don't think my sentiment on the matter has changed."

"You're too old to know the definition of the word 'change,' let alone how to do it."

His jaw clenched, Robin answered with silence and I continued to smirk in the same cocky manner. My arrogance was relatively short-lived, however. Robin savored a cup filled with schadenfreude the moment my weapons instruction commenced.

An open room typically used for meetings between Sabrina and the other vampire elders of our area facilitated our sparring sessions. On the first night,

Robin stood halfway across the room, nothing more than tiled floor between us with all tables and chairs removed from the immediate vicinity. Suit jackets stripped and sleeves rolled up, we held the blades Robin insisted we use. Two European swords; light, straight, and sturdy.

"Bring me to my knees again," he said, poised for attack.

Yet, he did not move.

I wrapped both hands around the hilt of my weapon, then leaped for him and swung the blade just as I had the night I bested him. This time, however, Robin ducked and shifted to the side. My swipe cut through nothing but air and my landing left me vulnerable.

I felt a sharp blade slice across my shoulder. Turning, I hissed at Robin. He smirked at me and rotated his wrist to swing his sword around in an idle form of mockery. "What the hell?!" I asked, freeing one hand to clutch my shoulder.

"You're lucky I am not nearly so incensed tonight, dear brother," Robin said. He smirked. "I could have impaled you through your back."

Gritting my teeth, I grabbed the sword's hilt with both hands again. Robin remained still, not bothering to motion one way or the other. He kept his sword lowered to his side with only one hand clutching it. The nonchalant posture infuriated me and I made another aggravated pass for him, aiming for his neck and too angry to care one whit over chancing his demise. But he merely perked an eyebrow at me before dropping to one knee. My blade sailed past, again, not connecting with anything.

The resultant momentum spun me around on my heels until I caught myself, and in that millisecond I felt the tip of Robin's sword pressed against my trachea. Robin rose to his feet while his eyes remained set upon mine in a deliberate manner. I felt the tepid blood beneath my skin seep down my throat. "Death blow number two," Robin said. "Care to make it a third, or have we learned our lesson yet?"

"What fucking lesson?"

Robin pressed the sword against my throat again and more blood trickled from the aggravated wound. I yelled, startled, wondering if he did intend to have my head after all. "I swear by The Fates and heaven above, I shall now start bleeding you a pint for every crass euphemism you employ. Now, as for what lesson; the very lesson I have been trying to teach you for days now."

"Yeah, yeah, finesse. Assassin. I get it." I growled. "Please lower the sword. That hurts."

He did as I requested, but still held a defensive position, as though not trusting me to hold back a cheap shot. "Precisely, but there is another lesson latent in this whole exhibition, Flynn."

I touched the weeping cut on my neck, glancing at the crimson staining my fingertips for a brief moment before my eyes rose toward Robin's again. "And what lesson is that?" My voice took on a subdued tone. I was angry, yes, but far more frustrated with myself than with Robin's attack. He had sent me crashing from my ivory tower back onto the ground in two blows. Perhaps I was not the prodigy Sabrina thought I was.

The smug expression on my older, more regal brother's face evened, the half smirk fading into a frown. I thought I caught a flash of sympathy cross his gaze, but it, too, smoothed itself out as though an unintended wrinkle in his otherwise polished appearance. "Respect," he said simply.

My brow knitted at the one-word response. "What do you mean?"

"You lack it to your downfall." He shook his head. "You claim I have been your antagonist from the start. I do confess, when I first had to carry your unconscious body from the street and into our coven, I decided you were a mistake and have acted accordingly. I might have been swayed otherwise, though, if not for your attitude."

"I don't understand. What attitude?"

"Never once have I detected an ounce of respect from you." His frown became a scowl, yet I did not sense absolute disdain in it as I had before. The man was bent to level with me and for once, he had my attention. "Not when I attempted to teach you your initial lessons," he continued. "Not from any subsequent time we passed each other in the halls. Had you not been an antisocial miscreant, I might have expected to see you snickering with the others behind my back. I may have made my disgust of you apparent, but you have done the same in spades."

The scowl relaxed. I lowered my hand from my throat, wiping the blood-stained digits against the fabric of my pants. "You probably think this is how I've always been," I said. "Rude and stubborn. Moody. I'll admit to. I'm not the Boy Scout I once was, but I'm not 'uneducated' or 'ignorant' either, as you put it the other night."

"And you think me nothing but pretentious."

"You definitely act that way sometimes."

"And you the same, but now we have something more than our petty differences to focus on." He raised an eyebrow at me. "Do you wish to learn how to do this all the proper way? Then assent me a modicum of respect. I have been alive over a century longer than you have, dear brother."

He and I stared at each other, locked within a silent stalemate with neither of us breaking eye contact. After a significant amount of time, I nodded. "Alright," I said. "I'll listen to you. But you should respect me a bit, too. I don't know what happened here before I came or why you think I was that big of a mistake, but it's not fair to take it out on me. The least you could do is tell me why you hate me so much."

Robin shook his head. His eyes drifted toward the other side of the room. "I don't hate you. And perhaps someday I will explain these things to you. But, for now, I made a promise and you accepted a commission." He turned his head to regard me once more. "You wish to please our mistress, don't you?"

The question shot a tingle up my spine, inspiring immediate agreement from my lips. "Yes." It also brought to mind the other notion nagging at me nearly as much as Sabrina's wiles. "And I want to know what I am. Everyone else seems to."

"You are a vampire," Robin said with finality, and I knew I would not hear any further explanation on the matter this night. "Now, raise your sword. And allow me to show you what you were doing wrong."

Sliding my shirt sleeve across my neck to wipe away the blood, I nodded and took hold of the sword's hilt with both hands. This time, Robin did not engage me. Rather, he walked around behind me to place his hands on my shoulders, adjusting my posture and stance. He bid me deliver a blow into the air afterward and corrected my failed attempt, stepping back to watch as I performed the action once more at his command. I glanced at him after he set his sword down on a table in favor of folding his arms across his chest. "Again," he said.

I nodded in response and complied.

.⊙℮ ℮☉.

Weeks persisted. Days lengthened and nights shortened while the weather turned from chilly to sweltering within the confines of our urban estate. Robin remained my shadow throughout the better part of the months which followed, first instructing and then overseeing when I began to eclipse his own ability. It happened much sooner than he anticipated – than either of us anticipated, for that matter. The level of skill and composure I achieved by summer's end could not be denied, though. A mortal familiar from Japan flew in at the beginning of autumn and the blade I first came to admire found its way into my hands once more.

The skill of a master. The focus of a far more patient man than I ever was before. That being hinted at by Sabrina started to fill my shoes and embody my tailored suits. I was a vampire's vampire by the time the winter months wrapped Philadelphia inside a blanket of frost and snow. Sparring with Robin, brother to brother, became common practice between us. Throughout the course of my instruction, we crossed the threshold from adversaries to friends, and the tenor of our sessions changed as a result.

Still stubborn and set in his ways, Robin held his European styled sword in hand while I whipped the curved blade of my katana from side to side. My sleeves rolled up, I stalked Robin as I had been taught, throwing occasional strikes without warning and anticipating the blows he issued in return. We conversed as this continued. "I am growing bored," I said, thrusting my sword forward while Robin parried, using his blade to deflect my shot.

"Define bored, dear brother," he said.

"Tired. Listless. My lessons are redundant." I intersected a counterstrike from Robin. "When do you think Sabrina will finally give me something to do with all this?"

"You mean an assignment?"

"Yes, an assignment."

Robin frowned. We engaged each other in several silent back-and-forth exchanges before he responded. "Flynn, I would not hurry into things. When we finally set you loose, you will have a target affixed to your back. You do not shed the blood of an immortal without there being consequences."

"I can handle it." I threw another strike his way. "I think I've proven my ability. My instructors have just about packed up shop and gone home."

"You mean you have mastered everything?"

"Everything. Every bloody thing."

Robin sighed. We crossed blades once more. "I still dislike it when you swear, regardless of what English dialect you use while doing it."

"Be thankful I stopped saying the other words in front of you." Steel caressing steel, I halted Robin's blade and held it in place, my eyes shifting from our swords to his eyes. "You're ignoring me."

"I dislike that you do it at all, and no, I am not." Robin stared me in the eyes for a few seconds longer before lowering his sword. I did the same. "Have you practiced with the knives?" he asked.

I nodded. "Yes, both close combat and throwing them."

"And what is your current level of aptitude?"

It was my turn to sigh. I freed one hand to scratch the back of my neck. "The same level as my sword skills. The same level as everything else. I stalk and take prey like a shadow. Nobody sees me whom I do not want to. Everything you taught me."

Robin drew in a deep breath, exhaling it slowly as he regarded me. "Brother, you have done well," he said with a nod. "You have done very well. I simply worry about a neophyte being exposed to the sort of danger you'll be exposed to. I never thought you would take so quickly to your lessons. I counted on this taking years, not months."

"I've done everything asked of me," I said. "You've commended me to Sabrina several times."

"I know. And I underestimated just how much your... nature... would factor into your proficiency."

I raised an eyebrow and adjusted my glasses. "What does that mean?"

Robin hesitated. He studied me, his mouth open as though willing something past his lips which was difficult to say. Just as it seemed actual noise would follow, the sound of stiletto heels clicking against the tile floor redirected our attention toward its source. I smirked at her the moment her brown eyes found me. "Good evening, fair Sabrina," I said, turning my back on Robin for the time being in favor of meeting her halfway across the room.

Stunning as always, the black suit she wore clung to all of the correct curves. Each time I saw her, Sabrina called to me like a siren and I found myself helpless to resist. What began as touches on my face and through my hair had become seductive brushes of her body against mine, her fingers sliding across my shoulders, her lips almost nibbling at my ear as my training fashioned this assassin of which she dreamed. I became more and more the item of interest to her and that night was no exception.

Sabrina's gaze wriggled into mine, ignoring the dark lenses protecting my eyes. If seduction could be made picturesque, it would have been as tendrils of smoke lacing across my body, wrapping around me like an anaconda seeking nourishment, strangling first before consuming. I died willingly within such an embrace.

"Hello, my devilish assassin," she said, her smile possessing the slightest hint of fangs. "How are you tonight?"

How much I longed for those teeth to find their way into my body the same way Rose's did each time we slept together. The vixen before my eyes could hardly be equated to the coven harlot, though. "I am well, Mistress." Bowing at the waist, my eyes remained set on her. "And you?"

She reached out as I straightened, hands touching the collar of my shirt and tracing their way down to play with the top button. "The night belongs to its predators." Her eyes shifted from her finger's play up to my gaze. "I am doing well, too, my dear. I heard you two were sparring and thought I would check on my prodigy."

A half-smile blossomed on my face, yet my eyes fell partially closed. I felt her hand slide across my chest and struggled with mental images of me taking hold of Sabrina and doing the wickedest things with her body. "Your dark son lives to serve you," I said.

"I know he does." Sabrina's head tilted to the side, exposing the pale skin of her neck. "You are eager for a kill, aren't you, Flynn?"

"I am." I motioned forward before I could stop myself. My lips touched her cool flesh in a feather kiss before pulling away. "What good is knowing all of this without having some use for it, after all?"

"Soon." Sabrina met my eyes with hers as I stood straight again. Her hands left a burning impression where they had been when she lifted them. I became aware of Robin's presence again when she turned to regard him. "How is he progressing, mentor?"

I pivoted to align Robin in my sights, catching a look exchanged between him and Sabrina that read of a thousand things. Robin's words hardly seemed a summary of any thought I saw in his eyes. "Remarkably well, Mistress," he said, his tone chilled without being frigid. "Prodigy does not begin to summarize it. We should have expected as such, though."

"Yes, quite." She raised an eyebrow. Her eyes shot venom at Robin before returning to me. At once, the flames of wrath settled into soft lights when we regarded each other. I noted the change with passing interest, lost inside her seductive stare once more as though a switch had been flipped. "Is he ready yet, then?"

"Yes."

"No."

Robin and I spoke at the same time – I affirming and he stating the negative – which jarred me from the trance. I turned and looked at him, furrowing my brow. "Brother?"

He stared at me, rather than looking at Sabrina. "You are too young for this," he said. "There are lessons only time can teach that supersede sword skills and knife proficiency."

"I can handle them," I said, frowning. I looked back at Sabrina as though pleading between two parents. "I don't understand what I still have to learn."

Sabrina looked at Robin, brow knitted. "Which lessons yet remain?"

Robin sighed. "Self-preservation. He minds his own, but he needs to do more than slip through shadows. He must be prepared for all ends and everything to possibly go wrong." His eyes finally settled on Sabrina. "You know what setting him loose will do. The moment somebody hears his name, he will become a public enemy, in more manners than one."

"I thought we came to an agreement on this several months ago, when it all started," Sabrina said.

"Yes, we did." Robin's eyes shifted back at me. "And the concerns I have now are ones I didn't have before. I did tell you some things might arise along the way."

"What else?" One of Sabrina's hands settled on her hip as she shifted her weight onto the opposite foot. "If that is your only concern, then we shall let the other six covens know that touching him means war."

"That is not as easy as you think it is, and you know it, Sabrina." Gone were formalities. Robin stared Sabrina down as a peer. "There are other things as well."

"Such as...?"

"Such as his mental state. I have been careful not to indulge his bloodlust nearly as much as he would like." I caught a quick shift of his eyes from Sabrina to me and back again. "He needs time to settle into immortality."

"I am settled," I said, interjecting.

"Brother, you do not know the half of it." Robin frowned. "You..."

"That is enough." Sabrina broke through our impromptu debate. We both looked at her as she sized each of us up. "I believe I am still the mistress in this coven, am I not?"

Robin muttered something in a foreign tongue, dropping his sword onto the ground in favor of walking off toward where his suit jacket laid. Sabrina scowled. Proverbial steam rose from her head, threatening to reignite the flames of wrath and consume Robin whole. "*Ne tournes pas le dos à moi,*" she said, answering Robin back in the language he spoke in hushed tones.

"*Pourquoi? Tu as décidé déjà.*" Robin slid his arms through his suit jacket, and then looked at me. "I will leave you to decide this with the Mistress," he said. "You are her child, not mine. Please know I do not doubt your aptitude, Flynn. There are only things about your mental preparedness which have me concerned. I would like to see you mature as a vampire first. It would put my mind much more at ease." Nodding, Robin looked away, leaving Sabrina and I the sight of his back as he hurried for the exit. I furrowed my brow at the display.

It lingered with me for the remainder of the evening.

Sabrina dismissed me shortly after Robin's departure. After indulging in a quick hunt, I returned to my room, my need for blood sated as the dawn sky threatened to intrude upon the matters of immortals. The air outside grew colder by the day as my first year as a vampire came to a close and I wondered just how many Robin thought I needed to weather. Five? Ten? A hundred, as he had? I shut my door with a bit more force than normal and leaned against it, arms crossing my chest while my eyes took stock of the room surrounding me.

What was once devoid of any blade of which to speak now boasted the beginnings of an arsenal. Several katanas, throwing knives, daggers, and short swords adorned the walls of my private quarters, with more housed inside the closet. Weapons with which I planned on experimenting had their place of honor on a side table. Everything Asian and all types of tools short of rifles, guns, and bullets. Had I been commissioned to be an assassin of men, those weapons might have had enough worth to be included, but I knew from the start who my victims would be. I would be killing other immortals. "A target fixed upon my back," I said, revisiting Robin's words.

I could handle it. I knew I could.

While I understood my brother's concerns, I also had a healthy sense of egotism throbbing through my veins as I plucked one of the swords off the wall. Swinging it as the others had taught me, I heard the streams of praise bestowed upon me echo in my ears. I was born for this. I was a natural. Handling the blade only seemed to confirm it.

I set my weapon down atop my dresser as the hour called me toward slumber. Yawning, I stole a quick glance inside a half-opened drawer where something shimmered from within. I found myself plucking it out and lifting it before I could stop myself.

The necklace I ripped from Lydia lay nestled in the palm of my hand. My fingers slid over its pendant while my eyes became distant and the mantra continued playing. I was born for this. I knew it as surely as I knew my name was Flynn; it had knitted itself with the killer instinct I possessed. Even as the sainted doctor, I had slain that which I loved with such precision, it would have made the surgeons I once worked with envious. What would it take to demonstrate to Robin that I could handle being an assassin?

Clutching the necklace in hand, I thrust it into my pocket, not entirely certain why I did such a thing except to keep the trophy close to my person. Throwing my belabored body onto the bed, I neither bothered to strip, nor did I tuck myself under the covers before succumbing to fatigue. Instead, I allowed the tidal wave to crest and carry me off in its wake. I should have been lulled into the soundest of dreams.

That morning, however, I weathered the most terrible nightmare I had experienced since my fledgling days. Despite months of cold cruelty and intense focus, there yet remained one voice that refused to surrender her mission to redeem my soul.

The ghost of Lydia Davies returned with a vengeance to haunt me.

CHAPTER SEVEN

I opened my eyes to find myself standing in the middle of a lifeless crypt. Heavy wool coat atop my black suit, I was dressed as though I anticipated an outing but could not recall ever leaving the coven. Adjusting my sunglasses, I focused on my surroundings through a darkness that had only part to do with any lack of illumination. Something rang familiar about it, though. I made out the presence of a lamp by my side and after I switched it on, light heralded far more than déjà vu.

My mortal living area. Fate transported me into my old apartment.

I perked an eyebrow. An immediate rush of memory swept past me, threatening to drown me in the undertow as the place I had not called home in nearly a year swam into view. A thin layer of dust rested on everything. Familiar pictures hung on the walls and every piece of furniture remained undisturbed.

That could not be right, though. Fingerprints had littered the murder weapon that killed Lydia Davies and would have led investigators here. Anything not nailed down should have been confiscated by the police, yet books and vinyl albums still rested on tables. Old mail lay piled on a stand in the entryway. The refrigerator hummed in the kitchen. A light blinked on the answering machine and the red, pulsing beacon piqued my curiosity. I strolled toward it and pressed play, listening as the tape rewound and settled into place.

A beep; a crackle. A moment's hesitation. Then, a voice.

"Hey, Pete!" a boisterous woman declared in opening. My mental Rolodex settled on a face. An obese, middle-aged nurse named Chloe Poole. "Pat and the Indian Mafia say you haven't been showing up for your shifts. Is everything alright? It's not like you to leave the ER hanging minus one doctor. I said I'd give you a call. Let us know what's going on."

The corner of my mouth curled upward in a smile. "I'm sorry, Peter won't be coming to work due to an acute case of vampirism." I rolled my eyes. Another beep punctuated the message, giving way to a short pause and another female voice.

This one, however, sent a shiver up my spine.

"*Peter,*" she said, but in that name alone, I heard so much more. Lydia. The tone of voice pleading, it plucked ancient heartstrings and caused me a start. "Please listen to me before you take another step. It's not too late."

I furrowed my brow, but remained silent; listening. She inhaled deeply and exhaled a shaky breath before talking again. "You have to stop," Lydia said. "She's deceiving you, but she has you too hypnotized for you to realize it." A pause. "I'm sorry. I should have called you sooner, but I've been trying to get you help."

I stepped closer to the answering machine on instinct and folded my arms across my chest. A few seconds passed before Lydia spoke again. "Remember what I told you? Remember... Two years ago, when we were lying on your bed? You looked into my eyes and I told you what I saw inside of yours, Peter? *She sees it, too.* You're a pawn in all of this... Oh God..." The shaky voice surrendered to a sob. I found myself swallowing hard and shut my eyes. That part of me was dead. She killed it with her adultery. I killed it with homicide.

"You're going to regret this Peter."

"No," I said. I inhaled deep, steadying breaths and shook my head. "You will not have your way again this time, bitch."

"I bet you don't even recognize yourself."

"I know what I am." I gritted my teeth. "Damn you, woman, I have known who I am for some time now. How dare you attempt to meddle in my affairs?"

"You've lost what you are, Dr. Dawes. Wake up. It's not too late."

"No!" My face contorted with rage as my eyes flashed open. "Oh no, no, no... I know what you are up to and it is not going to work. Do you hear me?! Not going to work!" In one, swift movement, I ripped the answering machine from the table and threw it across the room. The cheap plastic splintered into a thousand pieces when it hit the wall and the tape inside partially unwound as it remained attached to the mechanism. My fangs slipped from their hiding place and I hissed at the remnants of the unwelcome harbinger.

Two hands wrapped themselves around the small table where the answering machine once rested. It, too, splintered into pieces when I threw it. Wood shards rained down on the carpet, letters scattered from being displaced, and I stormed forward, eyes blazing fury, continuing to demolish the living room.

I tipped over the couch and hurled pictures around. A framed photograph of my parents hit the window, breaking glass. Another of Lydia met with a similar fate, shattering another window. Had I my wits about me, I might have noticed the cacophonous ruckus my actions created, but I had no concern for such a thing. I continued uprooting everything in my path like a hurricane until I reached the bedroom.

I studied the tousled sheets. Memories wished to surface. The one Lydia cited mere seconds ago nagged at the threshold of consciousness, but I did not allow it entrance. Using rage to blind my thoughts in a veil of burning white, I destroyed my old bedroom in the same manner I had the living room. Dismantling the final vestiges of my former life; destroying Peter Dawes himself. I reached in my pocket for my lighter. I flipped open the top.

In one deft movement, I ignited the flame and tossed it onto the bed. Fire licked at the bedclothes until they caught and a blaze spread outward across the sheets. Turning my back on the room, I adjusted my coat and began a brisk, purposeful stroll for the door. Stepping over fallen debris, I reached the entryway, but hesitated with my hand on the doorknob. I pivoted, lining up the pieces of answering machine in my sights, Lydia's voice yet playing in my mind.

"*Peter...*"

"Peter is dead," I muttered to the empty apartment, all of its fixtures uprooted by the immortal force of nature I had become. "My name is Flynn now, bitch. Deal with it."

Not now. Not while Robin still doubted my mental faculties; not while I was trying to prove to both him and Sabrina I was ready for an assignment after months spent in training. As I opened my eyes, beholding the pitch black of my heavily-shaded room, I found my head still steeped in something too palpable to be a mere dream. My body back at the coven, my mind was yet gripped by the heat of my fury. I gritted my teeth and sat up in bed.

If she wished to play a game, she was trifling with the wrong vampire.

Swiftly, I stood. Destroying the apartment in my dreams was not enough. There would be hell to pay and blood spilled if I had anything to say about it. I unbuttoned the shirt I had fallen asleep wearing and ripped my arms from the sleeves. Stripping my pants, I tossed my clothing onto a chair, then marched into the bathroom and turned on the shower. The water scalded and my anger boiled. How did one shake a ghost bent on being a conscience?

"Murder," I muttered through the haze of steam. "The same bloody way she met her end before." My fangs ached at the mere prospect of it. Death; I did not give one whit whether the mortal authorities whipped themselves into a frenzy over a pile of bodies on the street. I would relish the hunt that night with a particular form of sadism I had not entertained previously. I gave little thought toward whether or not Robin or Sabrina would tie a bout of carnage to me. I merely wished the adulterous wench silenced for good.

Plucking a fresh suit from my closet, I dressed quickly, but hesitated before putting on my suit jacket. My eyes surveyed the instruments of destruction on my walls, each waiting for a victim to pierce and bleed. I played by Robin's rules – used Robin's finesse and followed his guidance with religious fervor – while my dark side clamored within the confines of a self-imposed prison. What would happen if I released the monster for once?

A sinister smile spread across my face. Poison shot from my black soul and surged through my bloodstream again.

Opening a trunk filled with other accessories, I extracted a shoulder holster with slots designed to sheath daggers. After securing it around my arms, I reached for a set of matching throwing knives, plucking three from their display. One final adjustment and they nestled close to my body, whispering decadent thoughts.

I placed my sunglasses over my eyes and fastened my favorite sword by my side, strapping it around my waist. A full-length wool coat would conceal the obviousness of my weaponry, so I selected one from my closet. Black, leather gloves slid over my hands. Spiky hair stood aloft in gelled, organized chaos. By the time I departed from my room, I knew I embodied the word assassin and wanted the world to know that as well. Including the set of eyes fixed upon me from the cosmos.

"Ready for a show, Precious?" I muttered under my breath while alighting from the main staircase and strolling across the tiled floor of the foyer. Wing-tipped shoes did not make a noise. I did not pause to engage anyone in either conversation or eye contact. I passed by the doorman with cool indifference and held back my final proclamation to Lydia until the night air nipped at my face with its brisk bite. "Look me in the cold, blue eyes and tell me you see Peter now."

At once, I slipped into the darkness, just as I had been taught, the words of my mentor a sacred creed I was bent on both honoring and vandalizing. *Being armed within the city makes you conspicuous, stick to the shadows. Do not make eye contact with anyone. Do not allow anybody to see you unless you wish them to.* I almost muttered the words underneath my breath while following the scent of humanity and honing in on its tempting pulse.

Move swiftly. You are vampire, Flynn.

I jumped for a fire escape and pulled myself up for a better vantage point. My shoes made a slight sound on the metal platform when I swung over the railing, but I bounded up the remainder of the stairs in silence and leaped onto the roof of the five story building once at the top. The wind kicked around the ends of my coat and ripped through the strands of hair atop my head. The corner of my mouth curled upward in a devious smile. I jumped onto a ledge and extended my arms by my sides while closing my eyes, absorbing the wind and moonlight as though to steal its power.

'*Meet your new god,*' I thought as my palms rose heavenward. '*Bow to him and tremble.*'

A sound. My eyes opened and my head snapped in the direction of the noise. A man and a woman walking down the street, nearing a narrow passageway between two buildings. My grin broadened and my feet moved swiftly to intercept, dashing to the edge of one rooftop before leaping across the expanse and running along the opposite ledge. Climbing onto the precipice, I jumped and landed on the ground below, allowing my knees to buckle as I absorbed the impact.

Slowly, I stood. I reached deftly into my coat and slid one of the knives out with taunting care. Cradling the hilt in my hand, I stalked toward the end of the passageway, fangs slipping out as two heartbeats came closer... closer... closer still.

They were engaged in conversation when I struck.

Neither was prepared for what transpired. I grabbed the girl, wrapping my arm around her neck, and pulled her into the shadows with me. Her significant other ceased walking immediately, reacting to the startled yelp she issued before I cupped my free hand over her mouth. As he dashed into the passageway, he came to an abrupt stop when I raised the blade and pressed it against his neck. The mortal man's eyes widened.

I chuckled. "Pleasant evening for a stroll, is it not?"

He motioned to yell. I impaled his windpipe with the blade before he could do more than squeak. Blood ran down his neck and the startled look in his eyes turned to confusion. The woman I held made up for his failed attempt at noise by yelling into my hand. "There, there, love," I said, whispering in her ear, nearly salivating over her flesh. "You shall get your turn, too."

A final thrust severed the mortal's spinal column. He fell like a lifeless mannequin as I extracted my blade and flicked it to the side, splattering blood all over the wall of an adjacent building. The woman I held continued screaming and a sliver of moonlight caught the sheen of tears in her eyes, causing them to glisten.

I chuckled. "Now, it is just you and me. I like it so much better this way, do you not?"

A tear rolled down her cheek and over my leather glove while I raised the knife close to her neck. Tears became sobs and sobs shifted into wails the moment the cold blade touched her skin, starting her to bleeding as well. I chuckled while she struggled, pressing the knife against her throat in a more forceful manner. "Now, now. Hold still or I will slit your jugular and make this senseless violence with no purpose. You wouldn't want that."

She stopped, still weeping, but shook her head in an emphatic manner. "Just relax," I said, leaning close, my breath grazing her neck. "This will all be over in a minute."

The girl jumped when fangs pierced flesh. As I imbibed lustful swallows of her blood, however, she settled against me, given over to shock and then, unconsciousness. I fed from her over several minutes and pulled away once her heartbeat began to fade. Her head bobbed to the side, two puncture wounds still weeping blood in rivulets. I licked away the remnant and raised my knife again.

Dragging the blade over the bite wounds to conceal them, I then dropped her body on the ground. She landed atop her significant other, a gesture I thought only fitting as I stepped over them, cleaning the blood off my knife while strolling away. I slid the blade back into its sheath, adjusted my coat, and emerged onto a side street, crossing with a nonchalant air as I sought out my next victim. Not to imbibe, though. Heavens no.

Now, this was about murder.

I pinned the next mortal I found to the side of a building with one of my knives. After torturing him with another blade, I slit his throat before he could flirt with unconsciousness and allowed him to bleed out onto the gritty, Philadelphia asphalt. Collecting my weapons, I cleaned these, too, and continued onward.

My next victims were another couple, found walking through Fairmount Park. Knives thrown from a distance plunged deep into their backs, hurtling them face-first onto the sidewalk, where they came to a rest. Retrieving the knives, I licked them clean, a foreign laughter rising from my throat which threatened to become more drunk with power the longer I indulged it. My eyes rose toward the heavens. I wore the devil's grin even after my laughter had subsided. "Is this registering loud and clear yet?" I yelled.

I returned to the more populated part of the city where I stabbed one man in the gut for looking at me in an ill manner. Another, I ran through with my katana when he came upon the murder of my previous victim. After this, I found another woman, whom I lulled into the by-and-by with a prick of my teeth on a quiet, narrow street, my own thirst needing to be sated after witnessing so much blood spilled since my last meal. I tossed her lifeless body aside and discovered three people staring at me as I turned away.

Each of them pale, they parted lips to flash their identity through fangs. I smirked and slid my knife back into place. "Ah, familiars," I said, adjusting my coat and sweeping my hand across my mouth to catch any stray droplets of blood. "How can I help you?"

They regarded me in silence, three male vampires I begun to take for mute when they refused to respond. I raised an eyebrow at them. "Nobody here speaks English?" I asked.

"What the fuck do you think you're doing, neophyte?" one asked, breaking the silence. His long, brown hair was tied back in a ponytail reminiscent of Robin's.

I laughed. "I am sorry... What do I think I am doing?" Glancing at the downed mortal, I looked to my new friend then and shrugged. "Looks like I just murdered a woman. What do *you* think *you* are doing in asking me such an asinine question?"

"We were stalking this woman first. Has nobody taught you manners?"

"Many have tried. Few have succeeded." I folded my arms across my chest. "All three of you were stalking her? Fascinating. And were you all going to share her?"

He bristled. "That is none of your damn business."

"You were?!" My laugh rose in volume. "Good God, what kind of coven produces such pitiful hunters?"

"We are of Matthew's coven," another said, stepping forward. Shorter than his compatriot, he possessed shoulder-length hair hanging free of restraint. "And you?"

My attention shifted to the other vampire. I bowed in a sweeping, gentlemanly fashion. "I am Flynn, of Sabrina's coven. A pleasure to make your acquaintance."

As I stood straight, the first vampire laughed. "Sabrina? No wonder he's without manners, he has a wench for a mother."

I furrowed my brow. "I beg your pardon?"

He smiled. "You heard me, neophyte."

"First of all..." I held up a gloved hand, raising one finger. "... I told you what my name is and it is not 'neophyte'. Understood? Secondly, what type of disrespectful bastard do you think you are, insulting the mistress of a coven?" I snickered, arms lowering to my sides. "You know what? I think that is what I will call you. Bastard. Since *you* lack the proper manners to even tell me your name."

He made the mistake of baring fangs at me, as did his friends. The look in his eyes turned from indifference to malice and a growl underscored the words he spoke. "You have not earned the right to know my name, you piece of trash. And I will show you what we do to the garbage that wanders into our territory."

I rolled my eyes. "Fine. Bring on the lesson."

He hissed and stalked forward. My fangs slipped outward in response, my hand hovering over my stomach before sliding in a feather touch across my chest. The tall, long-haired immortal leaped for me, but I drew a knife and stepped back a pace just as he landed. Thrusting the blade through his chest, I sneered in his face. A look of shock enveloped his countenance as within seconds the immortal became dust. Uninhabited clothing and flakes of ash descended to the ground.

My eyes fastened onto the remains of what used to be a vampire, my mouth agape. Never before had I either facilitated or witnessed an immortal killed and with this virginity now broken, I reflected on just how I felt about it. Most vampires I knew spoke of the death of our peers with disgust. I, myself, had wondered if killing a familiar would be difficult when the time came. Instead of being repulsed, though, I found myself smiling. The devil himself must have been dancing in the shadow I cast, for when I looked up at the others, they both retreated one pace, their skin a bit paler than it had been moments ago.

My focus settled on the shorter one with shoulder-length hair and my grin became more pronounced. Fate reduced him from vampire to experiment in mere seconds and he must have sensed it, because he turned and began to run. I adjusted my hold on the knife's hilt, and then flicked it with the same focus I possessed while working with my instructors, yielding the same results. His back became a bull's-eye, his startled scream a death rattle. He fell to the ground, transforming into ashes as well, and I laughed as I regarded the last one standing.

He shook with fright and held up his hands, a man with short, blonde hair and piercing blue eyes. I hissed and reached into my coat again, but he ran to the side and disappeared into an adjoining alley before I could draw another knife. Rather than pursuing him, I flipped my hand in his general direction, my demeanor apathetic. The death of the others more than expiated my fury. I retrieved my knife and stared at the pile of remains, wishing I could leave behind a calling card.

Lacking an appropriate homage, I started back for the coven without the desire sated.

That one would have to wait.

When I returned, I beheld my brethren with different eyes, knowing I had turned a corner from whence I could not retreat. One night had changed me beyond being a mere vampire; I knew the demon I was capable of embodying with a new-found intimacy and I could no longer deny my carnal need to kill. It would remain part and parcel of my soul from that night forth.

As I shut the door to my room and immersed myself in darkness, I removed my sunglasses and nodded to the silent jury of my weapons arsenal, bidding them all a good evening. I took each down to practice, placing them back into position reverently before moving on to the next. Night hastened into day and the shades protecting my windows began to lighten, provoking a yawn past my lips.

I stripped my suit and slid into a pair of black, pajama pants, settling in for what would be a day of troubled rest.

⋅ₒ૭ℰ ৩ₒₒ⋅

The next evening, a knock at my door woke me, forcing me from the twisted choke hold of nightmares that lacked any form or substance to articulate. I trudged for the entryway, slipping on my glasses along the way. Not bothering to locate a shirt, I opted to greet whomever this was bare-chested, hoping that maybe it might be Rose so I could ease my frazzled mind with a proper romp in the sheets.

As I opened the door, however, I beheld something that did the exact opposite of soothe me. Robin stood before me, a serious expression on his face.

I furrowed my brow. "Is everything alright, dear brother?"

"Get dressed," he said tersely. "The Mistress wishes to see you."

I nodded, watching him turn and walk away. Shutting the door once he was out of my line of sight, I frowned at the darkness enveloping me in silence once again. The tenor of my older, more regal brother's words hung heavy in the air, his displeasure more than evident. I showered and dressed as though preparing for my execution, my deeds of the night prior still a fresh taste in my mouth.

And perhaps a foul taste in Sabrina's.

My gait to Sabrina's penthouse lacked the confidence of the night prior and although I strolled past her tall, stocky bodyguard, Paul, with an indifferent air I was preparing for the worst tongue-lashing of my immortal existence. I opened the door as slowly as possible before slipping silently into the vestibule. Quietly closing it behind me, I indulged in several steadying breaths before working up the courage to call out toward her living area. "Mistress," I asked, "Did you call for me?"

A deliberate pause preceded the authoritative voice of the siren who had gifted me immortality, the redheaded vampiress with a temper cleverly hidden beneath a veil of sensuality. "Hello, Flynn," she said in a tone I could not interpret. "Come inside. I would like to have a word with you."

Chapter Eight

I lingered in the vestibule for an additional moment, knowing I did so to my own peril. To keep the coven mistress waiting could mean my execution rather than my admonishment, but I found myself attempting to interpret Sabrina's tone as though reading tea leaves in a cup. Even the costly additional moment of pondering did not give me any additional indication of what I might face when I finally stepped into her room, so I switched tracks and took stock of as much of the living area as I could see from my vantage point. I perked an eyebrow at what I found.

In all of the times I had visited the palatial penthouse on the top floor of our building, a scattered collection of lamps had always been illuminated. This time, however, near darkness stared back at me. I stepped forward just one pace, casting a wary glance at the soft glow emanating from the corner of the room. When I saw it flicker, I reached up and did something I had never done before in any room besides my own.

I grasped my sunglasses and slid them from my face.

My eyes registered a slight tinge of pain from the candlelight, but it was not enough to burn. As such, I pocketed my glasses and stepped around the corner, into the sitting room where Robin and I had met with our immortal mother when she commissioned me to be her assassin. Thrusting a hand through my hair, I walked further into Sabrina's personal quarters. When I finally caught sight of her, my steps paused on instinct, my feet refusing to budge any further.

Sabrina stood near a heavily draped window, her back to me, a raised hand parting the curtains just enough for her to stare into the night. Her posture did not speak as many volumes as her manner of dress did. A blouse clung onto her slender, yet shapely, frame and even from my perspective I noticed a few unfastened buttons of a parted collar that hinted at how much cleavage I would see when she turned around. I swallowed hard at the sight of a skirt formed to her hips, ending inches shy of her knees, and the stiletto heels that shaped her calf muscles into sensual curves.

I began to suspect I was being seduced. And I did not mind it in the slightest.

"What is it, my son?" she asked, her voice soft and smooth as silk.

My skin prickled. I studied her, regarding the red hair cascading down her shoulders, and fought the compulsion to follow the sight of her into decadent thoughts. "Nothing, Mistress," I said, surprised at how subdued my voice sounded. "Why?"

"You hesitated. I called you in here, didn't I, Flynn?"

"Yes, you did." I nodded when she turned her head to line me in her periphery. "I am sorry. I simply did not know what to expect."

Sabrina released her hold of the curtain, allowing it to fall closed as she shifted to face me. The plunging neckline I had fantasized about her open blouse was offered forth as though meant to be a gift for my eyes. My gaze met hers and had I a pulse, it might have seized from the tension building in the air.

My mistress pretended she was unaware of it. "When I bid you to come," she said, "You are to come. Are we clear on this matter?"

I nodded. "Yes, Mistress."

"Good." Sabrina pointed toward one of her couches. "Sit. I wish to speak with you."

Nodding once more, I walked almost precisely to the place where she directed and sat, settling against the leather upholstery and hearing it creak beneath my weight. Sabrina sat opposite to me and crossed her legs. Her arm rose to drape along the complimentary sofa which was at once so close, and yet, so far away. Her hand touched her lips, which pursed while she studied me. "Do you know why I called for you?" she asked.

I suppressed the urge to jerk at the collar of my shirt. "No, I do not."

"You don't?" The corner of her mouth curled upward. "You don't even want to guess, my dear?"

Indulging in a deep, steadying breath, my mind traced across the events of the night prior. I scratched the back of my neck, engaging in an internal debate. Should I come clean or hold my cards close to my chest? I relaxed in my seat more and permitted the ghost of a smile to surface. "I believe I know what this is about, but am not entirely certain."

"You believe you might know?" An eyebrow lifted as her gaze locked with mine, refusing to relent. "Then enlighten me."

"You heard about what happened last night?"

"Did something happen last night, Flynn?"

"Yes." The ghost grin vanished, dissipating like smoke and giving way to an even expression I held on my face.

Sabrina nodded. "Assume I don't know and tell me anyway."

I nodded in turn and sighed. "I ran into three immortals from another coven. We exchanged words and things ended... poorly... for them."

"And what does that mean?" I could have sworn I saw the smile return to Sabrina's face, but it might have been a hint of amusement present in her eyes and nothing more. "Did you do something to them?"

Dipping my toe into the pool, I created a ripple to see where it would lead. "I was armed."

Sabrina did not crack a smile, but also did not cast a frown. "You were armed with a blade?"

"Several throwing knives." She did not need to know about the sword.

"Why were you armed?"

"Protection. Self defense." I paused. "To become used to carrying my weapons around with me."

Sabrina nodded. "And what did you do with these blades, Flynn?"

"I murdered two of the three." Inching forward in my seat, I held up a hand to stop Sabrina before she could shoot furious words at me. "But only because they were insulting you. They called you terrible names, Mistress, and insulted me in the process. When they threatened me, I retaliated." I hesitated, but only momentarily. The time had come to be truthful. "I do not regret it. Not at all. I would do it again, in fact."

"How did it feel?"

Her question took me aback. I furrowed my brow. "How did it feel to kill them?"

Sabrina nodded, but said nothing more. I looked away, considering the question for a few seconds before my gaze returned to Sabrina's and a sinister smile spread across my face. Her eyes glinted in recognition of this, almost reflecting evil as though a pool of water with me yet possessing a reflection. "I must confess," I said, a tone inhabiting my voice which hearkened back to the first mortal I ever consumed. "I liked it."

She perked an eyebrow at me, but her lips betrayed the neutral gesture by curling into a grin before my mistress could hide it by resting a finger against her bottom lip. My mind conjured the image of her licking the digit in a sensual manner, and giving way to double entendres flying between us until I took her into my arms and did the most erotic things to her. I swallowed hard. The thoughts seemed to be outside me and yet, I could not help but to succumb to their taunting. Her eyes melted into mine and although we both remained seated, I felt her presence overshadow me.

"I can tell," Sabrina said. "I have seen it in your eyes from the beginning. I still remember the first time you took that girl into your arms and finished her off. I knew I had a killer, Flynn. And a killer is what I see before me."

I stared, attempting to discern what it was I felt; what it was I wished to say in response. "Thank you, Mistress," I managed, "But I have only just begun this journey."

"I know you have. And you desire more." She nodded and stood, walking toward me while extending her hand. Our palms touched before I realized I had reached back to her. I furrowed my brow while she smiled. "Come with me, dark son. I have something I would like to discuss with you."

Standing, I nodded. "Where are we going?"

"To the balcony." Her footsteps slow, she tugged me in the direction of two French doors. "You may want to put your glasses back on, lest the moonlight hurt your eyes."

My free hand slid into my suit jacket, producing the dark spectacles which I secured over my eyes before we reached her balcony. Sabrina relinquished her hold on me to open the doors and as they parted, a gust of cold air blew past us, tousling my hair and kicking hers up behind her like a cape taking flight. I stood in the threshold while she strolled to the railing and only when she turned to peer back at me did I follow and assume a place beside her. Her gaze shifted back toward the distance and I looked in the same direction, losing myself in the sight of moonlight reflecting off the windows of a distant skyscraper.

"It's a rather interesting place, isn't it?" she asked. "I've been to Hong Kong and New York City, wreaked havoc in Boston and Chicago, but none of those cities enamored me as much as this place has."

I nodded, allowing my eyes to drink from the sight as though just as enthralled with it as I was Sabrina. "I have not traveled much," I said. "Only from home to my aunt's house and then to college. This is all I have known for the past decade."

"And to think you have forever to examine it all." Sabrina shot me a smile, directing my attention back to her as an amiable grin touched the corners of my mouth. No sooner did I gaze at her, however, than did her grin dissipate, a frown taking its place while her eyes lifted toward the concrete jungle surrounding us again. She sighed. "I have many enemies. You could live over a hundred years like Robin and not have my list, and I have only had thirty years in this place to develop such entanglements. They've had thirty years to plot my demise." She paused. "Jealousy amongst vampires is commonplace. The heads of the seven covens are not immune to it."

"I did not realize there was so much competition."

Sabrina issued a sardonic laugh. "We are a lot like the mafia. Our peace with one another is always tentative and the slightest thing could snap our precarious coexistence. We maintain order only for the sake of common interests. No other reason."

"Why do they loathe you?"

"They fear me." A smile surfaced on her face again. "They know I did not come here to be some subjugated puppet on a string. I came to lead a coven and to protect the interests of my immortal children. They see me as a threat because they are too incompetent to manage their own affairs."

I huffed. "The three I encountered were definitely incompetent."

Sabrina turned her head, her eyes meeting mine. "Were they truly?"

"Oh gods, yes." I laughed again. "I only spared the third one because I did not think he was worth chasing after. I could have easily caught up with him."

"Yet, you didn't." She paused. "Isn't it strange how fate works sometimes, my dear Flynn? How it brings us into these impossible situations and leaves us with an entirely different future as a result?"

"I do not understand." My voice sounded lost.

"Because you spared the one, he returned to his coven master and informed Matthew of what happened. My shadow in the night, you must not spare a one again, but this time, it was for a purpose. The name of Flynn has been spoken on the lips of an immortal quaking with fear. You have given them a reason to tremble."

Our gazes remained locked as Sabrina loomed over me, again without moving from her position. Rather, her eyes met mine and sank in deep, like teeth plunging through flesh to imbibe the lifeblood therein. I felt a chill run up my spine but confused warning with lust, allowing it to consume me. Our bodies drifted closer and Sabrina nodded as if to confirm we were bound in this death dance, mistress to fledgling.

"Your aptitude has proven your readiness," she said. "I have seen it with my own eyes as you and Robin have sparred and heard it from the mouths of your instructors. But now I must hear it from you. Are you ready to be my assassin,

Flynn?"

"Yes." My response drifted outward with ease. "I am."

"They underestimate us both." Sabrina's hand touched my shoulder. It slid across my back as she circled around me. I closed my eyes when another shudder assailed me, but her voice continued wafting a wicked lullaby into my ears. "Matthew thinks you a neophyte in need of scolding, but you are so much more than that, aren't you?"

"Yes, I am."

"What are you, Flynn?"

"I am a killer. I am your assassin."

"You live to serve your mistress, do you not?"

"Yes." My fangs slipped from their slumber. Her body pressed against mine from behind, her lips touching my neck as she leaned in close to me.

"And you desire me, do you not?"

"I do, Sabrina." I exhaled a shaky breath.

"You have for some time." I felt her tongue on my ear, caressing the lobe before she began to nibble on it. "Tell me," she commanded. "Tell me what you want."

My hands gripped onto the railing, knuckles white from how tight I took hold of the metal. "I want *you*, Sabrina. I want you more than I have wanted anything."

"No truces," she said. "No survivors. No mercy. Punish those I tell you to punish and I will reward you. Stain the streets red with the blood of my enemies and you will have all of those carnal fantasies you harbor. You are ready to be my killer and I will give you a taste of what your reward shall be." Her voice lowered to a whisper. "Claim what your loyalty has earned."

I felt drunk, pivoting to regard Sabrina with my lids lifting to mere slits. The sight of her entreated me beyond all self-restraint. Lust dripped from her gaze, her lips more of a temptation than I could resist, and I captured them as though starved for their sustenance. Sabrina thrust her body against mine in response, and as she wrapped a leg around my waist, I consumed her in violent, passionate kisses, tasting nothing but poison and craving each embrace. Sabrina grabbed hold of the lapels of my jacket and ground against me once.

Then she threw me onto the balcony floor.

Jumping on top of me, Sabrina kissed me once more before pulling away. I craned my neck to capture her lips again, but she used the opportunity to plunge her fangs into my throat, producing a howl of pleasure from my lips. At some point in the manic, tawdry episode which followed, my glasses were removed. I clenched my eyes shut, savoring with my remaining senses the thrill of having every unspoken desire consummated by Sabrina.

Oh yes, she had my loyalty. She had me wrapped around her finger and I was but a puppet on a string.

Later that evening, that sense of something changed carried with me while I hunted. As I took mortal life, it felt as though I had tasted fruit from the tree and made a pact with Satan himself. We exchanged wicked smiles when I returned home and I relished the knowledge of being her co-conspirator. Her assassin. No other held my affections nearly so pointedly.

With the exception of my brother Robin.

I returned to my room to find him standing by my door, leaning with his back against the wall as though he had been waiting all night for me to arrive. The vexed look in his eyes remained a fixture, shrouding his face and twisting my stomach in the process. I hesitated for a moment and then marched forward with forced confidence. "Robin?" I asked, my voice more cold than it had ever been to my brother. "What brings you here?"

Robin did not flinch from my tone and regarded me in silence until I stopped a few feet shy of him. "How did your talk with the Mistress go?" he asked evenly.

"Good." I paused. "She agrees that I am ready to assume my responsibilities as her assassin."

"Because you slaughtered two immortals in cold blood?"

"Because I defended her honor, dear brother."

Robin nodded. His hands slipped into his pants' pockets while his eyes shifted to the wall opposite him. "I see how little my opinion matters in this coven."

"With all due respect," I said, "I do not think I need to be as coddled as you want me to be."

"This has nothing to do with being coddled." His gaze returned to mine. "Flynn, you think, with all of the wisdom of a one year old immortal, that you understand the way this world works when nothing could be further from the truth. I walked the streets of Kilkenny before cars occupied roads. I sailed on ships when flying machines were the things of fiction. I am much more experienced than you."

I perked an eyebrow in defiance. "And you do not think I am ready for this? Even after I have proven I can hold my own?"

"This has *nothing* to do with holding your own and everything to do with the type of wisdom you lack." His eyes flashed anger as his finger rose to point at me. "The mistress may not give a care about this sort of thing, but I do. You are being thrown into a horde of enemies while lacking even rudimentary understanding of the ways of this world. You are being sent out there like a lamb to the slaughter and not because you have no notion of weapons and fighting. We have already established that the student eclipsed the ability of his master far before now. I hold no egotism. I admit my place as your inferior, but that is just it. You haven't the foggiest notion of why things are the way they are."

"And neither do I care to know!" I said, shouting back at him. I gritted my teeth, holding back the compulsion to bare fangs. "I am through with this cloak and dagger bullshit."

"Lang..."

"Fuck off, Robin." I narrowed my eyes at him. "I think you are jealous and are being spiteful because of it. I have proven and will prove myself. If I need a tutor at this point, it is trial and error."

Robin nodded. "Very well." The words spoken softly, the subsequent statement was issued with such harshness to be a stark contrast. "Since you have no further use for me, I shall find some place in this coven where I am needed."

He stood straight and began a brisk stride away. A frown surfaced on my face in a moment of clarity, long enough for me to say, "Wait," to him, though I did not move to follow.

Robin stopped. His back remained to me, but his head turned to line me in his periphery. "What is it, Flynn?"

"I never said I did not have any use for you." My statement was enough to coax him toward facing me fully, but he did not speak. I continued, "You are the only one in this coven who teaches me anything. I am going to need help. I simply do not want to be treated like an infant."

We regarded one another in silence until Robin nodded. "I will not leave you destitute," he said, "But you are to understand this." A pause punctuated his words. His stare became severe. "You will have to deal with the consequences of your actions from this point forth, Flynn. You chose this path. Now it is your burden, not mine."

"I never asked it to be yours in the first place."

"Indeed." Robin issued a short nod. "Now, sleep well this morning, dear brother. Savor every moment of it. Because I promise you, it is the last restful sleep you will ever enjoy."

He turned away again and this time, I did nothing to stop him as he made his way to the end of the corridor and started for the stairs. Instead, I remained standing in the same place, puzzling over his warning for a few seconds before shrugging it off and entering my room. Once inside, I closed the door and removed my sunglasses, sighing from relief over the darkness which wrapped itself around me like a cocoon. I leaned against my door. A sadistic smile spread across my face. I did intend to enjoy resting that night, and planned to do so every night regardless of what Robin had to say.

My dreams were not to be so accommodating, though. As I lay in bed, I tossed and turned while the vision of a white room materialized in my mind. A chill of dread settled in my bones, so much like the dream of destroying my old apartment I had weathered a mere two mornings ago, but no familiar furnishings surrounded me this time. I beheld the sterile, vacant place where my dreaming form found itself standing, turning around to survey his immediate area.

That was when I saw her.

Standing across from me inside the void, holding one of my swords, the ghost of Lydia regarded me with far more disdain than even Robin had. On her chest were bloodstains which marked the place where I shoved a butcher knife into her body. She lifted her chin, sizing me up. "I've been watching you," she said. "My eyes haven't left you even though I haven't said anything recently."

The sight of her brought loathe to the surface like bile rising to burn the back of my throat. I sneered. "Well, well, well. How fortunate does that make me to have an audience?" I raised my arms to my sides and bowed. "I hope you have enjoyed the show, Pet. Especially the night before last." Standing straight, I adjusted my suit jacket, a snide grin surfacing on my face. "That was for you. I thought if you wanted to fuck with me that turnabout was fair play. Lovely touch, placing me inside my old apartment, by the way. Especially with those pictures of you and my parents."

Lydia held an even gaze. "You speak just like a demon."

"I am a demon, mortal. You would do well to remember that and leave me alone from now on."

"You used to heal, Peter." She shook her head, lifting the sword as she spoke. "Now, you kill. You've been given unspeakable gifts and you're wasting them."

"So wrapped up in the past. Allow me to help you with that." I strode toward her. Lydia relinquished her hold on the sword in shock as I grabbed it from her hands and impaled her with it in one swift motion. Holding her close, I spat venom as I filled the air with the harshest whisper my lips ever produced. "Hear me now, you adulterous bitch, Peter is dead. He no longer owns this body and neither do you. I suggest you enjoy your afterlife and leave mine alone, or more people will die. Each time I sense your shiver or see your ghost, I will murder like a tyrant until you relent. Are we clear on this?"

"You have no idea," Lydia said, a pained grin on her face as her eyes returned my look of severity tenfold. "You don't see it yet, but you will. When we come back to finally deal with you."

"Lovely. Do be sure to drop in any time." I twisted the sword. "So I can continue doing this to you."

I did not expect her hands to rise, but they grabbed me by my jacket and pulled me even closer, noses a hair's breadth from touching while she shook her head at me. Her green eyes appeared almost ethereal. Her tone became sharp; stern. "You can't outrun your destiny," she said. "It's looking for you and it will find you... when you least expect it... "

Lydia's grip on me relented. Her body slid from the blade as gravity worked its wiles on her corpse and forced her to fall. I watched her crumple to the floor, an inner voice attempting to speak; a dying flame staring down at her, wanting to ignite again while failing miserably in its task. The ember surrendered its life in a puff of smoke and, within a few seconds, was no more.

I flicked her blood from the blade and strode off into nothing, satisfied with myself, thinking now this would be the end of my entanglement with the shadows of my past. Her threats held no merit and did nothing to sober me. I saw nothing more than the last breaths of a dead woman and regarded it with far less concern than I did Robin's words to me. When I woke, the evil consuming me yet thrived beneath my skin. I rose to greet the evening and plunder it once more.

A few days later, as I rummaged through my pants pockets, I found the necklace I ripped from Lydia's throat shimmering inside, staring at me as though possessing the stern gaze of its former owner. I held it in my fingers for a matter of seconds before thrusting it back where I found it and making a detour to a pawn shop. Mere days afterward, I received orders for my first assassination. The vicious glare in my eyes became a permanent fixture, a callous expression I wore each night with every murder I executed.

My sword stayed by my side. My coat concealed the knives I kept always on my person. My senses were attuned, my will as cold as steel and as sharp as a blade honed by the most skilled craftsman. I became the hit man of the undead, death personified and a force with which to be reckoned. Over the next four years, I established the name of Flynn through a testimony of ashes. All who stood against

Sabrina feared the day when they would meet me face to face. I reveled in it. I thrived within its confines.

The adage remained as true to me, however, as it does to all who possess a special calling. Eternity does indeed catch up with you. And it found me in the most unlikely of manners.

PART THREE

⚜

Four Years Later

"Autumn to winter, winter into spring,
Spring into summer, summer into fall,--
So rolls the changing year, and so we change;
Motion so swift, we know not that we move."

Dinah Maria Mulock

CHAPTER NINE

I despised when others kept me waiting.

My fingers twirled an unlit cigarette around before raising it to my mouth and inserting it between my lips. The bright orange glow of embers sparking to life followed a quick search through my pocket for my lighter, and had anyone been watching, they might have been impressed by the deft, fluid motions of one action flowing swiftly into the next. Instead, the thick crowd of mortals seemed distracted by other things – loud music, for one, and the putrid stench of their own sweat as they gyrated about the dance floor. I rolled my eyes behind the protection of my sunglasses and searched the area for my target.

Each day I permitted him to continue his pitiful existence, I was risking both my neck and my reputation. I should have never allowed it, lest my brethren speculate that the assassin might be growing soft or, worse, merciful. Even I pondered the paradox – if staying my hand indicated a latent weakness rising to the surface – but the compulsion which caused me to spare his life whispered the reason for the risk.

He had ways of locating desired items that left all the seven covens in awe over his scavenging abilities. As such, when Sabrina touched my ear with her cool lips and whispered his name as my next target, I knew I had to use this moment to its fullest. My mistress left for New York and the window of opportunity remained opened for three days. This was the last day, however. The time had come to settle debts with a man living on borrowed time.

I drew from the cigarette again and peered through the smoke, looking for the garishly dressed immortal that chose this location for our meeting because he enjoyed frequenting this club. My eyes scanned the crowd while I commenced questioning my sanity.

Four years had passed, ticking their interminable minutes and registering one more day following the one prior until the months began to stack up. Time itself held little significance but to count one more stroke upon the wall; one more day elapsed, one more year winding to a close. Such seemed to be the unbroken melody which made up my existence, underscored by the plethora of concerns an assassin could be expected to face. Robin's forewarning that my peaceful existence as a neophyte was to perish had proven apropos. I sensed it as I rose each evening.

I was a shadow and, yet, I was infamous. The name of Flynn possessed such a reputation to send shivers down every immortal spine within the city, and merely evoking it would garner a reflexive glance over their collective shoulders that bordered on superstitious. I relished it, savoring even the plots formed against my life by conspirators who met their eventual end by my hand. All who gazed upon my countenance by design found their time was through. Death saturated my life with crimson-colored decadence.

It evoked the slightest bit of unease, that I had become this monster after only five years.

"Losing your bloody edge," I muttered, dismissing the thought just as quickly as it had surfaced. I knew what caused this instability within – a dream which still taunted me, even after several weeks had elapsed since I woke with its images fresh in my mind. I relived it each time I considered what placed me on my current course; a memory from my mortal days I had never regained. To recapture something lost after five years was nothing short of a miracle.

I sighed and glanced at my watch, focusing my attention back on the task at hand. The urge to inspect the time surfaced and was dismissed a half-dozen more times before my quarry finally arrived. Had I been forced to wait any longer, I might have had to murder somebody to retain my sanity.

Through the crowd, I spotted him strolling across the dance floor. A stark contrast to the men and women dressed in shiny, modern material, he donned a crushed velvet suit. I rolled my eyes in response, stealing a moment to reflect on how often our kind indulged in the most garish fashions possible. His pale skin nearly appeared to glow from the combination of dark clothing and strobe lights; Anthony seemed only to lack a flashing sign to advertise what he was. The mortal woman holding onto his arm added to the absurdity with her too-thick makeup and promiscuous attire.

Anthony kissed her hand as he helped her slide onto a chair. I stepped from the shadows, drawing from my cigarette and exhaling a cloud of smoke large enough to give myself away. The movement and the puff of white worked their magic. Anthony turned his head, spotting me, while I shot him an impatient glare.

"Excuse me, my dear," Anthony said to his companion. "A little business to attend to." He winked at her conspiratorially before stepping away. She watched while he nodded at me and cocked his head toward the back. I stood straight, pivoting to stroll for the door to the alleyway running behind this godforsaken establishment without waiting for him.

Once outside, a rush of cold air hit me and I felt reborn. The door shut, drowning out the noise from inside. I strolled to the other side of the vacant street and leaned against an adjacent building, finishing my cigarette and flicking its remnant onto the pavement. No sooner did the depleted nicotine smash into the macadam in a display of sparks than the door swung open, bringing with it a painful reminder of the music and the stench from inside.

Anthony looked at me and smiled while the door clucked shut behind him. I breathed a sigh of relief as the night became still once more. "Flynn!" Anthony said, the tone of his voice making it sound as though we were long-lost friends. "I didn't realize you were to return so shortly! You certainly don't waste time, do you?"

"I told you two nights, Anthony," I said, without moving from my position. "And you agreed. It has been two nights and here I am."

"And I should have known Flynn is a man of his word." Anthony adjusted the cravat tied around his neck, another embellishment making his entire outfit look all the more idiotic. "I trust the arrangement we agreed upon is still favorable?"

My facial expression remained stoic. "Were you able to find it?"

Anthony chuckled. "I am able to find anything, given enough persuasion. I spent the better part of last evening interrogating mortals and bleeding them dry to find its current owner. One of my more daunting challenges, but, I found it."

"Let me see it."

"Tut, tut." Anthony lifted a finger, wagging it back and forth in a gesture which threatened to make me lose my self-restraint. With a tremendous amount of effort, I pushed aside my agitation. "First, the answer to my question. You told me that if I procured your trinket, you would offer me protection from Sabrina. Is this agreement still favorable?"

"I have not indicated otherwise." I glared as much as possible through the dark lenses of my sunglasses. Stepping forward a pace, I folded my arms across my chest, feeling the hilt of my knives press against my body from their position underneath my heavy wool coat. "Now, allow me to see it. My end of the bargain is contingent upon this being the item I requested."

"Very well." Anthony slipped a hand into his jacket and removed his wallet from his interior pocket. My anticipation mounted. "I recognized it instantly from your description, so I think you'll find this to be the charm in question." I watched as he opened the billfold and felt as though, if I had a pulse, it would be racing. The action of leather unfolding took on painful slowness, with my mind already envisioning the item I sold in haste four years ago. He reached inside, but then paused.

I could have spat acid when he closed the wallet again.

"You know, Flynn, I find it strange that an immortal with your reputation asked for something like this," he began, apparently emboldened by my affirmation that I still considered our deal favorable. Anthony dug into his coat again and produced a pack of cigarettes from within. "I've fielded some fairly unusual requests –" One stick wound up perched between his lips while he fumbled for his lighter. "– And discovered a great deal about other vampires as a result, but when you told me you wanted something so… feminine… I was taken aback." He chuckled, exhaling smoke through his nostrils while pocketing his lighter. "I thought, if anything, you would desire some sort of weapon."

Drawing a deep breath inward, I held it long enough to steady my anger. "Anthony, as I told you before, this is none of your fucking business."

"Come now, Flynn. Indulge me." He smiled. "Tell me of its relevance."

"I…" The word emerged through the precarious hold I maintained on my own rage. My sharp tone of voice turned vitriolic. "…Would sooner slit your throat and take your wallet while you choke on your own blood. Let us finish our business before I change my mind."

Anthony shook his head. "Now, no need to get snarky. It's a simple question."

"And my response a simple answer. Leave it the fuck alone."

"You know what your problem is." With one hand, Anthony slid the wallet back into his coat. The other hand pointed his cigarette at me while he spoke. "You're too intense, Flynn, for such a young immortal. You take your job too seriously and became reclusive and arrogant as a result. I can assure you, this will earn you no friends amongst the vampire collective."

"As if I desired such a thing." My arms fell to my sides. I began to step around Anthony, itching to instill the fear of God in him, now that the name of the game had changed. "You are all pompous bastards – the lot of you – and your ways irritate me. I could not care less about the opinions of such impotent mortal lovers."

Anthony's eyes widened first, and then narrowed. "What did you call me?"

The corner of my mouth curled in a grin. "I called you a fucking mortal lover. What do you have to say about that?"

Anthony gritted his teeth, tossing aside his cigarette. "I would say that if being something other than the monster you are makes me a mortal lover, then being Sabrina's trained pet makes you little more than the same brand of trash she is. Refuse." He scoffed. "Utter refuse. Chosen son of an inferior coven! You have yours coming to you someday, I can promise you that."

"Is this a threat?"

"More than a threat, it's a fact. Even I see the jealousy your brethren harbor for you. Such jealousy can only fester for so long. They'll surrender your head on a platter the first moment somebody offers thirty pieces of silver." He smiled. "You may have the exterior of a warrior, but you have the heart of a lap dog. And I will not be insulted by such a subordinate creature."

"You shall see the teeth of this lap dog soon enough if you fail to produce that which you promised me, Anthony." Two pointed teeth emerged from their slumber as I ceased pacing, balling my gloved hands into fists. "Or need I run you through to prove my point?"

Anthony hissed, his own fangs slipping out and his eyes shooting figurative flames of wrath. "Bare your teeth at me will you? I was eating the flesh of children before you were suckling on your mother's breast."

"And I have slain immortals for less arrogance than that." Faster than the action of lighting a cigarette, I slipped both hands under the folds of my coat and drew a set of blades, holding out both knives for Anthony to see. "Eager to die?" I asked. "Do you have any notion of how quickly I could make you dust on the pavement?"

Anthony sneered. "Where other men fight with fists, Flynn carries knives with him."

"Better a blade than a stake." I lunged with a knife, but missed on purpose. Anthony dodged out of the way, his grin turning smug while I held back any facial response – including the sadistic grin straining to emerge. "I find stakes idiotic," I continued. "Do you not?"

"Over-inflated mythological devises, much like you."

I lunged again, this time cutting into his jacket, forcing him to retreat a few paces. Anthony's eyes darted to the cut and back to me as if afraid to allow me out of his sight. I smirked. "Is that supposed to be an insult?" I asked. "Coming from a vampire who dresses like the ringmaster of a circus and takes the company of mortals to cover for his inadequacies? I hope to heaven that if I am as pitiful of a creature at your age, somebody does me the favor of sending me to hell."

He hissed once more. When he dove for me, I sidestepped the attack and threw him to the ground. He spilled out and moaned, but rose to his feet. I anticipated

Anthony's next charge, and kicked him in the chest with such force that his feet left the ground. His head impacted with the concrete of the wall; a solid thud preceded a long, pain-laden groan.

Springing toward him, I closed the distance between us and plunged a dagger deep into his stomach. Anthony screamed as I stepped back, watching him struggle. The hilt of my knife jutted from his abdomen. I had him pinned, and his wriggling merely served to injure him further.

I turned the other knife around in my hand, surveying the ruins of a vampire with my sadistic smirk only growing more devious the longer I regarded him. "My, what an uncomfortable position to be in," I said, shaking my head. "And to think, I have another knife here that... ah yes, wait..." I held up a finger and lifted the blade close to my ear. "Yes, yes, I do believe this one says it wishes to know how black your heart is, Anthony. I do not know if I will be able to stop..."

"Alright!" Anthony yelled. He moaned once more and gritted his teeth, eyes clenching in a grimace. "Alright, I won't ask any more bloody questions, Flynn. Just let me down."

"I beg your pardon?" I lowered the knife, twirling it around once before slipping it back into his sheath. "I believe you forgot to say please."

"Please! Please, please... Bloody hell, let me down. I'm begging you."

"That is more like it." Walking closer to Anthony, I wrapped my fingers around the knife's hilt, but leaned forward and made certain to bare fangs again as I spoke. "Remember who you are trifling with. I would slice you from neck to stomach and leave you bleeding on the street to watch the sun rise. I suggest, when I remove this blade, you give me what I came for quickly and stop wasting my fucking time."

I ripped the knife from his body before he had the chance to answer and watched with an apathetic air as he crumpled to the gritty pavement again. Strolling away from the wounded vampire, I produced a cloth from my pocket and wiped the blade clean, my eyes rising toward the sky to gauge the time. I frowned and sheathed this blade as well. "Some time before dawn, please," I said. "It is not getting any earlier."

"Fuck," Anthony muttered while clutching onto the building and coming to a tentative stand. Pausing to touch his wound, he winced and raised his crimson-coated fingers up to his line of vision. "I had best make this our last encounter. You just ruined a perfectly good suit."

I said nothing in return. Anthony rummaged through his coat again and unfolded his wallet without hesitation. As he opened it, that sense of time standing still drifted from the creases of the leather and his bloody fingers held my attention captive while they reached inside. A gold chain gradually came to view as he raised his hand, and when the pendant emerged from its hiding place I had to fight the urge to draw a sharp breath inward at the sight of what he held.

Anthony raised an eyebrow. "Is this what you requested?" he asked.

I strolled forward with more confidence in my gait than I possessed at the moment and snatched the necklace away. "Yes," I said, my voice subdued in such a queer manner, it even struck me as odd. I cleared my throat to mask the slip in composure. Staring at the pendant, I lowered it into the palm of my other hand

and allowed my thoughts to drift.

I visited another time and place. Back to when my name was Peter and I possessed the pulse of a mortal man.

It was supposed to be an engagement ring. That was why I withdrew several hundred dollars from the trust fund my aunt established before she succumbed to cancer. The money from my parents' life insurance policies and the profits from selling my father's farm were all meant to sustain me through medical school, but as my residency drew to a close, I came to the conclusion that the time was right to propose to my beloved Lydia. That was why I found myself at the jewelry store.

I emerged with something other than a ring, however.

On this side of my dance with immortality, I could not recall why I purchased the necklace for her until visited by the dream. Then all at once, this calloused heart felt a chill cross over its grave and relived the memory as though it had some relevance to the grander scheme of things. I recalled the jeweler looking across the counter at an indecisive young man, watching as I studied several diamond rings and rejected each one. Finally, he huffed and said, "Mr. Dawes, if you're not sure about this, then it's probably not the best time to propose to her, is it?"

Looking up at him, I furrowed my brow, glancing from his face to the counter and back again. I frowned at my hesitation, yet allowed myself to peruse the rest of his wares until my eyes settled on it. Gilded and Gothic, it fit her personality better than the cut pieces of stone I had been studying anyway. "Well, I need to get something for her," I said to the crotchety old bastard. "It's her birthday in a few days."

My eyes continued to admire the pendant, taking in all of its intricacies. Two hearts, one on top of the other, with a thorny rose draped across the two. It was something so intricate and yet, so macabre. At once, I knew Lydia was meant to have it. It was a perfect emblem for her.

I recalled purchasing it. I recalled giving it to her. That was another memory causing me some degree of...

"Flynn?"

Shaking myself from my thoughts, my eyes lifted to engage Anthony's once more. He clutched his stomach and scowled at me. "Is this what you were looking for?"

"Yes." I nodded and thrust the necklace into my pocket. "You are a clever bastard, I shall give you that."

"Good. Then our agreement is intact?"

"Oh yes. I shall ensure Sabrina does not touch a hair upon your head."

"Praise be to the Fates." Anthony sighed, glancing at his blood-soaked hand. "I feared when we first met that she had ordered you to do me in. Believe me, Flynn, I'll not be crossing your path again, except on accid..."

As he looked at me again, I reached underneath my coat and drew a knife. With a deft flick of my wrist, I whipped it toward Anthony, whose eyes became wide as the blade plunged deep into his chest.

I grinned. "No, Anthony. Not even on accident."

What had once been Anthony burned into dust and descended onto the ground as ash and discarded clothing. My knife bounced off the pavement with a clank and came to settle next to his remains while a gust of wind carried his remnant into the nether. I strolled toward the blade, exhaling a breath I did not know I was holding, and paused to clean my weapon again before I slipped it into its sheath. My eyes remained set upon his ashes, though. "I said Sabrina would not. I did not guarantee the same for me."

With a quick adjustment of my coat and a moment stolen to run my fingers through my hair, I set out with my pearl of great price. As I headed back for my coven, though, I knew I had just played a dangerous game and could yet face wrath for the indulgence. Sabrina's eyes extended through a network of spies who usually worked to my benefit. In this singular action, though, they became my bane. I had to do it, though; one memory hinted at other secrets lying in wait without telling me what existed behind the veil. All I knew was I wanted to unravel it. I wanted to know who I was at long last.

So, I lit another cigarette, and then slipped into the shadows to seek a proper victim before retiring for the day. And I hoped this small measure of insubordination would not come back to haunt me the next night.

CHAPTER TEN

The pendant felt as though it was burning a hole in my pocket as I returned to the coven house, bent on retiring for the morning and putting the whole sordid episode with Anthony behind me. I offered the doorman a cursory nod, masking my discomfort at smuggling contraband through the front doors, and maintained my typical casual gait as I crossed the foyer.

Wing-tipped shoes took the stairs two at a time while my mind remained fixated on Sabrina. My meeting with Anthony had marked the eve of my fifth immortal birthday, and the passing of the midnight hour brought with it memories of how my mistress enjoyed celebrating the anniversary of my awakening. I suppressed a shiver at the vision in my mind – Sabrina lying on her bed, her body's only adornment a cascade of flowing red hair shimmering in the candlelight. The thought of her hands exploring beneath my clothing troubled me, though, as it brought with it the possibility of the pendant's discovery.

Shaking my head, I continued up the stairs. The hour grew late and I needed to rest.

I passed my brethren without making eye contact, but caught glimpses of their facial expressions as I passed. The standard fare, it was what I had come to expect after years of debauchery. Cold stares. Distrust and a slight tinge of fear laden in the way they regarded me, knowing with what ease I could end each of them. The corner of my mouth curled upward. I finished my ascent, musing on the benefits of my station aside from a very small circle of friends.

My accommodations, for instance. No longer slumbering in a neophyte's closet, I sojourned in a spacious living area normally reserved for elder vampires. No, I had no need of Anthony's reminder to realize how much jealousy flew about me and how many hands itched for the tools to my undoing. Not a one of them dared to cross Sabrina, though, because they all knew better than to attempt and fail. Others had tried; none had succeeded. It discouraged repeat performances.

Still, as I approached the door to my room, the faint traces of perfume which wafted near my door reminded me I yet held favored status with some. I paused to remove my leather gloves and slipped them into my pocket. My fledgling smile blossomed into a full grin. I did not love the woman, this much was certain, but her presence pleased me nonetheless.

I reached for the knob. "Rose. Sweet Rose," I said as I stepped inside and shut the door behind me, blocking out the artificial lighting in the hallway. Darkness wrapped itself around me, broken only by the soft glow of a sparse collection of candles. I breathed a sigh of relief. "Came for a visit?"

The slender figure of a blonde-haired woman stood no more than ten feet away. Rose turned to face me, revealing a low-cut black dress hugging tight to her curves with her long hair spilling onto her breasts. She returned my grin with one of her own and closed the distance between us. "I haven't seen you for a while, so I thought I would claim the elusive Flynn first." Rose lifted her hands to slide my glasses from my face. "Happy birthday, darling."

"Thank you, my dear," I said as I blinked a few times, adjusting my eyes to the dim light. Rose set my glasses onto a table while I strolled further into my room, removing my coat as I walked. "I had a few matters to attend to before I could return, but had hoped to be back sooner."

"As did I." Rose slithered behind me, taking my coat from my grip and tossing it onto a chair before placing her hands on my shoulders. I felt her fingers run along my back and suppressed a soft groan. "You stayed out so close to dawn. Have you become suicidal or is it another brand of being fearless?"

I laughed. "No, it was that twit Anthony from Matthew's coven." I let Rose slide my suit jacket from my torso and watched it join my coat on the chair. "I had to finish my business with that overinflated piece of refuse before I could sate my own needs for the night."

"So it is done, then?"

Rose's hands caressed the blades against my body and I closed my eyes in response, as though she was stroking more than steel with those long fingers. "Yes, it is done. Though there is no doubt in my mind Sabrina shall be upset with me. I had at him twice before completing the act."

"Living life dangerously? You will need a very convincing tale to escape Sabrina's wrath." One of her well-manicured nails taunted at a button.

The corner of my mouth curled upward. "I will tell her I sought a trinket for you," I said as I turned to face Rose. "Something as beautiful as you, thus giving him an impossible task."

Rose smiled. Past her parted lips, I saw her fangs lying in slumber. "And now, Flynn flatters me," she said as she leaned close. Her voice descended to a whisper. "Tell me a story before you seduce me."

"What type of story?"

"What did you really ask Anthony to retrieve?"

"This is a boring tale with a disappointing ending. He was unable to locate what I requested."

"Then tell me he thought he had a chance to escape."

I chuckled at her schoolgirl-like enthusiasm. "Oh, he did." Reaching up with one hand, I brushed her hair away from her chest and allowed my gaze to drift southward. My fingertips ran along the edge of the fabric lying against her cleavage while my devilish gaze rose to intersect hers again. "I tore his garish clothing," I said, "And ran him through his gut while he bled like a stuck pig. Then I sank my blade into his chest and watched the wind carry him away."

She laughed. "Reduced to a pile of dust."

"Only ash and nothing more."

Her lips crashed into mine, our bodies pressing together despite the blades I yet wore. Rose pulled away from the kiss to whisper against my lips. "Tell me another story." The words dripped with lust. "Who did you kill before Anthony?"

Cupping the back of her head, I nipped at her bottom lip as I responded.

"Demetrius, again of Matthew's coven. One of his elders. The stupid bastard tried to ferret out information from Robin."

"Stupid bastard, indeed." We kissed once more. "Tell me you made his death slow. Tell me you made him suffer."

"He suffered good and proper, Pet." Stripping off my shoulder holster, I tossed my knives out of the way, and then took hold of Rose again. "I pinned him against the wall and rid him of the curse that was his head."

"Soon there will be nothing left of Matthew's coven."

"Not when I am through with it." Our mouths hovered dangerously close. "I shall kill them all, one by one. Their blood shall form a river of crimson underneath my feet and I shall laugh like a madman as they perish. How does that sound, Rose? Does this fantasy please you?"

Rose threw back her head and laughed before jumping into my arms and devouring me with kisses. We stumbled to my bedroom and fell onto the bed while she popped the buttons from my shirt and raked her fangs across my bare chest. Enraptured though I was, the fatigue of the hour began to make its presence known. So I rolled on top of Rose and took the reins, exchanging her typically slow, deliberate pace for one of my own.

I was sound asleep by the time she left, comatose within mere minutes of achieving our satisfaction. The scorn of Sabrina awaited me when I woke, but at the moment, the wrath of any being seemed far-removed.

Or, so I thought.

⚜

I had been asleep for a while when the ancient premonition returned.

The first thing I became aware of was a flash of brilliant white light, throwing me into a sterile environment lacking even walls. The bright illumination surrounding me should have had me writhing and praying for death, but pain remained conspicuously absent even without my dark spectacles to protect me. At once the solution became transparent, something impossible and yet, the only explanation I could conjure.

I was dead. One of my enemies slipped in as I slept and plunged a blade through my chest. If I had gone on into the hereafter, however, I could not help but wonder if the paperwork had been misappropriated. The waiting room surrounding me could hardly be described as the portal to hell.

"Hello?" I said, turning around only to find the same endless room surrounding me on the other side. "Would anybody care to explain where I am and what the fuck I am doing here?"

"I remember him," a voice said in response, one too familiar for me to ignore. My skin crawled as she continued speaking somewhere behind me. "But he wasn't this 'Flynn' person back then. I believe his name was Peter."

I sneered. "Miss Davies, it has been a while." Turning to face Lydia, I scowled at her while her emerald eyes shined defiance back at me. This time, my former lover possessed no sword of which to speak and none of the past wounds I inflicted bleeding through the white dress she wore. She held herself with an air of authority; not a victim, but a force.

"Yes, it has been," she said. "Four years, to be exact."

"Indeed," I said, "And I seem to recall telling you then that your Peter does not live here any longer. Now, have you come to bore me further, or do you have something relevant to say?"

Lydia held her gaze, even when mine turned sinister. "You looked for the necklace again." Moving forward, she strolled as though having all the time in the world. "If Peter doesn't live there anymore, then why did that dream haunt you so much?"

"So that was you?" I laughed. "I should have known, with such a memory returning after so many years locked away." Knitting my hands behind my back, I paced around her. "The adulterous wench returns. And she wishes me to recall such trivialities as a necklace. Why is this, Lydia?"

"Who says I was the one who gave you back that memory?"

"These things do not simply happen on their own."

Lydia smirked. "Are you sure about that?" She raised an eyebrow. "Maybe that meddlesome mortal you think died five years ago is still alive in there somewhere. Have you ever stopped to think about that?"

"No, dearest, I have been too busy entertaining notions of what I might do with this pendant." I stopped pacing and smiled, baring fangs at Lydia. "Perhaps I might drape it over the necks of the women I seduce right before I murder them. I could use it as a token to lure them to their deaths."

She scoffed. "Why don't you just wear it to spite me, Flynn?"

"Splendid. Perhaps I shall."

Lydia laughed. "I don't buy the persona. It's nothing but a facade."

"I can show you what a facade looks like." Walking closer to her, I raised a hand and touched her chin, pointing her neck toward me. Instead of plunging my fangs into her throat, though, I leaned close and whispered in her ear. "How about the facade of telling somebody that you love them and then whoring yourself like the slut you were? That you pretend not to be with your self-righteous bluster? How is that for a facade, Precious?"

"Why does Flynn care about that?"

"Oh, make no mistake about it, I do not give a shit about your mortal infidelity any longer," I stepped back, pushing her head away. "I have no lack of lovers. I can pick and choose whom I please and have my way with all of them at once if I wish. I am merely exposing your hypocrisy." Pausing, I waited for her gaze to return to mine. "Now, it is my turn for questions. Why have you visited me again?"

"Because I want to speak to Peter."

"And what do you wish to say to him?"

Lydia narrowed her eyes. "You're holding back his gifts."

I scoffed. "Gifts," I said. "Here we go with this cloak and dagger bullshit everybody feeds me without anyone explaining what the devil they mean."

"Kind of makes you think." Lydia grinned. "Doesn't it?"

The smug look on her face raised my ire at once. I sneered. "Fuck you, and fuck that name you keep evoking. Stuff these bloody gifts of yours; if you have answers for me, then I am all ears, but if not, then leave me alone and never come back." My voice rose in volume as my irritation grew. "I am *sick* of being touted as some special creature without being let in on the riddle. The last thing I need is another voice in the chorus."

My voice boomed throughout the room, a hush falling only as the echoes dissipated. Lydia held my gaze for a moment. We seemed fixed at an impasse until she said, "There are more things going on than you can begin to imagine. Things that have been in existence longer than there's been a vampire named Flynn. All I can tell you is that the answers are coming." Lydia frowned. "I only hope there's enough of Peter left in there to hear them."

I did not respond. Lydia turned to depart from my presence, but something caused her a moment's hesitation. She looked back at me. "Just remember, not everything is what it seems to be. If Peter is still there, past the violence and death, he will understand this phrase. '*The only thing worse than being blind is having sight, but no vision.*'" Her eyes fell to the ground. "And I never stopped loving you. You're the one who stopped loving me."

Lydia consummated her departure as though carried off by the wind; there one moment and gone the next. I stood in the midst of the white room with nothing but another riddle until the light began to fade. My waking eyes opened to reveal my slumbering body had never left the bed.

The darkness of heavy shades was not enough to fully mask that it was daytime and my retinas were none too thrilled with this fact. The ache rose to a burn, so I covered my face and slid out of bed, carefully maneuvering around the memorized layout of my room and avoiding a collision with several pieces of furniture along the way. '*Damn Rose,*' I thought to myself. '*She left my sunglasses next to the door.*' I muttered obscenities until finding the table in the entryway, locating my spectacles entirely by touch.

A sigh of relief punctuated shoving the dark lenses over my eyes, but from there I was unable to settle into sleep again. So, I showered, dressed, and whittled away some time staring at Lydia's necklace, wondering why I was entertaining her words as much as I found myself doing. Sight, but no vision. I remembered the quote as being one of her oft-recited proverbs, although I had no notion of why it was relevant to me. "Mortal nonsense," I said aloud, wrapping the chain around my fingers and allowing the pendant to dangle toward the palm of my hand. "That is all this amounts to." I shook my head and thrust the offending piece of jewelry into my pants pocket, rising from my chair to find something else to occupy my mind. Ghosts from the beyond, whispering their idle threats and veiled insight, were the least of my concerns on the fifth anniversary of my death.

I had a coven mother to face when the sun set.

CHAPTER ELEVEN

Robin ingrained the rules of being an assassin in me far before I set out to kill my first target. I could recite the three credos in my sleep. *'Be quick. Be accurate. Do not let one set of eyes spot you.'* I held them as dear as a religion and paid sacrifice at the altar of my god each time I drew a blade. As much as I enjoyed my position, though, and relished the sadism it ensconced me in, being a vampire hit man leaned itself to a peculiar conundrum.

After the first vampire I vanquished fell to the ground in a pile of ash, a disturbing notion had unseated the elation which followed. The more I thought about it, the more I realized that once my mission was complete, I had no way of proving I was the one who sent the departed packing from this mortal coil. Vampires are oft to wanderlust and can meet their end in a variety of manners. I wished to make certain all knew exactly what happened.

Anthony, of Matthew's coven, would be no different.

It seemed to take an eternity for the sun to set. I whittled away the hours by alternately reading and swinging around my newest sword, acquired after visiting a shop on the northern edge of Center City. A handsome piece of craftsmanship, the katana boasted of superior quality steel and a hilt styled with black and red adornments. I made certain to inform its maker of my approval before I left him bleeding on the floor of his establishment.

The sword hung at my side when I left my room and strolled into the corridor, headed for my brother Robin's private quarters. Not his original room either, it represented my brother's strange behavior as of late. I could only guess what occupied his mind, but Robin often provided me an ear of counsel despite his frequent misgivings with my personal code of conduct.

I approached his door and listened for activity inside his room.

Silence greeted me. I rapped my knuckles on the sturdy piece of oak, but still no sign of life made its presence known. Sighing, I adjusted the black, leather gloves on my hands and pounded on his door much harder. This time, a groan drifted outward and inspired a grin to curl the corner of my mouth. "Rise and shine, brother," I said. "Sunset waits for no vampire."

"Flynn," the groggy voice of Robin answered. "Please do not tell me you are waking me prior to sunset."

"Sunset passed a half hour ago, Robin." In a much lower tone of voice, I added, "Perhaps if you were not merely taking up space in this coven, you might be more aware of the time."

I heard his feet hit the hardwood floor and pad closer until the door swung open. The coven's second stared at me, disheveled and half-asleep. His shoulder-length hair fell alongside his face, not tied back as normal, and nothing but a pair of loose pajama pants kept Robin from standing bare before me. "What the devil brings you here so early?" he asked. "You're lying about sunset. I just checked my watch and it has not been a half hour."

My smirk grew more devilish. "A half hour, fifteen minutes, what does it matter? It is evening, brother, and once again you are wallowing in sloth."

Robin opened his door wider to permit me passage through before shutting it and surrounding us with darkness. I raised my hand to remove my sunglasses, but no sooner did I touch the hard plastic than my brother switched on a lamp and thwarted my plans. "Just because I did not bound out of bed does not mean I am lazy," he said, walking toward his closet, his voice still hoarse from sleep. "Not all the world rises two strokes past dusk."

I followed. "They should. Night perishes too quickly for us immortals."

"I hardly think that is the reason why you rose early tonight. I think it has more to do with what day it is."

"What would that have to do with it?"

Robin scoffed. "Oh come now, Flynn, I know how the mistress likes to thank you for being her angel of death. The entire coven has their designated moment when she spreads her legs for them and birthdays are yours."

"Well, somebody is in a mood." I perked an eyebrow as Robin picked a shirt and pair of pants out of his closet. "Do you have need of getting laid, dear brother?"

"Are you offering?" Robin shot me a look of annoyance before sighing and bringing his clothing to his bathroom. I lost sight of him, but heard the change in his demeanor when he spoke again. "I am sorry, brother. Last night simply wasn't a pleasant night for me."

I walked toward a wall and leaned against it. "What happened?"

"Nothing worth discussing. Give me a moment to freshen up. I'll be out as quickly as possible."

"Very well." No sooner did I respond than the bathroom door shut, severing our conversation. I sighed, glancing toward the heavy shades blocking his windows, already feeling the siren song of the night beckon me out for a kill. The blood thirst was not all that made its presence known in my consciousness, however. Embers of dread caught fire once more, playing an unfamiliar tune within my normally cool and focused demeanor.

I indulged in a deep, steadying breath just as the bathroom door opened. Robin strolled out, his hair tied back and a dress shirt and pants on his slender frame. Order reigned over his regal appearance. "So, brother," he said, walking back into his closet. "What did you come to discuss?"

"I wished to ask you a question," I said, drifting closer to my brother.

"A question." The words were spoken not as an inquiry, but a statement. I watched Robin select a tie from his collection and slide it around his throat, not bothering to tie it before moving onward to fetch a pair of shoes and socks. I began to think him ignoring me until he added, "Well, Flynn, speak your question. I can hardly read your mind."

"Very well, then." I took one step back, allowing Robin to exit his closet. "I wished for you to do me a favor."

"How did I know?" Robin huffed as he walked toward his sitting area. "I do not suppose this has anything to do with a black rose."

My grin turned cunning, the killer responding to his calling card. "As a matter of fact, it does. I must report to Sabrina, but while I do, would you see to delivering a present?"

My brother sank into a chair, placing his shoes on the floor. "Do I have much of a choice when it comes to you and your little errands?" He sighed, and began slipping on his socks. "Where am I headed tonight, Flynn?"

"I do not suppose you will be strolling by Matthew's coven again anytime soon?"

"Why? Who is the dearly departed?"

"His little scavenger Anthony is no more."

"Matthew will be thrilled about this." Robin frowned, moving on to his shoes. "No, I do not merely stroll past his coven. I already have the death of one of his elders on my head for the last time I came close."

"Yes, no doubt." My eyes returned to Robin. "The mistress is still quite suspicious of why you were speaking with Demetrius in the first place."

The words created an immediate reaction. A smile laden with bitterness touched the corners of his mouth, his eyes remaining set on the task at hand. "Yes, I imagine she is." Robin finished lacing his shoes. When his gaze met mine again, I had to frown at the way he regarded me. "Well, I ceased trying to please the mistress a very long time ago, Flynn. She can question me all she wants and find herself a new second if she so desires. I refuse to justify my actions to her."

I continued watching the cavalcade of sentiments within Robin's eyes until he looked away. Standing, Robin started to thread his tie. Silence fell between us. When Robin realized I was yet staring at him, he looked at me again. The frown which surfaced struck me as peculiar. "Be careful, brother."

I smirked despite myself. "When am I not?"

"Oh, you are plenty careful on the streets," he said. "Just not where it matters the most." Robin stood, plucking a suit jacket from an adjacent chair. He threaded his arms into each sleeve. "I see you have a new sword."

He glanced at the katana by my side. I grinned. "Do you like it?"

"It suits you." Robin adjusted his jacket and nodded. "You shall have to allow me a better look when time permits. In the meantime, I will leave your black rose on Matthew's doorstep and you shall see to the mistress. You know it is best not to keep her waiting."

"Yes, indeed." My eyes rose toward the ceiling, as though I could see through and into Sabrina's bedroom. Once again, my skin crawled slightly before I shook off the premonition. I looked back down at Robin and nodded. "Join me for a hunt afterward? We can slay mortals and drink brandy like brothers."

"I do not know." For the first time that night, Robin smirked. "Every time we go out together, you wind up corrupting me."

"I get you to remove that bloody stick up your ass, you mean." I smiled in return and felt somewhat more at ease when my brother chuckled and walked ahead of me to his door. He opened it, but paused to look back at me, his hand still on the door knob.

I perked an eyebrow at him. "What is it?" I asked.

Robin sighed and nodded. "I will look for you when my business is finished. To 'remove the stick up my ass' as you so eloquently put it."

I laughed, walking out to the corridor and strolling beside him when he shut the door. "Did you just swear, Robin?"

"No, I quoted you. There is a difference." His grin resurfaced and remained a fixture until we reached the stairs and headed in opposite directions. I nodded at him when he said, "Until later, brother," and watched him trudge down the first flight of stairs. Then, I turned toward the path to Sabrina's door.

Swift footsteps carried me upward and as I reached the top of the staircase, I took notice of a familiar face departing from Sabrina's room. My brother Timothy nodded toward Sabrina's guard and ran his fingers through his disheveled brown locks before looking at me. The grin on his face spoke a thousand words without a one of them uttered. I rolled my eyes and paused when Timothy stopped in front of me.

"Did you wrestle with a lion, Timothy?" I asked, impatience marking the inquiry.

Timothy chuckled, a smug grin surfacing. "You know, you're not the only one the mistress shows favor to, Flynn."

"Ah, Sabrina did this to you?" I perked an eyebrow. "So she is in *that* type of mood."

"Oh yes, she's a regular firecracker tonight. I brought her dinner and let's just say she came back for dessert." Timothy stared at me, but I failed to register a reaction to his words. His eyes glinted with a hint of loathe in response. "Rumor has it you're slipping."

"Oh, does it?" I shrugged, appearing more nonchalant about hearing such news than I truly felt. "Had to strike at the best moment possible. Not that you would know about such things." I flashed him a sarcastic smile.

Timothy bristled. "I know more about them than you might suspect."

"Undoubtedly, Timothy. A man of your skill and prowess could instruct even an assassin such as me." I bowed with a flourish.

"Fuck off, Flynn." A dismissive wave of his hand preceded a pivot toward the stairs. "I'll let you get to the inquisition I have no doubt awaits you. Happy Birthday, *brother.*" Timothy cackled. I fought off the urge to draw my sword and sever his head from the rest of his body, hand upon the hilt and eyes focused on his entire trek until he descended from sight. My mouth opened to rain down obscenities upon the ghost of his presence until another voice entered the fray.

"Flynn."

Knocked from a homicidal tail spin, I turned and directed my attention to Sabrina's guard as he cleared his throat and stared at me. Even Paul possessed the fear of me in his brown eyes when they regarded me. "Sabrina waits," he said.

I nodded in response. Paul opened the door to her penthouse. A shiver ran up my spine as I entered and the click of the door closing behind me bore an eerie finality to it.

At first it seemed my fears were unwarranted. As was tradition, Sabrina had lit the room with candles. I removed my glasses, slipping them into my pocket just in time for her to acknowledge my presence. "Is that my dark killer?" she asked, and had it been anybody else, I would not have been disquieted by the soft, sweet tone of voice she possessed. As it was, hearing it did nothing to quell my apprehension.

"It is I." I indulged in one last, steadying breath before continuing inside. Strolling through the sitting area without pause, I walked to her bedroom and leaned against the doorway. "Good evening, dark mother," I said, eying my mistress. "You look radiant as usual. I trust your time in New York was pleasant?"

Sabrina smiled. Sitting in a chair facing her desk, she surveyed the jewelry laid before her, her hands busy fastening an earring to an ear. I stood straight again and walked closer, picking up her necklace. Sabrina lowered her hands, yet sat perfectly still, allowing me to fasten the gold chain around her neck and place a soft kiss just below her ear.

She smelt like roses. Her cheeks were ruddy from a fresh feed. A soft moan rose from her throat as I stepped away. "Darling Flynn," she said with a chuckle. "You are debonair as always."

"Only for you, Mistress." I smirked as she looked at me. Her eyes caressed mine in a deep gaze reminiscent of ambrosia, delectable and decadent. I drank from it as we stared at one another. "My charms may seduce the mortals, but for you, they are a mark of my devotion."

"And devoted you are, dear." Sabrina turned in her chair to face me. "Five years has passed us by rather quickly, hasn't it? And you have only impressed me all the more with what a vampire you have become."

Bowing, I allowed my smile to become all the more sinister. "As always, I have you to thank for that."

She stood. "I only bestowed the dark gift, my son. You are the one who has become the face the seven covens see in their nightmares." Sabrina stepped close to me, placing a hand on the lapel of my coat, her gaze never straying from mine. "If I had to do it all over, I would slide my teeth into that frightened mortal and allow him to cross into immortality again. Your will is as sure as it was when I commissioned you to be my assassin."

Her chest touched mine and her lips hovered close. I felt my fangs slip from their hiding place as I plunged into a state of arousal. "And I would drink from your wrist again eagerly," I said, "Bathing my tongue with your blood."

"Oh yes, I know you would." I felt a hand slide down and cup me through my trousers. The groan I emitted brought a smile to her face. "You desire to kiss me, my killer?"

I shivered, my voice husky as I issued my response. "I desire to do far more than that."

Sabrina laughed in response. Her hand granted me an extra squeeze. "Oh, I know you do, but first tell me, my darling Flynn, if the task I assigned before I left has been completed?"

"Yes, it has." My hands burned with the desire to touch her as well, rising in a cautious manner beyond my own volition. A slow nod preceded a hard swallow. "A dagger straight through his heart, just as you requested."

"Very good." She leaned closer, tipping her head to entreat me. My hands landed on her back. Shutting my eyes, I moved forward to engage her lips with mine.

Until a hand wrapped itself around my throat.

My eyes flew open. Hers did as well. A look of malice replaced the seduction which had been present no more than mere seconds prior. "Insolent vampire!" she yelled, her fangs slipping out. "How dare you not confess your sins to me?!"

Before I had the chance to react, I found myself being thrown onto a chair, the hilt of my sword digging into my side as I spilled onto the seat. Sabrina slapped me across my face with such force it whipped my head to the side. Her foot crushed down on top of the arousal her previous actions brought about.

I screamed with pain, my vision swimming. Grabbing my chin, she turned my head to point my face in her direction again.

"For four years, I have come to rely on you, Flynn!" she said, her voice ascending to a shout from the start. I imagined the entire coven house could hear her as she roared, but I found myself nothing but thankful as her foot let up its pressure. "To do as you are asked and when you are asked to do it! I asked that you kill Anthony two days prior to when you finished the task. *Two days!* I had to find out from my spies that you extended Anthony mercy to go on a little hunt for you." Grabbing my coat with both hands, she lifted me to my feet, slamming me against her body. "May I remind you I have killed people for less insubordination?"

I sneered, pain radiating from my groin. "No, you need not remind me. I am usually the one doing the killing for you."

Sabrina hit me again, but held onto me to prevent me from flying back. I hissed at the affront, but she ignored the outburst and drew me close again. "I am embarrassed at you!" she said. "That I have to have a talk with you I normally reserve for the underlings. What do you have to say for yourself?!"

A growl rumbled from my throat. "I can only apologize for my lapse in judgment."

"Lapse?" Sabrina threw me back onto the chair and straddled my lap. Her fingernails cut into my skin when she grabbed me by the neck, drawing rivulets of blood. "A lapse in judgment would have been for you to kill him in front of a witness or to strike at an inopportune moment, not to hold off his execution for two days. So, let me ask, what was so damn important that you would consort with a traitor and an enemy of the coven?!"

Swallowing hard, I presented a half-truth to the only soul I had a hard time lying to. "I lost something and wished to have it back. Nothing more. There was no treason in my actions."

"Your disobedience was your treason. What was this item?"

"A piece of jewelry." I paused, attempting to make this sound convincing and thankful the more severe pain was disappearing. "Anthony was unable to find it, though. I promptly disposed of the piece of waste when he failed me."

Sabrina raised an eyebrow. Her grip relaxed, but only slightly. "Jewelry of what sort? And why was this important to you?"

"It was not important. Merely a trinket I stole from one of my victims, but sold in haste. I wished to give it to Rose."

She continued staring at me, her gaze searching and skeptical. I met the look she shot me measure by measure, a disarming grin ghosting at the corner of my mouth. "Mistress, surely you do not think I would betray you. I merely thought the bastard should be good for something before I ran him through." My smile broadened. "You would have been amused, watching him believe I would spare his life."

Sabrina's eyes remained locked for another precarious moment, until her scowl finally relaxed. She indulged in a deep breath and let go of my neck, her fangs retracting. I nearly sighed with relief when she smiled. "You are devilishly sadistic, my assassin," she said. "I should have known you were merely making sport out of him."

I scoffed. "Naturally, Mistress. I am nothing but loyal to you."

"Yes, you are, Flynn." Sabrina stood. She strolled back to her desk and sat in front of her jewelry once more. Lifting her other earring, Sabrina set about the task of securing it to her lobe. "It's a shame Anthony was not able to procure your piece of jewelry."

"Yes, well, we both know what a moronic waste of space he was." I rubbed my neck, feeling the grooves where Sabrina's nails had dug in. The scent of blood teased at my nostrils and when I lifted my fingers, the viscous liquid glistening on my glove verified the slight damage done. "He looked better as a pile of dust than he did as a vampire."

Sabrina laughed. "This better have taught you a lesson, though. When I say they are to die, they die at once and not a moment afterward."

"Lesson learned, Mistress." Sitting up in my chair, I wiped at the blood on my neck one final time. "Now, tell your assassin what he might do to make it up to you."

She smiled. "My darling Flynn. He does live for the kill." Glancing at me to wink, she turned her attention back to the collection of gold in front of her and slipped her rings on her fingers. "Well, there is one thing, as much as I was hoping to hold off on assigning you a task on your birthday. I think you will find this target in particular amusing, though, so consider it a present of sorts."

I perked an eyebrow. "Amusing? Do tell."

"There is a human who is causing me a great deal of consternation." She paused. "I want her gone before she meddles in my affairs any longer. Several members of the coven have caught her snooping around lately and one was successful in tracking her down. Now, I need my assassin to strike while the iron is hot."

"A human?" I laughed. "Oh please, Mistress. Tell me you are jesting."

"I'm not, Flynn, and this one is no ordinary girl." She raised an eyebrow in my direction. "So don't underestimate her."

"Underestimate her?" My laugh turned more uproarious. I shook my head. "The covens throw the best they have to offer at me and all of them meet with a swift end. I highly doubt some mortal girl is going to give me much trouble."

"As I said she is not ordinary. I believe she might be a sorceress."

"A sorceress?" This only served to tickle me all the more. "Has she attempted to call down hexes on the coven or turn one of us into a newt?" I continued to chuckle, but when Sabrina failed to join in my merriment, I sobered slightly. The grin remained affixed on my face, however. "Who is the girl and what harm does she mean you?" I asked.

Sabrina stood, walking back to where I sat with a look in her eyes which caused my stomach to churn again. Heavy-lidded seduction dripped from every step she took. She lowered herself slowly onto my lap again. Touching my chin, she lifted my head to ensure she had my full attention. This time, when her fangs slipped from their hiding place, my teeth slid out in arousal.

Sabrina grinned and leaned close. "Do you trust me, dark son?" she asked. Her lips touched my neck.

My eyes drifted shut. I nodded, whispering. "Absolutely, Mistress."

She placed a kiss further up my neck. The points of her teeth tickled at my skin. "And you still desire me?"

"Yes, I do."

"Your mistress has not forgotten your birthday kisses. I will reward you for your loyalty to me. But first, I need you to quiet your mind and listen to my words." She paused. Her lips found my ear and teased at the lobe with her cool breath as she spoke. "The girl must die. And my killer – my assassin – will do it for me without needing to know why. Instead, he will do the deed exactly as he was asked. When he returns, then I will show him my appreciation. This is all the motivation you need. Understood?"

A slow nod followed her words. "Yes," I said, speaking the word while hearing it echo as though through a tunnel. My mind seemed to be swimming down the current of Sabrina's ministrations, not tethered to my body. "I understand."

Her lips departed from their position beside my ear. She pulled back and, like a moon emerging from an eclipse, her face slowly came into view. Our noses brushed and mouths touched when she leaned closer, the contact tentative; teasing. I rose slightly to kiss her back, but she stopped me with a finger placed on my lips, pushing me against the back of the chair.

"My kisses will be here waiting for you," she said. "In the meantime, you will go to Temple University. You will locate a girl named Monica Alexander. She has brown hair with a blonde streak that runs down her bangs, and she resides in a small house by the edge of the campus." Sabrina's fingers slid into the breast pocket of my suit jacket, depositing a small slip of paper I knew would contain a more precise location. "Kill her quickly and silently, and bring me the scarf she keeps wrapped around her neck as proof of her death."

I swallowed hard. "It shall be done as you say."

"Good." Sabrina stood, severing the connection. I blinked, my head feeling as though it was surfacing from being submerged. Sabrina looked down at me, smiling as I stood. "Is that a new sword, dear?" she asked.

Glancing down at the katana, I furrowed my brow at the weapon, as though I had forgotten about its presence until that moment. "Yes, it is," I said, looking back at her. "I figured the red and black suited me."

"And its previous owner?"

My grin turned devilish. "Gone to meet his maker, I am afraid."

"Very good," she said. Sabrina turned and began walking away. "Humans are such contemptible animals, aren't they? Perhaps you can use that blade to do away with my nuisance."

I nodded. "I shall." Producing my glasses from my pocket, I adjusted my coat. "Contemptible, indeed. Thank you for freeing me of that curse."

Sabrina smiled in response and her parting words carried just as much enchantment as the execution order she presented. Dazed, I did not recall when I started for the door, except that within moments I found myself in the corridor once more, headed for the stairs. The stride which led me out into the night was a purposeful one, and such a posture continued unfettered until I emerged out on the street.

Standing before the coven's main entrance, I lit a cigarette and shoved the pack back into my coat. As I slid my gloved hand into my pants pocket, however, my fingers touched the hard metal of Lydia's necklace and took hold of it as if on instinct. Withdrawing it brought forth my lie, positioned right before me with moonlight reflecting from its pendant. A sinister smirk crawled across my face. Lydia's voice resonated in my ears.

"*Why don't you just wear it to spite me?*"

"Your wish is my command," I said. With a nod, I fastened the chain around my neck and hid it underneath my shirt. That done, my gait resumed its deliberate tenor, bound for Temple University. A slight shiver settled on my bones. The air about me took on a disquieting sensation. I did not know from whence it came, only that it was there and did not belong to either Sabrina or myself. The wind carried a premonition, without a face and without a name, and the questions yet whispered at me while I walked.

At that moment, I suspected I might be standing on the doorstep of revelation. Little did I know just how right I was.

Chapter Twelve

Smoke wafted from my cigarette, drifting toward the ceiling. My eyes were fixed on the building across the street from me, studying what appeared to be the sole occupied row house on the block. While my chosen shelter at least boasted an enclosed porch, the neighboring homes, including the one currently being renovated behind me, showcased boarded up doors and windows, their exteriors even more dilapidated than the address provided to me by Sabrina. It made perfect sense to me that my quarry was not home. I wished to be anywhere but there myself.

A quick glance heavenward revealed the time to be about ten, which meant I had been standing there for almost two hours. I growled, shifting my attention back to the house, and mused on my target once again. Snooping around the coven had never earned an assassination order for any other mortal – those caught were quickly dispatched as dinner and never spoken of again. This girl, however, had managed to raise Sabrina's ire, and details about her were woefully sparse. I only knew that she was a 'sorceress'.

Which I less-than-willing to believe.

Raising the cigarette to my mouth, I drew in deep and fought to ignore the aching in my body for warm blood. I had not hunted prior to arriving, so bent and determined to get this over with. Now, I suffered the consequences. "Where is this bitch?" I muttered. "Figures she would take her precious time getting here."

I exhaled a stream of smoke. Flicking the remainder of my cigarette at the ground, I succumbed to the urge to incline against the nearest wall, but misjudged the distance between my body and the newly colored surface. A paint-splattered sheet slid beneath my feet, causing an array of supplemental implements stacked precariously atop it to crash to the ground and make all manner of racket. Righting myself, I clenched my eyes shut and gritted my teeth. A deafening silence followed the entire debacle.

Frozen in position for several interminable seconds, it took what seemed like an eon before I worked up the nerve to open my eyes again. As I did, though, I discovered no crowd gathered to witness my mishap. Only a tall vampire with all the grace of an elephant, standing straight and dusting off his coat. "Losing your fucking edge, Flynn," I said, but any further words were cut off by the sound of shoes scuffing on the pavement. Immediately, my attention shifted back to the sidewalk leading up to the house.

I looked up in time to see her approach.

A cautious stroll punctuated the steps of a short, emaciated girl who appeared no older than her early twenties. Her hair just as Sabrina described it, its long, brown locks flowed down her back and a distinct patch of blonde framed one side of her face. She wore a tight, black shirt with a long, matching skirt, and the crimson-colored scarf tied around her neck concealed any patch of skin which might have otherwise been uncovered. I regarded the black gloves on her hands and studied her figure, deciding that if not for how thin she was, she might have almost been attractive. As it was, she was barely fit to be an appetizer.

She paused on the sidewalk directly across the street to turn her head and look around, prompting my hand to fall to the hilt of my sword in reflexive anticipation. Her eyes failed to settle on my hiding place, however, and passed over the quiet street without hesitation until she faced away from me, regarding her front door. I slithered into the shadows of the porch's open doorway while she ascended the stairs to her stoop.

Her heartbeat thudded in her chest. I listened to its cadence while she pondered a set of keys from her purse, becoming entranced by its siren song. My fangs emerged before I could stop them. Thoughts of disregarding my normal *modus operandi* and making this girl my snack polluted my thoughts with temptation. A little something to get me by, until I could return home and hunt with Robin.

I shook my head, not certain from where such a notion came. '*No, no,*' I admonished myself, '*One strike, one kill... like the samurai of old. Now is not the time to lose sight of my sacred credos.*'

She slid her key into the lock.

I drew my sword, taking the hilt in both hands while she twisted her wrist. The lock clicked. Readying my weapon, closing in on her brought with it a gust of breeze carrying her scent in my direction. Her sweetness wrapped itself around me; thoughts of my teeth puncturing her skin infected me with such a dire need that the compulsion to feed became a pounding ache. She removed her key and I lunged for her, thrusting my blade forward. Only, rather than impaling her, I pinned her to the door by the fabric of her scarf.

The mousy girl yelped. Leaning close to her, I cupped her mouth with my hand, hissing in her ear through protruded teeth desperate to claim purchase on her neck. "Hello, little woman," I whispered, drawing another deep breath inward, the intoxicating aroma of my new-found prey sending bolts of temptation rocketing through my senses. "Has nobody ever told you to watch out for strangers?"

I ripped my sword out of the door, taking hold of the girl by her shoulder and throwing her around to face me. Her eyes widened with surprise. I made certain she took a lingering look at the teeth which would soon be the instruments of her demise. Her pulse quickened in response. "Afraid, Precious? Just the way I like it." I raised my sword to eye level for her, showing her the razor edge. "Come now, Pet. Scream for me."

With one quick swipe, I cut her scarf from her neck. As it descended to the ground, I focused on the gash that had been inflicted, watching the decadent sight of her blood rising to the surface. The wiry girl screamed. A sweet symphony to my ears, it flooded my mind while I closed in on her neck, eyes shutting and aware of nothing more than her blood and terror. She flinched when my teeth touched her skin. As they did, though, she committed one desperate act of defiance and smacked the side of my face.

The impact sent my glasses flying. I heard them hit the ground. Opening my eyes on reflex, I subjected myself to maddening, acute pain in the process, and yelled as the familiar burning radiated from my retinas. "Fucking hell!" I said, dropping my sword and covering my face.

My target wriggled free for a moment, but I grabbed hold of her and slammed her back against her door. I opened my eyes long enough for her to regard their crystal blue color, but shut them before I could fully register the smug grin tugging at the corners of her mouth. My fangs plunged into her neck and warm blood spilled down my throat. I groaned in response, drinking deep until a disquieting sensation enveloped my entire body with sharp pinpricks of heat.

I ripped away from her, stumbling backward.

My eyes opened. Searing pain conspired with a sudden wave of dizziness and my vision became distorted. Before I could compensate, I tripped and spilled onto the porch, brought hard onto my knees and moaning as I was forced to catch myself with my hands lest I collapse fully. Her blood trickled down the sides of my mouth, burning my skin while my throat screamed enough agony at me to rival my visual handicap. Through the haze, I watched the figure of my target stroll closer, crouching to pick up her scarf and press it against the wound on her neck. Her voice possessed a strange dissonance to it when she spoke.

"Hello, Peter," she said. "I've been waiting to meet you for a while now. Didn't think this was how we'd finally say howdy, but hey, I'll take it."

I blinked, mouth and throat attempting to issue a response. Whatever her blood had done to me, it rendered me incapable of speech, bringing with it a creeping blackness which threatened to overtake me. Finding myself unable to fight against it, I slumped onto the ground, supine and at her mercy.

My last memory was of her crouching next me, touching my forehead.

After that, I remembered nothing more.

⋅◌◖◗◌⋅

"Good thing you didn't drink any more than that, Peter. It might've killed you."

The voice startled me into consciousness in a manner much like being thrown into a pool full of ice water. I found myself on my back, lying on a bed, with a slight tinge of pain radiating in my eyes from the glow of candles in the room. It provided sufficient illumination to cast shadows on the wall, yet shrouded enough in darkness for me to realize my vampire sight was not adjusting to my environment. I raised my hand to rub them, but jumped, startled when something caught my wrist and yanked my arm back down.

I tugged at the restraint. Hearing a rattle, I turned my head to look at it and groaned when I caught sight of a shackle wrapped around the sleeve of my shirt. I rolled my head to the other side to confirm its mate and moved my legs to discover that my ankles were likewise bound. "You best release me, little girl," I said as the hazy memory of crumpling before the sorceress came to mind. I kicked at the shackles on my feet. "Unless you wish to see one very pissed off vampire when I get..."

My words were cut off as metal shifted up my ankle, touching the skin of my leg past my sock. Rather than exhibiting the chill of steel, it burned, searing my flesh and provoking another holler of offense past my lips. Two hands slid the restraint back down again, away from skin. I paused for a moment to blink past the sudden onslaught, and then growled. My fangs descended. "What the bloody fucking hell was..."

"Peter..."

"Shut up."

A pause. "I beg your..."

"*Leave that name where you found it, bitch! Peter does not live here any longer!*"

At first, silence punctuated my words, but then, the witch began to laugh. I sneered at the mocking tone, not something I was used to hearing. Looking to my left for the small, mortal woman, I saw her standing beside the bed, dressed just as I remembered. A swatch of gauze covered the area where I had bitten her. I would have hardly guessed her injured, however, judging from the way she folded her arms across her chest and stared at me with unwavering confidence. "Oh come on, Flynn," she said. "What do you really think you're going to be able to do to me from there? Bite me again?"

I scowled and tugged at my restraints again. "We shall find out soon enough."

"I wouldn't do that. Unless you want a repeat performance of what just happened to your leg." She started pacing away from me. "The shackles are made from silver. It burns when it comes in contact with your skin, oh high and mighty vampire. I was merciful and at least made sure I wrapped 'em around your clothing, but if you keep wriggling like that, it's not going to matter. Kind of makes getting free a moot point."

I growled. "The pain would last just for a minute before I tore free and ripped out a piece of your throat."

"Doubtful you would tear free. For what, though? To be in the same position you were outside? Which, by the way... Thank you for making all that racket." She turned to face me again, smiling in a smug manner. "It gave me enough time to cast a protection spell."

"Stupid mortal nonsense," I spat. "Silver. Protection spells."

"Oh, I can assure you there's nothing stupid about it. You're staying right there until I say so." My unlikely nemesis strode back to the bed. The mattress dipped with her weight. I lifted my head to regard her as much as possible from my position as her eyes searched for mine. "Mommy vampire didn't tell her special boy much about me did she? I bet she's short on information a lot these days."

Hissing, I snapped at her, fangs exposed. She did not budge, except to lift her hand and narrow her eyes at me. I furrowed my brow at the glint which surfaced in her gaze, but had precious little time to do anything else. An invisible force threw me back against the bed, rendering me incapable of budging an inch.

My eyes had closed briefly with the impact, but I opened them again to find myself staring at the ceiling. The shadow of my captor crept against the plaster, the play of the candlelight making her loom more imposing than the wiry imp truly was. She chuckled. "You think you know it all, Mr. Bad Ass Assassin, but you've only been a vampire for what? Five years now? That's not enough time for you to have any clue what you're talking about."

I sneered. "And I suppose you are the scholar, Miss..."

"Miss nothing. C'mon, Flynny, we're buddies now. Call me Monica."

"I shall remember that for your funeral."

Monica laughed. "This is hilarious. You hate losing control of the situation, don't you? Ironic how often you let Sabrina take it away from you."

The mere mention of Sabrina's name sent my mind spiraling. Visions of my mistress perched upon my lap, speaking her final instructions to me, spun me around, reminding me I had a mission to accomplish. I moaned, scolding myself for screwing up and rendering myself at the mercy of my target. Slipping, yes. Perhaps Timothy was right. I was slip...

Monica snapped her fingers.

I opened my eyes without knowing I had closed them. Something ripped the thought of Sabrina from my mind as though eradicating it by force. Monica spoke once more, her voice subdued this time. "Damn, Peter," she said. "You're a real piece of work, aren't you?"

Blinking, I attempted to lift my head and discovered myself able to do so again. I looked to my right, seeing Monica standing there, hands on her hips and a look of grim concern on her face. I frowned. "Why are you looking at me like that?" I asked as our gaze converged. The way her eyes traced over me left me feeling as though a colony of ants were crawling around inside my brain. I shut my eyes to stop her. "Damn it, I asked you a question."

"I didn't recognize you at first," she said, her voice distant. "When you attacked me, I mean. I've seen pictures of you, but they were from before you were turned. You have no idea just how dark you look now. And your mind..." Monica issued one sharp, incredulous laugh. "My God, your mind is more screwed up than you can begin to imagine."

I opened my eyes again, brow knitted at the mortal sorceress. Monica's eyes regarded me in a normal manner once more. "You're a unique fellow," she said, "And yet, you don't know the half of it. Do you, Flynn?"

We stared at each other, until my lips twisted and a chuckle escaped from my mouth. The noise invoked a stream of laughter and within seconds, I sounded like a madman being driven over the edge. Monica blinked at me, her facial expression falling as I continued to chortle like a raging lunatic. "Oh, this is precious," I said. "We have reached the part where you talk about the gift, right? Oh, here comes the grand reckoning. The Fates help me; I am at the mercy of a witch."

Monica raised an eyebrow at me. "I'd think by now you'd be begging for the answers."

"*Fuck your answers!*" I said, snapping at her without warning. My mirth dissipated at once, given over to blind rage. "And fuck your psychological trash speak; your damn incantations and hoaxes. Hear me now, little bitch, I do not know what you expected to find, but all you have before you is death. If you knew with what you were trifling, you would be pleading for your life."

A smile tugged at the corner of her mouth. "I could stake you right now if I wanted to."

"So, why do you hold back?"

"I don't know, Flynny. I kind of like you." She sat beside me on the bed again, closer to my chest. "I'd only heard about this vampire egotistical bullshit before. Now, I get a front row seat to it." Monica winked. "Besides, if I stake you, I'll have to get your ashes out of my sheets and I hate laundry."

"Then humor me with your 'answers' or let me go." I glared. "Either way, I wish to know why you are holding me captive if not to kill me. I am hungry and grow weary of your presence."

"Yeah, the last snack didn't agree with you, huh?" Monica adjusted her black gloves and cracked her knuckles. The action struck me as odd; I watched her do it with a feeling of dread beginning to surface in the pit of my stomach. She smiled in response. "Beware of sirens, Flynn. I've been attacked more times than these pretty mortal women you seduce and I know how to arm myself."

Monica shifted closer to me. "You see, I *am* the scholar here," she said, "And you've been trapped in the dark for five years, convinced you're nothing more than this sadistic prick you troll around town being. You have your walls up to everybody but Sabrina and she only fuels it, while holding back who you really are. This is where I come in."

I perked an eyebrow at her when her grin broadened. "We could make a good team, Flynn," she said. "But first, we need to teach you how to see."

Lydia's words suddenly echoed in my thoughts – sight, but no vision. A queer notion originating some place outside me, it hinted at finally being able to discern that which I remained blind toward. Monica nodded as though able to read my mind and placed a hand on my forehead. "Do you want to know why Sabrina never tells you what this special sight is? It's because she wants to make sure you're completely wrapped around her finger before your abilities surface."

"Abilities?" I asked the question on impulse, captivated despite myself. Part of me still wanted to bleed the mortal woman dry, but another part studied her, listening to what she had to say.

Monica nodded. "Quite frankly, I don't think she even knows what it's going to look like when you get them. The important thing to remember is you were chosen for a reason. There's a game of chess being played out around you and you're the piece everybody's after. It has nothing to do with this egotistical demeanor you've created. That's all Sabrina's doing. She made you love to be a killer –" She positioned both hands on either side of my head. Dread escalated by leaps and bounds when I caught sight of the look in her eyes. "– Now, we're going to teach you how to do it right."

A flash of light threw my head back, the colony of ants evolving into a swarm of bees within the confines of my subconscious. I cried out on impulse as the witch's hands pressed harder against my skull and the sensation of synapses being redirected – files being reorganized – forced me into submission. The demon within me bucked and screamed. I settled, helpless, against the bed, until an inexplicable calm lured me toward slumber. Resistance, by then, was more than futile.

Monica lifted her hands. The sound of her cracking her knuckles once more became the final sound my ears took in, along with the distant resonance of the words she spoke. "Rest for a bit, Flynn. You're going to need it. Life as you know it has just gotten flipped upside down."

CHAPTER THIRTEEN

The sound of knocking ripped me from my dreams.

I shot to a seated position, surprised to find myself back in my room, surrounded by the pitch black of night. Blinking several times, I raised my hand to rub my eyes and began the standard survey of questions one indulges when disoriented. Was it still the same night? Some night afterward? How long had I been asleep?

The person on the other side of the door was not about to afford me the time to sort myself out, however. Another knock, this one more persistent, caused me to flinch. "Flynn!" the muffled voice of Robin yelled. "Brother, have you yet returned or are you still missing? Please answer; I would swear on my life I heard your door close no more than a few minutes ago."

"Yes..." The word came out sounding groggy and uncertain. I cleared my throat. "Yes, yes, I am here. Wait a moment, Robin." Running a hand through my hair, I smoothed back my disheveled locks and indulged in a deep, steadying breath. Flashes of my final moments of consciousness before slipping into sleep ran through my mind – Monica touching my head, the sensation of everything being reorganized within my brain. I blinked again and studied my hands, starting the self-examination there.

There was no evidence of the silver shackles on my wrists and my vision had not changed in the slightest. I still wore the same clothing, and did not feel different than I had before departing from the coven. The same attitude infected my thoughts and the same perspective lay behind my eyes. "Perhaps it was a dream," I said, both disbelieving the notion and desperate to take hold of it. Lowering my hand onto the bed, however, I touched something which shattered my theory in a heartbeat.

My katana. It laid beside me, placed atop my wool coat. Draped over the sword was Monica's red scarf. The sudden sight of both caused me to jump and reach beneath my shirt. The necklace yet dangled from my neck. I furrowed my brow. "Have I been screwed with by a sorceress?"

"Flynn?!"

"Yes! Coming, Robin!" Growling, I slipped the necklace under my shirt again and swung my legs over the side of the bed. I fought against a wave of dizziness while grabbing the sunglasses on my nightstand, and grumbled the entire way from the bed to the entryway. Opening the door, I leaned against the frame while adjusting the glasses on my face. "This had better be good, Robin," I said. "I was asleep before you started pounding on my door."

Robin furrowed his brow, stealing a few interminable seconds to stare at me. "Flynn, where the devil have you been?" he asked. "We thought you were dead when you didn't return last night." He paused. I winced at the concerned look in his eyes. "Did something detain you? You said you would come find me after your business with Sabrina, but nobody saw you return."

I sighed. "Yes, brother. Apologies, I did get waylaid." Standing straight, I moved aside and allowed Robin to enter. "I take it this is the next evening?"

Robin walked toward the center of the room, studying his surroundings as though examining them for the first time. A strange premonition followed in his wake, something which provoked a knit brow and a slight shiver up my spine. I closed the door while he spoke. "Yes." The word came out sounding subdued. His eyes shifted back to me. "And far later in the night than you typically rise."

"What time?"

"Eleven thirty, last I checked. Probably closer to midnight by now."

"Shit." I sighed. "Half the night spent already."

"Yes, quite." Robin looked me over, from head to feet and back again. "It's strange to see you sleeping at this hour. Did you just return?"

"I am not certain." Walking past Robin, I headed for the sitting area, issuing the implied request for him to join me. My knees weak and mind still reeling, I fell into one of the black, leather chairs and raised my glasses to rub at my eyes. After they settled back onto my nose, I pushed them up to where they rested comfortably. "Truth be known, I do not know when I returned or how I got back here. Only that I am here now."

"Well, you had the lot of us worried when you failed to show up." Robin remained standing, draping an arm across the back of an empty chair. "Sabrina went on a tear. She sent Timothy looking for you and ordered the rest of us to inform her of when you returned."

"Sabrina." I groaned in response to her name. "What the fuck am I going to tell...?"

"Language, Fl..."

I shot Robin a look of extreme annoyance.

Robin sighed. Sitting at last, he perched on the edge of his chair and folded his hands on his lap. "What happened? This sort of behavior isn't like you."

Leaning against the back of my chair, I tilted my head to regard the ceiling. "I am telling you the honest truth, I have no idea what happened. This is something I am still trying to figure out myself."

A moment's pause settled between us. I heard Robin shift in his chair. "Tell me what you remember."

I lowered my head to regard him once more. Thoughts of poisoned blood, unconsciousness, and captivity rose to the forefront of my mind, but before I could speak the words, a disquieting notion settled into my thoughts. How did I know I could trust Robin? Or anybody else, for that matter? My eyes widened behind my glasses, dread throttling to the surface of my psyche and whispering paranoia in my ear. "It..." I attempted to relax. "...Is a blur. I ventured out to fulfill a duty for Sabrina and cannot recall the rest."

Robin frowned. "You're lying to me."

I frowned in response. "Brother, it is the honest truth. I cannot trust what I recall about last night. I pursued a sorceress and she proved to be more than I bargained for."

"But you killed her?" Robin perked an eyebrow. "Right?"

Glancing toward my bedroom, I thought of the scarf lying on my katana. A slow nod preceded my response. "Yes." My gaze shifted back to Robin. "I bit her. Drained her and left her for dead. Her blood was tainted, though... It felt as though I had taken a hallucinogen and it left me in a weakened condition. I retreated into her home to sleep it off and must have yet been somewhat off kilter when I stumbled back here. It still has me dizzy, truthfully."

I studied him, looking for some hint that my story had come across more believable than it sounded. Robin nodded. "You should have run her through and sought to feed elsewhere. Witches cast spells against us."

"Well, nobody warned me of that." A wan smile cut through some of the edge in my voice. "I thought I was killing two birds with one stone."

Robin sighed. "You are right. I never taught you about witches. I thought I had plenty of time for that."

"Plenty of time?"

Robin waved his hand, brushing the words aside. "Simply not something neophyte vampires deal with on a regular basis. Even ones as prolific as you, Flynn."

I frowned, then nodded and looked away. "It was idiotic of me. And Sabrina shall be displeased. This is the second assignment in a row with an incident. One more and my days as an assassin shall be numbered."

"I think her greater fear is that the sorceress got to you somehow."

My eyes shot back to Robin. "Why would that be a concern?"

Robin's face took on a sober expression. "It's not my place to explain that," he said. "Better you bring it up to the mistress. She instructed the guards to beware, lest you start acting irrational, though, so be careful how you go about doing it."

I scoffed. "Acting irrational. That is foolishness."

He shook his head. "Not as foolish as you think. Even you must confess the notion of you acting irrational is enough to inspire legitimate fear." A smirk curled the corner of his mouth.

I sighed. Standing, I removed my suit jacket and started walking toward my bedroom. "Well, then I shall settle her fears. I have something to give her anyway." I tossed the jacket onto my bed as I approached. Plucking my shoulder holster from the night stand caused me just a moment's pause as I recalled I had been wearing this as well the evening prior. I shook my head and secured my weapons into place. The scarf found its way into a pocket and my suit jacket into my hands as I emerged into the sitting area. "Aside from being fearful over my mental faculties," I said, sliding the fine linen over my arms once more, "Is the mistress in an ill mood?"

Robin shook his head, his smile transforming into a halfhearted grin. "Otherwise, she is her same chipper self."

I chuckled. Giving one, final adjustment of my apparel, I glanced back at him. "Sarcasm does not become you, Robin. While I am thinking about it, though, did you finish the favor I asked of you?"

"The rose?"

I nodded.

Robin stood and proceeded to glance around the room. "Yes, it was finished as you asked. I had business to attend to..."

'...*Conspiring is more like it, you aged Irishman...*'

"...so it wasn't a problem whatsoever."

I blinked, studying Robin. While I heard the words clear as day, I failed to see Robin's lips speak them himself. "I beg your pardon?" I asked. "What did you just say?"

Robin's eyes returned to mine. He furrowed his brow. "I said it wasn't a problem, brother."

"No, no." I flicked the words away with a brush of my hand. "I mean, after you said you had business."

He stared at me, an eyebrow rising. "That is all I said, Flynn. I had business to attend to and completing your task proved to be no hassle." Robin closed the distance between us by one pace, and then stopped. His gaze turned searching. "Are you feeling alright?"

"I am not entirely certain." Narrowing my eyes, I studied Robin, seeing a lie placed before me without knowing how I could be so sure of it. I would have sworn on the altar of everything I held sacred, though. Those words had entered my mind with Robin's voice speaking them. Conspiring? Such a brazen declaration and yet, Robin had no idea what I was talking about. My hand came up to my head, my feet suddenly feeling unsteady. "I think I should lie down again."

Robin frowned. "See to Sabrina first, before she tears Philadelphia apart looking for you."

"Very well, I shall." Glancing at Robin, I noticed as an afterthought how soft my tone of voice had become. He regarded me all the more with concern and as I motioned for the door, he walked with me, lingering a trifle closer than normal. Somehow, I got the sense he feared I might tip over at any moment. Truth be known, the prospect seemed all too possible a reality. Something told me I was only beginning to fathom what had truly happened.

Together, we strolled out to the corridor. Robin paused to shut my door before resuming his place by my side. More than once, he asked if he should accompany me to Sabrina's room, going as far as to offer to procure something to eat. I refused his assistance as politely as possible. Partially an effort to mask my own discomfort, it reflected how much like an alien in my own skin I felt by the time we reached the stairs. I had to bite my tongue to stop from snapping at his offers to help, but he read enough of my annoyance to bid me a good evening.

I frowned while watching him descend the stairs toward the foyer. None of this was his fault, even if that unsettling air had coalesced around him while in my room and those taunting words had contained his voice. With a sigh, I lifted my head, shifting my focus to the second staircase which led upward. My stomach twisted into a knot and my hand touched the banister in a shaky manner. "The mistress waits," I said, my voice a low murmur. It took no less than two minutes for me to raise my foot to the top of the first stair.

My hand slid up the banister, my grip tightening on occasion whenever my feet became unsteady. The nervousness I harbored the night before could not hold a candle to the form of dread which settled on me with each stair I ascended. Agonizing, slow steps marked my progress to the fourth floor. I reached the top and wondered how pale I might have appeared as I stopped and stared at Sabrina's door.

Glancing at Paul, who was standing in his customary place, I noticed the same uncertainty present in his gaze Robin had possessed when he first looked me earlier. I shifted my eyes away at once, straightened my suit jacket, and strolled to the penthouse door. I suppose I thought pretending to be unaffected might soak through my pores and settle my inner spirit. Neither of us spoke to each other as Paul merely opened the door and left it ajar long enough for me to enter.

I indulged in a steadying breath. My gait slowed, caution returning as darkness enveloped me. I swallowed hard and called out toward the bedroom, "Mistress?"

Silence answered.

Walking into Sabrina's sitting area, I could not ignore the shudder running through my body, a far different sensation than I had ever experienced. My eyes glanced around the room, searching for any sign of my maker. "Sabrina?" I said. "Your assassin has returned. After a very harrowing night, I might add. Are you here?" As the last words escaped my mouth, I picked up on a presence without seeing it yet. The sound of light steps shuffling to the doorway reached my ears, but I did not turn around. Instead, I closed my eyes and watched a series of images play out in my mind.

I saw Sabrina regarding me from where she stood, warring emotions playing out in her gaze. Her piercing stare sent a shiver up my back and her full lips were pressed together in a frown. One eyebrow perked, she slid her hand deliberately behind her back. I watched her long fingers wrap around the hilt of a dagger, sheathed and tucked into the waistband of her pants.

My eyes shot open. I spun around to look at her as a surprised expression enveloped Sabrina's face. Her body tensed and we stared at one another, her gaze registering fear while mine attempted to mask the hurt of betrayal. I forced an agreeable smile to emerge and bowed, preparing for the performance of my life. "Sweet Sabrina," I said, "I understand I have caused you a great deal of concern. My most sincere apologies. I returned just as soon as I could."

Sabrina remained silent. I walked closer, weighing each step along the way while digging in my pocket for the piece of crimson silk. Once I reached Sabrina, I pulled it out, presenting it to her. "You requested a dead witch?"

The reaction was instantaneous. A smile lit Sabrina's face and her hand emerged from behind her back to snatch the scarf. "My darling Flynn, I feared she got the better of you," she said. Her eyes traced the fabric, focusing especially on the bloodstains remaining on the thin material. "A silly notion, wasn't it?"

I grinned. "Now, Sabrina, this is me we are discussing. When have I failed to come through for you?"

"Indeed." Craning her neck, she placed a kiss on my lips. Where such an action would have normally been met with desire on my part, a foreign form of repulsion surfaced. Its poison seeped into my mind as I fought hard not to violently pull away.

Unfortunately, Sabrina noticed.

Her eyes opened as mine did. "What is it, Flynn?" she asked. "Do you no longer want your mistress?"

Every profanity fashioned by man raced through my brain. "No, it is not that, Sabrina." My head felt as though it might rend in two at any moment. The lingering taste of wickedness left me chilled to the marrow, revolted beyond my control. I could not allow her to know it, though. "I did not return last night because I had to recover. I... was foolish and bit the girl. Her blood was laced with some sort of hallucinogen. It wrought havoc on my mind and I still do not feel like myself."

A maternal smile tugged at Sabrina's lips. "My child, you're fortunate it didn't kill you. Sorceresses are notorious for casting protection spells." She chuckled softly. "She must not have been as good as I thought she was."

"Either that or I have a strong constitution." My fingers ripped through my hair once more, my hand settling on the crown of my head. "Whatever the matter, I weathered a difficult night and only wished to sleep when I returned this evening. I came here because Robin visited. He said you were troubled."

Sabrina nodded. "I was, but am no longer. Rest, Flynn. I have no duties for you tonight."

"Thank you, Mistress." Lowering my hand, I touched one of hers and brought it to my lips. A forced grin accompanied the gesture, although I hoped Sabrina could not tell. "Have no concerns for your assassin. I shall be right as rain in short order."

She continued to smile. I studied her eyes for a moment, not trusting how genuine the expression she managed was. Sabrina reeked of nervousness, her hand registering a slight tremor when I let go of it. I suppressed the urge to frown and turned, walking for the door.

Her eyes never left me during the entire trek to the exit and it was not until I closed the door behind me that the sense of being a goldfish in a bowl dissipated. Even then, I could not help feeling I needed to get as far away from her as possible. Strolling away, I maintained my usual, nonchalant swagger and hurried down the stairs in much the same fashion, ignoring those I passed even when a few paused to stare at me along the way. I swallowed hard, shutting my eyes at one point and opening them only when I reached the ground floor.

If I yet had a pulse, my heart would have been pounding.

Somehow, I maintained my composure out the front doors, but once I emerged outside, I entered into a sprint, digging deep to use every measure of my vampire speed to get away from the coven house as swiftly as possible. The wind tossed my hair a million places and my suit jacket whipped behind me until I slowed and rounded a corner into a side street. My back hit the wall of one building, my eyes darting left and right to ensure I was alone. When I registered no other beings within proximity, I shut my eyes and indulged several shaky breaths while attempting to make sense of this all.

The encounter with Robin was unsettling enough, but it paled in comparison to my meeting with Sabrina. I had been forced to look her in the eyes and play actor to a role which came so naturally before. The fact that I yet possessed my life was sheer luck, but my fortune would soon run out unless I figured out what the devil had happened to me.

Had the girl cast a spell? I had no idea how the incantations of sorceresses worked. For all I knew, I might have been right when I assigned blame to biting the witch, her blood yet coursing through my veins, playing tricks with my mind. After all, I had not fed since that time and if my body was yet weakened, then the hexes she worked against me would no doubt be all the more effective. My eyes opened and I nodded. Yes, I needed to drown myself in blood. Then I would be fine again.

Standing straight, I ran my fingers through my hair to restore order to the short, brown locks. As if confirming my theory, I felt the slightest tinge of hunger nip at me, giving me all the impetus I needed to walk back to the main thoroughfare and seek out my first victim. Something young and lively; a wicked grin emerged as I thought about teasing her before driving my teeth into her neck. The city was full of such creatures, after all, and the night was still young.

Not more than an hour later, I found myself in the alley behind a night club, kissing a beautiful young woman while my hands ran across her curves. She threw her head back and laughed when I lowered my lips to nuzzle her neck, allowing my kisses to descend to her pulse point. "I normally don't... do this sort of thing," she whispered in a breathy manner, her body pressing against mine and her scent saturated with lust. "Moving so quickly. Do you?"

I grinned in a wicked manner. "Dear, life is entirely too short to be bothered with formalities." I licked her neck and suppressed a groan, bloodlust growing by leaps and bounds. It infected the core of my being until I could hold back no longer. Just as she began issuing a response, my fangs descended. No more than a few words made it past her lips before I drove my teeth into her neck, releasing a warm rush of crimson from the wound and into my mouth.

At once, a strange sensation crowded out even the taste of her blood.

Her name was Cecilia. She was a law student at Temple University. My eyes flew open as such details surfaced in my thoughts, my lips yet pursed around the wound and one hand cupped over her mouth to muffle her screams. I drew from the bite again, but doing so only made the deluge of facts and images all the more visceral. I saw graduation days and family, and heard the screams within her mind her vocal cords could not produce. She had never left the city. Never traveled; never been to Europe and now it was all going to...

Ripping away from her, I threw her onto the ground. Cecilia crashed into a pile of empty boxes next to a dumpster and placed a hand on her neck while I took several steps away from her. Our eyes remained fixed on one another, my right hand raising with a hard tremor as I wiped the blood away from my mouth. I could not help but to stare at this peculiar creature I now knew far too much about.

"Get the fuck away from me," I said, my voice a low rumble. I stumbled close to the night club and rested a hand on the concrete facade.

Cecilia sat up, regarding me with tears in her eyes. I could not bear the sight any longer. Pointing, I growled, my voice rising in volume, my frustration saturating each word I spoke. "*Go!!* Before I change my mind and cut you into so many fucking pieces, the coroner will need your teeth to identify the body!"

She whimpered and stood quickly, eyes afraid to leave mine until I hissed, my crimson-stained fangs offering a reminder of what I had just done to her. I did not even have the thought to glamour her, I simply wished her gone and the action served its purpose. She sobbed once before running in a hasty manner. I watched her, still clutching onto her neck, while disappearing from my sight. Once she left, I closed my eyes and my head began to spin. "What the fuck did that witch do to me?" I asked. "Bloody hell, I heard her thoughts."

"Did you know that a vampire can go as long as a month between feedings before completely losing their minds?" an irritatingly perky voice chimed. Lifting my eyes toward a fire escape on the wall across from me, I saw the wiry imp of a witch sitting on the edge, kicking her legs like a five year old sitting on a chair too tall for her stature. Monica grinned as our eyes met, her hand rising to wave. I noticed the manner of her dress was the same as it had been last night, with the exception of a green scarf matching her irises secured around her neck this time.

I narrowed my eyes and sneered. "You have a lot of fucking nerve appearing before me again, witch."

"Hey, I'm just giving you information that might be valuable to you in the future." She stood and, as fragile of a girl as she appeared to be, surprised me when she jumped to grab hold of the metal stairs above her and swung herself over the railing. Sailing into the expanse over the alley, she rolled once mid-air before landing on the street, her knees buckling, but her posture straightening after just a moment's pause. I blinked while she brushed at her sleeves and continued speaking. "Gymnastics classes paid off at last. Anyway, the olden ones have found ways of going as long as several weeks, but I wouldn't recommend a young vampire like you trying that."

Her nonchalant manner only served to enrage me that much further. I charged for her, grabbing her by the throat. Fangs bared, face contorted with anger, I slammed her against an adjacent building and spat in her face as I spoke. "I shall not be an emasculated vampire on your account, you meddling bitch. Now, either undo whatever spell you have cast on me, or I shall take great pleasure in ripping you limb from limb before sending myself into the afterlife."

"This isn't coming from me, Flynn. It's coming from you." The smile faded from her lips, but the bemusement lingered in her eyes. "The only thing I did was bring it out."

"Bullshit."

"What do you find so hard to believe? That you have any good left in you?" She chuckled. "That has to be it, because I have a strange feeling that if Flynn the vampire would have discovered these gifts on his own, he would have had a merry power trip, wouldn't he? But no, that humanity you thought was gone might not be so dead after all."

"And I think you are teetering on the edge of your last breath. Now tell me, what is this?"

"It's the sight." The smile returned, in all its mocking glory. "You're a seer. You read people's thoughts; you know what others don't. The next layer of things. Their intentions, their natures... Flynn, this is the gift."

I laughed. "Then I do not wish to have this power."

"It's not a choice either of us made. You were born with it." Monica attempted to wriggle out of my grip and I allowed her, too dizzy to issue a protest. She straightened the scarf around her neck and looked at me, sighing. "Listen, I brought it out prematurely for several reasons, not the least of which includes the fact that the voice of Peter is getting drowned out by your vampire machismo. Even as it stands today, I don't know if you'll use this gift for good, but it was going to emerge sooner or later. I'm just here to try to wake you up before she sinks her claws into you."

I perked an eyebrow. "I am being played around with, then?"

"In some ways. But, then again, you always have been." Monica lifted an eyebrow at me in return. "Why do you think Sabrina took you under her wing and made you an assassin? Why the hell do you think she made you a vampire in the first place?"

Just as a biting retort seemed want to surface, my mouth shut and brow furrowed as I searched for the answer to her question. Truth be known, Sabrina never told me why I had been turned and I had never asked her. I merely assumed Sabrina had her reasons for doing so and my service to her proved me invaluable. "Do you mean to tell me Sabrina has known I was to be a seer all along and refrained from telling me?"

"There's using your brain, Pete."

I muttered a low growl at her.

She held up her hand. "Yes, I know. I know. Not the Goody Two-Shoes name. We all know how he cramps your style."

I scoffed, my voice developing an edge to it. "Yes, please, let us discuss what a model citizen Dr. Peter Dawes was – the man who swore his life to helping the huddled masses and then murdered two people in cold blood." I shook my head. "Somehow in these hymns of praise every bloody entity in the cosmos wants to sing, that little detail gets overlooked."

"That's what this whole thing has been about?" The smile on Monica's face faltered. "You figure... What the fuck? You started off this way, why not go the full monty and shit all over life in general?"

As I looked at her, the expression on my face betrayed me, eyes becoming pained, words only previously thought drifting past my lips. "You have no idea what it is like to live under a curse. I do not loathe the name because it was my mortal name. I loathe it because Peter was precious little more than a hypocrite." My gaze shifted away. "He lived out his days pretending to be a healer, only to kill the thing he loved most."

Silence settled between us, neither of us apt to speak for interminable moments until Monica finally cleared her throat and sighed. "So, with that, the doctor becomes an assassin."

I indulged in a sardonic chuckle and glanced back at her again. "No, with that, the assassin becomes what he truly is." A finger pressed into my chest, just above my heart. "I am a killer. I feed from mortals. I live in blood... damn you, I am a vampire! And a vampire unable to kill is little more than the same sort of hypocrite

Peter Dawes was. The best fucking thing anybody ever did was to rid him of his cursed humanity."

A mysterious grin crept across Monica's face, her eyes not faltering in their gaze. "But here's a brain teaser for you, Flynn. Something I'd wager every mystical power in my life force you've never considered." She strolled closer to me, careful, calculated steps with a deliberate tenor to each one. Lifting a hand, she poked my chest directly where the pendant underneath my shirt hung. "Did Peter Dawes kill Lydia Davies? Or did Flynn?"

My brow knitted in confusion. "What kind of ridiculous question is that? I had not yet been turned."

"But Sabrina was already inside your mind. You've just been played like a fiddle so long, you don't know how to tell the difference."

Our eyes locked in a staring match. Unable to respond, thoughts waging war inside my head, I spoke the only words I could in my own defense. "I do not believe you. In fact, I believe you are the one attempting to manipulate me."

"If you truly believe that," she said, arms lifting from her sides. "Then put a knife through me, right now, and be done with it. End my incantation and go back to business as usual."

My hand rose, sweeping back my coat in a practiced motion as second nature as my hunger for blood. Fingers brushed the handle of one of my blades while my eyes remained fixed on Monica. If this truly was her sorcery, it would end with her death. A distinct part of my psyche could not help but to ask, though, if she might be telling the truth. In which case, what would I do with these new abilities? Would infatuation with life and humanity overtake me, or would I use them toward my own ends? Surely the voices could be dulled, my senses attuned to derive the same perverse pleasure from their thoughts I relished from their screams. I could have my vampire mistress and together, we would reign with absolute power.

That was precisely what Sabrina wanted, though. I recalled Robin stating that he feared for my well-being. It was not outside her capabilities to manipulate a mortal, turn them, and train them to do her bidding. The cold-blooded assassin within could not care less and wanted to embody the term 'killer' to the fullest, most inhumane sense of the word. A more distant voice, however, struggled to understand how he became what I was.

My hand lowered from the knife. I could not determine if I wished Monica's aid or if I purely intended to exploit her knowledge, but now was not the time to end her. "Put your fucking arms down," I said, frowning.

She grinned. "I knew you weren't that bad of a guy after all, Flynn."

I narrowed my eyes. "Do not try my mercy, woman."

"Very well, then. I'll leave you to your brooding." Monica played with her scarf. "I had to cast half a dozen spells to get you into your coven earlier, so I'll reserve our meetings for out here, on the streets." Glancing from the emerald green fabric back to my eyes, the grin remained a fixture on her face. "Besides, I got in Sabrina's cross-hairs once. If you told her that I'm dead, it wouldn't look good for us to be seen together."

"And if I need to find you?"

"I'll stay close." And just as I believed she could not grate on my nerves any more, she winked. The cocky gesture forced me to suppress an urge to grit my teeth. "Trust me, if you're in trouble, I'll know."

With a curtsey, Monica turned and begun walking away. I watched her take several paces before calling out, "Witch!"

Monica paused, glancing back at me with an upturned eyebrow. "The name's Monica, Flynn. What can I do for you?"

"Monica." Her name burned my lips like acid splashed on flesh, becoming just as vile to me as my mortal name had been. "What of this necklace? How did retrieving it after all these years force this torrent of nonsense to the limelight?"

"There's no such thing as a coincidence. You'll be mindful to remember that." She neither smiled, nor frowned – merely regarded me in an even manner. "It belonged to a special girl, let's put it that way. Somebody who's been looking out for you longer than you know. Try not to let Sabrina get her hands on it, okay?"

I nodded slowly as Monica spun around again and, this time, vanished from my sight. Even after she had departed, though, I found myself frozen in position, examining the air where she once stood as though the vapors of her presence yet lingered with riddled answers. I was confused, hungry, and tired, and the moment I broke my trace to regard the night sky, I realized the hour grew late. Not enough time to even attempt luring one of the late night stragglers someplace secluded. As if I possessed any desire to after that debacle.

So, I dug my hands in my pockets and strolled back to the coven house, opting to drain a few glasses of blood before retiring to my room again. The rays of the sun had not yet touched the horizon as I lay in bed, fingers tracing the pendant around my neck until sleep took me under. Somewhere in the back of my mind, I realized a battle for my soul had commenced anew, promising to be long and bloody. I could not figure out my posture on the matter yet. I simply knew one thing prevented the sinner in me from swallowing me whole.

Lydia. The push which sent me barreling over the edge in the first place was the same thread tethering me to my humanity. The direction of the wind hinged upon the death grip she had on the scattered remnants of Peter, but then again, a lot had always hinged upon her.

I simply did not yet have the eyes to see it when I was mortal.

PART FOUR

⌁⌁

THE SECRET

"For nothing is hidden that will not
become evident, nor anything secret that will
not be known and come to light."

Luke 8:17

Chapter Fourteen

I have never cared for the light. Even as a human, I rarely liked to wake early and often drifted toward late night walks and odd shifts at the hospital. This is partly what made the eternal darkness of being a vampire so appealing to me. While the mortal world basked in the dawn, I gloried in the dusk. Lydia often commented on what it did for my pallor, but then again, she was always a child of the morning.

We met under a pitch black sky, a most unlikely circumstance as Lydia hated being outside so late. She was a creature of superstition that way, always harboring the fear that some power or entity might do something to her when sunset found her outdoors. Whatever compelled her to leave her apartment that night sealed her hatred of darkness. It probably also sealed her death, because being out there led her to me.

A chilly wind blew past, forcing me deeper inside the protection of a warm, wool jacket as I strolled through a park in North Philadelphia. Looking for some sort of reprieve from my thoughts, I marveled over the tenor of my adult life. My parents were dead; my aunt gone and my uncle falling sick himself. Terminally alone, I felt content to be as such, but there were times when the burdens of the world weighed heavier on my mind than others. On those occasions, I would look around only to discover I had nobody with whom to speak. So, I indulged the habit of walking around the neighborhood.

My gaze often drifted to the heavens, regarding the stars for the answers to my private musings. I did not harbor any faith in a higher power; night after night spent at the hospital reminded me of the ills which befell humanity and prevented me from believing anything benevolent could exist. On nights like this, however, I still held out hope there might be a God, and that he could shine a little enlightenment down on me.

With a deep sigh, I stared upward, soaking up the moonlight with my bare eyes.

That was when she came slamming into me from behind.

The force caught me off-guard. I pitched forward and sprawled out on the ground before I could remove my hands from my pockets. My face impacting concrete, I added an extra grunt of offense when she landed on top of me. "Oh god," she said, scrambling to her feet. "I'm so sorry. I wasn't looking and I..."

"It's alright," I said, coming to a stand. My finger dabbed at my nose when I felt something warm trickling from it, but jerked away at the burst of pain radiating from the touch. Blood coated my digits. I frowned as I considered it might be broken, and then looked up at my unwitting assailant to discern what in God's name had just transpired.

As I did, two things about her caught my attention. Her eyes jumped around nervously, almost fearful, but their bright green color still appeared warm and inviting. Tempted to stare into them for a while, I caught sight of something which drew my attention to the side of her neck. I frowned at the rivulet of blood running from a deep gash. "Miss," I said, walking closer and reaching out to examine it. "This is a bad cut. You need to have it looked at."

Her eyes shot back toward me. She tensed, but failed to stop me as I continued inspecting the wound. When she did not respond, I lifted my gaze toward her emerald irises again. "What happened?" I asked.

"Someone tried to attack me," she said, tilting her head obediently to give me a better look. Her eyes shut and the breath she exhaled was rife with apprehension. "I'll get it looked at. I just need to get out of here first."

"I'm a doctor." I paused and corrected myself. "Well, I'm a resident, but I work at the hospital. Why don't we get you over there and see about patching you up? You'll be safe with me, I promise."

I backed away from her a little, allowing her to resume a more comfortable posture. She seemed to be weighing something internally, her eyes narrowing and a world away until some light of decision illuminated her face. Immediately, she nodded. "Okay," she said. "Thank you..."

"Peter." I smiled, placing my hand on her shoulder in some effort to offer her comfort as we walked toward the edge of the park. "But I could make you call me Dr. Dawes. A resident needs to get his ego trip somehow."

The comment made her chuckle and gave me a chance to see the finer points of her beauty, no longer shrouded by her flustered panic. She had long, brown hair and a delicate smile which curved upward at the corners of her mouth. It was just the right sort of expression to shoot a bolt of sunshine into the psyche of the beholder. She had me instantly smitten.

"My name's Lydia," she said, regarding me in return. "And your nose seems to be bleeding."

I laughed. Touching it again, this time gingerly, I spoke in a dismissive manner. "It's not like this is the first time I've screwed it up. Horsing around near farm equipment will do that, too." I paused to glance back across my shoulder briefly. "I'm more concerned about your well-being. You said someone tried to attack you?"

She nodded. I caught a shiver running up her spine as she answered. "Yes, I was. That thing came at me out of nowhere, but I think I scared it away."

"Thing?" I perked an eyebrow. "You mean, like an animal?"

When Lydia's eyes found mine again, her expression was almost harrowing. "No, nothing like that." Those words served to be her only response and I thought it rude to pry. So, I did not press her for further explanation. We walked in silence the remainder of the way to the hospital and I quickly slipped into the mentality of a doctor the moment we passed through the emergency room entrance.

My cohorts at the hospital regarded us with a bit of surprise, several stopping to ask what had happened as they took stock of my bloody nose and the gash on Lydia's neck. I heard a flurry of 'Pete!'s and offered a quick explanation to one of the attending physicians. He asked if I felt comfortable stitching Lydia myself and I nodded in response while leading her to one of the open beds in the emergency room.

Lydia appeared to relax as she studied the large group of people gathered around us. I puzzled over the tidal wave of relief which crested over her – evident by the change in her demeanor – but at least considered it a good thing she felt at ease there. She settled on the empty bed and I excused myself to wash up and clean my bloody nose. By the time I returned, she was able to smile brightly at me, ignoring the heavy-set nurse assessing her to watch me study a tray of equipment prepared for me.

Lydia was the first to speak while I slipped on a pair of surgical gloves. "So, do you always take women to the emergency room on the first date?" she asked.

The nurse, my old friend Chloe, raised an eyebrow while turning to depart. I thanked her quickly for her assistance, ignoring the knowing grin she shot my way before redirecting my attention to Lydia. "No," I said with a chuckle. I picked up a swab of rubbing alcohol and began cleaning Lydia's wound. "If I'd have known I was going to be on a date, I would've made dinner reservations instead."

Lydia winced a little while I worked, and then jumped slightly at the prick of the needle when I began sewing her wound closed. Still, a smile surfaced through the pain. "Dinner reservations? That sounds a lot better than a night at the hospital."

I could not help but to glance into her eyes once more before redirecting my attention to the task at hand. "Oh yes, with candles and everything. Might even include some flowers. Much better than a night at the hospital."

"Ah." She chuckled. "Somebody's a romantic."

I shrugged. "I just know how to treat a lady." My eyes were drawn to hers again, so I winked. "You look like the kind of girl who likes being doted on."

A contagious grin broke out on her face and I found myself mirroring it. As tempted as I was to continue gazing at her in such a manner, I forced myself to finish attending to her cut and drifted back into small talk until I secured the final stitch into place. Lydia offered the occasional response, but made it apparent her mind was occupied by more than our idle banter. I felt the weight of her stare on more than one occasion, though I did not mind the attention.

I removed my surgical gloves after securing a bandage over the freshly-patched wound. "You're all fixed now," I said, placing the gloves down on the tray. As we regarded each other, I found myself wishing it not to be over. I hesitated, considering how I could draw the moment out; how I could savor it before Lydia walked out of my life. A nervous fidget infected me as I struggled to remember if I had forgotten to do anything. "Um, you'll have to change the bandage at home. And come back in to have those stitches removed in a couple of weeks."

"Will you be here?" Her eyes remained fixed on me, her body still. I could only interpret her actions to mean she did not wish to leave, either.

I nodded. "Absolutely. There aren't many other places I go."

She smiled. "I'll ask for you, then."

"Sounds like a second date."

Lydia chuckled and I smirked, but the exchange only served to make me melancholy. It still felt as though we were delaying the inevitable, so I turned away while saying, "I'll have one of the nurses ready your paperwork so you can be discharged and..."

She cut me off by reaching for my hand, directing my attention back to her. I felt her fingers graze over mine and my heart leaped at the contact. "Peter," she said, her touch lingering, "You know what would make me happy?"

Her soft words and coy smile forced my words to descend to a whisper. "What would make you happy, Lydia?"

Lydia's grin turned all the more bashful. "Going out on that date with you. The one with dinner reservations, not the other one."

I laughed. She chuckled as well, before opting for a more concrete answer. "You make it sound pretty inviting."

"Then we'll have to make *that* the second date instead." I am not certain if my smile or eyes betrayed me, except to know the spark of desire the simple contact of her hand inspired blossomed into full-blown infatuation at the thought of our time together continuing. I had linked fingers with her without realizing it. "So, when are you available?"

Our conversation focused on schedules until we decided on a suitable time and day. It was a peculiar way to meet a woman, to have her crash into my life and invite herself to stay, but it epitomized Lydia. Nothing about her was subtle or ordinary. Riddles dotted her life, as did private treasures and personal pains she did not share with anyone else. Her eyes never failed to hold me in an aura of wonder, but her lips issued enigmas she would only allude toward before backtracking when it was apparent I did not comprehend what she was saying. Of the many stories I could regale involving Lydia and I, one weighed heavily in my thoughts as my struggles with Sabrina became more pointed.

It was the first evening Lydia and I shared ourselves with one another, bare skin touching bare skin as we laughed and rolled under my sheets. I could still see her face as she reached a climax and smell her scent as I buried my nose in the crook of her shoulder, just below the healing cut inflicted on her neck. Her hands held onto my back tightly and a breathy moan punctuated the crescendo of our coupling, our bodies still joined and the euphoria of afterglow taking hold. I kissed her skin and waited several lingering moments before parting from her. She rolled to face me when I settled on my side beside her.

I remember her looking at me in 'that way' again when our eyes met. While the evidence of our intimate union infected the way it surfaced that time, I could not deny its presence. She beheld me as though gazing at something more than her new lover. I kept silent and studied her in return, until she rolled on top of me and playfully bit my lip.

Chuckling, I nipped at the air above me, which made her laugh. My grin broadened, but as Lydia continued regarding me, her smile faded and her gaze turned inquisitive. I furrowed my brow at her. "What's wrong?" I asked, reaching up to brush some of her hair away from her face.

"Do you believe in fate?" she asked, her eyes not leaving mine.

I blinked. "I don't know. I've seen a lot of things called fate which were nothing more than nice coincidences. Not a lot of things that defy explanation, though." My smile turned playful. "Except for you."

Lydia giggled and leaned in to kiss me once more. When she pulled away, I shrugged. "I'm really not sure what I believe in," I said. "I don't give fate a lot of thought."

"I think we definitely cause our own fate sometimes." Lydia looked away, her fingers brushing through my hair in idle strokes. "It's the things that can't be explained I'm talking about." Her eyes met mine again. "Sometimes you stumble across something and you know you weren't supposed to find it. But it found you anyway."

I smiled. "Like somebody who makes you laugh? Whose eyes could break the deepest spell?"

Her smile sobered, but remained present nonetheless. "There are very deep spells in this world, Peter. Are you sure mine can do that?"

"I guarantee it."

"Then remember my eyes for me." She laid her head down on my chest and sighed as though releasing a heavy burden. "Because I'm afraid there's a lot of darkness waiting for you. You have rare gifts and the power-hungry will always seek to take advantage of people like you because of it."

Her words were a riddle and while I took them as a metaphor at the time, it did not occur to me to heed the larger warning which had been issued. It would not be the last time she would caution me against danger, but the skeptic within always thought her fears irrational. They were the things a lover speaks to the one they hold most dear and I offered them an obligatory smile without taking them to heart.

A lot of darkness waiting for me, she said as she lay in my arms.

She must have been talking about Flynn.

CHAPTER FIFTEEN

It would be quite rational to assume a lot of remorseful brooding followed my evening with Monica. Indeed, if one were so inclined, they could believe I spent the subsequent nights wringing my hands, wondering what to do with myself now that these mortal gifts had been brought to the surface. Such a notion, while noble, is incredibly fool-hearty because nothing could be further from the truth.

When water trickles from its source, it takes the path of least resistance. Likewise, when faced with a decision which calls for defying one's nature, the easier road always serves to be the most appealing one. So, I spent an evening licking my wounds, recovering from my brush with the unexpected. Then, I ventured back into the night to subjugate it.

Certainly, their voices rang inside my mind as I dispatched of body after body, and before too long I could summon their thoughts simply by touching them. After a while, I found ways to use this information for my gain. I looked them in the eyes and evaluated who they were, what they wanted and how best to lure them into my clutches. It made me that much more dangerous of a killer; a master manipulator. They tasted that much sweeter, were that much more satisfying to toy around with, and I became drunk on more than blood. Power wrapped its coils around my psyche. None of the miserable lot had the foggiest idea they had been duped by a vampire-seer until it was too late.

This deception would have been more enjoyable an experience if not for the return of my self-appointed conscience. Monica had the bad habit of surfacing in my life at the most inopportune moments. "Flynny," she said once, using that bastardization of my name I was growing to despise, "You mean to tell me you've learned how to derive some sort of sick pleasure out of knowing these people before you kill them?" She shook her head at me and sighed. "That's incredibly fucked up."

On this night in particular, I found myself standing in a back alley, laughing with arms extended and teeth bared. January had dissolved into late February and while the chill of the air had not dissipated, it seemed the wind which blew past me became all the more frigid with my words. "Incredibly fucked up does not begin to scratch the surface, Precious," I said. I grinned like a devil as Monica folded her arms across her chest, hugging a warm coat against her slender frame. "I can name them all to you. I can tell you where they lived, what their last thoughts were..." I swaggered close to Monica and bent at the waist, my face mere inches from hers. "Shall I begin with the girl I just murdered? Or would you prefer to hear about the couple I toyed with the night before last?"

Monica regarded me, trying her best to appear unfazed. "What are you trying to prove to me? That you're a sadistic badboy vamp? The act is charming, Flynn, but you're the one in denial."

I laughed and pressed one finger into her chest. "No, Pet. *You* are the one in denial if you still see me as anything but what I am."

"Running scared? Killing as many people as you can to silence your humanity? Do you think if you murder the rest of the world, you'll shut up Peter indefinitely?"

"No," I said, standing straight and allowing a brutal sneer to envelop my countenance. "It is much simpler than that. I am going to kill them one precious soul at a time and watch you suffer as I conquer the world with the toy you gave a vampire."

Monica studied me without speaking, locking us inside a stalemate. She held her expression steady while my declaration hung in the air. After what seemed like interminable minutes, she walked over to a stack of boxes poised next to an adjacent building and hopped to a seated position on top. "Then why haven't you told Sabrina about it yet?"

Her words whisked the smirk from my face. "How did you know that?"

Her grin turned mocking again. "Oh, I can read it loud and clear. I know what would have happened by now had you. In fact, I'll blow you one better. You haven't asked her anything yet. Not even why you were turned."

"Bah." I looked away. "What use is that information? Regardless of her reasons, she granted me the dark gift and I have worn it as though it was my natural skin. If anything..." My gaze returned to Monica. "I thank her for allowing me these pleasures."

"Now, I thought Flynn wasn't 'one to be trifled with' as you put it. That *is* what you told me, right?" Monica jumped down from her perch and walked closer to me. "It doesn't make you the tiniest bit annoyed that someone had the audacity to walk all over your free will?"

"I asked to be made immortal."

"That's what she wants you to believe."

"I do not give a fuck. So long as I am the one with the power, I shall take my lot and use it how I deem fit."

Monica smirked. "Not the least bit curious why she wanted Lydia dead? Just so long as you're the one with the power?"

Her question stunned me into silence. She nodded when I failed to respond. "You think this is all about you becoming a spoiled, licentious predator, but it's about a hell of a lot more than that," Monica said, pacing around me with her hands knitted together behind her back. I knew she was not referring to Sabrina when she added, "She saw it, didn't she, Flynn? What was it she said?"

"Darkness," I said. Lydia's words reluctantly drifted past my lips and inspired fresh echoes in my mind as some distant chorus grew in volume. "She warned me about the darkness. About those who would take advantage of my gifts."

"She warned you for a reason, and not because she's a good guesser."

My head turned, eyes studying Monica as I furrowed my brow. "Lydia was one of your kind?"

Monica smiled. "Remember, Flynn, there are more sides to this equation than you realize. You need to consider the possibilities. Was it truly Peter who killed Lydia or were you the assassin then as well? You haven't confronted Sabrina about it. You haven't told her about your abilities. You're not running to her to conquer the world, as you put it. Why is that?"

My eyes shot away from her, in an effort to conceal my one weakness. It was difficult for me to deny any misgivings, because while my lust for blood had been unaffected, my desire for Sabrina dwindled into nonexistence. Sabrina used to be able to snap her fingers and have me running to perform whatever duty she had planned for me that night. I would have traversed the seven continents to please my mistress and yet, whenever I found myself in her proximity in recent days, my thoughts were not steady, my reflexes not as sharp. For being such a murderous bastard, I could see a far more profound evil lying inside Sabrina, a predilection toward atrocities which eclipsed my own. The sight unnerved me beyond measure.

It should not have bothered me, but it did. I should have been savoring the thought of plotting the demise of her enemies, yet I knew what the end to such a thing would be. She would assign me a permanent place of worship, feared by all as a ruthless dictator second only to her as my queen. The neophyte would become a lord and master whose iron fist would capture coven after coven and claim them all for the woman who created him. I would assure nobody ever dared overthrow us. Yes, the thought should have been consuming me to the point of madness. But here I stood, playing parlor games with my gifts instead of surrendering myself to every vile thought I could conjure inside my twisted mind.

I spoke after a period of silence. "Why do you unnerve me, witch?"

Monica regarded me with sympathetic eyes. "I unnerve you, Flynn?" She grinned. "Maybe this is a sign your humanity isn't as dead as you think it is, if there's an evil you still fear. Why do you fear it?"

The words I spoke drifted from some corner in the back of my mind. "The consequences of Sabrina having such power would be grave." A frown enveloped my countenance. My gaze shifted to the ground. "Depart from my presence," I whispered. "I grow weary of your company."

Turning as though to leave, I realized Monica had not moved an inch. I glanced back her way again and found her eyeing me in an intent manner, with a heavy gaze that was refusing to waver. "Is this how it goes with you?" she asked. "Your worldview begins to unravel and you decide you can't take it anymore when it starts hitting too close to home?"

I scowled. "If you wish to be my helper, then do me the courtesy of leaving. I shall solve these riddles on my own."

A flash of rage surfaced on her face, but her expression quickly evened. She nodded solemnly at me. "As you wish." I watched her walk away, my eyes set upon her fading figure as my thoughts strayed back toward Lydia. Had she truly been a witch? Granted, I knew of her interest in the occult and supernatural, but never before had I thought there might have been anything behind it. As Monica turned down an adjoining road, I focused on her, attempting to employ my new-found talents to read the sorceress the same way I read the mortals I slaughtered. The moment I tried, though, I encountered a form of resistance, something my current level of experience could not bypass. Monica disappeared, leaving me with more questions than I had answers.

My hand drifted upward subconsciously, and my fingers reached underneath my shirt for the necklace which I kept secured around my throat. As I pulled it out, I felt energy buzzing from the pendant, something I had been daft to before. "Damn you, Lydia," I said. "Damn your ghost and your infidelity. Why do you continue to trouble me?" My eyes lifted toward the heavens, dark without even a hint of stars overhead. Sighing, I tucked the pendant back into its hiding place.

The entire episode angered me. I had started to derive some pleasure from my curse and now Monica had ripped it away. Disgusted with myself, with Monica, and with the entirety of the universe, I started back for the coven house. My gait betrayed my tumultuous, doubting thoughts, and I garnered more than a few stares from the sentries at the front doors as well as the brethren I passed on my way to the stairs. Placing a hand on the banister as I began my ascent, I winced when I heard a pair of feet rushing to catch up with me and a familiar voice calling my name.

"Flynn!" I ignored Robin and began a hasty trek up the stairs. Glancing back at him once, I saw him taking the stairs two at a time and grumbled as I increased my pace. Robin was not to be deterred though. "Flynn! Wait!"

Finally, I hesitated with the second evocation of my name. Pausing on the top stair, I turned to face him. "What is it, Robin?" I asked through gritted teeth, not bothering to mask my annoyance while my mind continued spinning. I waited for him to catch up before continuing, my voice lowering to a growl. "I wish to go to my room and do not desire your company right now, thank you very much."

"I can hardly believe your attitude." Robin ascended the last stair by my side and turned down the corridor with me. "What has you troubled these past few days? You've hardly been around and whenever we talk you act as though I'm doing nothing but irritating you."

"I have been acting no differently than normal." My stride quickened again. "Now, if you would kindly leave me alone..."

"Hardly. Not until you tell me what is wrong with you."

"What concern is it of yours?"

Robin shook his head, his feet more than keeping pace with mine. "I thought we were confidants, but I must have been mistaken."

"I have no confidants," I spat, "Merely a host of manipulators around me, trying to fuck with my mind. You all stand in line, both living and dead, to make a basket case out of me."

"What the devil are you talking about?"

"The devil." I laughed. "Yes, I imagine he is in on this as well. Just fucking call me Job instead of Flynn. It would only be fitting, seeing as though I am the prize to be won in an annoying cosmic dice game."

Robin scoffed. "I should almost call you Peter right now. You haven't acted like this since your first days as an immortal."

My steps ceased, though we were nearly to the sanctuary of my room. Turning to hiss at Robin, I bared fangs at him and spoke in the vilest tone of voice which had ever passed through my lips. "Call me that name one more time, you uptight Irish bastard, and I shall ensure you never speak another word again."

"You would bare your fangs at me? There truly is something wrong with you." Robin strode ahead of me, acting like a barricade between me and my door by pressing his back against the sturdy wood. "I demand you speak to me as my brother, or I swear to you I will run upstairs to Sabrina and tell her you've lost your mind."

"Get out of my way, damn it." My hand landed on Robin's shoulder, attempting to push him aside.

Robin growled and swung a fist around, landing a punch across my face. My sunglasses flew with the impact and light stabbed my eyes with blinding shards of pain. "Bastard!" I said as I covered my eyes. "Do you have any idea how much that fucking hurts?!"

I stole a quick glance at Robin through the cracks of my fingers, seeing his mouth hang agape. He struggled to speak. "Flynn," he said, his voice barely above a whisper. "Your eyes..."

"Yes, my eyes. They hurt, you moron." Bending over, I groped in a desperate fashion for my sunglasses, slipping them on the moment I located them. I stood once more and dusted off my suit jacket. "Or had you forgotten that in your abject stupidity?"

Robin failed to respond. I rubbed my eyes once more, and then regarded him, entertaining notions of unsheathing a knife and stabbing him enough times to make a vampire pin cushion out of him. The homicidal urge waned the moment I caught sight of how white his already-pale complexion had become. "What the fuck are you gaping at?" I asked. "You look as though you just saw the sun peeking through the windows."

He blinked several times. His mouth opened and closed in an effort to produce noise until finally producing a panicked hush. "Your sunglasses. They were concealing it, but I remember... I remember what color they were when you were turned. I..." Robin swallowed hard. He furrowed his brow. "When did you acquire the sight, Flynn?"

My facial expression sank. I asked the question, though fearing the answer. "What is it, Robin? What has happened to my eyes?"

One sharp, nervous laugh preceded my older brother's response. He placed a hand on my shoulder and leaned close to me. "What was once sapphire has turned to emerald."

I perked an eyebrow. "What the fuck is that supposed to mean?"

"Your eyes." Robin shook his head. "They used to be blue, but are no longer. Now, they've turned to green."

Chapter Sixteen

In case I have failed to mention it previously, the vampires of my bloodline have nothing in the way of a reflection. You can speculate all you would like as to what causes this phenomenon, but one item of amendment must be added to this fact.

This means we cannot see when our eyes have changed color.

I rushed inside my room with Robin in tow. He shut the door, but remained standing in the entryway, watching with confusion and awe as I ripped my glasses from my face and paced the room. "I cannot believe this," I said, knitting my fingers in my hair. "I cannot fucking believe this. What did that miserable wench do to me?"

"Who, Flynn?" Robin asked in a cautious manner. As though I had come unhinged and was ready to snap at any moment.

He would have been correct.

"That fucking sorceress!" I spun around to regard my brother, a strange premonition washing over me, brought about by knowing I possessed a visible mark of my hidden gifts now. It inspired a knot of dread which did not seem liable to unravel any time soon. "The little witch has been screwing with me and has finally gone too damn far."

"What are you talking about? I thought she was dead."

"She was supposed to be." Strolling over to one of my chairs, I fell into it with such heaviness, I should have broken it. Would have only been fitting, I figured. One more cosmic laugh at my expense. I leaned back and covered my face with my hands. "They never seem to die when you want them to. Instead, they cast spells which screw with your perceptions and change the fucking color of your eyes."

My words ceased in an abrupt manner. Robin made no motion to move or speak for what seemed like eons, causing an unsettling hush to fall between us. Finally, I heard his footsteps closing in on me. He sat in the sofa across from me and remained quiet for a while before speaking. "This is no hex, Flynn," he said in an even manner. "I am not sure about the witch and what spells she might have cast, but I know no sorceress able to give a vampire the gift you possess."

My hands fell on my lap. I sighed, lining my sights with Robin. "What the fuck are you talking about?"

He ignored my tone and frowned. "This matter with your eyes. The problems you've experienced with them from your awakening until now. Their change in color." Robin hesitated. I perked an eyebrow as he looked away. "Flynn, do you remember when I was training you to be an assassin and you asked what I meant when I mentioned your nature factoring into your sword skills?"

"Vaguely."

Robin sighed. His gaze met mine again. "I have done you an injustice. I can only hope you don't hate me when I tell you what I am about to say."

Instinctively, I slid forward in my seat. "Just tell me, Robin," I said, my voice lowering. "Please."

He nodded slowly, folding his hands on his lap. His eyes strayed toward the floor again while he indulged in a deep, steadying breath. "Brother, I've hidden from you what you truly are all these years, partly to protect you and partly to protect the rest of the coven. I was ordered by Sabrina, prior to your turning, never to speak a word of this under pain of death. The older you became, the less apt to come clean I have been."

I remained silent, eyes fixed on Robin. He shook his head, and then looked up at me again. "Sabrina and I were in San Francisco the first time I ever witnessed a seer with my own eyes. I'll not go into that story now. Suffice to say the impression was lasting and staring into the eyes of one almost always means a vampire's death. That we made it out alive is a wonder, but from that point forth, I paid attention to what the olden ones would say as they spoke of these... vampire hunters."

"Vampire hunters?" I frowned. "What the devil does that mean?"

"Your birthright." Robin issued a wan smile. "You were born to kill your own kind, brother. Seers come into this world with the ability to read thoughts and discern the intentions of those around them..."

I held up my hand. "I have heard this before." I paused. "Well, I heard about reading thoughts and have experienced this for myself. This is the first I am hearing about a seer being a vampire hunter."

Robin huffed. "The sorceress is apparently being selective in her information. Or cautious, which is not uncalled for when it comes to you." He nodded, his eyes becoming distant. "So, this would explain why you've been acting strange lately. I never thought to consider you had realized your gifts, but now it makes sense. The witch did this, didn't she?"

I nodded. "Yes," I said, my voice a whisper. Clearing my throat, I spoke louder and steadier. "Yes, when I was missing that night, she had me shackled in her room and laid hands on me. I do not know what she did, but it felt as though she was twisting my mind around and reorganizing everything. The gifts began to emerge afterward."

"You are fortunate Sabrina hasn't noticed this yet."

I closed my eyes and sighed. My voice lowered again. "Yes, I am. Those days are numbered, though." My lids remained shut. Monica's words coupled with Robin's to form a circle in my mind. Raising my hand to rub my face again, I allowed it to settle onto my lap while the charge levied by Monica finally gained enough urgency to make it past my lips. "Is this why I was to be turned, Robin?"

He swallowed hard and nodded. "One such as you was not meant to be one such as us." Robin sighed. "I know of no other vampire who has successfully turned a seer. To find one who hasn't realized his abilities is extremely difficult, if not impossible. The lot of you walk around like a ticking time bomb, eyes a different color with complete ignorance of what lies in wait. Then, suddenly, the bomb explodes and here you are." He raised his hands, pointing them toward me. "Emerald-eyed psychics snatched up by the mortals who employ you. Sabrina had a premonition about you from your first meeting, though. As a mortal, your eyes might have been blue, but they were the same shade. Her subsequent meetings confirmed her suspicions and when you woke with the infirmity, we took it as a sign."

"So, she was right." My gaze strayed toward the wall across from me. "The pearl of great price and here I sit, no longer ignorant."

"The witch has kept in contact with you?"

I nodded. "Yes. She locates me every few days, attempting to be my conscience." I scoffed, looking back at him. "Nothing she has said has stuck until now. I have reveled in reading thoughts and using my gifts to lure my prey, but..." Shaking my head, I sighed. "I do not think she shall rest until she has me utterly and completely confused."

Robin glanced away, gaze turning pensive, until it found mine again. "Why did she bring out your gifts?"

"The naive creature still thinks me capable of redemption." I laughed, incredulous. "And thinks my buried humanity will latch onto the sight. I confess, this has brought about some moments where I thought I might split apart and form two people from the madness of it all. The more I come to understand it, the more it confounds me." My words ceased for a moment. I frowned once more. "The only pleasure I have derived is from killing. After all, what good is a vampire who cannot kill? Precious little more than a deathless mortal."

Robin's expression turned pained and his shoulders sank. "You prick my conscience, brother. These are words I have hurtled at you."

I perked an eyebrow. "What do you mean, I prick your conscience?"

"Everything you are and everything you have become is due to me, in part." He sighed, his shoulders lifting again, but seemingly in defiance toward the melancholy which infected him. "You are not the only one who has served the mistress to their downfall. I did it when I agreed to train you. While doing so taught me to be the mentor I should have been from the start, I gave you the tools to become what you are."

"I do not understand. How are you responsible for what I became?"

"I have taught a seer to love to kill." He shook his head. "This world is part of a natural order; there are certain things which shouldn't ever come to pass. While I taught you what it means to be a vampire, I never revealed to you what you were before all this. And in doing so, I set you on a path which has made you more and more like Sabrina every day. For this, I will be judged mercilessly by The Fates."

I shook my head. "I do not know much about The Fates or about this natural order you claim exists, but Sabrina." Drawing in a deep breath, I exhaled it slowly. "As you pointed out, she knows nothing about this and thinks the witch is dead. Many times, I have tried to bring myself to killing Monica and each time, I have let her slip through my fingers without argument." I brought my hand to my head at the mention of Monica, as though I could develop a migraine at the mere invocation of her name. "She shows up and I become of warring minds. Curse that damn mortal and the day she entered my life."

Robin hesitated. I looked at him without realizing my gaze had strayed and focused on his thoughts, hearing them first as a whisper, then as a shout. As I concentrated on the one person inside my coven I trusted, I heard his private ruminations scream of distrust. Distrust of Sabrina; the thought that I was teetering on an edge and about to plunge headfirst into her arms so she could rip me apart. I saw an image of me being used before being tossed aside and frowned deeper at the notion. "You think me wise not to tell her," I said.

My brother glanced away, issuing a sardonic chuckle. "Ah yes. Hard to mask one's thoughts from a seer, isn't it?"

"This is the first time I have tried to read them." I leaned forward in my seat. "Why should I keep it from her?"

Robin sighed. "A century is a long time, Flynn. As I said to you before, I have a history with the mistress. It could take days to retell every story of our time spent together. One thing I can tell you, though, is that this coven has never been one large, happy family." His eyes met mine again. "When not infected with jealousy, it is compromised by its laziness and overindulgence. It hasn't made her any friends with the remainder of the covens and you were the straw which broke the camel's back."

I watched him stand and begin to pace the floor in front of me. Holding my gaze steady, I waited patiently for him to continue. "Sabrina's always been an ambitious person," he said, "But it became much worse forty years ago. That was when she became ruthless; willing to do whatever it took to gain whatever she wished. I left her side for ten years and returned out of duty to her as my maker, to be her second. I have never seen her use the level of deception she has employed with you before, though." He turned to face me. "She keeps you placated so you continue to use your blades in her service. I have caught her dabbling in things which she has no business trifling with and she has prided herself in turning a seer into a sadist."

For some inexplicable reason, the comment wounded me. "You think me a monster, Robin."

Robin frowned, regarding me in a solemn manner. "I think you're well on your way to becoming one and I fear it for everyone's sake – including yours, dear brother." He sighed. "When I was your mentor, I thought I was helping to give you a purpose to your existence. I had no idea how much Sabrina would exploit it. I served her blindly and I confess this to you. In the years which have passed, I realize what a grave mistake I made. You became more than a hunter, you are a killer. Instead of loathing evil, you love it. Continuing down this road, with the gifts you now possess, I see the potential for a monster far worse than Sabrina herself."

My brother and I stared at one another. While I felt the invisible knife which had just been thrust into my chest, I knew I deserved it. Swallowing hard, I nodded. "I do not deny the truth of your words." My eyes drifted away. "Sabrina's presence chills me now, though. I once desired her as nothing before, but these days, I cannot look at her without my gut twisting in revulsion. It has made being her assassin taxing, to say the least."

When I glanced back at Robin, I saw him grin. "The witch was saving your life, it would seem."

"More like condemning it. Knowing now what I do, Sabrina will not allow an insubordinate vampire under her roof, especially not one with an echo of his humanity in hibernation." Standing, I sighed. "Robin, for over four years my conscience has been free of remorse. I have experienced things, though, which have confounded me ever since the witch came into my life. I do not know why. Perhaps this seer still lives and has been woken by these abilities. I might be under some spell, for all I know. Or, this blasted necklace I procured from Anthony might be to blame for most of this. Who the devil knows?"

Robin raised an eyebrow. "Necklace?"

"Yes." I reached underneath my shirt and brought the pendant out where Robin could see it. He studied it as I continued to speak. "I had given it to my mortal girlfriend and retained ownership of it after I killed her. I sold it some years ago, but for some bloody reason, I asked Anthony to find it for me again and everything has been flipped upside down ever since. Sabrina shall seek my destruction if I continue on this path, dear brother. Her wiles have been useless against me."

Robin's eyes lifted from the pendant to meet my gaze. "The necklace is enchanted, which makes sense to me. Your mortal girlfriend was no ordinary human."

I tucked the necklace back into hiding. "That is what the witch tried to tell me. I don't know if this is to blame for my behavior, but Sabrina will notice it before she sees the color of my eyes. I have been walking a fine line as it is."

"Whether or not your abilities or this necklace are to blame for it, you'd be mindful to keep wearing it, regardless of how much it might trouble you." Robin's gaze turned severe. "I can only offer you my advice, dear brother. I'm certain my words will shock you, though."

"What is your advice?"

"Leave. Take your things, including some of your best weapons and get as far away from here as possible. Only, be merciful to me if we ever meet with you as the slayer."

I scoffed. "I refuse to be a vampire hunter, if this is what you claim my calling is. I only wish to be able to live as I once lived."

"None of us have that option any longer, especially not you. These gifts choose you, not the other way around. If your mortal conscience is truly coming to life once more, fulfill your destiny and stop tempting The Fates." He paused. A solemn smile managed its way onto his face. "Please, brother. Get away from Sabrina before she gets to you. It was wrong that you were turned in the first place, but this can't be undone. I'd sooner see you realize your human purpose than watch you continue to be Sabrina's puppet."

Nodding, I frowned. "What was it you once told me? I was a mistake?"

Robin's smile faded, lips arching downward into a frown. "I'm sorry I was so harsh with you before. I would like to think nothing in this world is a mistake, but knowing what I know about the natural order..."

I held up my hand to stop him. "Apologies are not necessary, brother." My hand lowered. I shook my head. "Robin, I cannot do what you say. I do not wish to assume any predetermined human purpose and I do not wish to leave. If I have any purpose left, it is here..."

"To subdue the enemies of Sabrina and allow her to rise to further glory in this city." Robin paused, tipping his hands such that his palms pointed upward. "And now, you will know all her enemies."

Unable to speak at first, I simply stared at him, the memory of those words I heard echo in my mind several weeks ago replaying. My hands found the back of my chair, yet my eyes remained fixed on my brother. "You are conspiring against her. This is why you were caught with Demetrius."

"Your words are correct." His gaze turned defiant without issuing any condemnation at the same time. "The other covens have spent months devising some way to end Sabrina and I haven't stopped them because I can't condone her actions any longer. I've lived a century, brother. I've seen both the best and the worst in vampire kind and this is nothing like what I imagined when I agreed to be second to a coven. I've lived with other nests and reveled in my nature with other immortals. Sabrina wants more. She would turn us into indulgent animals, from the higher mark of the food chain into sadists. We are wicked; I don't gloss over what we are in any way, shape, or form. There is an evil we cannot tolerate, though. Sabrina's quest for power has her blind and drunk."

We continued regarding each other, not speaking for what seemed like an eternity. I neither read his thoughts, nor offered him my own. Instead, I allowed my words to encapsulate my sentiments, the moment I summoned the will to issue them. "Robin, I cannot leave if this is to happen."

Robin's expression turned pained. "Flynn, please. By The Fates above, stop protecting that which your conscience is warning you against."

"Sabrina is not the reason why I cannot leave." I raised an eyebrow.

Robin blinked. "I do not understand."

Nodding, I lifted my hands from my chair, slipping them into my pants pockets. "I will continue my ruse as long as possible and conceal my eyes from her, until your deed is finished and my service to her ends. I do not know about human destinies or how I could fill such a role in my current state. If what you say is true, though, then Sabrina shall indeed become an insufferable evil if allowed to continue on her present course." I paused, feeling my stomach sink. "Especially if she finds out about me."

Robin opened his mouth to speak, but I interrupted by adding, "Only do it quickly. I do not know how long I can continue this charade."

He nodded slowly. "It will be done as you say."

"Very well." Lifting one hand to rub my eyes, I plodded around to my chair and sat once more. "You have extended a great service to me by telling me what you know, which is far more than I can say for any other player in this nonsense. So, I shall try my best to extend the same service to you."

"Thank you, dear brother." Robin glanced toward my door, and then looked back at me. "I will leave you to rest now. I'm sure your mind could use the reprieve."

"Thank you," was all I could say in return. Robin motioned as though to add something further to the conversation, but seemed to reconsider and merely nodded before saying good night. Once I heard my door shut, I sighed and sank deeper into my chair. Silence wrapped around me, but did nothing to settle my nerves.

Several times that night, my fingers reached to stroke the pendant around my neck while I sat alone in darkness. *'Damn necklace,'* I thought. *'Lydia, I have no idea why you chose this to be my anchor in the midst of a storm, but for the first time since this whole debacle started, I must thank you for it.'* Without pausing to add anything further to my expression of gratitude, I allowed my mind to go blank until it was time for me to settle into slumber for the morning.

Still, I had been left in quite a perilous position, to be forced to play the role of assassin and servant while becoming a participant in this conspiracy against Sabrina. My final thought before drifting to sleep caused my stomach to sink again. Knowing how cunning my mistress could be, I had no idea how I was going to pull off such a deception.

Chapter Seventeen

I remember the way Lydia's eyes danced when she opened the box and pulled out the gold chain. "Peter," she said, her smile widening as she looked up at me. "It's absolutely gorgeous."

"I knew you'd like it," I said, grinning back at her. Once again, I found myself becoming lost in her green eyes, beholding them as beacons set to enchant me beyond my inhibitions. "There's something about it that screams 'macabre yet beautiful girlfriend.' Must be why I was drawn to it."

She laughed, and then looked down at the pendant again. I recall the way she studied it, a mixture of adoration and curiosity present on her face as my girlfriend of two years regarded the trinket, lost deep in thought. "It's beautiful, but almost kind of sad. I see what you mean." When her eyes met mine again, I saw the melancholy present in her gaze. Such a look was standard fare for her. As quickly as she smiled, it seemed she frowned that much faster, as though something within Lydia prevented her from latching onto happiness for long. Sometimes, I wondered if she feared her joy would cause the world to tip from its axis.

I ignored it and took the chain in my hands, moving to drape it around her neck. As the clasp locked into place, I heard her sigh and perked an eyebrow. "You're not going to tell me, but I'm going to ask anyway. What's wrong, Lydia?"

Leaning down, I gently kissed at her neck. She turned to face me, her eyes closed at first and then opening slowly as her hand rose to touch the side of my face. "I love you," she said.

"I love you, too," I said in return, but I could not help but to be put off by her brooding. The conversation with the jeweler surfaced in my thoughts, as did a reminder of my hesitation to buy her an engagement ring. I had planned on it, being so close to the end of my residency, and yet the notion could not be brought to fruition. It was not a lack of money; my trust fund – what was left of it after tuition expenses, that is – afforded me more than enough resources. Perhaps I was afraid to be happy myself. Or, perhaps it had to do with the strange premonition which set up shop those days.

I knew one day I would lose her. As pessimistic as the thought was, it still existed and, I felt, not without good reason. Over the course of those final months, Lydia had become more and more distant. I blamed myself and my busy schedule; too many shifts at the hospital, trying too hard to be too many things at once.

"I make you sad," I said after a long pause. "Why?"

Lydia shook her head. "It's not you, Peter. It's me. I..." She trailed off.

I forced her attention back to me when she glanced away. "You what?"

She sighed. "It's my twenty-fifth birthday. I haven't been looking forward to this."

I smiled, in an effort to coax a smile out from her. "I'm three years past it and can promise you nothing happens. You just get another year older."

My effort failed. "And another year closer to death." Lydia frowned. Her eyes drifted away again and this time, I did not force them to return. "What if this is the last one?"

"You haven't been reading some book or listening to a lunatic tell you you're going to die at the age of twenty-five, have you?"

"You don't believe in the supernatural. It's hard for you to understand."

My breath passed through my lips in an exasperated sigh. "Just because I don't acknowledge it doesn't mean I don't know how it affects you."

"You really don't." Lydia moved away from me and walked toward the kitchen. "Peter, one of these days it's going to crash into you like a freight train and then, you'll understand. Until that happens, it's hard for you to know where I'm coming from."

"I just don't understand how you let these things get under your skin," I said, following after her. "Nobody knows the future and all this bullshit people try to pass off as being mystical amounts to a lot of parlor tricks from a bunch of swindlers. I don't see real psychics walking around giving credible advice to anyone, do you?"

I paused in the doorway to the kitchen as Lydia's steps slowed to a stop and her gaze fell to the ground. "There are things you don't see yet. The world has a whole other side to it." She looked up at me again. "It sees you, Peter."

A laugh preceded the condescending tone of my words. "What is that supposed to mean? You think one day I'm going to open my eyes and embrace a fictional world? Maybe when I'm senile or..." I pointed at the necklace. "...When that pendant becomes a magical talisman."

Her fingers rose to touch the pendant while her frown deepened. I could see tears welling in her eyes and felt my shoulders slump at her reaction. This time, I had gone too far. "Lydia," I said, speaking softly. "I'm sorry, that wasn't right of me. I just don't like seeing you get so upset over these things."

"Peter," she said, her voice developing an edge to it. "The only thing worse than being blind is having sight, but no vision." Her eyes shut. A single tear ran down Lydia's cheek while the words of her favorite quote lingered in the air between us. I opened my mouth to speak, but she cut me off by continuing. "I wish I could believe for you and be there to protect you, but somehow I know it's all going to come too late for me." She raised her hand to her face, brushing away the moisture on her cheek. "Damn it."

I walked into the kitchen and wrapped my arms around her, pulling her close to my chest. It was not the first time I forced myself to be patient with her superstition and I knew it would not be the last. "If I need help," I said, stroking her hair in a reassuring manner. "Then I know you'll be clever enough to figure out a way. I have faith in *you.*"

"I'm so afraid, Peter." Lydia buried her face into my chest, her arms wrapping tight around me. "Someone's going to hurt me and I don't have any idea who. I only know it's going to happen soon."

"If anybody ever tried to raise a hand to you, I'd protect you." Looking down at her, I touched her chin and raised her head so her eyes met mine. A reassuring grin surfaced on my face. "You have nothing to worry about."

Her eyes carried a measure of skepticism, but she nodded anyway and rested her head against my chest again. If she doubted me at all, she had every right to, for three months later I would be the one to do her the ultimate injury. No more than ten feet away from us was a block of butcher knives. My hand would be the one to plunge the blade into her chest. The knife would cut through her heart in the most literal way possible.

Lydia Davies would be no more.

⚜

The days passed, leaving me in the strange position of being a conflicted vampire. I was an assassin. My hands were the ones which snuffed out life so often, my actions had nearly become mechanical. Precise and unmerciful; lacking in compassion and utterly detached. What Robin said about the monster I had become could be proven time and time again and yet, after our talk, it became a bitter pill to swallow. If I had possessed a reflection, I might have become lost in the emerald green of my irises until I would have been tempted to gouge them out.

I vowed to perform the duties of a hit man, though. So as each night passed, I met with Sabrina and received whatever instructions she had for me, her dark killer. Maintaining a straight face, I kept my sunglasses on at all times, even when she kept her penthouse lit with her customary candlelight. I smiled at all the right times and sneered when I was expected to. I met her advances and learned how to pretend I did not realize how duped I had been for five years. Her seduction fell short of its mark. Her lips were acid and her body made mine wish to slink away in revulsion. In my heart of hearts, I knew the woman with which I dealt and my newly-acquired sight made being her assassin that much more difficult.

Fortunate for me, her advances never transgressed into the realm of skin on skin, so the necklace remained hidden. Each night, I came back to the coven home with another notch upon my belt, while my mind continued turning over my abilities and the talisman's effect on me. Neither helped, nor hindered, my assault against humanity. I still fed and still sensed their innermost secrets while I drank their life's blood. I continued to use the ruse of knowing them and even caring about them in order to make bloody work of them. In my mind's eye, I still saw each one as a hypocrite, with the doctor I once was being the worst transgressor amongst the lot. And my disdain only grew the more I learned about the skeletons in their closets.

The businessman who cheated on his wife.

The girl who seduced men for their money.

The fraternity brothers who raped a young woman.

I found myself wishing somebody would remove the curse which was humanity, regardless of whether or not that would mean my starvation.

Ordinarily, this would be the point when Monica would scold my double standards and delight in pointing out my care for their injustices proved my own conscience was not dead, but she remained absent. Several nights passed without one hint of the impish witch, adding itself to an already-growing list of absurdities. My previous attempts to rid myself of Miss Alexander had yielded no results and now she was gone through no action of mine. Still, I had more than enough practical matters with which to be concerned.

For how much of a mask I had to present to the others in the coven, though, Robin had to be that much more polished. Before I was even a glimmer in my mother's eye, Robin had been a trusted aide to Sabrina. Now that his thoughts had turned against her, he moved with all the cunning of Cassius through the courts of Caesar. We spoke to one another, much the same as always, replete with smiles and laughs for those who might be watching. He and I resembled the perfect models of our former lives. Late into the night, however, we would meet upon the streets of Philadelphia and engage in conspiratorial discussions. Such as the one we found ourselves embroiled in as late February found its way onto our doorstep.

"I cannot be the one to pull the knife, Robin," I said to him as my gaze lifted toward the night sky. I drew from my cigarette and exhaled a plume of smoke. "The one to do it must have a clear mind, not easily swayed by her wiles. I cannot vouch for my mental faculties right now."

"Cannot?" Robin scoffed, slipping his hands into his pockets. "You've successfully eluded her suspicions for over two weeks, brother. If anyone is mentally steady enough for this task, it would be you."

"I have far too many weaknesses presently. I am merely fortunate she has not discovered them."

"Such as your eyes? The pendant?"

"Amongst other things, yes."

Robin raised an eyebrow. "What else?"

I sighed. "Robin, my thoughts have been unsteady, even the ones which have nothing to do with Sabrina. I wrestle with my own demons too much to execute this plan with any clarity."

Robin paused, his eyes set upon me with a searching gaze. "You don't want to be the one to do it. After all this, the assassin still harbors some devotion to his mistress."

Drawing from the cigarette again, I frowned and flicked the depleted remnant away. My eyes drifted downward while I exhaled smoke out my nostrils. "Part of me is still enamored by her, yes. I am very aware there is a barrier which prevents me from being taken in by her charms, but I can still feel the other side of the wall. If she cracks through my defenses, I will not be able to carry out my mission."

"We have found the one creature Flynn cannot kill."

The verbal slap shot my gaze back to Robin. I sneered, tempted to speak through gritted teeth. "Robin, you wish your coup and I am giving it to you, even though I could pull a knife and drive it into your heart this instant. This is as far as my aid to you can extend." Forced to look away, I felt my gaze become distant as the whisper of a notion drifted past my lips. "I fear evil, but I do not hate it as much as I should."

"I would believe that, dear brother." Robin sighed. I looked toward him again in time to see him eye me as the stray sheep in the flock. "You are still of warring minds. One of these days, one of the two sides will have at the other and claim victory."

"I wish they would hurry it the fuck up and decide. This middle-of-the-road bullshit is taxing."

Robin chuckled and I could not help but to smirk in response. My disposition became sober once more, though, as I reached into my pocket for my cigarettes and tapped another into my hand. "So, tell me how you and your co-conspirators have this planned out, Robin," I said, lighting the end. A puff of smoke preceded the remainder of my words. "I wish to know how the amateurs do it."

"You would mock your teacher, Flynn?" Robin grinned. "I'll have you know I can still handle the sword just as well as I did when we last sparred."

"Which makes me fearful for your sake."

Robin laughed. "Then tell me, seer. Search my thoughts and interpret my plans."

I indulged in a long drag of the cigarette and turned to face Robin. Regarding him in a careful manner, I paid little attention to the smoke which I exhaled and focused on my brother. On the surface of his mind, I found an intense loathing of Sabrina present – a barrier clouding the rest of his plans – and felt a pang of concern for his sake. I ignored it for the time being, though, and proceeded further.

That was when the images assailed me. I saw a council meeting, with several elders and coven masters gathered together. I recognized such meetings as common place when the area vampires felt an important issue needed to be discussed and from Robin's thoughts, I gathered such a thing was soon to be announced. Sabrina would be the object of this meeting, without her knowledge. This would be when she would meet her end.

Just as quickly as I began to wonder how they would orchestrate their assassination, the still images came to life and formed a movie. Robin stood from his place beside Sabrina, but rather than speaking for her, he began to issue his complaints against her. My name was evoked, but defended and the council took a vote on how best to punish Sabrina. I saw the call for execution. I heard the masses cry for her ashes to be distributed amongst the covens as a reminder of the punishment for those who killed their own kind.

Shutting off the visuals, I looked into Robin's eyes and perked an eyebrow. "And how does this punishment get exacted, dear brother? Do you see Sabrina lying down and accepting her sentence as a convicted criminal?"

"No, I know she will resist." He sighed. "This is where I hoped you might be present to ensure the execution proceeds without incident. If you don't want to be a part of it, then I will have to make other arrangements." His gaze turned distant. He swallowed hard. "I might have to do it myself."

I frowned at the reaction. "I apologize for being unable to participate." As I raised my cigarette to my mouth again, I glanced away. "I hope to be far from this debacle, figuring out what to do with the remainder of my existence."

A hush settled between us. When I felt a pair of eyes fixed on me, I turned my head and looked at Robin again. He lifted an eyebrow at me. "I could use a bodyguard, Flynn. Not an assassin, but someone to help make the transition from

Sabrina's leadership to mine more seamless."

I could not help but to blink. "You plan on taking the helm?"

Robin nodded. "I am her second." His eyes turned soft, pleading. "Would you be my guardian as I have been yours these past few years?"

Staring at him, I regarded the seriousness of his words and the steady gaze he held. I used my abilities to search him for any hint of deception, but sensed none. Simply the request of a brother.

He continued speaking, as though sensing my hesitation. "No seducing. No manipulation. You wouldn't be my servant, you would be my friend. I only seek your defense, Flynn, not for you to be a strong arm for my whims." Robin paused, inserting another grin. "Unless your human destiny calls first to snatch you away."

"Bah." I flicked those words away with a flip of my hand. "Human destinies are for mortals and I am hardly mortal any longer." Studying Robin, I allowed the notion to turn around in my mind. "Only a bodyguard and nothing more?"

"As surely as you named me Robin and I named you Flynn, I will never ask for you to be an assassin again."

I nodded and glanced away, flicking my cigarette into the distance while I considered his words. Using my sword as a protector rather than an executioner was I prospect I never dared fathom, because I never thought such neutrality possible. Even the notion of exploring this so-called mortal destiny left me curious about what the future might have in store, but with my options laid out before me I was far more apt to take Robin's proposal over surrendering an eternity to The Fates.

My eyes met his again. "I shall not stand in your way as the assassination is carried out. And, when you are finished, my sword will be used for your protection."

Robin grinned. "You agree then, brother?"

Reflecting his smile, I nodded. "Yes, I agree, Robin."

My answer pleased Robin to the point that he walked forward and met me in a quick embrace. Falling into it in an awkward manner, I winced at his enthusiasm while he patted my back and pushed away, his hands rising to settle on my shoulders. "Very good, Flynn." He chuckled. "This is so much better than the thought of meeting you again someday as your adversary."

I laughed. "I should say so, for your sake."

A short bout of hysterics punctuated Robin's actions as he relinquished his hold on me. "I can't argue that much." The sigh which escaped his lips was rife with relief. "This is the best I've felt in decades. Finally this can all be put behind us and the covens can be at peace." Robin slapped my shoulder, provoking another grimace from me. "I won't ask you to play the actor much longer. The elders are stirring. We plan to meet soon."

I smoothed out my suit jacket to straighten the wrinkles brought about by his burst of brotherly affection. "The sooner, the better. I am walking a precarious line right now." My hand settled to my side and my gaze found the night sky again, surveying the hour and noting in the back of my mind I was due to report to Sabrina regarding my latest assignment. "Shore up your plans," I said, looking back at Robin. "Decide who your assassin will be. Sabrina, as you have noted before, is a crafty woman and shall sense your plans before you bring them to fruition if you are not careful. You might have to act swiftly, without the formality of charges."

Robin nodded. "I will make certain we have a few contingencies in place."

"Very well." I nodded. "I need to take my leave before Sabrina becomes suspicious, then."

"Good luck, brother." Robin continued grinning at me as I turned and started to walk away. My departure was interrupted, though, as Robin called out, "Flynn?"

I glanced back at him, perking an eyebrow.

He grinned. "It won't be much longer. I promise."

"Thank heaven for small mercies." I flashed a quick smile at Robin, then turned again to consummate my departure. It did not take long for me to stride back into the coven, past the sentries at the front doors, and well on my way to the stairs. I heard footsteps rushing toward me, though, once my hand touched the banister.

Rose appeared in my periphery, her eyes set on me. She smiled and waited until she joined me at the stairs to speak. "Flynn, you are just the devil I was looking for."

I chuckled. "Seek the devil and you will find him easy enough, dear Rose." My brow furrowed. "What did you wish of me?"

Her grin turned impish. "I have a message for you."

A sigh escaped my lips, sounding playful enough in its exasperation and concealing how tired I was. Indeed, I did not even have the motivation to plumb her thoughts for their contents, not expecting that I would find much. "Rose, you disappear on me for several nights and expect me to wait around for your little messages?"

She laughed. One of her hands rested on my upper arm, sliding to my shoulder. "Now, Flynn, you know I have many pursuits." As Rose tilted her head, the delicious sight of her porcelain skin directed my attention toward her neck. "My world does not revolve around you."

"I never said it did," I murmured. Knocking myself from a trance, I raised my eyes toward hers again. "Tell me your message while I walk upstairs to meet with Sabrina. I am late enough as it is."

"So I've noticed." The curl of her lips produced a wicked, sensual grin. Rose continued holding onto my shoulder as she looped around me to the stairs. I shivered as her fingers slid across my back. "Actually, my message is from Sabrina. She wanted me to tell you she had other things to attend to and will call upon you tomorrow evening."

"Ah, what a pity." The scent of Rose's perfume wafted toward me, her footsteps moving in tandem with mine as we began ascending the stairs. My baser nature took hold as I glanced at Rose and saw the plunging neckline of her dress, beholding the delicious sight of her cleavage and instigating a war within. I had been avoiding any carnal entanglements, lest they have something to run back and report to Sabrina. My internal strife, though, had also prevented me from taking advantage of the women I fed from as anything but my next meal. Something deep inside wanted to rip Rose's dress from her body.

I swallowed hard and found myself unable to fathom why I could not trust

Rose. Not with the truth, no, but she never gave me any hint she knew what a seer was, let alone cared about anything other than what passed down her throat and slid between her legs. '*Just this once,*' I conceded. "Well, all alone for the remainder of the evening," I said. "Whatever shall I do with myself?"

Rose's grin turned all the more sly. "My other pursuits are all occupied for the night. Besides..." We reached the top of the stairs. As she leaned close, I shut my eyes and felt her cool breath hit my neck while she whispered. "I want to hear about yours. They're always so much more exciting."

My eyes slowly opened, my head turning to regard her while my fangs ran down. Rose flashed her pointed teeth at me and within moments we found ourselves in my room, hastily divesting one another of our clothing. I lost myself in fanged kisses and needy actions after throwing her onto my bed. She might have taken more blood than our typical exchanges and might have been more wild than I recalled her ever being, but the moment I relaxed against the mattress, sated and spent, the siren call of sleep took me under. I had no energy left with which to question anything further that evening.

This must have been why I did not feel her deft fingers unclasp the necklace and did not detect her slipping from the sheets. I could be called the biggest fool in the universe for falling for her tricks, but at the time, I sensed none of the trickery which should have been screaming at me with overt obviousness. A strange premonition haunted me in my dreams, though, of the cold grip of dark magic dragging me into the depths.

The fact remained, my talisman was gone. Another vixen laid in wait to stake the final purchase on my soul.

Chapter Eighteen

"Do you know what drew me to you when we met, Flynn? You had the most radiant blue eyes and I knew there had to be something more than just a contemplative, young mortal behind them."

Her voice coaxed me from the chaotic embrace of unsettled dreams. My lids lifted without any thought and settled on the figure facing away from me, but seated on my bed. I regarded the long, flowing red hair and drew in a quick, sharp breath before I could stop myself. The action caused Sabrina to turn, her gaze settling on mine and the smile on her face broadening the moment our eyes met.

She reached for me tenderly, and I did not move when her fingers stroked the side of my face, but I had to suppress a shiver. Her actions were gentle enough to almost be soothing, despite being unsettling, until her nails settled against my skin and raked downward in a more tantalizing manner. I gasped despite myself, tempted to get lost in the erotic pain until a disquieting certainty rushed into the forefront of my mind.

Sabrina was working her wiles on me and I was falling for it.

Sitting abruptly, I fumbled for the pendant around my neck and panicked when I failed to locate anything but skin. Sabrina watched me pat the sheets around me and laughed in a fit of schadenfreude. As her other hand lifted, I beheld, to my horror, the gold chain dangling from her fingers. "Are you missing something, dear Flynn?" she asked. "My seer vampire, who couldn't even discern the thoughts of a wolf in sheep's clothing."

"Fuck," I muttered, feeling as though I should hear my heart pounding in my ears. Sabrina unclasped the necklace and raised it to her neck, fastening it into place before slowly, deliberately crawling toward me on all fours. Her palm settled on my leg, running up it over the thin layer of sheets separating skin from skin. I watched its northward path, fixated on her hand as it crept toward my crotch.

Sabrina leaned forward. Her lips touched my ear and her voice formed a sultry whisper. "I'll have you know, I find this absolutely delicious." I tensed when her hand caressed my already-hardening length. She chuckled. "To think you've possessed the gift and kept it from me. That you've played such a good boy and done my bidding while pretending everything was as it should be. Tell me, Flynn... How long would you have kept it up? Until the mortal's enchantment had you plunge a blade in my chest?"

She touched my chin and arched back my neck. Powerless to fight against her, I bared fangs in an expression of both defiance and arousal. My ambivalence clouded my judgment. The warring impulses shooting through me nearly left me shaking and once again, I felt ready to rend into two people. I indulged in a deep breath and shut my eyes. "Sabrina, your ways are wicked and your heart is black," I said in a half-dazed manner. "You would use me for your gain and the suffering would be great."

"That is the point, my dear Flynn." She kissed my throat and a shiver ran up my spine. "I spoke to you about the need to lay down the past and become a vampire when you became my assassin. You had Anthony find that adulterous bitch's trinket and have worn it around your neck ever since. Does Peter dull your senses so much you've forgotten the way you were injured by that woman; that contemptible mortal who could not even satisfy your desire to remain mortal in the first place? And yet, you would trust her magic?"

"Manipulation..." I trailed off as I felt her fangs rake against my skin. The next words came with difficulty. "I was... made to be this by you for your own profit. You sought to make a puppet out of a seer."

"I helped you find your potential in the form of something permanent. I freed you from the wretched stench of decay."

"I wanted nothing of your gift."

"Oh, you screamed for it." Her fangs raked harder. The scent of blood wafted to my nostrils an instant before I felt her tongue slide across the wounds she inflicted, provoking me to moan. "You *begged* me for it. You wanted death to embrace you in its dark arms and wanted to scoff at the mortals beneath you. I saw your powers and the possibility. I knew this day would come and you have killed like a master. Your blade strikes terror already. Now, your eyes will cause your foes to kneel down and worship you."

My resolve began to crumble while I silently cursed myself for falling for Rose's deception. I opened my eyes, only to have them roll back when she bit into my neck. '*Damn, sweet Rose.*' I might have been guarded against Sabrina, but I was not against the blonde-haired vampiress and had willingly tumbled into her trap. Sensing the evil surrounding me forced me to acknowledge that part of me loved it. Half of me wanted to bathe in it and drink of it – to embody evil, yes to personify it. In my heart of hearts, though, I knew the taste in my mouth was bitter.

I slid my hand to the side, beginning a slow trek toward one of my pillows.

Sabrina lifted her fangs from my neck, licking the wound closed. "Come now, Flynn," she said, whispering in my ear again. Her hand stroked up and down my length. "Don't fight this any longer. Do what comes natural. I will give you all you desire, you know this is true."

"I desire peace," I said, trying as steadfastly as possible to ignore the way her fingers wrapped around my cock through the barrier of sheets. My hand disappeared beneath the pillow, finding the knife I kept concealed there. "I desire to hunt in peace and as no man's instrument of wrath, be they human or immortal."

"And who could promise you such a thing?" She nibbled at my ear lobe. "Speak to me, dark killer. Tell me who our enemies are so that we might crush them."

Drawing in a deep breath, I moved so quickly, Sabrina had no time to react. I produced the knife and flicked off its sheath, pressing the blade against her neck. She froze in place and I growled, drawing blood as I pushed the sharp edge deeper into her skin. "You shall never have the chance to meet these enemies, Sabrina. I shall be the last one your eyes ever meet."

Her eyes shot to intersect mine. I felt her grip on me relax and nearly sighed with relief. "Your enemies seek to destroy you," I continued. "They petitioned my blade, but I refused until now. Hear me, woman, though, I shall not be made into a slave. Not by anyone."

"You fool yourself if you think you can have it any other way." Sabrina swallowed hard, but remained still. "You know it now, where these gifts come from, and I suspect you also know what they were to be used for in your mortal life."

"The mortals shall not have me either."

"They would accept your neutrality as readily as I would. There isn't any gray area in this, Flynn; there is only black and white. Either you are a god amongst vampires or the angel of wrath against them, but you are not afforded the ability to watch this war from the sidelines. The Fates wouldn't have it and the sorceress I told you to dispose of would hound you for the rest of her natural days."

"You lie."

"I hardly lie, Flynn. It is their way. Once the witch dies, another will follow and another and yet, your sword would be used for violence. And your conscience would rob you of the pleasure you derive from killing the mortals. Fighting against your nature – your strong, vampire instincts – for living as half a human; this is your only alternative."

"It is not." I scowled angrily at her. "I shall be Robin's guard when you are dust, Sabrina."

"Robin?"

"That is correct. Robin. You have sought your enemies amongst the other covens and yet house a conspirator under your own roof, sired by your own blood. My brother has promised me this neutrality I desire and there is not a damn thing anyone will do to interfere with it, do you hear me? I would sooner do that which I promised myself I would not do and be the one to murder you at last."

At first, Sabrina remained quiet. She smiled within a few moments, though, and once more, I felt her influence crawl into my brain. "You see there, Flynn. Did you hear what you said? '*That which I promised myself I would not do.*'" Reaching up, she took hold of my hand and pushed the knife away. I felt powerless to resist. She stole my weapon and commanded my attention with her eyes. "You still desire me, even after the witchcraft wrought against you. Where you could have already scattered my dust into the wind, you stepped aside and allowed your traitorous brother to find himself a killer. This is because Flynn knows where his loyalties lie. He knows his mistress's call and listens to it. And he will surrender this pretense of peace right here and now, won't he?"

She touched my neck, holding my head steady as she resumed her ministrations. This time, I felt the knife blade press against my chest and drag downward to start rivulets of blood running down my skin. I winced at the sensation, but my eyes closed and my fangs slid down again. Sabrina laughed. "Tell me, Flynn," she said as she gently pushed me back against the bed and straddled me. "Who else could make you feel this way? Could the wench you wanted to marry do these things to you?"

I groaned when her tongue slid across the cut she had inflicted. Her fangs scratched against my skin and my hands found the bed sheets, bunching them in my fists. Sabrina continued. "Would she send you to pillars of pleasure you could only fathom in your deepest, darkest dreams? Would she make you into something beyond immortal; beyond a man into something far more than a killer? Would she promise you power beyond your wildest dreams? Answer me that, Flynn."

"No," I said, my voice a husky murmur. "No, she would not."

"Why is this?"

"Because she was mortal." I arched my back, a loud, drawn-out moan escaping my lips when the knife blade slid across the side of my neck. Sabrina's tongue dragged across this wound as well. "An adulterous mortal."

"And what are mortals?"

"They are weak and finite." I felt the darkness encroaching and not only could not stop it, I wished more of it. The tips of my fingers started to slip from the ledge, with a chasm of wickedness waiting to swallow me whole. "We are the higher beings."

"That's right, Flynn." Sabrina lifted her head. I felt her lips brush against mine. "Come and say it, dark son. Say it and my body will be yours."

"Ask and I shall do it, mistress."

"I want you to conquer our enemies. I want you to assassinate Robin."

"It shall be done as you say."

"I want for Peter to die once and for all so that Flynn can come forth and reign in terror with me. I want the blood of the seven covens to fill the streets. I want power. I want you."

My lids lifted and a slow, sinister grin crept across my face. My eyes danced with madness and a wild impulse shot poison into my veins as I regarded my venomous mistress. I nodded, the glint in my gaze bearing a form of wickedness even I had never experienced before. "It shall be done as you say, Sabrina."

Sabrina laughed and kissed me in a passionate manner. I flipped her onto her back and ripped her shirt open, starting what would be a torrid and fevered coupling between us. With each stitch of clothing rent and each moan rising toward the ceiling, I felt my humanity ebb away. I had come so close to grasping the mortal buried deep within and yet, in that moment, I hungered to be everything Sabrina desired. A cold-blooded killer. A vampire without a conscience. A demon personified. The Devil himself.

My green eyes blazed as the monster took over, shoving Peter into a cell and binding him with chains. I fell away from the ledge and the chasm loomed deep as I became a terror beyond a mere assassin.

I became evil incarnate.

Chapter Nineteen

That night, I sought to the streets and slaughtered like a newborn vampire. The selection of my victims was far more varied than murderers, rapists, or other degenerates. Rather, I killed out of sport. Their corpses dropped to the ground and I laughed over them before making my way to the next conquest. As much as I disliked them before, it had become a matter of weighing the whole race and finding them wanting. And I was bent on disposing of them one miserable soul at a time.

In the days which followed, Sabrina took me as her lover many times over. She gloried over the power I now possessed, desiring it in her presence as much as possible so she could bask in the afterglow. For as ambitious of a woman as she was before, her head now throbbed with megalomania. I found the behavior infectious to the point of emulating it.

I would ask her constantly when I could make good on assassinating Robin. Sabrina smiled as she ran her nails down my bare chest. "Flynn, I'm certain I could request his ashes right now and you would present them to me on a silver platter. Remember, though, all things are to happen at the right moment. Especially if we are to stake our claim over the other covens."

"You speak of the meeting, then?" I asked as I touched the pendant dangling from her neck. It no longer held any power over me. In fact, I found myself reveling in the irony of Sabrina wearing it. "Is this when we are to make our move?"

"There exists the soul of a conniver within you yet." She chuckled, drawing herself closer to me as we lay upon her bed. Her eyes met mine in a deliberate manner. "Yes, the meeting. I have a bloodbath in mind, my darling. Robin and I walking in, he seated beside me as if he still belonged there. I will allow them to conduct their business and listen to Robin rail against me as you said he will. Before they can carry out my sentence, though, you will come in and surprise them."

"And what shall you have me do then?"

Sabrina smiled. "I want you to kill them *all*, my assassin. We will collect their birthrights and rule the city."

I smirked deviously. Later, when I retired to my room, her words carried me off to sleep for the day.

The next evening, I rose and went about the normal tasks of grooming and dressing, strapping my katana to my side before threading my arms through my suit jacket and setting out for the halls of the coven house. Thirsty for more killing, my footsteps felt possessed, as though I walked amongst clouds of darkness raining down blood, the evening mine to drink. I approached the stairs, but stopped the moment another figure ceased her ascent right in front of me.

"Rose," I said, my eyes glinting devilishly behind my dark spectacles. The blonde-haired vampiress took a half-step backward and I stalked forward. Rose's eyes widened and her back hit the wall. Descending one stair in a menacing manner, I raised my arm and pressed the palm of my hand on the wall next to her head. "I have seen less and less of you these days. Have you ceased enjoying my company?"

She tilted her chin in defiance, though her eyes told another story. "I will not entertain the bed of a traitor."

I leaned closer to her. "Ah, but I have seen the light. In fact, I own the light and keep it in my pocket with all the other trinkets I possess." My other hand lifted and I delighted in her reaction as I slid my fingertips across her cheek. "Perhaps I will possess you as well, Rose. Would you like to be one of my trinkets?"

Before she had the chance to issue a response, the hand on her cheek took hold of the base of her throat, pinning her in place. My fangs slid down and nails dug into her skin while Rose gasped. Her hands shot to my arm and began attempting to push me back. "Sabrina has called us upstairs, Flynn," she said. "Let me go or else she will begin to worry."

"Who is 'us'?"

"Timothy, you, and me. Timothy was supposed to find you."

"Well, he obviously has not, otherwise I would have known what the fuck you were talking about." Grinning broadly, I tightened my grip. "He fears me. I can smell it every time I pass. Do you fear me yet, Rose? Do you quake when you think of the secrets I can make myself privy to within your mind? The control I have over you now that I can lay your innermost desires out like an open book?"

Rose clenched her eyes shut. "I fear the monster you've become."

Her confession provoked me to laugh. I leaned all the closer, finding her ear and whispering, "Thank you for helping to free the demon, sister. Your service shall be repaid tenfold."

She attempted to speak, but I pulled away before she could, relinquishing my grip and allowing her to crumple as her knees gave out on her. Her hands found her neck and rubbed it while I slipped a hand into my suit jacket, producing my black, leather gloves. "Get up and compose yourself, woman," I said as I threaded my fingers into one. "If Sabrina has murder on her mind, we should not keep her waiting."

Rose slowly came to a stand, her eyes shooting hate at me. I growled sharply and the action was enough to light a fire beneath her feet. She scurried up the next flight of stairs while I brought up the rear, smoothing the last glove over my hand before resting it on the banister. Rose neither glanced over her shoulder, nor slowed her pace, but her posture remained rigid and tense. I grinned. '*Only the beginning, Rose*,' I thought at her. '*If payback is a bitch, then revenge is a vampire named Flynn.*'

She shuddered in response. I hummed in a satisfied manner. Together, we reached the top of the stairs and strolled toward Sabrina's penthouse.

Paul opened the door for us, his eyes lingering on me. I paid him no mind and walked ahead of Rose, into the vestibule and toward the sitting area without any pause. Sabrina appeared in view, sitting on her couch alongside Timothy and holding a glass of red wine in her hand. She smiled when she caught sight of me. "My darling Flynn," she said. "I see Rose was able to find you. I was just about to send Timothy to locate you."

Timothy glanced upward at the mention of his name. His eyes met mine and I saw the same anxiety latent in his gaze which had been in Rose's. Had I been able to feed from fear itself, I could have become drunk merely from the way my two older siblings regarded me. I smiled in response, an expression which, judging by his reaction, chilled him to the bone. "Well, a serendipitous thing Rose found me, then," I said, glancing at Rose. "Is it not, dear sister?"

Rose ignored me, but finally walked to the opposite side of the room and sat in an empty chair. Sabrina watched her as if noticing the same thing I did. Her eyes read of supremacy and delight when she turned her head back to me. "Sit with us, please," she said, pointing to the couch in front of her. "We have plans to make."

I nodded, strolling to the unoccupied piece of furniture and sliding back into it. One leg lifted and settled on my knee while I leaned my elbow on the arm of the couch, a casual enough pose despite my inner demon's eagerness to find some manor of corruption to entertain. "What plans are these, darling mistress?"

"I've received word from the council." Sabrina lifted her chin, turning her head to glance at us all. "They will convene this week. Robin himself delivered the message no more than an hour ago."

Unable to control the impulse, I snickered. "Bloody fool."

Sabrina's eyes met mine again. "Oh, quite a fool, but not oblivious." She raised an eyebrow, her grin fading. "He has noticed your absence and asked if I was keeping you busy. I told him I had several tasks for you."

I nodded. "What might I do to assuage Master Robin's curiosity?"

"Do nothing. Don't allow Robin to see you until the meeting and avoid me altogether, lest he become suspicious. We need him to think we are all ignorant of his plans."

"Will that be enough?"

"Oh, I genuinely have a couple of tasks for you." The grin returned to Sabrina's face in wicked splendor. "This will at least lend some truth toward you being busy, my assassin. Your black roses and the uproar from the covens will prove it." She paused. "I assume ending a few troublemakers won't cause you too much burden, will it?"

I grinned. "It shall be done as you say."

"Excellent." Sabrina winked at me, but then directed her attention to all three of us when she spoke once more. "My enemies want me dead. Timothy and Rose, you have heard whispers of a conspiracy and Flynn unveiled the treason of the bastard I have called a son. I thought my children trustworthy, but I know better now and look to you three as the only ones I can depend upon. There are those who would, no doubt, embrace the reign of Robin over my house. Charles and Louis converse with him often enough for me to believe Robin has them in mind for leadership, and the rest are just lazy, stupid sheep who follow the direction of the wind." She nodded her head toward us. "You three are loyal. You have demonstrated your loyalty in being a part of this. I won't forget it any time soon."

Sabrina stood. She began to pace with a lithe and contemplative gait. "In four days, the masters and seconds of every major coven in this area are set to meet at Matthew's coven in Society Hill. Undoubtedly, the stodgy bastard is still upset at me for having one of his elders disposed of, so I'm certain he finds a delicious irony in hosting my undoing."

"A shame he has not liked the roses I left him," I said.

Sabrina chuckled. "You taunt him with your roses, Flynn. I'm sure the only reason why he doesn't want you dead as well has to do with your brother." Her gaze met mine in a deliberate manner. "I want Matthew to be the first to die."

"As you wish, mistress."

"Very good." Her attention shifted back to us all. "Their actions against me are intended to make a point. Anyone who vies for power will be exterminated by the collective will of the covens. I intend to make a counterpoint. That to transgress me will mean the lives of whoever tries to stop me. As the council convenes, I want you all to be waiting in the wings, away from the watchful eye of Matthew's security. Timothy will help me escape and Rose..." Her eyes shifted to the vampiress. "You are to help slip Flynn past the guards in the front."

Sabrina placed her hands on the back of the couch where Timothy sat. This time, I found myself the object of her focus. "My dear Flynn," she said, "After they begin their charges against me, you will infiltrate the meeting room and start the bloodbath. I want every single elder and master disposed of, trapped like rats and ended like the vermin they are. Arm yourself as heavily as you must. Show no mercy to any, including Robin. He signed his death warrant when he turned his back on me. I want him to join his co-conspirators as nothing more than ash."

A slow, sinister grin spread across my face. "Not only shall it be easy, it shall be very satisfying."

"For both of us, dark killer."

"Indeed." I paused, perking an eyebrow. "When shall I be needed and what duties do you have for me in the interim?"

"I will have Rose fetch you when the time is right. Remain close to your room that evening. In the meantime, dispose of Vincent of William's house for me. First, do away with his human slaves over the course of the next two evenings, then kill him the night before the meeting. The pretentious twit is expendable and should make for an easy kill. Remember, we are offering a distraction. Keep your wits sharp."

"I always do." Standing, I walked toward Sabrina and stopped just shy of her. "I shall take my leave, then, and see to your orders."

Her eyes rose to meet mine, her body drifting close. Her hand slid against the front of my shirt while I felt her wickedness caress my psyche. "Say it to me, my seer." Sabrina's voice lowered to a whisper. "I enjoy hearing those words drift past your lips."

I bent enough for our mouths to hover close. "It shall be done as you say, my mistress."

Sabrina shut her eyes as I shut mine. A deep, lingering kiss commenced between us, fueled with energy so palpable, I struggled with the impulse to throw her on the couch and fuck her right in front of Rose and Timothy. I heard whispers of their thoughts, which provoked me to grin like a devil as Sabrina pulled away.

Her fingers toyed at the buttons of my shirt. "When we meet next, on the other side of this debacle, we will have our enemies cowering at our feet."

"Yes, we shall." Offering Rose and Timothy a parting glance, I turned and made my way out of Sabrina's penthouse, passing Paul once again and feeling the weight of his gaze settle on my back. Power pulsed through me, rousing an infectious temptation to stroll past every member of the coven and lord over them. I suppressed it and descended the stairs, headed for my room.

Along the way, however, I paused by the door of the one person yet to fear me as pointedly as he should. Chancing an encounter with my older brother to eavesdrop on him, I placed a hand on his door and felt first for his thoughts. When I found no sign of any suspicions he might have harbored as far as I was concerned, I allowed the words he spoke in hushed tones to drift toward my ears.

"Yes, I pledge my life to you that Flynn will not interfere," he said. "My brother has committed himself to our cause, just not as a participant."

"Then how do we know he won't honor some pledge to Sabrina at the last moment, Michael?" I recognized the voice, even through the minor distortion of the phone held to Robin's ear, as belonging to Matthew.

"He's been made aware of how grossly Sabrina has manipulated him. As I told you before, he still plays the ruse of an assassin so Sabrina doesn't become suspicious. It will all end once we execute her. He has given me his word."

There was a pause on the other line, followed by a sigh. "We are investing a lot in your word because you are an elder, and a trusted one, at that. Please realize, though... If you are wrong, I fear it will mean all our deaths that evening. You included."

"We won't die. I promise you. I know my brother well and know what thoughts trouble him. By next week, there will be order amongst the covens again. You'll see it with your own eyes."

A slow, wicked grin curled the corners of my mouth. Turning away from the door, I strolled for my room with an unaffected air. My brother was ignorant of walking into his own grave and while his co-conspirators remained skeptical, they were mice following the Pied Piper's tune. I settled in to rest that morning, allowing a lingering thought sing me to sleep like a macabre lullaby.

No, Robin did not know he was to fear me yet, but he would the moment his house of cards came tumbling down around him.

Chapter Twenty

It was as I returned from killing Vincent that she confronted me again.

"The vampire Flynn," she said, announcing herself with a mocking tone. I halted what had been a casual stroll, my eyes tracing across the back alley I had been taking for a shortcut, looking for her position. Seeing nothing, I furrowed my brow and spun around to peer behind me.

"This is how it is, Flynn. Sight, but no vision. A gift wasted by the selfish desires of an immortal who should be a guardian of people. A guardian of his brother." The voice paused. It shifted location. I turned to follow it, but did not yet see its owner. "You think it's about power, and I'm sure Sabrina fed you that line of bull, but it's about purpose. Be careful you don't learn that lesson the hard way."

"Come out!" I said, baring fangs. "Stop playing games and face me."

"Not yet. Consider this warning the last one you'll receive." Her presence drifted away just as quickly as it had surfaced, leaving the quiet to surround me in an eerie manner with her words yet resonating in the stillness of the night. I frowned.

The encounter bore the earmarks of a sorceress and as I only had one alive in my life at the moment, I sneered while looking toward the last place she had been speaking. "Come now, witch. Teach me my lesson. I wish to toy with your body and slit your throat." My hand rested on the hilt of my sword, but it became apparent before long that Monica had delivered her message and departed.

"Coward," I muttered, and resumed my walk back to the coven.

Little did I know that Monica remained hidden on a roof, sitting on the hard concrete while holding her breath. She exhaled slowly, peering over the side of the ledge that had shielded her from view. "Everything is the hard way with you," she said, watching me leave. "It's time for you to get a heavy dose of the truth."

Monica brought herself to her feet, her eyes taking on a solemn look. "Don't worry, Peter. This isn't over yet. One way or another, we're going to get you back to where you belong."

⋅ೋ෴ೋ⋅

The next evening arrived much the same as every other setting of the sun, only this time I opened my eyes knowing the single most daunting assassination I had ever orchestrated laid before me. Rising, I stretched and surveyed my room, realizing I would need to be heavily armed. Walls and shelves arrayed with weapons ensured this would not be a problem. As such, I began my ritual.

I showered and plucked a fresh suit from the closet. The act of dressing took on methodical undertones; I meditated on each button and studied every article of clothing with calm focus before moving on to the next. The shirt, pants, and shoes were the simplest elements to assemble. The equipment which followed became the meticulous part.

Fetching my shoulder holster, I threaded my arms into their respective holes and secured it into place. Three knives found their way into three different slots, each positioned with the utmost care after being cradled for a moment in my palm. I slipped a sheathed knife into the waistband of my pants and strapped my katana to my side. A shorter sword found itself fastened to my back. I procured a trench coat to cover my collection of weapons after settling everything into place, and nodded with approval.

My fingers caressed the hilt of my katana before I wrapped them around the red and black braiding. I drew it seamlessly and swung it around once before snapping it back into its sheath. A cold, sinister grin crept across my face. Armed to the teeth, the assassin was ready for battle.

A knock ripped me from my thoughts.

I turned and strode for the entryway. Twisting the knob, I opened the door and perked an eyebrow once I spied Rose standing on the other side. Her eyes ran over me, fear distilled in her gaze. "The council is about to convene," she said. "Sabrina and Robin have departed and Timothy left just behind them."

"Very well." I stepped out of my room and secured the door closed. Gesturing a command that she should proceed first, we began to stroll down the corridor. I reached into my coat pocket for my black, leather gloves and slid them over my fingers in the same methodical manner as I had my other accouterments. "Have any concerns or changes cropped up?"

"All is as planned." Walking ahead of me, Rose's posture stiffened as she summoned some form of backbone to continue the conversation with less fear in her voice. "We will wait until the meeting convenes before dealing with Matthew's guards. Sabrina asks that you kill them quickly before we sneak into the meeting room."

I scoffed as we started down the stairs. "This is not my first kill."

"You seem to have problems keeping your focus. Especially when strange sorceresses come calling."

Her comment provoked a sneer. "Keep careful watch over your words, Rose. When I am your master, I might collect tenfold for your disrespect."

She motioned to speak again, but quickly shut her mouth. Rethinking her response, however, opened her mind to me without any effort on my part. I read the curses issued in thought as though they had been painted on the walls. She could be a fiery vixen when she wished to be and her temper was evident in every ill word she conjured. We reached the bottom of the stairs in silence, but she stopped and turned to face me. I held an even gaze. "Walk ahead of me," I said. "Unless you are waiting for some fanfare to precede you."

"I do not trust your eyes on me from behind." Rose pointed toward the main entrance. "You first, please."

I laughed. "That would hardly be wise, Pet. To see me coming ahead of you would arouse suspicion."

"Until we arrive, then."

In a flash of anger, I took her by the chin and shoved her body against mine. "Rose, do I need to be crass and insulting in order to make a point with you? After tonight, looking at me means gazing upon Sabrina's right hand. More than a mere assassin, I shall be the lord of this manner and the second most powerful vampire to grace your presence. Now..." I leaned closer, my face hovering centimeters from hers. "If I were you, I would learn more about respect. Or else, I shall chain you in shackles for the rest of your days with only the blood of rats to sustain you. And my new ritual, before I retire every morning, shall be to beat you and fuck you until you forget there ever was a being named Rose inside the shell of your body." My eyes conveyed the seriousness of my threat, and she quaked against me. I smirked. "Are we crystal clear or must I offer you a demonstration?"

Rose's expression regained a modicum of defiance. "Sabrina wouldn't let you. I mean too much to her."

"Sweet Rose, have you not figured out by now you are just as expendable as every other immortal in this coven?" I grinned in a sinister manner. "Remember, I own your thoughts now, woman. The moment you think anything ill toward either me, or Sabrina, I can have you eliminated."

Rose pushed herself away and I laughed as she stormed ahead of me. "Good girl." The guards at the entryway held the doors open for us to pass as we made our way out to the streets.

The excursion to Matthew's coven took a matter of minutes. I spent the time focusing on my litany of weapons, assessing each one's functionality and versatility. Soon my training would be put to the test as never before and I relished such a challenge. Rather than dampening my confidence, knowing success hinged entirely on my precision and capability fueled my arrogance.

Once we arrived, though, an ill wind blew past, causing the hair on the back of my neck to stand aloft. I ignored it as much as possible while we approached the exterior gate. Rose slowed her pace and asked, "Now, how do we go about this?"

I stole a moment to glance around the empty, landscaped yard, listening for any sign of movement. "The guards must be protecting the meeting room," I said, speaking in a hushed tone.

Rose nodded and together we walked further up the walkway to Matthew's coven house. The disquieting sensation that had greeted me became more pronounced, but I pushed it aside again in favor of further assessing our surroundings. The entire path was lined by dimly-lit sconces interspersed between trimmed hedges, and opened up to a columned entryway. I crouched upon reaching the bend in the path that would put us in full view of the front door. That is when I heard them.

Cautiously peering around small amount of cover afforded by the shrubs, I spied two male vampires standing watch outside a set of sturdy wooden doors. Both stared forward, neither catching sight of me before I ducked back behind the bush.

My eyes shifted to Rose and a chilling, sinister grin surfaced on my face. '*Sweet Rose*,' I thought at her, not wanting to risk any volume of speech, '*I believe I have found meaning to your useless existence.*'

She swallowed hard, her eyes widening with fear.

With that, the first phase of my mission commenced.

I recognized the guards as being James and Martin, two of Matthew's immortal children, and savored their reaction when the peace was shattered by the sight of a blonde-haired vampiress running toward them. Rose cried blood tears, clutching herself as though she had been violated and acting every bit the part of a damsel in distress. I slipped into the shadow afforded by one of the columns while they directed their attention to her.

"Please help me!" she said, her voice shaky as she threw herself at them. James clutched onto her and she, in turn, grabbed fistfuls of his shirt. "He's gone insane! He'll kill me alongside of you if you don't stop him."

James blinked at Rose as I slithered behind his partner, baring fangs in anticipation. She tilted her head so her eyes met his and James spoke just as I ran Martin through with my sword. "What is it, Miss? Who did this to you?" he asked as, unbeknownst to him, ash flaked to the ground. I stalked forward, just out of his periphery, and readied my weapon.

Rose motioned to answer, but I interrupted by thrusting my sword through James's back, far enough for the tip to protrude from his stomach. Rose yelped and jumped backward; the sharp steel stuck out far enough that it nearly cut across her abdomen, impaling her as well. Smiling, I snaked an arm around James's neck while holding the sword steady with my other hand. "I believe that would be me," I said pressing my face against his head while speaking harshly into his ear. "You know who this is, right, James?"

"Flynn," James managed, grunting through the pain.

"Very good. And that is Rose. She is a good actress, is she not?"

Rose eyed me in an apprehensive manner. I flashed fangs at her and winked before turning my attention back to James. "She is a skittish thing, I must say. Very easily frightened. I believe I shall have to educate her on how to properly conduct herself in my presence, what do you think?"

James grunted. "What the fuck do you want, Flynn? If you've come to kill me, do it and get it over with."

"Now, let us not be too hasty, James. You are going to tell me a little story and if I am amused enough, I might allow you to crawl away on your hands and knees." My hand slid around to his neck, fingers pressing hard into his throat. He winced again, trembling with pain. "Now, there is a meeting of importance convening inside this house and I intend to crash it. The last thing I wish is to waltz into the soirée blind, though. As such, you are going to tell me how many people are inside."

"I don't know the full number."

Twisting the blade inside James, I provoked a moan of agony from him. "Do not toy with me. I want a number," I said through gritted teeth.

"About twenty," he managed, nearly choking on the words. "The master of each coven, with their second-in-commands. A handful of bodyguards, too."

"Are there any stationed between the front door and meeting room?"

"Two pages. Another guard stationed in front of the meeting room doors."

"And the meeting room itself?"

James paused. "What about it?"

Slowly, I pushed the blade further into James, relishing the wails of misery he produced until the sword's hilt touched the back of his shirt. James trembled, glancing down at the blood-stained metal protruding from his body before clenching his eyes shut. "Closer…" He paused, inhaling sharply. "Closer to the back of the house. Past the stairs and down the corridor. I swear."

"Very good." A cold grin spread across my lips. "Two final questions. Is there only one set of doors leading into the meeting room or are there other methods of escape? And where are the others in your coven? The house seems quite barren and I dislike surprises."

James indulged in a steadying breath. "Why the fuck should I tell you?"

I scowled. "Because I have a sword in your stomach which says you should. And can have a knife at your throat helping you to bleed out before I end your miserable life. Is this enough incentive for you?"

"Yes." James swallowed hard, seemingly forcing the words out. "There is one other method of escape. A side entrance which leads to the back exit. The others are away so they wouldn't eavesdrop on the meeting. Matthew wanted absolute secrecy."

"Thank you, James." Raising my foot, I pushed him from the blade and sent him tumbling face-first onto the ground. "I hope you shall understand when I say, appreciative as I am, you still must die."

James moaned, rolling onto his back. "Robin believed in you." He clutched at his stomach, his gaze meeting mine. "He told us you would be his brother and stand by him."

"Which makes him a fool, does it not?" I raised my katana, both hands wrapped around the hilt. A sinister grin crept across my face. With one, quick swipe of my sword, I rid James of his head and after flicking the blade to the side, I snapped it back into its sheath. "Death has come to this house tonight and he has come to collect."

Lifting my eyes to meet Rose's, I saw them flash with fear before she composed herself again. Her gaze shot to the door, both needing something else to focus on and moving to the next logical step in our journey. "Well, you managed your *information*, Flynn. So help me if you ever…"

"Shut up, Rose." I straightened my coat, allowing the folds to conceal the hilt of my sword again. Turning for the door, I crouched low before twisting the knob and pushing it inward. A dark foyer greeted me, with nobody in my immediate line of vision when I peeked inside. "Follow me and be quiet about it," I said to Rose as I crept into the house. Once she entered, I shut the door behind us, listening for the soft click of the lock engaging while pivoting to face the estate's interior.

The house appeared as barren as James had stated, with nary a soul anywhere in our vicinity. I moved further inward, avoiding the moonlit corners of the entryway and seeking the shadows away from the sparse amount of light provided by one lamp lit near the stairs. Plush carpet muffled the sound of my steps, yet I still moved cautiously, approaching a wall and pressing myself against it while slithering closer to an adjoining corridor. Voices filtered from the other end of the hallway, no doubt belonging to the two pages about whom I had been warned. I risked a quick glance around the corner and spotted them standing far too close to the intersecting path leading, I assumed, to the meeting room.

Ducking back, I frowned pensively and surveyed my surroundings. Dark wood accented lighter-colored walls where a host of framed portraits and landscapes hung. Other decorations were sparse, and scattered amongst a small collection of tables and chairs situated closer to the windows. My eyes found Rose again, who blinked at me and motioned to walk closer.

I held up a hand to stop her. *'Stay there,'* I said, speaking within the confines of our thoughts. *'You have one last task to complete before I send you on your way.'*

Rose opened her mouth, hesitated, and finally narrowed her eyes. *'How does this mental communication of yours work?'*

'Precisely like that, my dear sister.' A condescending smirk curled the corner of my mouth. *'You had a question?'*

'More like a directive.' Her hands settled on her hips. *'I agree to help under the condition you not scare me like that again.'*

'Which shows you how much you know about this sort of thing. And how attentive you truly were when I spoke of my assignments. Had you been more of a listener and less of an empty-headed whore, you would know the very wrong thing to do at this moment is cause a panic. Now, order me again, and I will slip and slaughter you with the two pages we are to murder.'

Rose tilted her chin in defiance, but wisely did not respond. I nodded, stealing a quick glance down the corridor again before peering back at Rose. *'You are to step outside again, then enter and shut the door more audibly. I wish you to call into the house to get their attention and ensure both pages make it into this room so I can dispose of them without arousing further suspicion.'*

'What should I tell them?'

'That you have a message you need to hand deliver. Tell them the front guards permitted you entrance.' If they did not fall for the ruse, I would have to move quickly, but the chance at secrecy was worth the risk.

'Very well.' She sighed and turned toward the entrance again, stepping forward and opening the door. When she peered back at me, I nodded, and moved closer to the stairs as quickly and soundlessly as possible. She shut the door more forcefully while I ascended the first few steps and crouched behind the banister. "Hello?" she said, calling toward the corridor, adding to the charade by craning her neck as if looking for someone.

Footsteps sounded down the hallway, although as they approached, I discovered she had managed to attract only one of the pages. A blond-haired man, he appeared confused when he caught sight of her. "Miss? Can I help you?"

She attempted an agreeable smile. I could have murdered her on principle alone when she glanced in my direction, but she recovered before the page noticed. "I have a message. It's rather urgent and needs to be hand delivered to my mistress."

He nodded, albeit in a skeptical manner. "Alright. Either give it to me or tell me what it is, and I'll make certain she is informed."

Her eyes flicked in my direction again. I stifled a groan. *'Start to motion for the hallway,*' I said, utilizing my telepathy once more. '*Let him stop you. Perhaps the other page might take notice and come.*' My hand settled on the hilt of one of my knives. I slid it from its sheath, preparing to toss it at the page and quickly intercept his compatriot should the need arise.

Rose focused on the page again and strolled closer to him. "No. I insist I be the one to deliver it."

"Who is your mistress?"

"Does it matter?" Rose lifted a hand, pointing in the direction of the meeting room. "I know she's in there. Let me pass; I won't be but a minute."

The page shifted, coming between Rose and the hallway. "I'm afraid that's out of the question. The meeting has already begun."

Rose raised an eyebrow at him and shoved forward. The page muscled against her, providing enough resistance to knock her back a step. "You are not allowed back there, and that's final. I'll summon the other page and have *him* deliver the message."

"Why not you?" Rose asked, rolling her eyes.

"Because now, I don't trust you won't try to slip past me." The blond-haired page glanced back down the hallway, lifting a hand to snap his fingers and then motioning for his compatriot to wander over. Whatever silent communication transpired between the two of them must have been enough. The other darker-haired page appeared out of the hallway, glancing between his friend and Rose with a quizzical expression on his face. "What is it?" he asked, his eyes settling on the other page.

"It's this woman," he began. I did not bother listening to the rest of what was spoken because I knew I had to move swiftly. I slipped from my hiding place and managed to attract Rose's attention just as I raised the blade I held between my thumb and forefinger. She stepped backward and tripped, landing on her backside with an audible thump and provoking the blond-haired page to swing around and look behind him. I released the knife the moment our eyes met and produced my sword before the blade had even plunged into his chest. He turned to ash, as did his friend when I decapitated him.

The remnant of both vampires fell on and around Rose. She squeaked with disgust and stood swiftly, brushing off her clothing as though the ash was corrosive. Opening her mouth to talk, she began to say, "I can't believe you did…" before I closed the distance between us and poised the tip of the blade at her throat. Rose immediately stopped when she felt the sharp edge cut into her skin.

"Speak again," I whispered harshly, "And I shall ensure it is a long time before you say anything else." My fangs slipped down once more, a menacing scowl enveloping my countenance. "Return to the coven. I have no use for you here any longer and do not wish to explain to Sabrina why I ran you through if you speak that loudly again."

My immortal sister swallowed hard, and then stepped backward. My eyes remained set on her in a deliberate manner, until she opened the door and shut it softly behind her. Alone in the foyer, I knew I was still on borrowed time to eliminate the next being on a rapidly-shortening list standing between me and my finest hour.

I collected the knife I had thrown and clutched it in my hand. Stepping confidently down the carpeted hall, I gripped the hilt tight and paused at the corner, knowing the guard to be there and listening carefully to how close he was. A few, tense moments later, my patience was rewarded by a faint shuffle as the man shifted his weight, placing him mere steps away. I moved with deft swiftness, first around the corner, then behind him after dodging the awkward grab he made at me, and ending with my arm wrapped around his torso, pressing his back against my chest. Before he could regroup, I slit his throat and watched him flounder for speech, grinning broadly when he failed to produce sound. '*It is called your vocal chords,*' I thought at him, caressing his neck with the bloodied dagger. '*And this is telepathy. Tell me all your secrets. I have a meeting to crash.*'

Had he the ability to create more than a gurgle and a squeak, he might have alerted the others to what was taking place. Instead, he wriggled against me while I held him firmly in place and entered his thoughts with little care as to how violently I did so. I saw Matthew at the end of the table, closest to the doors directly behind me, with Sabrina seated opposite from him. A host of other faces I did not recognize or had only seen in passing filled in the bulk of the other seats. Matthew's second, Eunice, was stationed beside him and Robin sat beside Sabrina as though he belonged there.

'*Excellent. That shall do.*' Pushing the guard away from me, I spun him around and thrust the dagger into his chest. He furrowed his brow at me before disintegrating into ash and crumpling onto the floor with the rest of his possessions. I slid the blade back into its sheath and strolled closer to a set of double doors separating me from the group of people I had seen in the guard's thoughts.

While the doors latched from the inside, their handles provided a wide birth and a quick glance around the immediate area inspired an immediate solution to my need. I grinned and walked toward an ornate floor lamp, proceeding to unplug it from the wall and remove the shade. The length of it slid nicely between the handles and secured the meeting room's main point of escape. I suppressed a chuckle while examining my handiwork. They would be trapped, with one exit remaining for Sabrina.

Indulging in a deep, steadying breath, I glanced toward the corridor again and nodded to myself. With that, I made my way to the back, my nerves steady and my conscience still as absent as it had been since losing Lydia's necklace. The preliminary tasks had been finished.

One more round remained before my mission would be complete.

Chapter Twenty-One

Lithe steps carried me to the side entrance, my hand poised atop the hilt of my katana as I prepared to slay another of Matthew's guards. As such, when I peered around the corner and caught sight of Timothy standing alone, it took me aback. I stepped more confidently toward him when he turned his head to regard me. "Did Matthew leave this entrance unsecured?" I whispered.

"One guard; I took care of him," he said. A snide grin surfaced on his face. "Did Flynn think he was the only one capable of killing vampires?"

"Not the only, merely the best."

"So you think." Timothy scoffed. "And what of the guards at the other door?"

Directing my attention to the barrier separating me from the events to come, I answered in a sharp hiss. "I am an assassin, Timothy. I know how to do my job, thank you very much." I paced closer and raised my hand to touch the wood. Inside, voices already spoke in raised tones, although I could tell the true festivities had yet to commence.

Timothy glanced around and furrowed his brow. "Where is Rose?"

"How the bloody hell should I know?" My eyes found his and a scowl formed. "Could you please be quiet and allow me to concentrate?"

Timothy nodded, saying nothing further. With that, I turned my focus back to the meeting room and closed my eyes, attempting to form a mental image of what was transpiring.

⚬૭ළ ૭ૡ⚬

Inside my mind's eye, I saw Sabrina settle back into her chair, her crimson lips spreading in a grin as she folded her hands on her lap. "Some concerns, dear Matthew?" she asked, a feigned hint of surprise latent in her voice. "By all means, please list these concerns for me."

"Sabrina, I know you are one of the oldest members of this council," said the stately-looking Matthew, with hair so dark, it could have transcended black. I recalled his pallor being a perpetual state of near white, as though he only fed when absolutely necessary and at no other time. I saw his brown eyes blazing intense at my maker while he spoke. "We are peers in age and as such, I will treat you as my equal and not insult your intelligence. Since forming your coven, you have been nothing but trouble, but in recent years you have utilized the services of an assassin." The room fell silent. Matthew's tone of voice became all the more vitriolic. "In this, you have crossed the line. Now, you must be dealt with for your insubordination."

"Insubordination?" Sabrina laughed. "I am nobody's subordinate."

"You are subordinate to the collective will of the seven covens, Sabrina, and to me as the recognized leader of this area. Before you arrived, we lived in peace and cooperated freely to maintain the interests of our kind."

"And done nothing to further these interests, I might add," she said sardonically.

"Damn it, even you know this is a delicate balance." Matthew sighed in an exasperated manner. "Vampire kind and human kind. They have their champions and yet, you would risk the Supernatural Order dismantling us all. For what? So you can prove to the rest of us how superior you are?" I heard him fall into his chair and listened to silence until he gathered himself and spoke again. "You jeopardize our very existence. For four years, we have told you to rein in your neophyte, and you answered by having him decimate our ranks."

Sabrina chuckled. "And this is where you are wrong, dear Matthew. Flynn has been my protector. Those he has killed have been your agents seeking to undermine me. You would have seen me dead before I even turned him. Should I take such a threat lying down?"

"You've had him kill without any provocation! Many times, out of sheer paranoia. If there are others who wished you ill, you should have summoned the council and presented your concerns to us."

"And how would you have handled it?" Sabrina paused. I imagined her glancing across the faces of each person gathered. "All of you have meant me ill. All of you! Anybody I would have presented to the council as a threat would have been slapped on the wrist. By now, I would have been ashes!"

"Because you are a threat to our safety and anonymity," said another elder, whose voice I recognized belonging to John-Mark. The second-in-command of a coven in Southern New Jersey, he would have been seated beside his maker, Emily, and resembled a mortal in his mid-forties. "Your complete lack of regard for common decency leads to blood baths. We are only trying to preserve our very existence, yet you accuse us of being spineless man-servants."

"I merely call it as I see it."

"You call nothing, Sabrina. That your coven was ever allowed in the council was a grave mistake."

"John-Mark, please. Let us hold our composure," Matthew said, interjecting. "We will handle this with the dignity of vampires and not lower ourselves to bickering and insults. Besides..." Matthew trailed off and a quick glimpse into his thoughts revealed where his gaze settled. My hand tightened around the hilt of my sword. Robin. "Her coven isn't a complete loss."

I heard a chair slide out and imagined Robin standing before the rest of the vampires gathered. "Gentlemen," he said, projecting his voice across the room. "I acknowledge and understand your concerns. As such, I wanted to formally separate myself from the rule and oversight of Sabrina. As an elder, I have that right, and as a distinguished vampire of this region, I refuse to condone the actions of my maker."

"Treasonous bastard," Sabrina spat. I felt the unbridled anger she had been holding back finally direct itself toward my older brother. "You would have seen my demise not soon after your awakening, you ingrate."

"I think we both know that isn't true." Robin paused. "I returned to your side when I didn't have to, why? Merely out of duty? No. You gave me immortality and I have been grateful for this even when you have been nothing but condescending toward me. I did not fight nearly hard enough when you sought to turn my brother, and while I have treasured his friendship, you and I both know The Fates are not done with you."

"What do you mean, The Fates aren't done with her?" Bruce, another coven master, called out from close to where Matthew sat.

"A very good question," I said, opening the door at last and making my entrance. A gust of air opened my coat enough to flash the hilt of my sword, with the other blade strapped to my back being more than enough of a warning I entered this discussion armed. I strolled toward the center of the room and stopped, turning to engage each set of eyes which fixed upon me. I grinned, and then looked toward the brown-haired vampire who spoke last. "Master Bruce, it is a pleasure to meet you." I bowed. "I am afraid my duties do not bring me close to your coven in Delaware. Otherwise, we might be better acquainted."

"Brother, what brings you here?" Robin asked, his voice subdued.

I turned to face him. "How could I stay away? After all, this all centers around me, does it not? The assassin. The neophyte Sabrina has failed to rein in." My eyes found Matthew in acknowledgment of his words. "The bloodthirsty murderer who threatens the safety of the seven covens. I felt I should be here to help our case, dear brother."

Matthew shifted in his seat. "Please explain."

"Gladly." I looked away, nodding at the group as a whole. Alarm resonated through each of their thoughts, which only made this all the more satisfying. It was all I could do not to laugh. "I, who was once Peter Dawes, was born for a task I had not yet realized upon becoming a vampire. In changing the course of my destiny, Sabrina fashioned an immortal seer. Not to protect the covens, though. To protect herself."

A collective gasp echoed throughout the room. I nodded. "Indeed, ladies and gentleman. I was never meant to be a vampire and yet, Sabrina knew. Before her fangs plunged into my neck, she realized the type of being I was to become and turned me to use my power as hers." I turned to face Matthew again, staring to pace toward him. "That is what this is about, after all. Power. Who holds the highest hand of cards and can use them to further their interests. What would ensure power more than having a seer trained to be an assassin?"

Matthew looked at Sabrina, raising an eyebrow. As he addressed her, I slipped around the table, headed in his direction again. "Is this true?"

Sabrina shrugged. "Isn't it time the mortals granted *us* a bit of favor?"

"Alas, I have been but a pawn in this play," I said, drawing the attention away from my mistress, "When I have simply wished to end the power struggle between the covens once and for all." As I stepped behind Matthew, my gaze met Robin's and my older brother regarded me with a hint of fear in his eyes. They widened when my hand closed around the hilt of my katana. "You see, I desire peace as well, Master Matthew. Only, I have other methods of ensuring it."

Robin extended his hand toward me, as though he possessed the ability to cease my actions. But before he could in even a single word, I slid my sword from its sheath and impaled Matthew through the chest, catching the elder vampire completely unaware. My fangs descended as Matthew turned to dust before the eyes of his compatriots, my gaze still fixed on my traitorous brother. "Peace shall come when I stand with Sabrina as the second most feared vampire in this city."

My actions sprung the others into a flurry of panic. Sabrina stood, unimpeded, as the back door flew open, and clutched Timothy's hand when he ran in to fetch her. Together, they flew from the room while the other elders belatedly came to their feet. Sliding my katana back into its sheath, I took hold of two knives just as two of my would-be victims raced for the only open exit. Each knife met their target, who became dust within moments.

The door slammed shut. The lock engaged with an audible finality, leaving me as trapped as the rest. I glanced to the side, reaching behind my back for the shorter sword secured there as a crowd of three bodyguards came at me while their masters attended to the doors. I impaled one, and then spun around to decapitate another. The third had produced his own sword, but lost it as I slashed through his arm before he could mount a proper defense. Kicking the blade up into my hand and ignoring the ashes dusting its hilt, I used both swords to slice off his head. My attention turned to the rest.

"Flynn! Don't do this!"

The voice calling through the haze of murder did nothing to deter me. I ignored Robin, grinning devilishly at the elders as they struggled to break through the doors after discovering both exits well secured. Spinning both swords in my hands, I sent the sharpened steal of one plunging into the first elder I encountered. I sliced through the neck of another with my shorter blade and kicked one backward who attempted a charge for me. A set of greedy fingers clawed for my borrowed sword and managed it from my hand as I assessed my attackers. I turned swiftly. My remaining sword slid through his chest and his ashes fell to the ground, along with the blade he had taken.

I had no time to fetch it before the trapped vampires descended upon me.

Abandoning their doomed attempt to leave, the vampire elders bared their fangs, an obvious mask for their fear and one which hardly intimidated me. Producing my final knife, I poised it in the palm of my hand as they formed a circle around me. My movements were fluid and unerring. I threw the dagger at the chest of a vampiress, simultaneously swinging my sword and claiming another head in the process. I pierced the heart of one and severed another's spinal column. Body after body fell to the ground as ash, until finally there was only one in my line of sight. I threw my short sword as he attempted to retreat and watched him disappear just as the rest had.

The hairs on the back of my neck stood aloft. Wrapping a hand around the hilt of my katana, I drew it and spun around just as I became aware of the threat from behind.

Metal impacted metal. Robin stood behind me, holding a bodyguard's discarded sword and presenting himself as my final opponent. I grinned. "Well, if this is not a familiar posture. A bit of nostalgia for the evening?" I asked amiably.

"How could you fall for her treachery, brother?" he asked, his sharp teeth fully exposed and his face contorted with rage, underscored by disappointment. Despite the obvious emotion saturating his expression, Robin held his sword steady and threw a trained blow at me. "I thought you were cured of her control."

Our swords impacted. "Well, you know what they say. In order to be cured, one must first see their condition as being a problem." Both blades crossed and pressed together as our bodies came in closer proximity. I stared Robin down. "And I rather like myself this way. You do not approve?"

Robin pushed me from him and swung his sword again. I crouched and raised my katana to block. "Damn you!" he shouted. "You don't understand, she is manipulating you. These are not your actions, they are hers. She has been controlling you far longer than you could dare realize."

"Did you just swear, dear brother?" I freed one hand to waggle a finger at him. "Language, Robin."

He gritted his teeth and thrust the sword for me. I turned out of the way at the last minute and laughed. "I think you underestimate me," I said, clutching my katana with both hands again. "I am more than capable of my own evil intentions."

Robin held his sword steady, but made no further motion with it. He frowned at me. "She made you what you are, Flynn." The expression in his eyes turned pained. "Stop this nonsense for a moment, and let me tell you more about your rebirth."

He began to speak, "I know why you killed your mortal lover..." but the words came too late. I was already in motion, thrusting my blade forward when he dropped his defenses. The oversight on his part left him unable to block me in time. Cold steel ran through his chest. A thousand thoughts assailed me, forming a picture which turned into a movie playing in my mind. An entire ocean of explanation impacted me – who I was, what I had been. With vivid color, a landscape opened up before my eyes.

I saw Lydia. I saw the night she was murdered.

And finally, I understood who it was that killed my beloved.

At once, my humanity rose up from some distant corner of my psyche, but did so just in time to stare into the eyes of the demon's final victim. My sword had impaled Robin through the heart; the deluge of truth had been his final lesson. With his last breath he said, "I loved you as a brother, Flynn."

Then he turned to dust. Robin was no more.

The room turned deathly quiet. Nothing but ash surrounded me as Peter glanced around the room for the first time, beholding the crypt he had fashioned. I clutched my sword, but my hands began to shake and once more, I recalled the feeling that had ushered me into immortality. Bare before the world, the foolish man who had slaughtered the last thing left which meant something to him in this world. The katana dropped to the ground, falling to my feet with a clank which echoed all about me. My knees became weak. My legs caved in and I crumpled to a kneeling position, bringing both hands to my head.

"What have I done?" I asked, as though the ash surrounding me could answer. "How could I have been so blinded for so long? How..." Blood tears formed in my eyes despite myself. "How could I have let this happen?"

I broke down into sobs, greeted only by the cold embrace of every atrocity I had committed. Finally, I understood what had been done inside me, after five years of failing to see it.

Yes, I was a vampire. This much was true and could not be denied. Peter Dawes, however, was no willful murderer, a fact which resonated as images from Robin began to play again.

PART FIVE

HUMANITY RESTORED

"A man cannot do good before he is made good."

Martin Luther

CHAPTER TWENTY-TWO

In my thoughts, I saw Robin, back when his name was still Michael and he knew no such being as Flynn. He stood before Sabrina, his brow furrowed. "What do you mean you spared the mortal?" he asked. "That seems out of character for you."

Sabrina's penthouse materialized around me, with my body situated in the center of the room as though I had been present for these events myself. I wore no sunglasses and possessed no fangs, once again the human to witness the path toward my demise, but only a specter. I frowned, watching Sabrina pace by me, completely unaware of the fact I even stood there.

She folded her arms behind her back, an air of amusement following her as she walked. "Oh, dear Michael," she said. "There is a method to my madness." Pausing by her liquor cabinet, she produced a glass and proceeded to fill it two-fingers full with brandy. Sabrina swirled around its contents once, and then sniffed it before allowing the amber-colored liquid to slide down her throat. Her eyes met Robin's again. "The boy is no mere boy. I looked into his eyes and knew what sort of creature I gazed upon, even without the emerald green irises."

Robin raised an eyebrow. "I don't understand."

Sabrina's grin widened. "The mortal is a seer. One who has not yet recognized his abilities."

My brother scoffed, slipping his hands into the pockets of his pants. "Sabrina, the Order themselves cannot pinpoint the seers before their time. How did you suddenly gain the ability to do so?"

"Oh, I know." She chuckled and polished off the rest of her drink. "If you saw him, you would know what I meant. His eyes are blue as the clearest ocean, the same shade as the green they become. The way he holds himself and even the contents of his thoughts scream of it. They are centered on change. Mortality." Sabrina shook her head. "He is one of them. I just know it."

"I think you're merely infatuated and want to turn him."

"Oh, I want him immortal, I won't argue that point, darling Michael." Her gaze met his measure for measure. She set the glass down, and then settled her hands on her hips. "Think about it, if I am right. We could possess the gift. Finally, those bastards could pay for what they did in San Francisco."

Robin frowned, sitting on the arm of one of her couches. "Sabrina, don't start this again. San Francisco was a long time ago and I will tell you now what I told you before I left you in Boston. Your fixation will be the death of you someday, and all the more if you are even thinking of turning a seer. The Fates themselves could strike you down where you stand."

She flicked her hand in a dismissive manner. "I fear no Fates. What are they anyway, but mortal deities? Besides, how would they strike at us if we possessed one of their own?"

"Don't." He sighed, bringing his hand to his forehead. "You know damn well I'll be no accomplice to you if this is the path you have chosen."

"Why not?"

"Why not?!" Robin laughed. "Sabrina, words haven't been invented to express my opposition to this idea. If you want to retaliate against the seers, then kill him and be done with it. Let us continue living as we have been without upsetting the balance of the natural order."

Sabrina gritted her teeth. "The mortals filled your head with nonsense during those years we were apart."

Robin came to his feet. "I seem to recall you being the one who instructed me on the natural order before you lost your mind to ambition."

"Which you lack to your detriment." She scowled. "If you wish to continue being my second, then you will do as I ask. Find out about him. Find out about his lover and whether she is one of the Order's puppets. If I could see the gift in him, I know I'm not the only one who could."

"Absolutely not."

"You will do as I order. I am your maker."

"Sabrina, I've followed you to the ends of the earth. I refuse to do this."

Abruptly, Sabrina raised her fist and pounded down on the surface of her liquor cabinet hard enough to splinter wood. Even I jumped at the action, which spurred Robin back into a seated position. His eyes widened as she pointed a finger at him. "You ungrateful Irish bastard, do not make me regret the day I offered you my wrist. I don't care whether or not you think this is a bad idea, he will be mine and you are going to help me." Her gaze turned wild, her fangs descending. "Fuck The Fates. Fuck the Supernatural Order. *I* will become the Supernatural Order."

As Robin regarded Sabrina, I saw a pain in his eyes I had never witnessed before. He indulged in a deep breath, shoulders straightening as it seemed he exhaled past whatever knife had pierced his heart. I frowned on impulse. "This man," he said, his tone of voice turning cold. "This healer, as you described him... How do you propose to lure him? Supposing you are right and he is a would-be seer, his natural inclination will be to resist being turned. You know this is the truth."

"Then we shall make it all the more desirable to him." Sabrina grinned again, something unholy taking up residence on her face, replete with wicked glint and fanged sneer. In it, I saw the mirror image of Flynn. "He flirts with the darkness and has a pliable mind. I've already begun wrapping my fingers around his subconscious without him realizing it. By the time we are ready to turn him, he'll fall willingly into our arms." She lifted a perfectly-manicured fingernail and tapped her chin. "In fact, I think I know the best way to begin working on him."

Robin raised an eyebrow. "And how is that?"

"The girl," Sabrina said. "The pathway to our young seer will be this woman he calls Lydia."

◦◦◦

Immediately, the scene changed, and once again I found myself along for the ride. This time, Robin's old room materialized around me, along with all his old furniture and possessions. I watched him converse with Rose as she lounged on his couch.

"It's just as Sabrina suspected," he said, pacing the room. "The girl is a member of the Supernatural Order. She cares for him, I know this much is true, but I don't think her care for him is simple emotional attachment." He paused and turned to look at her. "I fear we're getting in over our heads."

Rose arched an eyebrow. "So, the mortal is indeed a seer?"

"I am not sure, but the presence of one of her kind seems to suggest this might be the case." He shook his head. "Going any further down this path will result in nothing but trouble, but Sabrina fails to see the severity of her actions. If she doesn't leave him alone, the girl might catch on."

"And you think she would cause trouble?"

"The girl is a watcher, Rose. A sorceress. Yes, I think she would. She could even go so far as to help him discover his abilities prematurely."

Rose blinked. "I didn't think that was possible."

Robin sighed. "They're capable of worse things than this, sister. And if she does that, his anger at our coven would be severe. He would collect our ashes as punishment if he suspects for one moment what our mistress has planned." He glanced away, folding his arms across his chest. "I wouldn't be surprised if the girl has already sensed us. If she is a watcher worth her salt, then she has to know something is amiss. This is all wrong."

"Then we must do away with the woman."

His eyes returned to Rose, an intense scowl surfacing on his face. "No, Rose. We must stop playing this game."

She chuckled. "Oh, Michael. You get so worked up over nothing. If the watcher is gone, we can strike. He will be ours without any interference."

"I can't believe I am listening to this." Robin paced closer to Rose. "Turning a seer – a *seer* for the love of all things. We might as well all sign our death warrants."

"Sabrina knows what she's doing. She always has." Rose stood, flashing a disarming smile at Robin. "I believe we should inform her of this news and see what she has to say about it."

"Rose!" Robin called out, as she turned for his door and opened it. Not to be deterred, Rose dashed from his room and left him to chase after her. I turned and motioned to follow them as well, but the room transformed again before I could and one step forward only placed me back in the middle of Sabrina's penthouse, a little further into the future. I whipped around and regarded the sitting area, stopping my examination at once when I caught sight of Robin again.

He laid on one of the couches, hollering in pain as the coven's physician removed his shirt. Slashed to ribbons, the fabric fell away to reveal several deep gashes across Robin's chest, as though he narrowly escaped being cut in half. "The wretched mortals attacked me," he said, his breaths labored in the throes of agony and his fangs down. "Damn you, Sabrina. Damn this plan of yours; you nearly had me murdered."

"You bloody idiot," Sabrina said as she stood close, regarding my wounded brother with annoyance. "The whole point of surveillance is not to be caught. Now, you've left us in a terrible position." She scoffed. "If you expect sympathy from me, you have come to the wrong place. Perhaps you should seek it from that man you bedded last night when you were supposed to be minding our prodigy."

Robin sneered. "That was a one night encounter, Sabrina. And the mortals knew I was coming! How could I have been any more careful?"

"Listen to me, Michael. I will say this once and only once before I lose my patience and have you killed." Sabrina shoved the physician aside and dug her fingernails into Robin's neck. "I am *this close*, do you hear me?! *This close* to having the seer in my pocket and now, not only does his watcher know we're stalking him, the other members of their council do as well."

"And don't you see what I am telling you?" Robin's voice strained through the added insult of Sabrina's grip. "They already knew. She'll do what I warned you she would do and we'll all be dead because of it."

"Then we must kill her. Before she has a chance to bring the seer into enlightenment." Sabrina shoved Robin's head back against the pillows of her couch and smoothed out the wrinkles in her form-fitting pants suit. "The girl is little more than a petty nuisance. My guards could be done with her in short order."

The physician inched toward Robin again. Robin scoffed, closing his eyes. "Her people would expect us to strike right now. It would be a massacre." Slowly, his lids lifted again. "Sabrina, it would take turning the seer against her for us to have a chance. That's how long of a shot you have."

Sabrina turned to face Robin again. She furrowed her brow. "Turning the seer against her?"

"Which I assure you is impossible." He indulged in another labored breath, his gaze turning severe. "Sabrina, I beg of you... Kill him. Have us relocate the coven before the Order sends another seer after us."

"Never!" Sabrina shouted, her fangs beginning to emerge. "I will *not* bend a knee to them and I refuse to cower because of them again. Never... I swear to you, Michael, I fought tooth and nail to establish this coven before I called you here to be my second. I will not give it up now that our security looms imminent."

"Security?!" Robin laughed. "There is nothing secure about any of this! You are going to have... us... *slaughtered.*"

"Oh yes, there is. There most certainly is." Sabrina relaxed enough for her fangs to slip back into place. "Inside this mortal lies the will of a killer and the talent to execute. We will help him discover enough of that for him to use it against his lover."

"How do we go about doing that?" asked another female voice from the far corner of the room. I turned to find Rose standing against the wall.

Sabrina tilted her head in Rose's direction. "What is the one thing that can turn one lover against another, my dear? Betrayal. She will betray him and he will murder her. When he has finished this task, we will reward him with immortality."

"You'd sooner part the ocean than to get the watcher to betray him," Robin said, interrupting.

Sabrina turned her focus back to my injured brother. "We don't need the act, only the appearance of it." She pointed a finger at Robin. "Heal. Feed. Do whatever you must to get back in top condition and we will strike while we have a chance. I will get inside his mind and twist his thoughts. You will set his bitch up for the fall exactly as I tell you to. When these two events converge, then we will have a new vampire in this coven."

I released a breath I did not know I was holding. Suddenly, it all made sense. I never doubted Lydia's fidelity until I met Sabrina and everything I feared grew with exponential gravity almost overnight. The darkness present in me amplified; my paranoia mounted and the anger and aggression became its own being manifest within me. "Flynn," I whispered, bringing a shaky hand to my head as my thoughts drifted to that fateful night again. Only this time, Robin's memories helped me fill in the final, missing pieces.

My mind's eye transported me to Lydia's living room while Robin stood outside, silently observing the events which unfolded. I glanced his way, seeing him stare through the parted curtains leading to Lydia's balcony and read the resignation in his eyes clear as day. My brother may have been a participant, but he did so despite every instinct within him screaming to force Sabrina to understand. I knew, though, such a task was impossible. I swallowed hard and whispered, "I forgive you, dear brother."

If only I could have asked him to do the same for me.

Turning my focus back to the apartment's interior, I found Lydia sitting at her dining room table and had to draw a shaky breath as I recognized the clothing she wore. Her glasses were affixed on her face and her eyes scanned the pages of an open book while she raised a coffee mug to her lips. I studied the spines of each tome piled around her and felt tears well in my eyes. They all had something to do with dark magic and witchcraft. The gesture eclipsed even her typical interest in the occult and now, I knew why. There was a threat surrounding me I neither saw, nor believed in, and she had to try and save me from myself.

I frowned. "Lydia," I said, even though I knew she could not hear me. "I am so very sorry for never believing you. I should have known you were right, but I..."

A knock interrupted me. Lydia and I both looked up. She removed her glasses and placed them atop one of the books before rising to answer the door. Walking closer to the other side of the apartment, I glanced down at the volumes on her table once before lifting my eyes to regard the entry. I did so in time to hear Lydia gasp. "Liam!" she said, speaking a name I instantly recognized. "Oh no, Liam. What happened?"

The man hobbled into her house, looking as beaten as Robin had in the previous scene. Robin's wounds were minor in comparison, though, because this man was mortal. Mortal and still existing in the realm of the living, yet only for a few minutes longer. The realization forced me to sit where Lydia had just been.

Lydia examined the tall, middle-aged man, her eyes fraught with panic. "I was attacked," he said, revealing a British accent as he spoke. "That vampire we found mucking about the Council on Monday ambushed me on my way over."

"Oh no." Lydia lifted one of Liam's arms and draped it across her shoulders.

"Come on. I'm going to lay you down on my bed so we can take a look at you. Can you make it?"

"I've made it this far." Liam winced, leaning part of his weight onto Lydia. "Bastard. I wish I knew why he just ripped into me. I should be dead."

"The vampires in that coven are all acting insane. I've never heard of anything like this before."

"Well, they've managed to do the impossible, so they're probably feeling bloody smug about it." Liam walked into the bedroom with Lydia's assistance. I stood, following right behind them and becoming all too aware of the mistake I was about to make.

Lydia lowered him onto her bed and began taking a better look at his injuries. "Liam, I'm going to grab my first aid kit and a few washcloths. Take off your jeans and shirt, if you can."

"I'll give it the old college try." Liam winced as he started unbuttoning his shirt. "I don't know if there's much you can do, dear. We might have to wait it out until sunrise before I can check into the hospital."

"I know." Lydia walked into the bathroom and pulled out a first aid kit from beneath her sink. I recalled giving it to her in jest, an allusion to what we coined our 'first date' and could not suppress the frown at seeing her need to use it. "I'll do what I can for you here," Lydia said, placing the kit next to her sink and turning for the linen closet. "But then, I'm calling Peter."

"Would it be safe to pull him into this?"

"I'll tell him to come in the morning." She pulled out a stack of washcloths and tossed them in the sink. "If we have to, we'll call an ambulance and have him meet us at the hospital."

"Alright." Liam grunted in pain as he pulled off his shirt and started on the button of his pants. "What are you going to tell him?"

Lydia hesitated. She turned on the water and immersed the washcloths in silence. "I don't know," she said finally. "He's still in the dark about everything going on, in more ways than one."

"Sometimes, it takes seeing to believe." Liam gingerly slid his jeans down past his hips before giving up and settling against the bed again. "Fucking vampire. I'm afraid I've done all I can do." He gazed toward the doorway to the bathroom. "Lydia, every seer I've ever met spends the first two decades of their life in blissful ignorance, and probably many of those just as skeptical as your Peter. He will believe one day, I promise."

"He might not have enough time." Lydia walked back into the bedroom with her materials and placed them on her nightstand. Picking up one of the wet washcloths, she dabbed at one of Liam's wounds. "I think we should draw out his powers. Bring him into protective custody and lay it all out to him. The vampires are going to keep this up if we wait for the High Council to send another seer."

"Lydia, we can't." He winced. "We have to be sensitive to the natural order. Drawing out a seer's powers before their time is a dangerous game. There are scales which need to stay balanced."

"But you said it yourself, Liam. They're acting smug and we both know they've become dangerous." She frowned, wiping at his chest. "Damn, he got you good."

"I still would like to know why the bloody hell he left me alive."

"I don't know. But Peter... I've sensed something off about him for a while. He's been acting funny when I see him. He's a lot shorter with me and a lot more... Well, we even..." She paused, and then shook her head. "Sorry, that's too personal. Anyway, if we don't draw out his powers, they'll not only kill us, they'll do God only knows what with Peter. He doesn't see it coming."

"You think the demons mean to turn him?"

Lydia nodded. "I've caught him talking to this vampiress..." She trailed off and sighed, tears forming in her eyes. "She looks at him like some trophy, some pet she wants to have and there's not a damn thing I can do about it. She would have killed me if she knew I was watching."

Liam frowned. "If you've known you have a seer on your hands, you shouldn't have gotten romantically involved with him. The life of a seer isn't an easy one. This won't be the first time you'll see him in the middle of danger, dear."

"This is different, though." Lydia set down the washcloth and raised her hand to touch the pendant dangling from her neck. "He gave this to me for my birthday. Do you know how frightened I am? I put a spell on it to offer him protection in case that vampiress kills me. I keep seeing my death and I know it's going to happen before I get to be his watcher." She sighed. Her tone of voice turned entreating. "The natural order's flown out the window, Liam. Let me get Peter in tomorrow and let's finally tell him the..."

The front door slammed open, interrupting them. Both Lydia and Liam gazed past my invisible form into the other room. I could only shiver, knowing who this was. Far more than that, I found myself trapped in the surreal notion that I knew what he meant to do. And regardless of the fact that this was me, I could not do a single thing to stop him. Lydia whispered, "Oh dear God, is it them?"

Liam could only shake his head before their attacker entered the room.

Lydia froze when she saw me standing there, clutching a butcher knife with a white knuckle grip. "Oh no. No, Peter..." she said, but as I regarded my past self I saw murder pouring from his gaze – evil glinting in his eyes – and knew I was seeing Flynn for the first time. Every person I murdered over the course of five years would have recognized the being standing there. Before I ever became an assassin, I had realized my dark side. This would be his maiden voyage.

At first, I turned away in revulsion, but was compelled to look again when Liam shot to his feet and hobbled forward despite his injuries. He struggled to pull up his pants, tripping in the effort. "Peter, stop!" he said. "You don't know what you're doing." He came to his feet, but my past self charged forward, looking to intercept the perceived interloper first.

"No, Peter! This isn't what you think!" Lydia yelled, her hands coming to her mouth when I thrust the knife forward, plunging it into Liam's stomach. This wound alone would have been mortal, but my past self was not yet satisfied. He removed the blade only to slit Liam's throat.

Lydia began to tremble. She stood as I turned my sights on her and all I could do was watch as my past self advanced toward her. She looked down at her former mentor in shock. "Oh God. Liam..."

Fury overtook the mirror image I no longer recognized. He thrust the knife deep into Lydia's chest and looked her in her eyes as she gasped and gazed back at him, a single tear trickling down her cheek. "I'm so sorry, Peter," she whispered.

"Burn in hell," I said. My past self stared down at her coldly while she fell to his feet.

I could no longer watch in silence. "No!" I shouted, running forward and collapsing next to Lydia. Tears streamed down my face as I touched her dead body, trying to feel her skin and will her back to life. My inability to so much as stroke her hair only served to break my heart further. "Why did I do this to you?" I asked, raising both hands to my face. "Oh God, why did I not see this before?"

"Peter the blind. Sight, but no vision."

I looked up when I heard the voice. My past self had vanished, leaving me alone in the room with the two corpses who were bleeding out on the carpet. I furrowed my brow when I saw neither body speaking, and then glanced around again. "Who is there?" I asked.

A familiar voice emerged, entreating me back to the present.

CHAPTER TWENTY-THREE

"I'm sorry I did this to you, Peter, but it was the only way I could reach you. You were lost and I had to get you out of there somehow."

Opening my eyes, I discovered belatedly that I had removed my sunglasses. "Shit," I said, clenching them shut while groping around the floor. When my fingers found something hard and plastic, I picked up my sunglasses and thrust them onto my face. Then, I lifted my lids once more.

Monica stood in front of me, frowning, again with an emerald-colored scarf tied around her neck. The same shade as Lydia's eyes – as my eyes now probably as well. "I won't blame you if you hate me," she said, her voice soft and lacking its normally-present sarcastic edge. "It was time for you to see the truth, though, and I knew you wouldn't believe it coming from me. This was the only way I could get through to you."

I regarded Monica, noting distantly that her presence no longer annoyed me. Rather, she seemed a sight for sore eyes. "Monica," I said, my voice sounding weak. "What have I done?"

She closed the distance between us and crouched by my side. Her hand rested on my shoulder. "Peter, you've been lost for a while. You've been controlled by a powerful vampire who..."

"I remember it, Monica. You do not have to explain." I brought my hands to my head, struggling to make heads or tails out of all the memories crowding in on me. Acts I remembered committing; remembered, even what I had been thinking and feeling while committing them. People, places, and events which had been a part of the past five years. Victims, innocents. Sinners. Vampires.

Vampires.

Oh God, I was a vampire.

It was a fact I knew quite well – something I had even thought to myself mere moments prior – but the recollection of my acts only served to bring this observation to the surface again. It felt as though I had woken from a long sleep to discover these fangs I now possessed and the insatiable temptation I harbored to use them. I knew what terror I had wrought with them. Flynn. That was what they called me. The monster residing inside my body. The monster who was me.

"My head is swimming," I said. "I cannot make any sense of this."

Monica nodded. "Like looking at a two-sided mirror, only with different reflections."

I nodded. "Precisely." Looking up at her, I frowned. "Who am I?"

"You're a man waking up from possession, Peter. Do you see what I mean now?" She paused to sigh. "You've been manipulated by these people. They've called you a son and brother, but even Robin here was part of the deception for a while."

"He tried to stop it."

"I know he did." A soft, sympathetic grin surfaced on her face. "Even vampires can have a conscience sometimes."

I blinked. "Is that what I am now? A vampire with a conscience?"

Monica sighed. "You're... a little too unique for a category."

"You are calling me Peter. Am I Peter again?"

"I don't know. I guess that's for you to decide."

"I was tricked." I furrowed my brow, my speech mirroring the jumbled progression of my thoughts. "They tricked me into killing Lydia because she was protecting me." Gazing at Monica, I studied her, confused. "You are a watcher as well?"

Monica patted my shoulder and stood. "Come on, Peter. Let's talk somewhere else about this stuff. I don't know when Sabrina's going to figure out you're missing and your mind's too fragile for her to see you this way."

I nodded, coming to a stand. My limbs felt shaky and the room around me seemed liable to start spinning, so I clutched onto Monica's shoulder as I took my first few steps. "I should retrieve my weapons," I said.

Monica nodded. "I'll grab the ones from the other side of the room. You do what you can over here, okay?"

"Alright." I glanced down at the floor, picking up my katana first and sliding it into its sheath. Not too far from there laid the remains of what had been my brother. My stomach twisted, forcing me to look away so I could continue scavenging for my remaining blades.

I found two of my knives closer to the double doors at the front of the meeting room. Monica met me where I stood, waiting patiently for me to holster my weapons before handing me my short sword and remaining throwing knife. She held out my trench coat, but I stole a moment to produce the sheathed knife from behind my back after securing the other blades into place. I passed it to her while accepting the coat. "Please keep this for now," I said, threading my arms through the sleeves. "Just in case you need it for protection."

"From what?" she asked, taking the weapon.

"From me." I gave her no chance to respond before lumbering forward, heading for the now-opened back exit. She jogged to catch up with me, and in a matter of moments we found ourselves outside.

Neither of us spoke at first. The short, young sorceress and tall, male vampire strode through back alleys and crossed carefully from one shadow to the next while making our way through Philadelphia. As I regarded the city around us, I saw it through changed eyes. The vitality of the mortal population beat like a pulse of possibility, with the electricity of life running through each person as a current. It was something my vampire side was blind to, but I became aware of through my rediscovered humanity. Yet, it communicated to me I still stood apart from these beings who had once been my peers.

"It's the sight," Monica said, breaking the silence. She looked up at me. "The gift of being a seer was always meant to be used for their protection. I'm sure it was hard to grasp before."

I nodded and allowed the quiet to overtake us again. Monica honored my implicit request and kept her observations to herself for the remainder of our excursion. It only took a few minutes more for us to find our way to a house nestled on the northern edge of Center City. I perked an eyebrow as she jogged up a short flight of stairs. "A new hiding place?" I asked.

She nodded while producing a set of keys. "Yeah, the other place wasn't safe, what with coven mistresses knowing my address and all." Monica flashed a grin at me, then unlocked the door and swung it open. I watched her stroll inside, but paused at the entry, refusing to take another step.

Monica looked back at me and perked an eyebrow. "What is it, Peter?"

I frowned. "Are you certain you trust me enough to allow me to enter?"

She nodded. "I do for now. Come inside and close the door." She waited for me to do as she instructed, then held up the knife, still grinning in a disarming manner. "I'll keep this close to me, just in case."

"Might not be a bad idea." Stepping past the entryway, I stripped off my coat and draped it across the back of a dilapidated couch. One piece at a time, my arsenal of weapons fell to the ground until it left me clad in only my black shirt and pants. I settled into the sunken cushions and sighed as I reached for the frames of my sunglasses. The dark living room afforded me the chance to uncover my eyes, so I placed the dark lenses atop an adjacent end table, relaxing as much as possible.

Monica strolled to the doorway separating the living room from the kitchen. "You didn't feed before all that, did you?"

"No, I did not," I said, looking at her. "Nor do I care to right now."

"Well, all the same, you should have something. The next few nights aren't going to be daisies and roses for you." She sighed and I watched as she walked into the kitchen and plucked a glass from the cupboard. She set it onto the counter, and then rolled up her sleeve first before unsheathing my knife. Monica winced as she cut a gash into her arm. Blood ran into the glass.

I frowned. "Monica, please do not..."

"It's okay." She indulged in a deep breath and allowed the rivulet of crimson to continue filling the glass. I fought against the fangs which wished to descend at the sight. "And in case you're wondering," she said, "I didn't cast any protection spells, so I'm not trying to poison you."

"It was the furthest thing from my mind, actually. I doubt you would have brought me here simply to trick me."

"Good. Maybe we're starting to trust each other." Monica slid her arm across the rim of the glass before setting down my knife. Using her now-freed hand to untie the scarf around her neck, she wound the silken fabric around her arm and knotted it tightly into place. Her good hand took hold of the glass. She walked back into the living room and handed it to me. "It's not much, but it'll take the edge off."

I accepted the glass and drank down its contents. Pausing for a moment afterward to allow my head to clear, I fought my fangs once more and drew a deep breath inward until the heady rush passed. I opened my eyes without knowing I had closed them. "I thought you said we could survive without blood for a few weeks," I said, directing my focus back to her.

"You can, but you have to condition yourself for it first." She frowned. "And I wasn't talking about a vampire who's both as young as you and as used to feeding the way you are."

"How will I manage this, then? Living this way? Even if my mind comes to terms with my humanity once more, my physiology shall make the struggle that much more difficult."

Monica nodded, sitting across from me in a chair resembling the couch on which I sat. "I've had to think about that. Not that I was counting on a miracle, but I figured if I managed to reach you, I'd have to help take care of you somehow." She sighed. "I'm not going to lie to you, Peter. The next few days are going to be difficult for us both while we figure things out."

"You do not intend to allow me to stay here, do you?" I frowned. "Do not trust me under the same roof. You could be signing your own execution order."

"We don't have a choice." Monica eyed me in a deliberate manner. "I'm your watcher. I knew Lydia before she died and she made me promise I would take her place if something happened to her. Lydia loved you a lot, Peter. Poets could have written books full of poems with the things she told me about you." The smile which had begun to surface dissipated as it seemed an unpleasant thought sprung to life inside her mind.

I read the thought and nodded. "Except that your promise has led you to care for a bloodthirsty assassin. Not the love of your friend's life."

Monica issued a wan smile. "I guess we have to play the hand we're dealt, right? Both you and me." She stood and paced around the room as though floating on a pocket of air. "They say there's a first time for everything. I just keep trying to tell myself everything happens for a reason. I don't understand The Fates, but there was some method to their madness when they let you be turned. We just have a few more challenges to overcome." Her eyes found mine again. "We *have* to overcome them, though, Peter. We have no choice. I can't let Sabrina get her hands on you and you can't step backward now after finally making it this far. You're too dangerous and have too valuable of a gift."

"Monica..." I sighed. "I cannot sense this purpose toward which you allude. From where I am sitting, there is merely madness. I see only what I have become and the things I have done."

"There's a lot more on the line now. Especially after what happened tonight." Monica returned to her chair and placed her hands on its back. "You might be the only hope we have left. The local council's been crippled for years. They haven't had a replacement elder since the one you killed, and they lost..." She pointed at me. "One of the most powerful seers to walk the planet. Not to mention a very talented sorceress. Sabrina has been nothing but a growing threat and more than once, they've discussed having another seer brought in to kill you."

I blinked. "They have?"

"Oh yes. Yes, they've wanted your whole coven blown into next Thursday, but I stopped them." Her eyes met mine in a deliberate manner. I felt them dig deep into the innermost parts of my psyche as though driving a message home. "I staked a claim on you, Peter. Because what Lydia said about you was true. I waited for a sign and when you made your first move, I jumped in with both feet, because I believe

Peter Dawes was meant for bigger things than to be some she-vamp's bitch." She paused to grin. "And, tonight, you finally proved me right."

Nodding, I allowed my eyes to fall to the ground, knitting my hands together on my lap. "I do not know. I have been what I am for so long, I do not know how much of what I did was Peter and how much was Flynn. There is a distinct part of me which looks back on the past five years with utter revulsion, and another part which savors every moment of it."

Monica nodded. "So we're going to have to reprogram you a little. You're still a vampire. Nothing's gonna change that. But if we can use your vampire abilities to our advantage, we could make you one hell of a force to be reckoned with." She waited for my gaze to return to hers and offered a soft, reassuring smile. "You have the hard part behind you already. You've faced death, you know violence, and while it's made you jaded, you can still work that to your favor. What we're doing now is teaching the killer how to tap into his humanity. Because in the humanity lies the seer."

We stared at one another until one of her thoughts drifted into my mind as though on a wisp of wind. "First, we make it through the next day," I whispered. "And the next day after that, until we piece this splintered being back together."

"I hope I exonerated Peter enough in your eyes to make that possible."

"Either make it possible or baffle me further, I do not know." I sighed and allowed my gaze to become distant. "The demon has been injured, but he yet lives. I sense him in there."

"And he might never die entirely. It might be something we have to deal with for a long time, but I think you can do it. It's just going to sting like a bitch at first."

My eyes focused on her again. "Please be mindful of your protection until we know if he can be beaten back. Do not be so open with me again past this evening."

"I won't. At least for now." Monica nodded in the direction of the hallway. "I have a room for you. Typical room, but with a sturdy door and a few hexes placed on it."

"Hexes?" I perked an eyebrow.

She chuckled. "Yeah, I'm not completely stupid. Once you enter the room, I have to invite you into the rest of the house for you to get out. It's just so that you don't snap and kill me in my sleep or that you don't roam the house in a bloodlust-fueled tirade." Monica smirked. "I'm sure you've thought this stuff was only folklore, but you'll discover there's more to magic than the myths."

I rose to my feet and nodded. "Well, then I suppose you should lock me up for now. I doubt I shall sleep all that much, but I am mentally exhausted and need to think matters through."

"Okay." She stood and walked ahead of me, taking the lead as I followed her to the end of a short hallway. Pointing to the room, she grinned. Monica waited for me to enter before snapping her fingers twice. "There you go. You'll be secure in there. I have books and candles in case you want to read, but all your weapons'll be kept out here so you don't do anything to yourself." She paused, and then added. "Or me."

"Very well." I gazed at her across an expanse which constituted only a few feet, but might as well have been miles. She looked back at me, offering a solemn grin before shutting the door and locking me inside. I surveyed the four walls of my new classroom, regarding the bed and heavily shaded windows. The faintest embers of moonlight were filtering through, causing me to wince slightly. Once I ensured the shades were firmly in place, I sat down and sighed, knowing this first day would probably be the hardest I would weather from this point forward.

Chapter Twenty-Four

It was the first thing I became aware of when I opened my eyes. Hunger; pure, insatiable thirst demanding to be requited.

I shut my eyes and indulged in a few steadying breaths, exhaling each in a slow manner as I began to realize the scope of my newest foe. I had waged war against the nightmares which marked my attempt at rest, and stolen precious moments of sleep were captured when exhaustion finally overwhelmed me. Now, however, the night was upon me, and sunset left me wrestling my nocturnal appetites.

"Fuck," I whispered, burying my head into a pillow. Reducing my blood intake would take time, and I expected it to result in some form of withdrawal. Knowing this, though, did not stop my head from swimming and my fangs from descending, drumming the cadence of palpable desire. Yes, it was time to feed; time to seek nourishment and savor the pleasure of a proper hunt after only nipping at scraps the night before.

Of course, Monica standing outside my door was not helping.

"Monica, you would do well to depart from my presence." I attempted to steady myself. For as much of a physical battle as this would be, I knew it would be a mental one as well, and I had no choice but to win it.

She hesitated. "Do you need me to find you something to...?"

"No!" I shouted, not meaning to chastise her, but to assert past the demon screaming, '*Yes!*' inside my mind. "Do not expose the addict to his addiction before he is able to break his need of it. If I become weakened, I shall inform you. For now, I simply need to concentrate."

"Would talking to someone help?"

With a sigh, I sat up on the bed and ran my fingers through my messy hair. My shirt cuffs were unbuttoned and my shirt tails hung loose. My pants were wrinkled and I looked every bit the worthless piece of refuse which I felt like at the moment. I had to confess, though, that engaging my mind might be a good idea. "Open the door, but do not come in. I am not faring well at the present."

I heard the lock turn and the door creak open, but refused to open my eyes. Instead, I scooted my legs into a bent position, resting my head on my knees while focusing past the onslaught of her tempting pulse resonating in my ears. Knowing she stood on the safe side of the threshold became my only comfort when I realized that having her company would also inhibit my fangs from retracting back into place.

I felt the weight of her gaze before hearing her lean against the door frame. "You're either really brave or a closet masochist, Peter," she said, a hint of humor in her voice. "I intended to have you wean yourself, not go cold turkey."

Breathing deeply, in some effort to calm my nerves, I shivered when the action brought with it an unhealthy dose of Monica's scent. The perfume provoked a deep moan to rumble from my chest. "Fuck." I rubbed my eyes. "Perhaps a masochist might be more apt than assigning me with any form of bravery. At the same time, I spent the past twenty-four hours weathering the memory of every victim I have killed since acquiring my abilities. I have no desire to add another to the collection."

"I didn't say I'd let you kill anyone."

"Right now, you would be hard pressed to stop me."

"Good point." Monica sighed. "I understand."

"Please..." I swallowed hard. "Talk to me about something other than feeding, unless it is your intent to drive me insane."

She chuckled. I heard her settle on the floor and could not help but to smile at the way she laughed. It might have been the most human response, besides conciliatory remorse, I had manufactured in years. "Insane?" Monica asked. "No, we can talk about something else." She paused, either to study me or adjust her position to get more comfortable. "Do you have any questions for me?"

"Many, but so few which could be answered."

"Well, start with the ones I can answer."

I nodded, summoning the gumption, somehow, to retract my fangs. Lifting my head, I kept my eyes clenched shut, in the event the now-open door brought more of the offensive moonlight with it. "Well," I said. "I suppose the first question would be to ask where my sunglasses are."

"On the stand next to the bed. I put them there while you were asleep."

Frowning, I sighed. "I could have woken up."

"I knew what I was doing, Peter."

"Quixotic imp." Reaching to the side, I fumbled for where the nightstand was, only vaguely recalling the layout of this unfamiliar room. It added one more item to the list of new things toward which the assassin had to adjust. "Where the bloody hell is...?"

"Hold on, Peter." Monica paused, and, for a moment, I thought the madwoman daft enough to enter. Instead, I heard her crack her knuckles and shift her position. "I'm going to teach you your first lesson as a seer. You ready?"

I sat straight and nodded, wondering what precisely she intended.

"Alright." She paused. "You've had that euphemism about sight and vision thrown at you a lot, but it's for a reason. Seeing things as they are involves more than just the use of your eyes. It involves your mind, too. Now, I'm looking at the stand your glasses are on, and I'm pointing at it. One of these things will help you and one of these things won't."

"Well, with my eyes closed, I can hardly see your hand."

"So, use my mind."

Nodding, I focused my thoughts on Monica and attempted to see the world through her eyes. A mirror reflection of me seated on the bed formed in my mind, along with an image of the rest of the room. The perspective I borrowed showed me the stand and, poised atop it, my sunglasses. I reached to the side and captured the spectacles in my first attempt.

Slipping them on, I opened my eyes and erased the mental map which had formed, but her lesson had been learned. I turned my head to regard Monica. "So, I'm to see the world through other sets of eyes, then?"

"Well, think of it this way." Monica stood and brushed off her skirt. "When you see how other people look at the world, you can see where their motives lie. Sometimes, it's as simple as where their focus is."

"Fascinating ability." I nodded. "So, if the way others regard the world says something about them, then what does my visual impairment say about me? I never cared for the light even as a mortal, but becoming a vampire seems to have given it an especially painful level of contempt. Why?"

Monica tucked the blonde patch of her bangs behind her ear. "I don't have an answer for that, unfortunately. The sight of a seer and the soul of a vampire are two totally different things. I don't know if that explains anything, but imagine this might be part of it."

I nodded. "It is possible Lydia herself would not have known."

"She might have. She was pretty sharp." Monica smirked. "Plus, she knew you for two years. I've only known you for a few weeks."

The comment struck me. I looked away. "Before I ask the question, allow me to preface it by saying I know Lydia loved me. That being said... Was our meeting happenstance or did she get too close to me?"

"Nothing's happenstance, Peter. Lydia might not have planned to run into you that evening and probably wasn't the first in line to become a watcher, but those facts don't change what happened. It was for a reason."

"Was she told what I was, though?"

I glanced back at Monica. She grinned. "No. She knew when she looked into your eyes. And by that point, she had already fallen in love with you."

Nodding, I acknowledged Monica's assertion, but was in no mood to expound upon it further. The hunger started to encroach again as we conversed about inconsequential things. When it became too difficult to handle, I asked Monica to lock the door and not let me out, regardless of how belligerent I became. She agreed, albeit with no small amount of reluctance. The night wore on and my mind became consumed by the insatiable desire to kill.

"Damn you, Fates," I muttered at one point, clawing at the sheets and close to the verge of hyperventilating, useless breaths or not. "Damn purpose... damn reason... damn it all." By the time exhaustion took me under, I was a mess in all senses of the word. That evening was only to be the tip of the iceberg, however.

Four days of hell followed. Over the course of each evening, my condition deteriorated more and more. I knew Monica was listening. She neither spoke to me, nor intervened, which only served to piss me off. "Fuck you, woman!" I yelled. "Let me out of this room at once!" On the final evening, I found myself punching through one of the walls, leaving a gaping hole in the plaster.

I had oscillated through so many different emotions, one might have been convinced I had gone fully mad. It started with throwing things and turned into ripping other things apart. I went so far as to destroy pieces of furniture. My room looked as though a zoo full of animals had paraded through it. I drove my fist into the wall again and hissed when my knuckles hit a wooden beam.

"Fuck!" I yelled, retracting my hand and clutching it. My eyes drifted to the crimson liquid oozing from the deep gashes inflicted on my hand and I shuddered. "Damn it." The red contrasted against my pale skin, mesmerizing me after days of not having my thirst sated. Before I could stop myself, I licked the wounds eagerly, groaning as all my senses were held hostage to the need. I collapsed onto the ground, slipping into the fetal position.

I held myself in a tight embrace, shaking and clenching my eyes shut while the room began to spin around me. Fangs down, I felt them ache while the knot forming in the pit of my stomach tightened. "When shall I be rid of this curse?" I asked, not expecting an answer, but still wishing one could be afforded to me. After four nights of shouting obscenities, I felt weak; tired. Nearly to the point of throwing myself upon my katana if just to end it all. Whatever would free me of the chaos in my head.

Even if it cost another mortal life.

"No, I must not do that." Somewhere in the back of my mind, I heard Lydia speak of how much she admired my profession as a doctor. "*You heal people,*" she had said once, a glint of wonder and respect in her eyes. "*I don't think there are many jobs with a higher calling. It represents the kind of person you are.*"

I recalled asking her what kind of person that was, and receiving one of her typically-mysterious answers in return. "Very few people are called to do what you'll be doing. Healing people, yes, but saving them as well." She smiled. "It makes you a hero. That's what you are, Peter Dawes."

It was difficult to think of myself as much of a hero while I shivered on the floor. No, if I was honest with my self-criticism, I was more like a whining vampire, lamenting his enslavement to his own nature. "I have to stop this," I said, placing my hands onto the ground while indulging in another series of deep breaths. "I am not a monster. I am not an addict. I shall not give in to these desires, no matter how badly they afflict me." Swallowing hard, I managed to retract my fangs at long last, unable to recall the last time in the past four days when I had been able to do so.

With this task completed, I forced my useless breathing to slow and sat up. Crawling toward the bed, I reclined against it and leaned my head back as I settled into a seated position on the floor. My hands shook, but I clenched my eyes shut and inhaled deeply once more. This was the defining moment. Break the addiction, or die trying. "The Lord is my Shepherd, I shall not want," I murmured, recalling the oft-cited Bible verse my parents enjoyed quoting when I was a young boy. I spoke the words not to evoke a higher power, but to do *something* other than dwell on my weakened condition. Latching onto the thought, I continued. "He maketh me to lie down in green pastures. He leadeth me beside the still waters."

My hands gradually ceased their shaking as the words poured from my lips, running together on an infinite loop. I felt my tense body begin to relax, bringing with it a tremendous wave of fatigue. My vampire nature had been lashing out with such sound and fury, I had not realized how starved I truly was. Still, I could not bring myself to call for help. The calm washing over me felt too euphoric for me to disturb it yet.

"Though I walk through the valley... of the shadow of death... I will fear no evil..." My eyes fluttered shut. My arms slackened and hands lifted from the floor. "… For thou art with me." The black of unconsciousness engulfed me in its abyss. I hit the carpet just as it pulled me under. Lying on the ground, I fell asleep at last, completely unaware of the world around me the moment my body relaxed.

Had I been any closer to lucid, I might have heard the door open or sensed Monica standing on the other side of the threshold. As it was, when she walked into the room, I did not stir, and as she lowered to a crouch, I remained as still as a corpse. She sighed and touched my forehead. "It's about damn time, Peter," she said. Lifting her hand, she cracked her knuckles. "I was beginning to think this would take all week."

A grin tugged at the corners of mouth. Extending her hands, palms facing upward, she lifted my body without touching me and pushed me gently toward the bed. I settled limply onto the mattress, my head resting on a pillow and eyes shut tight while sleep still held me soundly in its throes. Monica snapped her fingers to release her spell, then brushed her hands together and glanced at the wall. "Wasn't bad enough that you broke everything else? You had to go and punch the wall, Peter." She shook her head and frowned. As she glanced back at me, she raised an eyebrow.

Monica strolled closer to where I laid and sat beside me. The ghost of a smile resurfaced. "I have no idea how I'm going to hide those holes, but I suppose I'll worry about that later. For now, you need some uninterrupted rest and I don't trust you fainting will keep you under the way it should." Wiggling her fingers, she positioned them on either side of my head and closed her eyes to concentrate. After a few deep breaths, she whispered the words, "Now, sleep," before folding her hands atop her lap.

An indescribable calm washed over me, something I sensed from even the deepest recesses of my subconscious. After weathering the storm, a dreamless sleep would carry me through the remaining days of my recovery.

Chapter Twenty-Five

"I know how you feel about this, but you have to eat something. Now wake up, tough guy. That was only round one."

My eyelids fluttered open in response. Darkness shrouded the room around me, an extra sheet draped over the shaded windows to block out any excess light which might have otherwise peeked into the room. I blinked, reaching up to rub my eyes with the idle thought that my glasses must be on the nightstand again. As I turned my head to look for them, though, my gaze froze when I spotted something on the wall in front of me.

All of the weapons I had on my person upon arriving at Monica's house hung from the wall, partially concealing the holes I created with my fists... the previous night? Several nights before that? I could not tell. I felt rested, albeit weakened, and remained skeptical that I had only been asleep for one day. Still, the sight of so many weapons so close unnerved me. "Monica, take those out," I said, seeing her standing in the doorway. "I could hurt..."

"You won't," she said, walking over to me. Monica sat on the edge of the bed. "Do you want to know how I'm so sure of that?"

I furrowed my brow, noticing the absence of a scarf around her neck. I could not deny the sight of her bare skin enticed me, but miraculously, I held my fangs at bay. "How?"

She smirked. "You haven't eaten in a week and haven't noticed the glass full of blood next to your bed yet."

My gaze shot to the nightstand. A glass filled near to the brim with an opaque, crimson liquid sat beside my sunglasses and this time, my sharp teeth slid down, the scent of blood an intoxicating essence after so many days without it. Still, I did not dive for it immediately, which struck me as peculiar. Instead, I glanced back at Monica, an eyebrow perked. "Where in the heavens did you get that?"

She chuckled. "Not from me. I have a friend down at the blood bank. It's a special donation for a doctor in need."

"I hardly qualify as a doctor any longer."

Monica shrugged. "Some creative lying." She pointed at the glass. "Go on and drink it. I said you could go a couple of weeks. Didn't say I recommended it."

Smirking, I reached for the glass and brought it to my mouth, imbibing the precious offering and savoring it as though it was a fine wine. With each swallow, I felt my weakness wane, the soreness of days of struggle being soothed with every drop. I closed my eyes and paused with the glass yet half-full. Licking my lips, I allowed a pang of bloodlust to pass through me and lifted my lids once I was certain it had dissipated.

Monica nodded. "Yes, you're going to have to deal with this for the rest of your life, Peter. Still, the fact that you've made it this far says a lot. Your need for blood is like my addiction to oxygen. You can't ever be totally rid of it. Still, we can help you keep it under control."

"How?" I asked, raising the glass again to finish my drink.

"We'll keep you away from biting people for a while, at least. Only have you feed every few days unless you get injured or something like that. You were pretty fucking hooked on it, but you've only been killing for what? Five years now? Nobody taught you much about glamouring and sipping, I guess."

"Robin might have tried, if I would have listened." The invocation of my older brother's name inspired an immediate frown. I looked away, clutching the glass with both hands. "I truly killed him."

I felt the air between us change, becoming heavier. Monica sighed. "That part wasn't a dream, Peter. I'm sorry."

"You have no reason to apologize." Staring at the goblet in my hands, I admired the remaining droplets of blood with an apathetic air. My stomach felt twisted in a knot, my heart somewhat emptier. "I was the one who plunged the sword into his chest."

Monica inched closer to me on the bed, provoking me to make eye contact again. One of her hands reached for one of mine. "No, I do have something to apologize for. I could've stopped it. I knew what you were about to do and let it happen." She frowned. "Call it the last desperate act of a witch."

My hand closed around hers, apt to accept the comfort being offered. "Permitting something to happen is a far different sin than being its cause." My gaze lingered on her for a few moments, and the longer I saw the contrite expression on her face, the guiltier it made me. I managed a small grin. "I think your advice in minding my feedings is rather sage. I certainly do not wish to weather that experience again."

Monica laughed. Freeing her hand, she patted mine and then settled hers on her lap. "That makes two of us. Listening to you shout and throw things isn't what I'd call a good time."

"No." Indulging in a deep breath, I stood, pausing a moment to survey to room around me with fresh blood coursing through my system. I glanced at my injured hand and watched the fading wounds on my knuckles disappear altogether. A wave of calm settled on my psyche and I focused on relishing it, knowing I would not have many days from this point forth given over to such pleasantries. The notion turned around in my mind during an extended period of silence, until my voice found unction again. "I suppose part of my rehabilitation involves becoming familiar with what it is I am supposed to be doing." I lifted my eyes to regard Monica again.

She nodded, but did not answer right away. Instead, she smiled. "Take a shower. Change your clothing. I'm sure you want to clean up. We'll talk more after that, okay?"

"Very well."

Monica stood and winked at me before strolling toward the hallway. Turning the corner, she disappeared from sight and I allowed my posture to relax without realizing I had been so tense. My eyes skimmed over the bed before lifting to regard a chair I thought I had broken in the midst of my tirade. Placed atop it was a neatly-folded stack of clothing I could only assume Monica had procured for my sake, complete with a suit jacket draped across the back. The sight caused me to perk an eyebrow. "Surely you did not..." I stopped the thought mid-sentence, not wishing to know if Monica had been so foolish as to slip into my coven again.

Instead, I plucked the clothing from the chair and entered the bathroom, set upon the task of cleaning a week's worth of filth from my body. I spent more time than could be deemed necessary standing beneath the stream of hot water and dressed slowly when I was finished, meticulous about the way I threaded my arms through each sleeve and secured the belt around my waist. Draping my suit jacket across the crook of my arm, I walked into Monica's living room and fell into one of her chairs.

Glancing up at her, I waited for her to meet my gaze while regarding the way she huddled on the couch. Quiet and closed in; she appeared to be a thousand miles away and the silence became uncomfortable rather quickly. "I suppose I could attempt reading your thoughts," I said, shifting my position to face her. "But I shall extend you the courtesy of telling me what you are thinking."

"A courtesy?" She grinned, looking at me. "You vampires are so giving."

I perked an eyebrow. "I did not intend to be condescending."

"I know. You have the right to know what I'm thinking anyway." Monica sighed, her grin fading. Sitting up straighter, she nodded. "Well, I don't know how to say this any other way than blunt, so here we go. I made a decision a few weeks ago when I told the Order I encountered you. I could have lied through my teeth, but I told them I brought out your abilities and a giant clusterfuck followed."

Her gaze drifted toward her hands as she continued. "Some of them yelled. A lot of people called for me to be removed from the Order and shipped back to Seattle so I could be punished. They, at least, disqualified me from being a watcher and thought you should be killed on the spot." Once again, we peered at one another. "You're their fuck up, Peter. Not to be mean, just being truthful. Letting you get turned wasn't our shining moment."

I nodded and looked away. "I am certain it was not."

"But it happened. And while they've been keeping their distance from you ever since...You're on their radar screen again."

"Yes, undoubtedly." Raising my hand to rub my eyes, I felt a weight deposit itself on my shoulders. "This creates a sticky situation for them. Where they gambled on the unknown with a vampire assassin, now they have a vampire seer with which to contend. One who murdered a watcher and..."

"... an elder, yeah." Monica nodded. "That was one of the reasons why I changed where I was hiding. First, the Order wasn't happy with me. Second, Sabrina would come looking for you. And you need some time to sort things out before you can face either of them." She lifted her arms, palms held pacific. "So, we have this place."

"Only now there are worse problems." I knitted my hands together, my eyes lowering to the floor. "I murdered every other vampire master besides Sabrina, and all their second-in-commands. Sabrina might not have me any longer, but she has the balance of power. Precisely what she wished to have."

"Yes, I know." Monica sighed. "I wouldn't devalue your purpose in her economy, though. She might have done away with the masters, but she needs you to ensure she gains control over the whole city."

I frowned. "You think she means to come after me?"

"Oh, I know she will, Peter. You're too good a prize to pass up. I don't have to be in her inner circle to know she's spent the past week looking for you. If she's smart, she hasn't told the other covens you're missing. Just that you're lying in wait, ready to murder whoever would challenge her."

"Yes, but such a threat shall only last for so long. You are right." I looked up at her again. "They fear my name enough to take her threat seriously, but when the time comes to squash an insurrection..."

Monica nodded. "She's going to need to put her money where her mouth is." She frowned. "We could argue all night about who created this mess. Me for bringing out your powers, you for killing those people at the meeting. Hell, we could even blame Lydia for forcing me to promise her I wouldn't let you go without a fight. The point is, before we can deal with either of them, I have a seer who needs to have a little more faith in himself."

I sighed. "Murder, I can accomplish, Monica. I have done it enough times to orchestrate an assassination in my sleep." Raising a hand, I ran it through my hair and shook my head. "But if you are asking me to guard against Sabrina's wiles, I do not know if I can."

"And this is where I come in."

I perked an eyebrow at her.

She smiled. "I'm your watcher, Peter. I'll be here to help you every step of the way. We have a mess to clean up before you can even look her in the eyes, anyway." Her smile softened. "You're not the only person who's ever had to wrestle with a vampire's seduction. Or himself, for that matter."

"Yes, but has a vampire-seer ever existed before? A being at odds with their own nature from the start?"

Monica sighed and shook her head. "No, I don't remember ever hearing about this happening before. Seers aren't usually recognized before they gain their powers and even then, they wouldn't agree to be turned."

"Agree to be turned?"

"There's power in words, Peter. Just keep that in mind." She fell quiet, lost in thought for a moment before she looked at me. "It's possible you're the first, but that doesn't change the fact that human nature has always involved wrestling with darkness. Every one of us has to face our demons."

"Monica, all this philosophical talk of human nature is no use to me. I know what I am."

"I'm sorry." She stood and began to pace. "I'm just saying we're not completely flying blind. And as for Sabrina, she'll definitely be trying to whisper sweet nothings to you because she wants you back. But the 'seer' part of the vampire-seer title you now so auspiciously hold is going to be your best friend through all that. She'll be trying to tug at the vampire. What's carried you through seven days so far will help fight against that."

I followed her with my eyes while allowing her words to imprint on my mind.

"Peter, this is what it means to be a seer. I know I sound like a broken record, but you have to understand it. You see into things; layers into things. Sometimes far more than even I can. You have the ability to dive past thoughts into intentions, into tricks, into exactly what this woman is trying to poison your mind with. When you learn to see that, you'll be able to cut through the bullshit and fight against it."

"How was she able to entice me after you brought out my abilities?"

"She found the right buttons to push. How was she able to seduce you when you were a mortal?"

I mused upon the question. "She saw my doubt and darkness."

"And that's what she feeds on." Monica sat on the arm of her couch, regarding me sternly. "You've come a long way, but you're not out of the woods. You'll never be without the darkness, but you can recognize the light now. Keep walking toward it. Even if it hurts your eyes."

I nodded, musing on her metaphor. What I had to be would fly in the face of everything I had been for five years. I had to continue finding greater pleasure in penance than through immersing myself in decadence. I had to be a seer and a protector – not a cold-blooded killer. I might not have been able to call myself mortal any longer, but I chose to align myself with them just the same. The humanity within me knew this was merely the start of many changes that had to occur.

"Monica…Teach me this, then. Instruct me further on how to see past evil, as I had before my life became shrouded in blood." Glancing away, I sighed. "It is such a distant echo to me, what I had been like in those days, but it reverberates just the same. I know it can be found again."

"It's not as far away as you might think." Monica stood once more and motioned for me to do the same. "C'mon, let's go for a walk. You saw a little bit of it last week when I brought you here, but you need to see more of the world." She grinned. "Call it a field trip."

I perked an eyebrow, but stood and hurried back to my room to fetch my sunglasses. Affixing them onto my face, I also slid my arms into my suit jacket, and met her at the door. "Is this safe?" I asked as I watched her tie a green scarf around her neck. "Shall I bring a weapon for our protection?"

She considered that for a moment, then looked at me and smiled in a cryptic manner. "I think we'll be fine. Besides, Sabrina's spies won't think to look for you where we're going."

"And where is that?" I asked.

Monica opened the door, and then looked back at me. "To the hospital, of course." Her eyes glinted with mischief. "Dr. Peter Dawes."

CHAPTER TWENTY-SIX

It was the first moment I stepped inside Temple University Hospital as an intern, in my first year of residency. The first day of what would be a long three years, or so I thought at the time. July had never seemed hotter, and the ink on my medical school diploma had barely dried. The world expected me to apply my knowledge in the gravest of manners, though, in the emergency room of a hospital located in the heart of Philadelphia.

For the past eight years, I had been surrounded by textbooks and teachers, cadavers and skeletal models, diagrams of veins and capillaries. The endless hours of tests, lectures, and dissections led me to the point where I signed my name on the dotted line to specialize in emergency medicine. I wished to save the world, one human at a time, after losing the two people who had brought me into it.

They remained heavy in my thoughts as I strolled into the hospital.

It was survivor's guilt that had placed me on the path of medicine when I determined which career I would pursue. For months on end, I remembered wrestling with nightmares of the last moments of my parents' lives. Years later, I could still hear my father and mother laughing together while I sat in the back, seat belt unbuckled and not a care in this world. Thirteen years old during the summer of 1967, my cares and concerns extended no further than my chores around the farm. It all shattered around me within seconds.

I recalled the deafening sounds of metal impacting metal as tiny shards of glass showered us with crystalline rain. I was thrown forward into the back of my father's seat, my leg bending at an unnatural angle as the world twisted about me, pain shooting from the point of impact intensely enough to make the world go black for a few moments. By the time I opened my eyes again, there was a copious amount of blood staining my pant leg and, more terrifyingly, coating my mother's window. My father's head rested against the steering wheel. Neither of them moved.

I thought I heard the sound of labored breathing while drifting in and out of consciousness. I would find out later, as I was pulled from the twisted remains of my father's vehicle, we had been hit head-on by a drunk driver and it had taken the police an hour to find us. My father's sister drove to the hospital and later broke the news to me. John and Marjorie Dawes had died while we waited for help to arrive.

Two surgeries and a lifetime's worth of scars later, I was an orphan. My aunt took me in and I went from living in rural Pennsylvania to piecing together the remnants of my existence in Abington, a bustling suburb of Philadelphia. Amidst the struggle to figure out what to make of life now, my mind continued revisiting the accident and I wondered, what if I had been able to help my parents? The notion found its genesis while I sat in the hospital and gained fruition when I started school that September. By the time I received my high school diploma, I had been accepted into Temple University's medical program.

The work ethic of life on a farm translated into my studies with devoted obsession. I made all of my classes and studied as hard as possible, as though I would be able to teleport back to the accident and save my parents. Eight years of schooling had now culminated in this purpose.

And I was scared to death.

Senior residents barked orders at me. The entire world seemed tipped on its axis while spinning quickly at the same time. My first week provided me precious little sleep and by the second week, I wondered how I would make it to the other side of three long years. One especially frustrating shift found me sitting in the locker room, holding my head in my hands. Two weeks in, and my nerves were already shot to hell.

As I strolled back into the emergency room, I passed a nurses' station and found myself scowling at the women as they tried to speak with me. I was not vexed with them so much as I was simply angry with the world at large and bent to take it out on everyone. A portly, middle-aged nurse raised an eyebrow at me, but I turned away before she could speak. The intersected gaze was enough, though. She stood to give chase and I sighed, aggravated enough to spin on my heels as I sensed her approach.

She smiled in the most disarming way possible, extending a hand. "Well, hello there, young man. I'm assuming you're one of the new interns. We haven't been properly introduced." Pausing, she nodded. "The name's Chloe Poole. Who would you be?"

I mustered as much of a grin as I was apt to reciprocate. "Peter Dawes," I said, shaking the outstretched hand. "Yes, I'm an intern."

"Thought as much." Her grip was firm, almost a challenge or a dare, but relaxed within seconds. "Those senior residents work you fellows ragged. I always have pity on the interns."

"Yes, they've been..." I sighed and ran my fingers through my hair, peering at the other doctors before regarding Chloe again. "This behavior's normal for them?"

Her grin became a smirk. "Honey, it's a tradition. The world likes to shake you up and see what you're made of from time to time."

"So noted." I frowned. "I don't know if I can take much more of this. It trumps even the shit my instructors used to put me through."

"Well, this is life in the E.R., Pete." Her eyebrow arched again. "Why did you become a doctor?"

I sighed, recalling the first time in my medical school career I had been asked that question. "Because..." I said, reciting the same thing to her I had told my teachers. "I lost my parents in a car accident. Couldn't help them, but I wanted to be able to help somebody else."

"Ah, you're one of the idealists." Chloe started to walk, motioning for me to follow her. I did so, glancing around while listening to her speak. "I see it happen so many times, Pete, when pre-med and med school doesn't take the luster out of an intern's eyes and they get thrown into this lion's den without instructors to hold their hands. It's not the gold medal marathon the movies make it out to being, but when you help somebody who needs helping..." Her smile brightened. "It's worth all the other horse shit you need to shovel along the way."

I nodded. "I haven't gotten to the part where that's happened yet."

"Then you're looking at it the wrong way." She pointed toward one of the occupied beds. "Granted, it's hard to find something noble about treating the same alcoholic who fell down another flight of stairs, but even the people who come in here with minor sniffles and sneezes aren't wasting your time. They're everyday people and they might not be bleeding and broken, but you're helping them get on with their lives."

Turning my attention toward another bed, I saw a young woman raise her eyes toward me in an apprehensive manner, a blanket pulled up to her shoulders with dark circles framing her eyes. Chloe slapped a chart against my chest which I reflexively took in hand while shooting a glance toward the nurse.

She smiled. "Go save the world, Dr. Dawes. Don't get cynical like the rest of us."

Nodding slowly, I watched Chloe walk away and opened the chart she had handed to me. Inside, I found the information taken down by whoever had first spoken to the patient. Persistent insomnia. No medical insurance, but a quick note scrawled across the bottom said it had gotten to the point where she had nearly been involved in a major car accident. My heart sank to think about what could have happened. Did she have a family who could have been harmed? Could she have been like the drunk driver whose car impacted ours all those years ago? Looking up at the young woman, I drew a deep breath inward and started my examination.

She left not too long afterward with a prescription and a few bits of additional information regarding her condition. The next patient complained of persistent stomach pain, and I determined he had a burgeoning ulcer which would only get worse if left untreated. He thanked me while confessing the stress he faced every day and even as I sent him on his way, he spoke of a wife and children dependent upon his income to make ends meet. Each patient, it seemed, had some story to tell which struck a chord with me that night. When I entered the hospital for my next shift, even the badgering of the senior residents could not deter me from grasping firm hold of my new-found perspective.

Not that every night from that point forth bore a resonance of 'sacrifice for the greater good', but it helped me limp through the months until I met Lydia. From that point forth, she constantly reassured me that I was a noble person, even when a hard day of work failed to make me feel accomplished. The universe seemed bent to affirm her, though. I can yet recall saving a woman's life and following up with a compulsion to check on her the next evening.

As I said, "Feel better," to her I caught sight of something which caused me a moment's pause. She wore a wedding band, replete with a matching diamond, and had a dozen red roses poised beside her on her tray table. I excused myself to continue my shift, but happened upon the thought several times that night that I had helped mend somebody's wife. Perhaps that is why I held Lydia a little tighter that evening. It could be I was simply glad it had not been her. Whatever the matter, I experienced a moment both sobering and vindicating at the same time.

The idea of helping the helpless infatuated me, this much I could not deny. It had been a small, but very real, slice of pleasure I relished until I met Sabrina and started down into an endless spiral. Monica was quite astute, though, to think my old place of employment would be the best place to take me. No matter what transpired, I knew exactly what job I had to do and how to handle the challenges presented to me.

It would be a valuable lesson as I faced a test of a different sort.

⋅⊙ℂ ℊ⊙⋅

Strolling into the building, I found myself staggering from the wave of nostalgia which impacted me. It was hard to believe it, but there I stood, in the middle of a hospital which used to be my second home.

I did not bother looking at Monica when I spoke. "Are you certain this is the best place to bring a vampire?" I asked, perking an eyebrow.

"No," she said, "It's definitely the wrong place to bring a vampire." As I turned my head to regard her, I saw the corner of her mouth curl in a grin. "But it's a great place for a seer to be. Call it a moment of perspective, Peter, because that's what we're here for."

She swatted me on my back. I frowned and continued walking with her, glancing about the vicinity in as idle of a fashion as I could manage. When one commits double homicide and then becomes a vampire, one does not have much of a chance or inclination to notify their place of employment they shall not be returning. As such, I speculated on what the other doctors might have thought when I vanished.

Had they heard about Lydia's death? Were they questioned by the police? My stomach twisted and I wondered why the hell Monica had been so foolhardy as to bring me there. My old friends would recognize me and I would be forced to do something idiotic to avoid being detained. Suddenly, my temples throbbed despite the absence of a pulse.

Raising my hand to adjust my sunglasses, I kept my gaze fixed on the ground while burying my hands inside my pockets. I did my best to avoid making eye contact with anybody, but this did not prevent somebody from stopping in the middle of the hall. I winced as they called out my name.

"Pete?!"

Monica ceased walking, but I continued onward. The woman who recognized me was not to be deterred, though, and I knew why the moment she spoke again. The all-too familiar voice sparked mountains of recollection my simple brush-offs would not assuage. I realized I would not be able to escape.

"Dr. Peter Dawes? Is that you?"

The footfalls hurrying toward me broke into a jog. I sighed, resigning myself to the imminent conversation and turned to face my pursuer. Mustering a halfhearted smile for the short, chubby nurse was as cordial of a gesture as I could manage. "Chloe, it has been ages," I said, hoping she did not hear the strain latent in my words. "You look well."

Truth be known, she looked tired – far more than I recalled her being when I worked with her. She huffed and shook her head. "Oh, stop bullshitting me. You always were a terrible liar." Reaching forward, she threw her arms around me without hesitation and I froze in place. "You're a sight for sore eyes."

Reluctantly, I embraced her in return, weighing myself against the knowledge that this was my first physical contact with a mortal since my detoxification. Granted, I had taken company with Monica, but Chloe knew no protective incantations and unknowingly exposed herself to a moment of closeness with a predatory sadist. The part of me which was yet Flynn scoffed at tainting his lips with her blood, though, which might have been Chloe's saving grace. "It is surreal to see you as well." Pulling away before the temptation became too much, I nodded. "I hardly know why the sight of me would constitute being 'for sore eyes', but thank you just the same."

"Are you kidding?" Chloe laughed. "We all wondered what happened to you. You wandered out of the E.R. one night and never came back."

"I have had... an interesting five years, Chloe."

"I'm sure." She glanced at Monica as the sorceress strolled carefully toward us. "What brings you back here?"

As if on cue, Monica's face contorted and she clutched her gut. I perked an eyebrow at her. "Ow. Oh shit... It's starting to hurt again." A gloved hand reached to pat my upper arm, then returned to its position on her stomach. "Thanks for helping me to the hospital, *Pete*," she said. Her eyes glinted with mischief when they met mine. "I think I can find my way to the reception from here."

I resisted the urge to growl at her as Monica hobbled away. "You are... welcome," was all I could manage, teeth gritted and feet rooted in position for the lack of a better reaction. I found myself staring at Monica until she rounded a corner and disappeared from sight.

Chloe furrowed her brow, watching with me. "Should you tell her she just turned the wrong way?"

"She shall discover this eventually." My gaze returned to the nurse when I felt I could relax my facial expression. "She has been taking far too many liberties in trying my patience lately. If she gets lost, it is her fault."

"Seems like a strange girl." Chloe shrugged and turned her sights back to me. Her eyes traced up and down my body and for a moment, I felt somewhat self-conscious, wondering what I must look like. Black suit. Pale complexion. Dark sunglasses over my eyes. She frowned, just as I thought she might. "Running with the Goth crowd these days?"

"No." Despite her frown, I was amused, though I tried hard not to smile and jar her with the sight of my fangs. "But I can see where you would assume that especially to look at her as well." Clearing my throat reflexively, I pointed toward where Monica disappeared. "She is... ah... a friend. Monica has been complaining of stomach pains for the better part of the evening, so I persuaded her to finally receive a proper examination."

"I see."

"She shall be alright." I shuffled my feet and dug my hands into my pockets. "It is probably a case of indigestion or something of the like."

Her brow smoothed and this time, it appeared she believed me. The smile returned to her face, albeit in a solemn manner. "Well, whatever brings you in here, it's good to see you nonetheless." Chloe stepped closer. I fought the urge to groan when she placed a hand on my shoulder. "I heard about what happened to Lydia. I'm so sorry."

My eyes shifted to the floor. "Thank you, Chloe. I apologize for never saying goodbye, this has been..." I reluctantly looked toward her again. "... A dark period in my life."

She nodded. "I know. I'm just glad you're not dead or something. A few people thought..." Chloe stopped abruptly and shook her head, nervously shifting a chart from one hand to the other before tucking it under her arm. "It's not important. It's just funny how things happened. Everything hit the fan right after you left. Things started getting strange. The morgue has seen some freaky shit and we've been treating odd patients."

Nodding, I stared at her and skimmed her surface-level thoughts. Images of conspicuous gashes and odd puncture wounds drifted into my mind, many of which reeked of my handiwork. I frowned, confronted with the reality of the monster I had become. "I am sorry."

"It's just a weird city, Peter. Always has been." She lifted the chart. "Take this girl, for example. She came in covered in scratches and animal bites, and she's been catatonic the entire time. I'm supposed to get personal information from her when she can't even say what happened."

"How was she brought in?"

"Ambulance. Somebody found her and called 911."

"Might I take a glimpse at her chart?" I extended my hand. Chloe nodded and handed it over. Flipping it open, I begun paging through the notes already penned by the paramedics and her attending physicians. She skirted close to the edge of hypovolemic shock, and if the loss of blood had not been alarming enough, the scratches from a struggle and eerily placed puncture wounds were enough to inspire even a skeptic toward belief in the paranormal. Some vampire had done a woeful job of attempting to dispatch of her. I felt revolted at their sloppiness.

"How do you see with those sunglasses on?" Chloe asked.

"I had an accident shortly after Lydia's death which makes me sensitive toward light." The lie came easily, though I was far from proud of it. Glancing up at Chloe, I perked an eyebrow. "I know I am not a doctor here any longer, but if you wish me to speak with her, I could. I think I might know how to help her."

Chloe perked an eyebrow. "How?"

I frowned. "Hard to explain without sounding insane, but I can help." I paused. "If you still trust me, that is."

She studied me intently. I could hear it turning around in her mind, all the questions I expected. Were the rumors of me killing Lydia true? No, of course not, she thought. This was Peter. Peter had simply been so traumatized over the loss of his girlfriend that he buried himself in a pit for five years, even if his disappearance reeked of guilt. I fought the urge to confirm how close to the truth she was.

"Okay, Peter," she said, motioning for me to follow. We strolled together down a corridor, in silence at first, until Chloe looked up at me again and sighed. "What happened to you? I mean, I recognize you, but barely. You look like you haven't seen the light of day in..."

"... Five years?"

Chloe tensed at the comment. I nodded, looking straight ahead. "I am not certain what you are looking for in the way of answers, but I have none for you which you would care to hear. I only have my pledge that I shall not harm this girl."

"Why did you disappear, though?" She stopped walking and turned to face me. "One minute you were here treating people and the next... Poof. You were gone. People have said terrible things about you being involved in Lydia's murder and I..."

"Chloe." I sighed, looking at her. "That is not a question I can answer to your satisfaction."

"Please tell me the truth." She frowned. "The Peter I knew wouldn't have harmed a hair on anybody's head. I know something's changed, and I doubt you could give me an answer any weirder than the stories I've been hearing lately." Chloe shook her head. "Every time I think I've seen the strangest thing possible, something else happens and I just... want to know how bizarre things truly are."

"No, you do not." I perked an eyebrow at her. Leaning close, this time of my own volition, I attempted to ignore her scent as I whispered, "The things being said about me might all be true. Far worse things might be true as well. There might be things out there which you do not wish to believe in and I shall only confirm them to you. Whatever the case, if you have any sense, you shall continue helping these people and stay far from the darkness." I nodded. "I shall not burden you with my presence past tonight. Please allow me to be of some benefit to you before I depart."

Chloe stared at me for what seemed like an eternity, her mind a discordant wave of thoughts too confusing for me to sift through. Her eyes pierced right into me as though she possessed the same abilities I had, until she nodded and looked away. "Alright, Peter," she said, starting to walk again. I followed her without responding.

We paused by the door of one of the rooms nestled at the edge of the emergency area. I stole a glance down the corridor, at the flurry of activity in the main thoroughfare, another sense of nostalgia nipping at me like an unpleasant harbinger. "This is it." Chloe's voice stirred me back to the task at hand. "If you can do anything, it'd be a huge help to us."

I nodded, handing the chart back to Chloe. Without another word, I opened the door and closed it behind me after I entered.

The woman lay on a bed, but she was not the first thing of which I took notice. The fluorescent lights overhead conspired with the sanitary white walls to make the room far too bright even with the protection of my sunglasses. I raised my hand to touch the wall, hesitating when I remembered this to be the room where I stitched Lydia's wound all those years ago. "The more things change, the more they remain the same," I mused aloud.

Switching off the lights, I also locked the door and motioned forward.

The woman barely stirred. I removed my sunglasses and folded them into my pocket. "My apologies," I said, issuing the statement to her without knowing if she even understood me. "This hospital has been giving me a headache since I entered. Between the scent of you creatures and the stark white all around, I wonder how in the heavens anyone remains in this area without going mad." Walking toward the bed, I pulled a chair close to where she laid and sat in it. My elbow rested on the arm of the chair and my chin settled in my hand while I studied her from my vantage point. "You certainly do look pale, I shall grant you that. Had I passed you on the street, I would have moved on to something with a trifle more substance. Herein lies the question, though. Who are you and why did they allow you to live?"

Standing, I examined her closer. A thick bandage covered her neck and the sight of blood soaking through forced me to recoil and assemble my wits about me again. Indulging in a deep, steadying breath, I looked back at her and nodded. I cracked my knuckles – as I had seen Monica do – and touched the sides of her head while shutting my eyes to focus.

Images slowly filtered toward me. At first, they made no sense and seemed to have no relevance toward anything in particular. The deeper I sank, though, the more form they gained; I saw the face of her attacker and shook my head in disgust as I recognized him from one of the area covens. The leaderless immortals were getting brazen and downright idiotic with their conquests. "Disgraceful things," I said. Concentrating harder, I continued my pursuit into Miss Joann Griffith's mind.

Joann Griffith. Her name emerged from the depths. Thirty years old. She told people she was twenty-five and worked as a legal secretary. No spouse. No children. She had been walking alone when attacked and left alive only for two reasons. For one, the vampire was a neophyte. Secondly, he had been interrupted by a man who subsequently called the paramedics. I frowned at the trauma wrought against the woman's psyche. How many people had I sent into shock prior to ending their lives?

"It would have been better had he finished you anyway, Miss Griffith." Leaning closer still, I ignored the tempting scent of her blood wafting toward me and whispered in her ear. "Wake up. The only monster in here is me and I am not going to harm you."

Joann blinked twice. I saw the lights switch on within her gaze and smiled, lifting my hands from her head. Once our eyes met, she gasped, using some hidden strength and a surge of adrenaline to slide away from me in revulsion. "Who...?" she began. Pausing, Joann swallowed hard. "Who the hell are you and what're you doing in here?"

"I am an ally and nothing more." Stepping backward, I nodded. "Please, allow these people to treat you. You are safe now, Miss Griffith."

I turned to leave, but she interrupted, "Wait a minute." She frowned when I looked at her again. "You're one of those... things... aren't you?"

I perked an eyebrow. "If you mean a vampire, then the answer is yes."

"Why aren't you attacking me, then?"

"Because humans are off the menu for now. Consider yourself fortunate, I was a prodigious killer in my time." Nodding, I glanced away momentarily. "I shall not bother you any further. I simply did not wish you in a catatonic state for the remainder of your days on account of my kind's sloppy workmanship. The nurse shall be in to see you shortly."

I produced my sunglasses again and slipped them over my eyes. She nodded at me, still the most confused creature I had ever seen, but far more lucid than when I entered. I flashed a quick, subdued grin at her and furrowed my brow when a small, tight smile tugged at the corners of her mouth. It appeared as though she wished to speak. I waited patiently for her to summon the courage.

Joann sighed. "I don't know if I should even be saying this to you, but... Thank you." The slight smile vanished. "I was trapped in a maze and... couldn't find my way out. I knew I was dying. I was just waiting for..."

"... It all to end?" I nodded. "I experienced it once, so I am familiar with the condition. Yours is the first story I have examined since regaining the inclination to empathize with a human. Thank you for allowing me that."

She nodded, but eyed me in a perplexed manner. "You're welcome."

I offered her as much of a grin as I felt apt to muster and motioned for the exit. Joann did nothing to stop me, yet I could feel the weight of her gaze settle on my back until I shut the door between us. Chloe stood waiting on the other side. "What happened?" she asked as I turned to face her.

Shrugging, I pointed back toward the room. "Your girl shall be fine. Her name is Joann Griffith and she has had a harrowing night. Allot her some time to work through what transpired before you label her a lunatic."

Chloe shook her head. "How do you know...?"

"I simply do, old friend. Remember, at times ignorance is bliss." I paused. "With that, I shall depart."

"Wait." Chloe sighed, glancing at the adjacent nurse's station. Holding up a finger implying I should linger where I stood, she dashed toward her compatriots and conversed with one of them briefly, passing Joann's chart to them. Then she jogged back as fast as her short legs would permit. "There, that's been taken care of." Shaking her head, she touched my arm and coaxed me toward a corridor. "Come on. It's been five years; you could at least catch me up a bit."

I frowned as I glanced at her hand, wondering if I could ask her to kindly let go. "There is not much else to say, Chloe."

"Alright. Playing coy." She sighed. Her arm finally lowered to her side. "I'll at least let you know how things have been here. Sam and Dave are still around, although they're usually on the day shift. Mark has off tonight. He probably would have freaked out if he saw you here."

The corner of my mouth curled upward despite myself. "The man was always afraid of his own shadow."

"Tell me about it. He still hits the ceiling anytime somebody codes." Chloe continued peering straight ahead. We neared the waiting area by the emergency room entrance and stopped, turning to face each other. "Other than that, everybody's gone their separate ways. Rashi and Maryanne both work in Jefferson. Bill's somewhere in New Jersey. Have a whole new collection of interns and residents and the world's still going to hell in a handbasket."

"The world does seem to do that, Chloe." I glanced toward the automatic doors as something caught my eye. A few feet away, a group of men approached the hospital and a shiver ran up my spine in a manner I had never felt before. My already-pale complexion whitened while the hairs on the back of my neck stood aloft. In the background, I could faintly hear Chloe continue to speak, but my focus remained fixed on the doors as they parted and the first of the collective strolled inside.

"Pete? Pete, what the hell is the matter with…"

Without thinking, I took hold of Chloe. Forcing her away from the corridor, I pinned her to an adjacent wall. Her eyes widened. "What are…?"

"Silence," I whispered harshly as I released my hold on her. "Stay there and do not move. Do you hear me?"

She nodded slowly. I cast a stern gaze at her, then walked toward the corridor again and peered around the corner. Ten men, if they could even be called that, gathered by the entrance. There were tall, strong, and by the way they glanced around the room, they gave the distinct impression they were not here for medical assistance. I watched one open his mouth to reveal sharp fangs hiding in slumber and their throats produced a collective growl which caused the humans gathered to stop cold and stare. "Bloody fucking wonderful," I muttered. "A pack of emasculated ruffians. What a bed I have made for myself."

I sighed and looked toward Chloe again. Inching closer, I whispered, "Chloe, there are a group of dangerous beings in the waiting area. Do not walk anywhere near this corridor and do not allow them to see you, but I need you to procure something for me."

Her eyes shifted from the hallway back to me. "What do you mean 'dangerous beings'?"

"I have no time to explain. Fetch me anything sharp. Scalpels, preferably."

"Peter, you're not going to…"

"Yes, I am." I frowned. "Chloe, I am afraid the answers I wished you to be ignorant of shall be forced to come to light. I need you to trust me, though. Fetch me the scalpels and return swiftly, but do not allow them to see you. Are we clear?" She remained frozen in position. I shook my head. "Chloe, if you ever counted me a friend…"

"Alright." Chloe swallowed hard and stepped away from the wall. She eyed me skeptically for a moment before hurrying toward one of the storage rooms and disappearing inside. I indulged in a steadying breath and focused my attention once more on the pack of vampires. Sorry bastards. They did not know what a gross error they had committed in coming there tonight, but soon would.

I closed my eyes and concentrated on the assassin I had been no more than a week ago. With that, a little of Flynn rose to the surface and prepared for an attack.

Chapter Twenty-Seven

I did not have to bore too far into the ringleader's mind to learn his name was Mathias. He had been an elder in one of the area covens, but now led a pack of rogue immortals, evidence of a new epidemic within Philadelphia. Without masters, he and others like him had been set loose to create havoc amongst the populace.

"Just fucking wonderful," I said from my hiding place, speaking just below a whisper. I sighed and continued to watch, knowing myself to be largely responsible for this sordid mess.

Mathais looked around the room, his lip curled in a snarl. "A late night snack before we go in, boys. What do you think?" he asked. Nine others stood beside him, all with fangs straining to descend, judging from the tips I saw prominently displayed. Malevolent eyes fixed themselves on the humans gathered and the sight seemed to instill enough fear no one dared to move. This left them all little more than sitting ducks.

"I detest the sick," one shorter, more Victorian-looking vampire said. A quick glimpse into his mind revealed his name to be Christopher. "I always have to chase their blood with a bottle of wine."

"Ah, but there are plenty here who are healthy." Mathias strolled ahead of the pack and nodded to the humans gathered before bending in a sweeping bow. "Greetings, inferior creatures, allow me to introduce myself to you." He stood straight once more. "My name is Mathias and I am a vampire. No doubt you've already figured this out, but to make the point much clearer, I'm going to inform you of our intentions. We intend to feed and add to our ranks. I will allow anyone interested in being turned to step forward first. Then, we will rip the shit out of the rest of you invalids."

"What a magnificent proposal, Mathias. Do sign me up for that."

Mathias swung around. His eyes met mine as I emerged from my hiding place and his face paled the closer I walked toward him. "Flynn?" he asked, his voice laden with disbelief. "I thought you were dead."

Pacing forward, I folded my arms behind my back at waist-level. Each hand held a scalpel with more pressed against my back, tucked into my belt. But he did not need to know about those just yet. "Dead?" I chuckled. "Mathias, I have died so many times, I cannot begin to know the difference any longer. As for my corporeal form, I assure you I am no mere apparition."

He raised an eyebrow. "Why are you hiding amongst the humans?"

I ceased walking and shrugged. "On occasion, I humor myself with a hobby. Immortality grows weary when one is not busy, does it not?" My eyes skimmed across the face of each mortal, insuring not one of them appeared about to do anything foolish. Their faces were marked by equal measures fear and confusion, but they stayed frozen in place. "Whatever the matter, I might ask what the lot of you think you are doing barging into a hospital of all the godforsaken places, and preying upon the infirmed. Does that not seem insulting to you?" I chuckled. "A pack of vampires so inept they must procure their meals from amongst the weak?"

"Yes, well... I might ask you why you are here, then."

"Touché." I grinned, revealing the tips of my fangs. "If I came to feed, I would be as pitiful as the lot of you, but this is not why I am here."

"Oh yes?" He furrowed his brow. "And why are you here, then?"

My grin turned wicked. Lowering my arms, I spared no chance for Mathias to see what I held before I deftly threw one scalpel for Christopher's heart. It plunged deep into his chest from the velocity with which I threw it and within seconds, the Victorian relic fell to the ground as nothing more than dust. Assured of his demise even before my makeshift weapon found its target, I had already hurtled another into the chest of the next vampire in my sights. It killed him instantly as well.

Sliding my hands behind my back, I plucked two more scalpels from their hiding place and grinned. "Believe it or not, Mathias, I am here to protect these creatures."

"You've lost your fucking mind." He glanced at the vampires remaining. Then his eyes met mine just as his fangs finished descending. "You'll protect nothing, you turncoat. There are eight of us remaining and only one of you."

"Oh good, then maybe you might give me a challenge." I sneered. "Although, I highly doubt it."

They hissed and rushed at me *en masse*, no doubt with the theory their numbers might overwhelm me. The humans finally began to scatter, retreating away from the action as fast as they were able. I ran directly for the vampires, waiting until the last moment to drop to my knees and topple two of them over as though they were bowling pins. Springing to my feet, I plunged one of the scalpels into the chest of a vampire I had not downed, then turned and kicked another advancing behind me. The blow caused him to stagger, but he remained standing. I had my first challenger from amongst the pack.

He took hold of a chair that had been within reach and swung it in a violent arc for my head. It forced me to retreat a pace and arch away, but I whipped a fist for him. The impact forced him back again and a kick to his stomach sent him crashing onto the ground. Just then, however, I sensed one of his compatriots nipping at my heels. I leaped onto an empty chair and turned, aiming a kick to his jaw which caught him entirely off-guard. He spun around and landed hard, sprawling out onto the tiled floor.

Stepping down, I plunged a scalpel into his chest before he could recover. He transformed into dust leaving me holding the scalpel. When I lifted my eyes from his remains, I counted my remaining adversaries. Six. My first opponent rejoined the others still crowed around Mathias and I smirked as they studied me with obvious intimidation in their gazes.

"Peter!" A female voice called out behind me.

I turned. Monica stood close to the corridor where Chloe and I had been hiding a few minutes prior. She had crouched and lifted her skirt, revealing a sheathed knife strapped to her thigh. Pulling the blade from its holder, she tossed it toward me. I caught it and lifted an eyebrow at her.

She shrugged. "Hey, you were the one who suggested I protect myself," she said. Then, Monica pointed toward my opponents.

I swung around in time to see Mathias run for me. He leaped to attempt a tackle, but I crouched down on the floor fast enough for him to miss. Another came at me as he sailed past and I plunged the knife into his chest, releasing my grip on it so I could angle myself to fire the scalpel in my other hand at another of Mathias's pack. Both descended to the ground as ashes and left only four remaining.

Mathias charged for me again. I threw him onto the floor, where he landed atop the remnants of one of his compatriots. Standing, I watched as one of the others confiscated Monica's knife from the pile of ashes it had created. He attempted an untrained, but accurate, retaliatory throw, that I caught by the hilt. "Many thanks." I sent the blade hurtling back at the vampire with a practiced flick of my wrist. It flew as it was meant to; with enough speed he was unable to catch it despite his attempt to recreate my feat.

The knife sank deep into his chest, and then hit the floor with a clank covered in ash as another member met their demise. Mathias came to a shaky stand and glared at me, but I laughed in response. I had one scalpel remaining tucked behind my back and the knife lay on the ground with three vampires remaining. "I *would* present you a chance to surrender," I said, a slow, devious grin tugging at the corners of my mouth. "You know me, though, Mathias. I am hardly the type to permit anybody to walk away from their encounters with me."

"Yes, Flynn the killer," he said, hunched in a defensive posture. His eyes remained fixed on me. "I must say, I'm impressed. You're every bit as formidable as your reputation."

"You flatter me, sir."

Mathias relaxed his posture marginally. I tilted my head, assessing him. "Such a skilled assassin shouldn't bother with underlings like me," he said, lifting his hands in an almost plaintive manner. "We're only vagabonds, hardly the type of target worthy of a man of your skill. Let us be on our way and we promise not to return."

I grinned, attempting to hide my amusement. He was not the first to ever attempt such a tactic and probably would not be the last, if I continued down this path. "Yes, dregs such as you do sully my name. You have forced my hand against you, however."

"Hardly." He grinned. "Not one human has been touched."

"Yes, this much is certain." I took step toward Mathias and then stopped, appearing nonchalant in the gesture. "I was attacked, though, and I take that quite personally."

"Surely you can allow for self-defense."

"Granted." I touched the corner of my mouth with one hand while the other drifted slowly behind my back. Fingering the scalpel, I nodded. "I did manage to singlehandedly decimate most of your gang. Do tell me, however... What would I receive in return for allowing you to walk away, besides your pledge not to return?"

"My word that nobody will know we've seen each other." Mathias nodded. "If it is your business to protect the mortals now, I won't take exception to that. And I won't inform the others I know you're still alive."

Nodding, I feigned looking impressed. "Well, this certainly is a compelling offer." A notion tickled my mind from somewhere outside of me. Monica. I heard her ask what the hell I thought I was doing and could only smirk. Ignoring her, I shrugged and paced forward a few additional steps. "It would please me not to have to murder three additional souls this evening. Heaven only knows I have had my fill of this." I flashed my most disarming grin. "You have a deal."

He stepped forward. Extending a hand, he seemed pleased with himself.

That was until I produced my last scalpel and plunged it into his chest. The look of happiness on his face transformed into shock within seconds. I shrugged. "On second thought, perhaps you should just die."

Mathias failed to produce a sound before his ashes descended to the floor. I wasted no time in throwing the scalpel at the second-to-last vampire and watched him disintegrate as well. This left just one.

The remaining foe gazed at me, wide-eyed. He turned and ran for the doors, but for how quickly he moved, I was much faster. I dashed for the knife, plucked it from the ground, and flicked it for the scoundrel's back all in one seamless sequence. By the time I ceased moving, it was over.

My final adversary fell to the ground as ashes. I grinned, satisfied, and then cast a quick glance around as I dusted off my suit jacket. The eye of each mortal fell on me with a mixture of awe and apprehension, none of them seeming to know if they should thank me or fear me. I caught sight of Chloe in my periphery and turned my attention to her, offering her a wan smile. "Sometimes the questions are not worth the answers, are they?" I asked.

She failed to respond. I merely nodded and turned toward the door. Monica jogged up to me, pausing to pick her knife up from the ground and return it into its sheath before joining me outside. We walked toward one of the side streets and turned down it without one word exchanged between us. I waited until we were into the shadows, before stopping and leaning against a building, my eyes shutting.

Monica walked up to me, but remained quiet. I spoke first. "For a few minutes, I almost recalled what it was like to be human" I opened my eyes to regard the night sky. "I felt such a wave of nostalgia from being there. Almost as though I was Peter once more."

"I'm sure." She smiled. "You wanted to rediscover the part of your life that wasn't darkness, so that's why I brought you here." When Monica's grin faltered, I raised an eyebrow. She sighed. "Well, alright, I brought you here for other reasons, too, but I'm sure you've figured that out by now."

I nodded, studying her. "You knew they would be there, did you not?"

The corner of her mouth curled upward in a coy manner. "Precognition. I don't get it all the time, but it has its moments." Her eyes gravitated toward mine. She raised an eyebrow. "I bet you think that last bit was the assassin and not the seer, though. Don't you, Peter?"

"I suppose you are going to tell me I am wrong if I confess this."

Monica nodded. "Being a seer isn't about having a few parlor tricks and seeing into the unknown. Those are all tools to help you protect other people. Part of that is searching into their thoughts or reading their intentions, but the other part is standing up and fighting when you must. That's the other lesson I brought you here to learn." Reaching out, she patted my shoulder. "Trust me, Peter, even your past self would have stepped up to protect those people. He might have died trying, but he would have done it."

I sighed and nodded. "I suppose you are correct." Glancing at the building behind me, I cocked my thumb toward it and grinned at Monica. "I do not believe I shall be welcomed in there again, though."

Monica smirked and tugged at my arm, directing me back onto the path toward her house. As we walked, I could not help but to acknowledge her point. My former self assuredly would have leaped into the thick of things, even if it had meant his death. Still, another pressing concern made its way past even my existential ruminations; the notion that the area vampires were forming into marauding bands and rogues were wandering about forging covens. I knew I needed to deal with this problem swiftly, before disorder led to abject chaos.

The vampire Flynn and the seer Peter yet stood at odds, but there was no time for them to make further amends. Reining in the city's vampires was not something that could wait.

Chapter Twenty-Eight

My fingers coasted across the red and black hilt of my katana, my eyes following the braided, silk wrapping as I caressed it in a ginger manner and recalled the reason I was drawn toward it. When Robin named me Flynn, he had bestowed a metaphor upon my shoulders – a title with the word red within its very definition. As such, to see my color intertwined with black seemed a fitting homage. Death marked my footsteps and hung upon my shoulders as a coat. In a mere five years, I became the devil.

I had to wonder if it was wrong for me to still possess the sword.

I spilled innocent blood to procure it and scoffed at the corpse of its maker. The vampire within held no remorse, yet seeing such a piece of art laid out on my bed stoked the embers of conscience, reminding me the funeral pyre of my humanity had not yet been extinguished. Still, it symbolized how at odds I had become with myself. The sword was a vestige of the vampire, but fate had summoned me to be a guardian of mortals.

"Sometimes, irony royally pisses me off," I murmured to myself.

Standing, I lifted the weapon and slid the blade from its sheath. I admired the gleaming steel before swiping the air a few times and spinning the sword around with a turn of my wrist. Pivoting on my heel, I raised the katana and challenged an invisible foe with it, holding my position as I stared down my adversary. I attempted to imagine who he might be. Timothy? A quick, upward swipe would decapitate him. Rose? Thrusting the blade forward would impale her through the chest. Paul? The bodyguard had never intimidated me. I would run him through before he could as much as blink.

Sabrina?

Indulging in a deep breath, I relaxed my position as I exhaled. The sword lowered slowly to my side and my eyes drifted toward the floor. Head bowed, I recalled when Robin asked me to slay her, and realized how weak and inadequate she made me feel. I could not pledge my hand in assistance for the very reason my dear brother met his end. She knew how to play me like a fiddle. Her eyes would gaze into mine and her grip would tighten around my soul. Without Lydia's talisman to protect me, my humanity would be torn away and she would drown me in darkness. And I would enjoy every moment of it.

"You'll know what to do when the time comes."

I nodded and turned to face Monica, watching her lean against the door frame. She held a cup of coffee in her hands and regarded me in a solemn manner "I am certain you believe this," I said, reaching for the sword's sheath and slipping it over the blade before gently placing the katana back onto the bed. "I pray your faith is strong enough for the both of us."

"It's not my faith that's going to win the battle. You need to have some yourself."

Monica raised the cup to her lips and indulged in a drink. A smile lit her face. "Maybe you can borrow it from somebody who once had a lot of faith in you."

I sighed. My eyes gravitated toward the hilt of my katana again. "Lydia visited my dreams in the past, but has been absent in recent days."

"I'm not sure how the other side works, but I doubt she's given many chances to use the telephone." Monica entered the room, but hesitated a few feet away from me. "I do know one thing about visits from the grave, though. They're done for a specific reason. When you need to hear from her the most, that's when she'll appear."

"Very well." My eyes lifted from the sword to the wall across the room. I drew in a deep breath. "The sun is setting. What does the night have in store?"

Monica sat on the edge of my bed. "Well, while Mathias and his band of merry vamps are just a few hours in the life of a janitor now, I doubt he's the only one trying to make a grab for power." She looked up at me. "I'm sorry I tricked you, by the way."

"No. It is a fortunate thing we were there." My gaze shifted to Monica. "How shall we go about subduing the others?"

Monica paused to reflect. "What happened when Mathias first entered the hospital last night?"

"What do you mean?"

"I mean, did you feel something?"

I perked an eyebrow. "You know I felt something?"

She smirked, drinking from her mug again. "I wouldn't be much of a watcher if I wasn't keeping an eye on you, Peter."

"Granted." I ran my fingers through my hair, and then paused for a moment, searching for the right words. "It was... a disquieting sensation. I knew they meant ill before one of them so much as snarled. The hair on the back of my neck stood on end. I dare say, that had never happened to me prior to last night."

"So, it set off an alarm?"

"Yes." I furrowed my brow. "It was as though an ill wind had descended upon me. I sensed the evil..." I trailed off as the gravity of my words finally impacted. "Monica, I detected it as though it was removed from me."

Her smile widened. I mirrored her grin and laughed despite myself. "Amazing," I said. "That came absolutely out of nowhere."

"Now, the question is..." She placed her coffee cup on the stand beside my bed. Monica rose to her feet and folded her arms across her chest. "Can you do it again, seer?"

My grin turned cunning. "Is this a challenge?"

Monica shrugged. "You could call it that."

"I could and I shall." Plucking the katana from the bed, I tossed it upward and caught it with my other hand. "I do not back down from a challenge. I shall seek them out from the crowd using this newfound sense." I pointed the pommel at Monica, "And I shall send those bastards packing into the hereafter, mark my words."

She chuckled at my enthusiasm. Closing the distance between us, Monica patted my shoulder and smirked. "Let's wait for the sun to finish setting first. Or else, the only one being sent to the hereafter will be you."

"Sage advice." I watched her wink and turn toward the corridor. The corners of my mouth remained curled in a grin. "A pity my gifts cannot assist me with that."

"We work with what we have." Monica paused in the doorway. Her eyes evaluated me while she touched her arms with her gloved hands. "Are you sure you're ready for this?"

My grin broadened. "Do not attempt to dissuade me, Monica. I mean to embrace this destiny."

She chuckled. "Very well, then." Her smile faded. The ironclad barrier around her thoughts lowered for a moment, permitting me a glimpse inside before she erected the wall once more. "I have a couple of things I need to do. We'll set out in an hour or two, okay?"

"Yes, this is fine." I held an even expression until she disappeared down the hallway. Once she was out of sight, though, my grin dissolved and a slight wave of trepidation settled on my demeanor. I nodded, sitting slowly on the bed, and settled the weight of my katana across my knees. "Yes, the Supernatural Order. I am certain they wish to know how black my heart remains."

Gazing at the sword beneath my hands, I forced myself to consider the question. How wicked was I yet? After the previous night's events, I could not deny a chasm of detachment between whom I was and who I had been. The exercises were helping. Being able to save those people opened, and no doubt would continue opening, pathways toward the light. Were those things enough, though, or did they merely tip me toward my human side with the demon yet lying in wait?

The Council, assuredly, had their doubts.

My eyes remained fixed on my sword. It might have been an assassin's tool, but I was as much Flynn as he was me. It simply amounted to who held the keys at any given moment. I subdued his lust for blood. His perspective had been altered and now I embraced that which I once loathed. Would his vehemence ever rise to the surface again, though?

I frowned as I realized I could not give the Order an answer with any degree of certainty. My words would never be enough anyway – from my discussions with Monica, I knew they viewed vampires as precious little more than masters of deceit. If anything, my actions would be the clincher; both in maintaining a hold on my personality and convincing others my motives were pure.

What better way to accomplish this than killing a few miscreants?

Standing, I unsheathed the sword, grasping it in one hand and swinging it around once more. As my eyes closed, I lost myself in its rhythm, feeling what could only be described as the pulse of life. I whipped the steel through the air as though conducting a symphony and opened myself up to the world around me. Breaths and heartbeats. That notion of fighting for an existence, of facing adversity and subduing it. Minutes elapsed as I continued swinging the sword, swept up in the thoughts of nights to come, of opportunity and purpose waiting to be realized. When I stopped, it was with my sword clutched in both hands, poised at-the-ready.

My eyes opened. My smile turned unholy. The time had come for the vampires to fear my blade for an entirely different reason.

⋆◦҉◦⋆

The wind whipped my hair around as my eyes scanned the night sky, searching for stars obscured by the iridescent glow of the city. Beside me stood Monica, who was leaning against the railing of a fire escape. "Yes," she said, responding to a question I had just posed to her. Her gaze remained fixed on the ground below as she sighed. "I should know better than to let my guard down while in the presence of a seer."

I grinned. "Well, you were practically screaming your secrets to me," I said as I waited for something to summon my alarms. "Do tell me, then, what your Council would have you do with me?"

"They're still upset at me, but they'll be glad to hear you're coming around. The next couple of weeks are going to be a little tense. They're trying to figure out what to make of you."

I scoffed and glanced down at Monica. "If abandoning me becomes necessary, I shall understand. Do not continue to hold this obligation if it shall result in disciplinary action being taken against you."

"That's not it." Monica glanced quickly at me, and then looked away again. The wind tossed her hair about, the strands intermingling with her green neck scarf as both sailed behind her. "This has nothing to do with me. The worst thing that could happen is they'd dismiss me and strip away my powers."

"This does not sound like a minor thing."

"It is compared to what I fear the most."

"And what is that?"

"You."

I perked an eyebrow. "I assumed as such, but..."

"You being killed."

Monica's eyes met mine as I gazed down at her. She sighed. "They're not exactly convinced letting you live is a good thing. Given your past, they're trying to decide whether or not they should strike you down now while you're in a 'weakened condition', to use their words. It's a philosophical debate. Kill the monster, or thank the Fates for a reclaimed seer and just embrace his new quirks."

"Fangs, a blood-only diet, and an aversion to sunlight are quirks?" I chuckled and glanced away again. "I do suppose I would take some getting used to. Amongst the lot of them, though, they should have enough protection spells not to fear my presence."

"It's not that, Peter. They don't want you killing..."

"I know what they fear, Monica. I was jesting."

I directed my attention toward Monica again and nodded. "It is a warranted fear and a sage debate. I would not be ready to accept me with open arms either." My smile faded as I paused. Reflexively, my eyes lowered to the ground below. "I am not certain how long I wish to continue existing. My mind is being kept occupied enough for the time being, but the longer I possess a conscience, the harder it shall be to wrestle with myself. If my deeds constitute some form of punishment, so be it."

"That doesn't make you unworthy of mercy."

"I neither deserve, nor request, mercy. I merely ask for the chance to undo what I have done before they demand my ashes." Jumping onto the railing, I crouched and glanced about the alleyways below as something started tickling my senses. "When I have the situation resolved, I shall surrender in chains if they request it. For now, I have a mission to accomplish."

Monica looked first at me, then down toward the city streets. "Is something coming?"

I nodded slowly, eyes scanning the area while a shiver crawled up my spine. The air about me went from pleasant to chilling and the hair on the back of my neck stood on end once more. "Yes," I said in a distant manner, my focus becoming completely preoccupied. "Five of them, though I am not certain from where this notion comes, simply that it is truth."

She raised an eyebrow. "Going in with both guns blazing?"

I smirked and adjusted my coat in an effort to conceal the shoulder holster which held three knives securely against my torso. The katana would be impossible to hide, but I did not feel the need to anyway. Any vampire who knew my name knew how much I favored the sword. Seeing me without one might have proven more suspicious than having it openly displayed. "No, I believe I shall chat with them first. Wait here." Springing from my perch, I fell to the ground below and bent my knees as my feet impacted the asphalt. I straightened to a stand, walked toward an adjacent building and produced a pack of cigarettes. Tapping one out, I lit it and waited for the group to emerge.

They rounded the corner, laughing amongst themselves as I exhaled a plume of smoke. I scanned the group and noticed they numbered seven, not five, which perplexed me until I realized two amongst them possessed pulses. Humans. The five vampires dressed in finer attire, with an air of superiority in the way they held themselves. The two mortals were women dressed in black. Ironically, they noticed me first.

I grinned at one, a brunette wearing a dress with a low neckline. She raised an eyebrow and nudged the side of one male vampire before pointing at me. "Devin," she said, glancing at her companion. "There's some strange guy over there staring at us."

I raised the cigarette to my lips again. Devin, who had been conversing with two of his associates when nudged, turned to face me. The moment our eyes met, he abruptly ceased walking. I could not help but to laugh. "Devin," I said, drawing from the cigarette and exhaling more smoke. "A rather unusual name for one of our kind. Turned recently, if I had to guess?"

Devin swallowed hard, his brown eyes refusing to look away. "Flynn," he said, exhaling my name and punctuating it with a chuckle. "I didn't realize we were in Sabrina's territory. If you want us to go somewhere else, we will."

"Well, in light of recent events, she claims all of Philadelphia as her own. I dare say, there is hardly a stretch of asphalt your shoes could touch which would not offend me, is there not?"

The brunette eyed Devin in an inquisitive manner. "Sabrina?"

"Never mind, Marie." Devin shot her a sideways glance, only averting his eyes from me for mere seconds. The moment they met my gaze again, he grinned. "Please, Flynn, we're merely going about our business, the same as you probably are. We've done nothing to upset you."

"Not yet anyway, which is the only reason you still have your lives." I glanced at the women, then back at Devin. "Dismiss the humans."

Devin laughed. "Flynn, you can't ask us to..."

With my free hand, I brushed back the side of my coat, brandishing the knives concealed underneath. Devin ceased speaking and I grinned after taking a long drag off the cigarette.

He nodded slowly. "Ladies," he said, still staring at me. "If you could please head back to the club? We'll catch up with you later."

Marie looked from me to Devin and back again. I watched her eyes survey me, from wing-tipped shoes to unruly brown hair. Then they settled on my sunglasses. "Devin, who is this?"

"You need not worry about who I am," I said, spreading my mouth in a wide grin which exposed the sharp tips of my fangs. Her eyes widened. I nodded. "Do as he said and flee, or else you shall be made privy to an encounter you shall not soon forget."

Marie took hold of the other mortal's arm, a redheaded woman whose expression read of the same shock her friend's did. They began to pace backward. I growled and allowed my fangs to slip down.

They screamed in unison. Turning around, both ran faster than I had seen a mortal run before, one losing a shoe in the process and not pausing to retrieve it. I laughed and allowed my fangs to slip back into slumber once more. "I grow loathe to conduct the business of immortals in the presence of humans," I said, watching the two women round a corner and disappear. My gaze drifted back to the collective and this time, I stole a moment to assess each of them. One she-vampire and four males, all looked to have been the same mortal age when turned. They were all, undoubtedly, from the same coven and each regarded me with identical measures of fear.

Perhaps reputations were not such a terrible thing after all.

"Anyway," I said, continuing. "You state you have not transgressed the House of Sabrina, but seem surprised you could be inside our territory right now." I flicked my cigarette away. "Why is this, young sire?"

Devin narrowed his eyes. "I'll have you know, I'm a year older than..."

I growled to silence him. "I do not wish to argue your maturity in the ways of immortals, insubordinate." My hand drifted to rest on the hilt of my katana and my tone of voice became sharp. "Now, shall I get nasty with you? Do you wish to lose your head arguing age with me?"

"No," Devin said, shaking his head and stepping back a pace. The remainder of his collective stumbled back as well. "I'm sorry. I meant no disrespect. Please forgive me."

I stepped forward to compensate. "Then answer the fucking question and do not force me to reiterate it. When I have to repeat myself I become very, very cranky."

"I am sorry. I just..." Devin became visibly flustered. He paused for a moment to inhale a steadying breath. The rest stared at us, mute. "I... I, it's... not that I don't know about it, but there are territorial wars and immortals trying to establish minor covens. I mean... We all know that Mistress Sabrina is ruler over all covens, naturally, but this doesn't stop the others from arguing over turf. So, I didn't know if Sabrina had allotted this neighborhood to you."

"And had you half a wit, you would know all Sabrina possesses is mine as well." I paused, perking an eyebrow. "Territorial wars, you say?"

"Yes, Flynn. I don't know the extent of Mistress Sabrina's knowledge, but we are a small group, formerly of David's coven. Jessica, Stephen, Mario, and Thomas are my kindred here, all turned around the same time by different immortals. We were friends as mortals, as well, and only assemble as a pack to feed, not to challenge Sabrina's reign."

"This would explain your involvement with the mortals, then?"

Devin blinked. "Yes, we still feed. We are vampires."

I sighed, exasperated. "I meant that you were not meaning to turn them." Shaking my head, I frowned at Devin. "You shall never be confused for the brightest star in the night sky."

"Oh." Devin scratched the back of his neck. "No, we are far too young to be turning anybody. Anyway, that isn't something one does flippantly."

"And yet, there are those who ignore that." I stepped one pace closer. "Are there not?"

Devin hesitated.

I perked an eyebrow. "Are there not?" My hand closed around the hilt of my sword again as I advanced closer still. My smile turned cunning. "Do tell me, do you know of any who seek to do such a thing? I shall allow you to be made privy to what my mistress does know. We are aware rogue covens seek to unseat her by increasing their progeny. She wishes to know who, young one, so if you wish to keep your heads, you shall tell me."

At first, Devin remained silent. Then he glanced at my sword and frowned. "What they say is true. When one encounters Flynn, one doesn't walk away."

"There is one certain way to find out."

"There are three," said Jessica, speaking up for the first time. I directed my attention toward her quivering form, reading the mind which screamed the three vampires' identities. She spoke them aloud as their faces marched across her thoughts. "Justin, formerly of our house. He has been prowling around University City..."

"Jessica!" Devin hissed.

She ignored him. "A-and on the South side, there are several from William's coven... the leader of that gang is Philip. The final one prowls around the Northeast. I believe her name is Suzanne, but I'm not sure."

"You're signing their death warrants, Jessica," the one named Stephen interjected, scowling.

"Better theirs than ours."

I held up my hand to stop them. "Enough!" Turning my head as if annoyed, I frowned and looked back toward Jessica. "You have done a service to me. I thank you for this information."

Devin sighed. "Are we free to leave?"

"Self-serving you might be, but not a true evil. I shall spare your lives. However..." I stared at them, my gaze severe, allowing whatever power of suggestion I possessed to emanate from my eyes and slither into their minds. "If I catch you so much as seducing a mortal with the intent of harming them, then you shall be punished in kind."

Devin raised an eyebrow. "I don't understand."

"You are a fool, Devin. I do not expect you to understand. All of this time, however, you have been speaking to a seer, and one who would kill his own kind if necessary. I shall show you mercy, but do not misconstrue my mercy for weakness. Now, go and live the remainder of your existence away from my sight or, so help me, the next time we meet, it shall end with your ashes on the ground."

He stared at me for long moments, and then burst into a fit of laughter. Glancing at the others, he then acquired equal measures of brazenness and stupidity in the way he spoke to me. "So, all your talk about Sabrina has been bullshit." He stepped forward, as though to challenge me. "You know, Flynn, I find this hilarious. What they've said about you is true."

I smirked. "And what might that be?"

"That you killed the heads of all the covens, except for Sabrina, and the experience drove you insane. And here, we have the evidence before us." He turned to face his brethren. "A vampire who fancies himself a seer. What a ridiculous bunch of bull..."

Devin started to twist to face me again, but I drew one of my knives and waited. The moment he faced me, he ceased speaking and watched, mouth hung agape, as the blade flew through the air and plunged into his chest. With only enough time to scream, Devin turned to ash and was no more.

The knife hit the cold asphalt. I glanced at the others, an eyebrow upturned. "Does anybody else think me lying?"

Devin's group all turned and ran without as much as a beat between my words and their action. Scattering like their compatriot's ashes in the wind, the four disappeared in mere seconds, something which brought a smile to my face. I relaxed my posture and strolled to where my knife laid. "Was that unwise?" I asked, directing my voice toward the fire escape, knowing Monica could hear me.

She clapped as I plucked my weapon from the ground. Pushing away the side of my coat, I slipped the blade back into its sheath while she spoke. "I think you did very well. Bravo, Master Peter."

Bowing in a sweeping fashion, I then stood straight and walked toward her position. Monica vaulted down the stairs, and then leaped to the street below. I grinned. "What do you think, dear? Am I mad?"

"Stark raving," she said with a wink.

I chuckled. "And no doubt, they shall spread the tale of my madness." Nodding,

I glanced toward the night sky again. "I think this is a rather good thing for us."

Monica blinked, raising an eyebrow. "How do you figure that?"

"Let them think I lost my mind." My eyes met Monica again. "When they face me, they shall know precisely what they are up against. I might have been feared by the others as an assassin, now let them think me a madman." My grin turned devious. "I shall shortly become their worst nightmare."

PART SIX

✧✦✧

THE LAST TEMPTATION

"Lust is to the other passions what the nervous fluid is to life;
it supports them all, lends strength to them all.
Ambition, cruelty, avarice, revenge, are all founded on lust."

Marquis De Sade

CHAPTER TWENTY-NINE

One by one, they fell, victims to my sword.

Over the course of the next five evenings, I orchestrated my assault on the vampire population of Philadelphia. It started with Justin, as he and I had a history and I knew all too well how he conducted himself amongst the mortals. Justin maintained the reputation of being the bloodiest vampire outside Sabrina's coven and the second most of all the covens, period. The prestigious honor of being first belonged to me.

He did not see it coming when I descended on his fledgling coven and killed the entire lot of them – more than a dozen strong. I saved Justin for last and allowed him to stare into my eyes before I ran him through.

"The gaze of a seer," he said. "God help us all."

As he turned to dust, I grinned. "God shall not be of any aid to you bastards." I strolled away from the empty room with an air of satisfaction. As much as my memories burdened me I found respite in the kill, as though I could atone for the wrongs I had committed through my blade. It afforded me the chance to scope the extent of my abilities, even if I suspected I was just barely scratching the surface. With each encounter, I relished the accomplishment and pushed myself further into self-discovery.

Suzanne heard the reports, but still seemed surprised when I appeared and made quick work of her grab for power. I stripped her of her immortality with a slice through her neck before walking away, shaking the dust of nearly two dozen vampires from my shoes.

Philip proved to be a bit more of a challenge.

By that point, reports of the past week had been circulating around, becoming more urgent with each occurrence. Each collective I downed formed a stone on a pond with the ripples expanding outward, forcing the stragglers to assemble and flock to Sabrina's wing for shelter. The pockets of resistance steadily declined and Philip departed from his previous location, taking his fledgling coven into seclusion. While a part of me relished having the lot of them running scared, I realized this also made my task that much more difficult.

Monica and I spent the next three evenings scanning the area, questioning any vampires we managed to locate and casting whatever incantations Monica could utilize for our benefit. Finally, The Fates allowed us to sniff out Philip in the far northwest portion of the city, in an abandoned warehouse seated in a gang-riddled neighborhood. When I showed up, he was not nearly as surprised as the rest.

"Flynn, I have information I will divulge to you if you let me live," he said as I pressed a knife against his throat. Arms wrapped around him, I clutched his back to my chest and felt him shake in a manner which should have brought a sadistic grin to my face. As it was, I could not claim any sort of amusement at the moment. I simply wished the bastard dead.

"What information is this?" I asked, sneering at him.

"First you must promise me you will not kill me."

"Now, you know better than that, Philip, or have you forgotten the order of things? I am the seer. You are the enemy. This dictates where my course of action is headed, does it not?"

"This information is worth sparing me. I promise it."

I hesitated. "Speak. I shall decide whether or not it is."

"Sabrina knows," he said, struggling. My grip tightened. His eyes shut and his body quaked all the more when I pressed the blade harder into his throat, drawing blood. "She knows all about you. That you have deserted her and become a seer."

"Good," I said, leaning close enough to issue a harsh whisper into his ear. "And I sincerely hope she is petrified, because she is next."

"Flynn, there's more. Other immortals..." I pushed him away from me and he turned to face me with hands extended in surrender. Philip stepped backward as I slipped the knife into its sheath. His expression shifted from wary to terrified when my hand settled on the hilt of my katana. A final attempt at bartering for his life spilled from his lips. "No, Flynn... the others. They know about your powers. They..."

Quickly drawing my sword, I advanced on Philip and aimed a swift arc for his neck, ridding him of his head and rendering him to dust. I whipped my blade to the side to flick the blood from its sharp edge and slid it back into its sheath. As my weapon snapped into place, I heard footsteps advancing and turned my head to regard her in my periphery.

Monica frowned, glancing down at the remains of Philip. "What do you suppose he meant by that?"

"I am not certain." My eyes drifted to the ground as well. Monica paused by my side as I mused on Philip's last words. "I did not spare him a moment to read his thoughts and am not apt to trust him."

She nodded. "I'll have to ask the Council if they know anything." Monica drew a deep breath inward and glanced up at me. Her hand rested on my shoulder. "Come on, Peter. It's been a long night. I'll call them tomorrow and see if they'll meet with me then."

"I shall accompany you of course?" We began to stroll away from the warehouse-turned-crypt. I plucked my weapons from the mounds of dust which encompassed Philip's downed compatriots and paused to secure them back into place. I then offered Monica my arm and led us out into the night.

She shook her head as we began a sedate pace down the street. "Not a good idea," she said. "I still don't know if you're safe being seen by them. We've come a long way, though." Monica paused. Her eyes found me again. "When Sabrina's dead, I'm sure they'll be more agreeable. For now, it's best if I spoke for the both of us."

"Very well, then." I nodded, falling silent for the majority of our stroll back to the safe house. All the while, I mused on Philip's warning, wondering what to make of it without knowing the answer would find its way to me in due time.

For Sabrina's eyes scanned Philadelphia that very moment. It would not take long for her to find a watcher; one who would lead her to a seer.

.｡෯ℰ ℐ෯.｡

She glanced over herself before setting out the next evening. I watched, amused, while Monica patted herself down and gestured with her hands. "Okay," she said, exhaling a deep breath. "The Council is expecting me. Protection spells have been cast. Knife is secured. What am I forgetting?"

"To calm down," I said, grinning. "You look as though you are marching off to face an execution squad."

"Feels like it sometimes," she muttered. Monica's eyes met mine before narrowing. "You know, when you were mortal, I bet you were still a pain in the ass." Her lips betrayed her words. A smile tugged at the corners of her mouth. "Try to keep yourself out of trouble while I'm away. No slamming your fist into any more walls or anything."

I placed my hand over my chest. "I cross my silent heart and vow to save any pent up aggression for the vampires."

"Good." Monica winked, and then straightened herself out. She nodded. "Alright, it's time. The Council gets snippy when I keep them waiting."

Shifting in my seat, I watched Monica pass me on her way to the door. "Are you certain a protection spell shall be enough to ensure your safety?"

"It got me into your coven." She fetched her red scarf from the back of the couch and tied it around her neck. "Besides, it's all I have for now. You can't join me. I promise I'll be careful and won't talk to any strangers."

"Especially ones with pale complexions and fangs."

"Yeah, look what happened the last time I did that." Monica offered me a smirk, allowing it to serve as her parting shot before leaving. I merely grinned in response, my gaze fixed on her departure until the door shut behind her. Drawing a deep breath inward – in an attempt to settle a nagging apprehension which had taken root – I convinced myself all would be well with her. I strolled toward my room, plucked a book from one of the tables along the way, and read to occupy my mind.

It did not take long, however, for a disquieting shiver to run up my spine. A chill followed the shiver. Reclining on my bed with Monica's volume open on my lap, I paused, lifting my head and perking an eyebrow over the queer sensation. I glanced around the room in an attempt to discern its cause but nothing in my immediate surroundings had changed. Slowly setting aside the book, I swung my legs such that my feet touched the floor, and as soundlessly as possible, I stood. I crept toward the doorway and took hold of the sword propped against the wall.

Removing it from the sheath, which I threw onto my bed, I poised the sword in both hands. One foot moved in front of the other in quiet, deliberate steps, marking a cautious exit from my sanctuary and into the adjoining corridor. My ears attuned themselves to every sound in the house, my eyes scanning for what might be lurking. At the same time, something seemed to be hindering my abilities, clouding my vampire senses and seer talents. I drew a deep breath inward and exhaled it slowly, realizing I was about to face an unknown force handicapped.

I reached the end of the hallway. Pausing, I studied what I could of the living room from my vantage point, part of it obstructed from view by the wall. I motioned to take a step forward, but stopped and spun around when I heard a noise behind me. This proved to be my undoing. A figure advanced before I could react and a sword plunged into my unprotected back, provoking a scream of pain. My eyes lowered and I beheld, in horror, the tip of a blade protruding from my stomach. I yelled, as much from shock as from pain.

The voice which spoke made it all abundantly clear. "Hello, darling Flynn." The words caressed my ear in her familiar tone of voice, the simple greeting agony enough to rival the physical pain. "Is this where you've been hiding from me?"

My eyes closed. I struggled to maintain my composure. "Hello, Sabrina," I said, my voice shaky. The katana dropped from my hand beyond my own volition. "Fancy meeting you here."

"Stranger coincidences have happened. Of course, we would be assuming our meeting is a coincidence, wouldn't we?" She twisted the blade inside me. My vision swam and another scream lodged in my throat. "Wayward son, it's time to bring you home."

I laughed despite the torment, forcing my eyes to open. "Sabrina, you might as well drive that blade through my chest. I shall not be going anywhere with you."

She smirked. I did not even have to see it to know, I could hear it distinctly in the way she spoke. "Oh, you'll be coming with us, seer, unless you would like your watcher's death to be your final vision before being sent to hell."

Using the sword, she swung me around to face the living room. Sabrina raised a foot to my back and pushed me from the blade, causing me to topple onto the floor. I coughed a few times and instinctively clutched my violated stomach. "You lie," I spat as I motioned to stand.

Sabrina's foot settled on my shoulder and forced me back down. Bending forward, she gathered a fistful of my hair and tilted my head so I had no choice but to look up. "See, Flynn? I am a woman of my word."

I gazed upward and beheld it with my own eyes. Timothy held Monica in his clutches with Paul standing directly beside him. Both of them smirked in a satisfied manner when my face registered a reaction to seeing Monica. She could barely stand. The reason for this became clearly manifest when I saw the bite marks on her neck still weeping blood, her scarf completely removed. Her cheeks pale, I could tell she had already been drained of as much blood as they could without killing her. "Monica!" I called out.

"Don't worry about me, Peter," Monica murmured, fighting to keep her eyes open. "Just stop her. I'll be... fine..."

"Now, isn't that noble?" Sabrina asked. Her breath hit the side of my face as she spoke. "I find it sickening, personally – this martyr complex the humans seem to have. They want to think themselves heroes. But you're not like them... Are you, Flynn?"

I shut my eyes and coughed again, my blood slowly pooling beneath me on the floor. I could feel it, Sabrina's tendrils attempting to wrap around my mind once more, entrancing it with her siren call. Gritting my teeth, I fought against her. "I am no more like you than I am the mortals I defend. There is, however, one apt comparison I can make. Monica is selfless and vigilant. You, on the other hand, are a vile, contemptible bitch."

"The mortals you defend. Listen to that." She laughed, her grip on my hair tightening. "An emasculated vampire, this is what you've become. The Flynn I knew would have sooner met the sun than to act the way you have."

"Then kill me and put me out of my misery."

"No, no, no..." Sabrina kissed the side of my neck, her fangs scratching and provoking a shiver I attempted to mask. She nipped at my ear as she whispered. "We're going to talk first and my assassin is going to return to me. It is this festering humanity inside you I want dead. Not the vampire."

I laughed. "I am not nearly as weak-minded as I was before."

"Then why don't we begin with a little incentive?" She looked up at Timothy. "How much more do you think we can bleed from her, Timothy? Does she have another pint left in her before she withers and dies?"

Timothy grinned, revealing his elongated fangs. "Oh, I think I could get at least another mouthful or two from her, Mistress."

Sabrina leaned close to me again, releasing my hair. "Refuse me and the girl will die and you will be forced to watch. Or... even better..." She chuckled and looked toward Timothy once more. "My dear Timothy, how would you like to turn your first child? I don't think it would take long for me to break through her defenses and force her to beg you for it."

"No!" I shouted, attempting to force myself to my feet again. Sabrina's grip shifted to the back of my neck and proved to be too strong, however. The loss of blood had left me weakened. "If you dare try it..."

"You'll do what?"

I continued struggling, but was forced to give up when my efforts yielded no results. Having nothing to retort, I remained silent.

"Do we turn her, or do you surrender?"

I lifted my eyes to regard Monica again. She forced her eyes open, gazing back at me. I read the fear in her expression, but she shook her head anyway and whispered, "Don't, Peter..."

I could not allow it to happen, though. In an instant, I relived the experience of watching Lydia die by my hand. I saw the countless mortals I sent to their graves with impunity. I stared at the one standing before me, and every fiber of my being screamed against the outrage of her being forced to become a vampire. "Leave her alone," I said, my eyes lowering to the floor. "I shall come with you. Promise me, though, that neither of you shall harm her. This includes an attempt to turn her."

"Oh, you have my word, darling Flynn," Sabrina said as her voice became saturated with seduction once more, "But I won't have to do a thing to harm her when all is said and done. Do you know why?"

I forced my eyes shut and swallowed hard. "Do I have a choice?"

Sabrina touched the side of my face. "Because, my killer, by the time I'm through with you, you will be the one doing it. And I will take great pleasure in watching it happen."

Chapter Thirty

Thrown into a dark room, I could still sense the eye of every member of the coven settle on me when I landed on my knees. My naked gaze remained fixed on the floor, my sunglasses having been removed upon entering the building. I twisted my hands a few times to test the strength of my ties – arms at my sides, wrists bound in front of me – but whatever incantation Sabrina placed on them made the effort useless. I had been brought to a place of trial and there would be no escape.

After indulging a few deep breaths, I looked upward, searching for Monica. Just as soon as I caught sight of her, though, Sabrina stepped between us and took hold of my chin. She turned my head to ensure we stared at each other. "The witch is alive. That is all you need to know. Now, it's time for us to have a chat, darling Flynn."

I tried to look away, but her gaze held me hostage. "A chat with you, Sabrina, is hardly ever a pleasant thing. What do you intend to do to me?" I mustered a smirk. "Tell me what a bad boy I have been?"

She laughed, but I scarcely had the chance to react before she slapped me across the cheek. The impact threw my head to the side. I groaned and Sabrina roughly turned my face to force my eyes toward hers again. "Oh, you've been a *very* bad boy, Flynn, and you know it. You've become enchanted with the mortals and abandoned your mistress and lover. Such acts of treason should call for your death."

"You are not my lover, Sabrina. And, I dare say, I rebuke your leadership over me. I had a love once, a pure one you tricked me into murdering. I know no other love than hers."

Sabrina bared fangs. I could sense the first wave of assaults upon my will as the growl she emitted threw suggestions in my brain. I blocked them as best as possible, but they still stuck long enough to begin a loop of hypnotism. '*Obey,*' they told me. '*Give in to your base desires. Lust. Rage. Hate. See in these fangs a mirror image of your true nature and fight against it no longer.*' I sneered, but made the mistake of making eye contact with Sabrina again. "You shall need to do better than that amateur spell casting," I muttered. "My will is stronger than it was before."

"Oh, you think it is, because you're infected with this sense of self-righteousness." She grinned, still flashing her pointed teeth at me. I found myself needing to look away, lest mine descend as well. "You killed the upstarts. My enemies, by the way, and I thank you for that service, dark son." She leaned in closer. Her lips hovered above my ear, her voice descending to a sultry whisper. "My assassin is ensuring my power struggle is a success by slaughtering the competition."

"An act of judgment, nothing more." I shut my eyes. "I am not your assassin any longer, loathsome bitch."

Sabrina threw me onto my back. Standing, she gazed down at me as I opened my eyes again. "That doesn't change what you've done and how well you've done it. Over the course of your two week pity party, the casualties you've amassed have only helped me rein in the rogues. The people gathered around you are now aligned under my name, with countless others throughout the city. They fear me and they fear you. Why fight the power when it is there for the taking?"

"Because I no longer seek your power."

"I don't believe it. I believe somewhere deep down inside, you enjoy the power." Sabrina paced around me. At once, the room began to spin and my eyes had trouble tracking her. "Come now, Flynn, be honest with the one who has been your mistress for five years. The one who gave you the immortal gift. Every time you've plunged the blade into a vampire, either as an assassin or a seer, you have *reveled* in it. The sensation of killing. The satisfaction of sating your lust for blood. Surely you realize the monster you truly are."

I shut my eyes once more. My hold upon the mental ledge I dangled from became precarious. I could feel my grip weakening, my footing starting to slip. I fought harder against it. "You would have me believe I am yet a monster only for your gain."

"For *our* gain. I have seen it in your eyes, Flynn. I saw it when you killed Matthew and tore through the other elders. You bathed in their ashes and delighted in it."

"As I shall delight in your ashes when they descend to my feet."

"Now, you don't really want that, do you?" I heard the sound of footsteps and a blade sliding from its sheath. I refused to look, though, lest Sabrina meet my gaze again. "Search your heart of hearts. You have the knowledge and the ability to slay me and yet, you have butchered the tail instead of severing the head. Two weeks, Flynn, and you have not darkened my doorstep. Why is that?"

I winced. She had exposed my weakness too quickly. "Because I wished my work to be complete when you met your end."

Sabrina laughed, her voice growing closer. I heard something whip through the air and could only guess this to being the blade she now held. The sound of its strokes sounded overly familiar, though. "Do not con a con artist, dark killer. I've heard many reports. Those you spared for information told me you still called me your mistress. In a convincing manner, no less."

"I was acting."

"You were always a terrible liar, Flynn."

The swinging sounds stopped abruptly. There was a pause before a piercing pain racked me from head to toe, finding its genesis in my stomach. I cried out in pain and opened my eyes to see my katana protruding from me, pinning me to the ground.

Sabrina smiled as she continued holding onto it. "My, this sword does suit you, doesn't it? A clean cut. Very strong and steady." She pulled the blade from inside me and flicked my blood from its edge. I moaned. "I imagine this injury is making you hungry. Care for a bite?"

"Fuck you." I winced.

Sabrina raised the sword and brought it crashing down again. This time, it buried itself into my shoulder and forced wails of agony from my mouth once more. She laughed with relish. "Oh, now we've descended into hurling obscenities? My, that *is* the old Flynn." Ripping the blade from me, she tsked. I shut my eyes against the excruciating pain assailing me. "Come now, vampire. Feed and be healed. You're losing blood. I can tell from your pallor you haven't been taking care of yourself."

"I require nothing," I spat. "Save but for you to burn in hell."

Once more, Sabrina brought the sword plunging down toward me. Its tip buried into the ground beside me, with the blade cutting into my neck, but in a superficial manner. Still, I felt the pain and knew the wound to be weeping blood. No, she did not mean to kill me. She meant to bleed me until I became too thirsty to hold back. I had to stop her. "Is this the best you have?" I asked, forcing out a laugh.

Sabrina leaped on top of me. Again, I made the grievous error of looking her in the eyes. She held a knife, with it hovering above my cheek. "Silly, silly vampire," she said. Pressing the edge into my skin, she drug it downward slowly, tracing a line which sent sparks of electricity up my spine. I groaned, uncertain of whether I should be writhing in pain or entranced with pleasure. She laughed as she watched my reaction. "You should know my bag of tricks runs deep by now, Flynn." The blade lifted. She leaned close. Her breath hit the side of my face. "Into pits yet unexplored."

Her lips touched my neck. She licked the blood which trickled from the wound. I shivered, and then yelled again when she plunged her fangs into my throat and imbibed a deep, lusty drink. It became more than I could stand. My fangs descended and I hissed.

She paused her drinking, but did not lift her head. "Fight it no longer, Flynn. Those daggers emerged to feed. You remember that, right?" When she licked the wounds closed, I felt the points of her teeth rake a path gently up toward my jaw. A tantalizing sensation, it jarred my already precarious footing. She was right. I only became hungrier with my fangs exposed and the thirst mounted the longer they remained down. "The base things," she continued. "The pleasures. You remember how good it feels when blood coats your tongue, warm and with the pulse of your prey still resonating in your ears? My Flynn remembers how these things brought him pleasure."

Attempting to retract my fangs proved useless. "The pleasure is passing. The evil remains." My words as much to myself as to Sabrina, I spoke them with as much conviction as I could. "Your evil remains, and I cannot suffer it."

"Oh, but you can, Flynn. You can." Sabrina's trek up the side of my face paused when she thrust her body against mine and taunted my lips with hers. When she began to kiss me, her fangs cut into my bottom lip and brought the taste of my blood onto my tongue. I kept trying to fight, to pull away, but she persisted and I found myself enjoying the crimson dripping into my mouth far too much. That illicit thing I had to avoid as much as possible. The single greatest weakness a vampire could harbor. I wanted more. God, I knew I should not, but I did anyway.

"No, Peter! Fight it!"

I heard Monica's words as though they drifted down a tunnel and opened my eyes. Sabrina pulled away, though, only to laugh. "How precious," she said as she straddled me. I watched her bite into her own wrist. "She uses your mortal name as if that is what you really are. But you and I know better than that, don't we? You are no mortal. You are a killer. You are no seer; you are the devil himself in vampire form. Flynn the assassin, ready to stand with his mistress at last."

Her wrist hovered over my face, dripping blood into my mouth. I could bear it no longer. I imbibed the droplets in a lusty manner, bathing my tongue in her crimson offering. Sabrina pressed her wrist against my mouth and I drew hard from it, becoming immersed in desire, wishing to become one with it again.

I opened my eyes. A wicked laugh rose from my throat. Sabrina pulled her wrist away and mirrored my grin. "Sweet crimson," I said. "Sweet Sabrina. Save your devil from this undoing."

"There is only one thing which can save you from her wiles."

"Speak it," I said, my head swimming. I locked eyes with Sabrina and this time, did not fight against her powers of suggestion as they crashed into me again. My eyes wavered only once, to see the pendant dangling from her neck. Then, they returned to meet her gaze. "It shall be done as you say."

Sabrina touched my chin and turned my head so I could regard Monica. Monica looked back at me, fear latent in her eyes. "Do you see that vile thing, Flynn?" Sabrina asked.

"I do. Her veins run thin, but blood yet courses through them."

"Yes, blood does indeed. Mouthfuls of it. Merely drinking her blood will not free you of her curse, though, for her spirit will haunt you much the same as the other woman has." Sabrina leaned close, licking my neck again before whispering in my ear. "Make her one of us, dark son. I give this gift to you. You will turn her as the first of many and father your own coven."

Monica motioned to scream, but was cut off by Timothy. He cupped his hand over her mouth and pulled her close against his body. I grinned, fangs still exposed. "You would have me turn her?" I asked, my eyes dancing with excitement.

"I would relish it," she said, pressing her cheek against mine as we both regarded Monica. "I would watch it and revisit it in my most pleasant dreams as we conquer the city. As we make them all our servants and take from the Supernatural Order all of their kind, to either feed upon or to turn. Would you not relish it as well, my assassin?"

I grinned. "Yes. All of their fucking kind, from this city to the next."

"Bastards, all."

"Yes, bastards." I looked back at Sabrina as she lifted her head. "Only, I wish to be the one to turn their kind, so they might look into my green eyes and see their own power being used against them. That they might be put into submission by me as they once sought to make me submit."

"I think it only fitting." Sabrina kissed me once more. I drank deeply from the embrace, savoring every taste of her wickedness. Her hand drifted down my chest and pulled at the fabric of my shirt in a tantalizing manner. She sat up, then forced me to my knees, pressing her breasts against me and brushing her fingers across my cheek. I leaned close, kissing her neck and nipping at her skin, but then allowed my eyes to gravitate toward Monica. I scowled. "Let me have the human," I said. "I wish to do your bidding now."

"Very well, my dear." Sabrina stood, plucking her dagger from the ground where she had left it. She walked around me, bending forward to cut my ties and stood straight once the task was completed. My arms fell free. I glanced at her as she continued speaking. "Do not allow her heart to stop before you force your wrist at her. Just draw from her once or twice and allow her to drink from you. She will stop when the change has taken hold and be lulled into sleep."

"Very well." My eyes remained fixed on Monica; my scowl turned even more menacing. I barely paid Sabrina any mind as she handed me her knife and stepped back to observe. Instead my gaze turned obsessive while I came to a stand. Monica swallowed hard as I approached. I stole a few moments to ensure she could read nothing but malicious intent as we regarded each other. So convinced was Monica, she clenched her eyes shut to avoid looking at me.

My grin turned more sinister. "Good," I said. "You see you have misplaced your faith in me, you reckless imp. I have spent nights thinking of stripping you and laying you bare before me and now, there is nothing you can do to stop me. I shall have you however and whenever I would like. And you shall please me, or you shall die."

A sob racked Monica. I watched her chest rise and fall with anxious breaths. Timothy stepped away once I took hold of her and I licked my lips while staring at her pulse point. Slowly, teasingly my hand slid across her shoulders. Then I wrapped my arm around her and pulled her against me so hard that had I been aroused, she would have sworn I meant to penetrate her. She yelped and I laughed. "Come now, witch, and embrace eternity with me."

Monica jumped when I pressed the knife against her neck. Dragging it downward, I formed a superficial cut which immediately wept crimson rivulets like tears streaming from a fractured soul. She flinched as I pulled the knife away and the pause which followed contained the entirety of her human existence.

Hesitating no further, I plunged my teeth into her neck and took the first drink of pure, live blood I had savored in two weeks.

CHAPTER THIRTY-ONE

Within the deepest portions of my soul, the memory of Lydia gazing at me after the first time we made love is still crystal clear. I had said her eyes could break the deepest spell and, in return, her facial expression turned solemn. "There are very deep spells in this world, Peter," she said. "Are you sure mine can do that?"

"I guarantee it." I had spoken the words in a half-teasing manner that sought to instill some measure of my feelings for her. As much as I had enjoyed our coupling for carnal reasons, I knew she had also claimed part of my heart. I truly believed I would always be safe so long as I could reach out and touch her. Even when I knew she and I would not enjoy a happy ending.

A part of my being wanted to believe in her. Prayed I could.

"Then remember my eyes for me," she had said as she rested her head on my chest. "Because I'm afraid there's a lot of darkness waiting for you. You have gifts, and the power-hungry always seek to take advantage of people like you because of it."

The grip of the hungry, seeking to make my power their own. How enslaved I had been to such a spell for five years of immortality. I had been its willing thrall, serving its will rather than exploring my true nature. Truthfully, I enjoyed it. Sabrina had taught me to find euphoria in doing its evil bidding. Then a peculiar thing happened to this creature.

He stepped into his birthright and claimed it for his own. Not for the Supernatural Order. Not for his Mistress, for she was that very darkness his former lover had warned him about. No, he did it for himself and found that while the years of bloodshed had stained his hands, he could yet find solace in the light. The satisfaction of being a seer far eclipsed the decadence of being that demon assassin, and for two blessed weeks he touched his humanity once again.

The evil was returning, though. Bent to drag his soul into the depths.

Sabrina used my weakness to spin me dizzy and forced me to wrestle against my black heart once more. She had almost won, but then I saw the pendant dangling from her throat and found the will to subdue the demon. I distantly recalled when she took it, the last time she had steered me away from the path I was walking so I could do her bidding. I felt the loss of my brother Robin anew; stared at Monica and, though I scowled in the most villainous way possible, saw the chance to turn away before I lost control.

In the end, the joke fell on Sabrina. She freed my tethers and set a seer loose in her house.

When I rose to my feet, my head swam and the first steps I took were extremely precarious. Sabrina had sought to incite bloodlust within me, to make the desire to feed on Monica so palpable I could not withstand it. She slashed me to ribbons. She teased me with her blood. And while feeding on Sabrina revitalized me enough to stand, I needed more if I was to fight. I hated doing it, knowing she had already been bled, but Monica remained the only mortal in my presence and with two dozen vampires watching my actions, I had to convince them all the assassin had returned.

Monica trembled beneath my grip, but just before my teeth sank into her neck, I sent a thought to her.

'*Trust me, Monica. I know what I am doing. Just play along.*'

She leaped when my fangs penetrated skin. My eyes shut as I felt her blood trickle down my throat. '*Just a couple of sips,*' I reminded myself, '*Enough to get my head on straight again.*' I drank slowly, forcing my fangs to retract while my lips remained pursed against her neck. I would have to move swiftly to make this work.

With a quick, downward swipe of the knife, I cut Monica's ropes and threw her down onto the floor. I spun around and plunged the weapon deep into Timothy's chest, but did not wait for him to turn to dust before pivoting and hurtling the blade at Paul. Leaping over Monica, I slid onto the floor and plucked the knife from Paul's remains as soon as he disintegrated into ash. My eyes shot back to Monica, the spring which brought me to my feet deceptively fluid. "Get away from here as fast as you can," I said.

Monica crawled away. My gaze shifted to Sabrina. A smirk curled the corner of my mouth as I lifted my empty hand to wipe Monica's blood from my chin. "Do not con a con artist. Right, Mistress?"

She narrowed her eyes at me. "Bastard." Her fangs descended again and her face contorted in a sneer. "The humans have bewitched you beyond the point of reform."

"I honestly wish that were true. Your magic is no longer sufficient to bridle me, however." My grip around the knife's hilt tightened. "So, what shall you do with me now?"

Sabrina plucked my sword from the floor and swung it around. In the five years I lived under her roof, I never fancied her as much of a swordswoman, but she handled the weapon more adeptly than Robin ever had. "We kill mortals and their vermin in my house, recalcitrant vampire," she said, stalking forward. "If you do not stand with me, then you die by the tip of your own blade."

I stepped to the side, flashing a quick glance at the vampires standing around before focusing my attention on Sabrina. She followed my movements, her eyes searching me as though to predict my first action. I grinned. "You think I fear death," I said. "Quite to the contrary. I know I have my reckoning coming to me. If you are the one to send me into the afterlife, then so be it. I shall not die, though, without ensuring you meet your end as well."

In my periphery, I spied one of the other vampires advancing. Spinning around, I plunged my knife into their chest before quickly turning back to face Sabrina again. "Your children all seem to have a death wish."

"He's mine, you idiots," Sabrina called out to the others.

As Sabrina glanced away, I averted my eyes, peering across her shoulder toward the back of the room. There, I saw a familiar door, and within the span of seconds surmised that if I could buy myself enough time to make it the weapons room, my confidence would be backed by more than bravado. '*Just need a bloody sword.*' I frowned. Shifting my eyes back to Sabrina, I pivoted and flicked my wrist. The knife in my grip sailed toward her chest. I knew she would deflect it, but the distraction served its purpose. I ran and Sabrina lost her footing in the effort to avoid my blade as I ran for the door.

She tumbled to the ground and the rest of the gathered throng froze, uncertain of what to do. Their inaction afforded me enough time to kick open the door to the weapons room and dash for the wall. "Get him!" I heard from the other side, but by the time the others roused from their stupor, I made it to my destination. With one hand, I fetched a short sword. With the other, I took hold of a katana. As I held both, I flicked their sheathes away and ran for the common area again.

Two challengers waited for me on the other side of the threshold. I struck them down with little effort. The others retreated and I grinned at Sabrina as she stood and narrowed her eyes at me. "Oh no you don't, little boy," she said.

I raised the short sword and smirked. "A pity I never knew you could handle a weapon before. Our nights together might have been much more spirited."

"I lived in the Orient before you were a glimmer in your mother's eye, traitor." She growled. Placing one foot in front of the other in a studied manner, she stalked forward while I reciprocated. Slowly, but surely, the gap between us began to close.

I chuckled. "Had Robin do your bidding, then? My, but having him as my mentor backfired in your face, did it not?"

"The only satisfaction I have is that you finally rid me of that Irish derelict."

"Yes, I imagine so." My grin faded, given over to a serious expression. We began to sidestep once within striking distance of one another, but neither of us motioned to claim the first blow. Rather, we seemed to be feeling each other out. "You are rather good at allowing others to soil their hands to do your bidding. Lydia... Robin... Those countless immortals from the other covens I assassinated..."

"A pity you cannot end yourself." Sabrina whipped the katana in a trained blow; swiftly enough that it set me back as I used my short sword to block. I retaliated once she retreated, but she reacted just as fast, swinging for me again, determined to score a strike. Strands of Sabrina's hair flew from the tight bun she wore it in and her fangs remained elongated while her eyes blazed fury. I matched her mettle, but she was in far better condition.

I decided to even the score.

I swung the katana while thrusting the short sword forward. Sabrina twisted away and raised her sword to intercept the blow. I readied the short sword again before she had a chance to recover. It sliced across her chest, cutting through her shirt and gashing across her breasts. Sabrina stepped back a few paces and freed one hand to touch the bleeding wound, scowling. "You will pay for that."

My smirk turned devious. "Then come and collect."

Sabrina lifted the sword with a hiss and brought it crashing down. Her impatience cost her, though, as I caught her blade with the katana in my hand and I plunged the short sword into her stomach. I laughed as she doubled over and pushed her off, watching her fall onto the floor. "You call that a collection?" I raised the katana, eyes lowering to her neck. "Allow me to properly demonstrate a collection, dear Sabrina."

"Rose!" Sabrina yelled. "The lights!"

The lights? Oh fuck. I could instantly hear Robin's voice chastising me for failing to keep my infirmity in mind. The world afforded me one mocking second with which to line Rose in my sights. It was just enough time to see her grin and flick a switch that immediately filled the room with bright, blinding light. I screamed as an unholy amount of pain lacerated my corneas. The short sword dropped from my hand as I tried desperately to cover my eyes, to little effect. I fell to the ground, writhing in agony. "Damn it to fucking hell," I muttered, still clutching the katana, but now lacking the ability to use it.

I heard Sabrina come to her feet. The sound of a blade cutting air closed in on me and I at least had the presence of mind to raise my sword to intersect the easily anticipated strike at my neck. I could not see to where she retreated, however. I did not know her position or how she would next attack. I was left a sitting duck.

'Peter!'

I rolled away and attempted to stand, my eyes still clenched shut. Sabrina kicked me in the jaw, and I toppled back down onto the ground.

'Peter!! Listen to me, damn it. Remember the sight. My finger's pointing at Sabrina, but my eyes are fixed on her. Which of the two's going to help you right now?'

I furrowed my brow, realizing the voice in my mind belonged to Monica. The lesson; she was attempting to remind me of the lesson, and suddenly I realized I had another weapon at my disposal. "Sabrina," I said, realizing I needed to stall. "Tell me, before you cut me down in my weakened state, what it would have been like had I surrendered to you." I began to feel for Monica, honing in on her thoughts which screamed at me as if attempting to be heard over a multitude. "Would everything have happened as you have said, or was I being played like a fiddle to the end?"

Sabrina stepped forward one pace as I locked onto Monica. At once, the room exploded with detail. I saw the faces of everyone watching, each gaze beholding me, waiting for the demise of Flynn. They all knew better than to move, which would have made me smile if it would not have revealed my ruse to Sabrina. A coven of slothful, decadent vampires and Rose remained the only one apt to lend a hand. It suddenly made sense to me, why my maker kept the masses lounging about, complacent and sated. They were easily ruled.

Rose strolled closer to where Sabrina stood, undoubtedly to secure a front row seat. I spied her through Monica's eyes, but kept my attention on Sabrina. She stood in front of me, holding my katana as though it had been meant for her. Like the pendant around her neck. Like the man lying before her. Everything she possessed, stolen from something or somebody else. I rolled onto my back, preparing to steal from her in return.

The sword laid by my side. My hand tightened around its hilt.

Sabrina walked two more paces forward, staring up the length of my body from her position beyond my feet. "Flynn, you should know by now how it works," she said with a smile. "I live only to serve myself. Oh yes, we would have enjoyed many bloody years together. You would have savored the affair and I would have reveled in the covens you destroyed. Once I had what I desired, though, I would have killed you in your sleep."

I laughed. "The coward's way out. My life has always been forfeit."

Sabrina raised her sword, but paused. "A pity you have to die now. You finally figured it out."

She grimaced and motioned to administer the death blow. I waited, ready, and rolled to the side at the last moment. Raising my foot as the blade slashed by harmlessly, my kick caught her in the chest. Unprepared, she flew backward. The katana fell from her hand and Rose rushed for it, but I came to my knees and plunged my sword into Rose's chest.

Rose stopped. I smirked. "Goodbye, sweet Rose," I said, releasing my grip on the sword to snatch my katana from the ground at long last. I came to my feet just as Rose's dust descended to the floor. Clutching the red and black hilt of my weapon, I focused on Sabrina, knowing it had to end now.

Sabrina realized it as well. She came to her knees and, in a blur, plucked the other sword from Rose's ashes. I raised my katana and aimed for her neck.

She thrust. I swung. I felt cold steel run through my chest as the sharpened edge of my weapon severed Sabrina's head from her body. Pain sharper than any I had experienced before overwhelmed me and I crumpled onto the ground, losing consciousness. Somewhere in the haze of white light, the room faded from view.

Just as surely as I had died to be reborn a vampire, I began to suspect my second death had come to embrace me. But rather than facing the demons, an angel greeted me instead.

Chapter Thirty-Two

The next sensation I became aware of was both comforting and confusing at once. A hand brushed the side of my face and a voice spoke softly. "Peter, how long are you going to avoid looking at me?"

My eyes snapped open. A strange feeling washed over me, heightening a sense of tranquility and giving it more depth. The room surrounding me contained no form, much like the white room in the dreams where I had seen Lydia. The ground beneath me was flat, and I could make out nothing in the way of walls from where I laid. I sat up, aware of a woman crouched beside me, but noticed several strange points of interest first.

I touched my mouth and failed to feel the points of my fangs. My finger slid across the top row of my teeth and when I discovered them reverted to their duller state, my eyes widened. My senses were normal, not as sharp as they had been no more than a few moments ago. My lungs filled and a laugh of wonder floated past my lips. I was human once more.

I turned my head to regard the woman. Lydia. Her face brightened when we made eye contact and I could not help but mirror her grin. Lydia threw her arms around me and I wrapped her tight in mine. "Oh Peter," she said. "My heart's broken so many times for you."

Clutching her against me, I shut my eyes. My fingers threaded through her hair and I could not help but to be lost in wonder. "Lydia," I said, laughing once more. I pulled away to look at her, cupping her face in my hands. "Is it truly you?"

She nodded, tears dancing in her eyes as she laughed. "It's me." One tear escaped her eyes and ran down her cheek. She reached up to swipe it away, and then rested her hand atop one of mine. "It's really me."

"Oh, thank heavens." Without waiting for permission, I pulled her close and kissed her in a deep, lingering manner, allowing myself to get wrapped up in the moment. Our lips touched a few times before Lydia broke away and chuckled. I grinned, resting my forehead against hers. "This has been one long, horrible nightmare I have been stuck living."

"I wish it was." She sniffled. Her eyes opened to regard me. "I'd like very much to tell you that it's all been a dream, but I'd only be lying to you."

I nodded, pulling her close once more. "I am sorry I doubted you when you tried to warn me. I wish I could go back in time and force myself to believe you, but I cannot." My fingers combed through her hair, and I drew a deep breath inward. "How in the heavens do you wish to be close to me right now after all of the things I have done?"

"What matters is that you believe now." She pulled away from me again. "I'm just glad to be able to see you. Even if it's only for a short visit."

A glassy haze obstructed my line of sight as my eyes met hers. "My sins are too great for me to linger with you in heaven. It might have been the monster, but I was a participant nonetheless." I sighed. "I understand and had expected as such."

A smile broke out on Lydia's face. "No, Peter," she said, visibly holding back a laugh. "You're not dead. Well, not dead again, anyway."

I blinked. "How did I survive? I could have sworn Sabrina..."

"Got you through the chest?" Lydia nodded. "But not through your heart, so you are pretty badly hurt. You're just resting at the moment and I needed to talk to you." Her grin turned coy. "Now that you'll actually listen to me again."

I nodded. A frown tugged at the corners of my mouth as I looked away. "I had hoped it to be over, to be perfectly honest." My eyelids drifted shut. "God, I would have preferred eternal damnation to waking as a vampire again, if there is such a thing as hell."

Lydia touched my cheek, forcing my eyes open again. "You're right about having a lot to make up for, and your job isn't finished. If I could, I'd sneak you off with me, but I don't have a say in the matter. You have other places to go. Other challenges to face. A long road ahead of you."

"A long road wrestling with the demon."

She nodded. "I'm sorry, but it's true." Pausing, she considered me for a moment. The look in her eyes turned deliberate. "You have to listen to me, though. There're a lot of things waiting for you. I've brought you this far, but I can't help you with what lies ahead of you. You'll need to rely on Monica and your wits to carry you the rest of the way." I detected a hint of sadness in the way she regarded me. "I wish I'd been there to see you through it."

"You have, Lydia." My grin broadened. "Far more than you realize."

She smiled. "Then my work here is done."

Nodding, I raised a hand to touch her hair one final time before dropping my arm back to my side. "When shall I see you again?" I asked.

"Not until you reach the other side."

I drew a deep breath inward. "Then let your lips be the last which call me Peter. Flynn has much to atone for and such shall be his task now, until my days on Earth are finished."

Lydia sighed. "I don't envy your position, but I admire your strength." She leaned forward and a soft kiss touched my forehead. "I wish you blessings on your journey, Peter, as well as the hope that you can endure the challenges you'll have to face. I can't tell you more than what I've already said, but don't count 'Peter' out just yet." She nodded. "I'm leaving you to Monica's care now. Take care of yourself, okay?"

"I shall do my best." My eyes shut as I pressed my lips to hers again, allowing the moment to linger as many seconds as The Fates would allow until the world around me shifted. I felt myself being swept away as though a leaf upon the wind.

Without further warning, consciousness returned to claim my immortal form.

◦◦◦◦◦

Pain. The first thing I became aware of the moment lucidity began trickling toward me again. Darkness was the second thing I noticed. The lights in the room had been turned off once more.

I grimaced despite myself. "Bloody broken body," I murmured. "Put me out of my misery, Monica. I am no use to you anymore."

She chuckled, but it sounded weak, as though she could manage nothing more than that. "We're both a mess," she said. "You've been stabbed so many times, I've lost count, and I've been bitten twice. *And* I just had to shoo away a bunch of vampires thinking I was fair game."

"How did you manage that?" Opening my eyes, I verified I was still resting on the floor of the common area, where I had fallen. I touched my chest and winced. The slowly-healing wound yet seeped blood. Sabrina had missed my heart only by a hair's breadth.

Monica stumbled over to me and sat where I could see her. I had no desire to attempt standing, so I remained flat on my back. "I have a few tricks up my sleeve," she said as she moved my hand away. I watched her study my wounds. "Have I ever told you that you're a lucky son of a bitch? Because you are, Peter."

I frowned. "Please let that be the last time you call me that."

Monica raised an eyebrow. Her eyes lifted to meet mine. "The last time I call you a lucky son of a bitch?"

"No. Peter." I closed my eyes and sighed. "He yet resides within me, but so long as I possess this body, I shall always be Flynn. And I shall always have too many things to atone for before I reach the other side."

"You can't atone for it."

I opened my eyes to regard Monica. At first, she looked away, but then her gaze shifted back to me as she continued. "That's the harsh reality of all this. You can't look at this as atoning. It's what you were born to do."

"Regardless, I shall petition for redemption until I exist no longer."

"Fair enough, I guess." Monica frowned. "You had me worried for a minute there, you know. I didn't think you were acting."

"I wish I could say it was all an act, but then I would be lying." I finally motioned to sit. The effort laborious, I felt overwhelmed with dizziness and hunger at first, but managed to suppress both in favor of looking toward Monica again. "There is much work to be done. This much I know. Lydia visited me for what she said will be the final time and informed me there are trials which lie ahead. Perhaps, if I make it through, The Fates can at least rend me in half and have mercy on Peter. Until then, it would appear you are stuck with this conscience-laden immortal, watcher."

"Have a little faith. Like you said, we have a lot of work left to do." Monica nodded. "I understand, though. Even if calling you Flynn all the time'll take some getting used to."

I smiled wanly, as did Monica. She reached forward, patting my shoulder. "For what it's worth," she said, "At least you beat Sabrina. That's a very good start, Flynn."

I nodded, furrowing my brow as a strange thought entered my mind. "Monica, how was Sabrina able to get her hands on you in the first place?" I asked. "I thought you cast a protection spell."

Monica's smile turned timid. "I lied."

"You..." I shook my head. "What do you mean you lied?"

"I mean exactly what I said. I let myself get captured, so you'd finally have to confront Sabrina. The Council wouldn't have been able to tell us shit. They told me the next time they saw me I'd have a lot of explaining to do, so I wasn't going to count on them to help us. This was the only resolution I could think of."

I blinked. "Monica, how could you do something so bloody quixotic? You nearly met your end because of it."

Monica patted one of my hands, while struggling to a stand. "I had faith in you." She took her first precarious step forward, and then motioned for me to follow. I rose to my feet as well, collecting my katana and Lydia's pendant before making my way to the back exit with her. "I knew the seer would win out in the end. Even if he scared the shit out of his watcher."

"Do not ever do that again, or I swear I shall strangle you myself." She laughed and we walked, side by side, out of the coven of my rebirth for what I assumed would be the last time. I had no desire to return and finish the others; they might have been lazy and decadent, but they were not evil. No doubt there might be a day I would face the unruly ones, I thought to myself, but I had a lot to recover from and many lessons left to learn before then.

After all, I had a prize in my sights. Pleasing the Fates enough to merit some way free from the curse of being a vampire, or earning my rest somehow. I wanted it so much I could taste it.

And I felt it worth all the pleading in the world.

"There is no person so severely punished, as those who subject themselves to the whip of their own remorse."

Seneca

EPILOGUE

"So, you have finally come to speak to us about this vampire named Flynn," the man said from his position on the other side of the room. The area itself the sanctuary of an old church, it came replete with seven chairs poised where the altar used to be. Six elders from the Supernatural Order occupied seats. One chair remained empty, as it had for five years.

I was absent from the meeting, situated on the other side of the stained glass windows. Using Monica's eyes to witness the events, I filled in the remaining details with my ears and smoked a cigarette in an effort to mask my apprehension.

Monica regarded each elder and inhaled deeply. "Yes, I have, Richard," she said to the man with salt and pepper hair who had addressed her. Her voice cracked, though she recovered quickly and worked to regain her confidence. I could envision her, however. Shuffling her feet. Looking down at the floor before lifting her gaze to regard her superiors. "I know I've angered the Council with my actions as of late, but I have news I hope will justify my actions."

"Speak the news," said a female seated a few chairs down.

Monica directed her attention toward her. "The vampire covens of this city have been quieted by Flynn. He's realized his position as a seer and put out several fires they started. One of the vampires he killed was his maker. It was difficult for him to accomplish, but the fact that he was able to do it shows how far he's come."

"What of Peter Dawes?" the woman asked in response. "Why does the seer continue to use his other name?"

"Because he feels the need to. It's a complicated issue, Joan, but I promise the Council the Flynn they've known has been suppressed."

"Suppressed?"

Monica sighed. "So long as I'm his watcher and he's under my guidance, I'll do what I can to ensure his conscience remains steady. He's already come a long way toward holding his instincts at bay for good."

"But he's not at that stage yet?"

"He's still a vampire and a fledgling seer. That makes his condition unsteady, but given the time, he'd..."

"So he might strike at humans again?" asked another elder, seated closer to Richard. A blond-haired man. He raised an eyebrow at her.

Monica held up her hand. "Please, Lewis, I ask the Council to give him a chance. Any of us have the potential to become wicked. Granted, I know, in Flynn's case, it's much more volatile, but he wants to learn more about being a seer. He's been an attentive student and faced all the unique challenges of what he is with determination. His dependency on blood has diminished. He doesn't feed on live hosts and I..."

"Show us your neck, then."

Monica turned to look at the only other female, a brunette. "I beg your pardon, Beverly?"

Beverly leaned forward in her seat. "I asked you to remove your scarf and show us your neck."

Monica hesitated. "I don't see why this is relevant."

"Now, Miss Alexander." Beverly lifted an eyebrow.

"Alrighty then." Monica sighed and untied the scarf. Her eyes were downcast when she removed it altogether, revealing the scars on her neck.

A hush settled across the room. Beverly shifted in her seat and pointed. "Please explain this injury," she said, in a sharp tone of voice.

Monica looked up at her. "I placed myself in danger and was bitten. It wasn't Flynn's fault."

"Then who bit you?"

"Timothy, of the House of Sabrina. He's dead now."

"Only him? I see two sets of marks and what looks like a cut."

Monica shut her eyes, rendering me blind for the time being. "No, Flynn did, too. He'd been injured and needed my blood to be able to finish the job. This was three days ago and he hasn't made any move to harm me since then."

The room fell silent once more and yet, I could feel the eyes of the Council upon Monica as though they gazed at me instead. Monica lifted her lids once more, in time for us to watch Richard lean forward in his chair. He shook his head. "Monica, I shouldn't need to remind you of this... thing's... sins again. He killed a member of our Council and his first watcher before even being turned."

"In his defense, he was coerced. Sabrina used dark magic. You all know that. I've *told* you that."

Richard eyed her in a stern fashion. "Nevertheless, that doesn't dismiss the fact that he killed them in cold blood. And his deeds as a vampire are legendary. In five short years, he's killed hundreds of humans and countless vampires still acting in accordance with the natural order. The only vampires he *didn't* terrorize are the ones we would've targeted ourselves. The Seattle office has wanted him dead for five years. The only reason why we haven't sent punished him for his atrocities..."

"... Which were likewise influenced..."

"... is because somehow, you convinced your parents..."

"... by Sabrina. Dark magic, Richard. I swear to you he..."

"*He is without excuse.*"

The outburst shocked Monica into silence.

"Your parents have been informed of the situation. They lifted their hand of restraint." Richard frowned in a paternal manner. "Child, will it take being drained to death for you to see what this creature is? I know you want to think the best of him and I know the promise you made to your sister, but this Council has never bound you to the soul of Peter Dawes."

"I've done this of my own free will," Monica murmured defiantly. "And I'll continue doing it, even if it means being removed from the Order."

"It might come to that."

Monica stared down Richard. "Please don't do this. Not when we've come so far." She lifted her hands, as though presenting an offering to the six people who would decide our fate. "I know you think it's the right thing to do, but you haven't worked with Flynn like I have for the past few weeks. In that time, I've seen a sociopath become a penitent. He is a determined seer, Richard. That, in and of itself, is a miracle. Yes, I defied the Order in bringing out his powers. And, yes, the catastrophe that caused was terrible, but Peter's spirit has been restored and all that mess has been cleaned up... *by him*. He has a conscience and has used that conscience increasingly since getting it back. What more does he need to do?"

Richard sighed. "Our orders come from the High Council, Monica. They don't see him being worth the risk. He possesses enough power to become one of our worst enemies if we don't do something about it right now." He paused. "And I agree with them. Our minds are made up and the vote in both Seattle and London was unanimous."

He drew a deep breath inward, before nodding. "It is the decision of this council that you be arrested and stripped of your abilities. We further rule that the vampire Flynn, formerly known as Peter Dawes, is to be turned into the Order and executed. We make this decision in accordance with our solemn oaths, and for the protection of the human race.

"May The Fates have mercy on his soul."

SPECIAL THANKS

FLYNN'S LISTS FOR SUPREMELY SANGUINE SORTS

"Favored Prey"
Brandee Crisp

"More Than A Snack"
Leslie Kisler
Heather Watson

IN ACKNOWLEDGEMENT

As I'm sure the more astute of you have gathered, there is no Peter Dawes. (Though telling him that is often a matter of intense debate and always amusing to witness if you happen to see it.) I'm not the only one behind this madness; there exists an entire group of people who have contributed to the delinquency of this author. Thus, I thought it fitting to cast a smile in their direction.

Peter was born one evening as I sat in my office wrestling with a comic series and its accompanying set of novels. I found myself so disenchanted with the third book, I opened a blank document in Microsoft Word and begged the literary gods for some stroke of genius. They gave me a man who had committed a murder, and although I questioned it at the time, the further I delved into the piece, the more I learned about him. His girlfriend uttered his name with her dying breaths and he fell into the hands of an ambitious vampire mistress at the end of the scene. That very first piece is now Chapter One of this book.

Five years later, he's still with me, in a collection of novels, short stories, and daydreams that have slowly and methodically made their way onto paper. As such, I only thought it fitting my very first hat tip should go to you, Peter. You've been an amazing accomplice so far and I can't wait to show the world the further exploits you have in store for them. Let's give them hell, seer.

The list of co-conspirators grows from there. There are the first brave souls who read earlier drafts and fell in love with the characters. (Even begged me to bring one back to life.) There are allies who stood behind my right to pen whatever I pleased, even if the content was unsavory to some. There are the Sisters in Ink, who have constantly supported me throughout the years and revisions made to this tale. Don't be surprised if some of you make the occasional cameo in these books.

There are the myriad of fans I've shaken hands with at conventions, who gave me the courage to continue believing. There are the host of detractors who attempted to censor me, and the God who never let the world break me, even if I felt sorely bent at times.

To my mother, I say... Look, I finally have one finished! Here's to hoping for two and three and fifteen. (And perhaps a coin or two in my pocket to show for my trouble.)

To my younger brother, I say... The reason why I know what the love of a brother looks like – the very reason I can depict it – is because of you.

And to my muse, I say... I may be your Poet, but you are indeed my Maestro. If I had the vocabulary to capture how grateful I am for all the things you've done and continue doing for me, I'd pen a hundred tomes and yet not scratch the surface. As I lack the words, I'll simply say... Thank you. This is our world, our dream, and our future. And I am the happiest person on the planet in being able to share it with you.

I love you with all of my being.

I am a blessed fool for having all of you, friends and enemies, admirers and naysayers. You never truly know you can do something until somebody says you can't. Then you set your sights to the stars, grin and say, "Just watch me."

June 1, 2011

Keep reading for a preview of

Rebirth of the Seer
Book Two of The Vampire Flynn Trilogy

PROLOGUE

From the first moment I laid eyes on him, I knew I was going to murder him. And I wished it to be a particularly bloody death.

While the statement could be called prophetic, I was certain of this only because I knew myself. He regarded me with skepticism as I entered his shop, making him more astute than most, and the wiser tended to meet a swifter demise than even my normal playthings. Still, I ignored the short, Asian man as he tracked my progress, knitting my hands behind my back and allowing my eyes to scan from one shelf to the next. Each piece – from the short swords to the eclectic collection of daggers – was a masterful work of art, but none held my attention more than the katanas. I drifted toward them as if being summoned.

"Can I help you, sir?" he flatly asked.

I stole a grin at the increased tempo of his pulse. "No, I am merely browsing," I replied. My focus was already locked on the Japanese steel as I became lost in admiration. I could not remember what compelled me into the store; I already possessed an arsenal back at the coven, all utilized with skill and precision. I plunged each sword and dagger into human and vampire alike, licking the blades clean as I conducted the dark orchestra which was my life in Philadelphia. They were more than instruments of death to me. They were trusted confidantes who made up the short list of friends I had as an assassin. Perhaps why I felt inclined to add another to my collection.

My blue eyes scanned each katana from behind the protection of sunglasses. "Very fine blades you have here," I said, breaking the silence. "The hands which crafted them are quite talented."

The man emerged from behind the counter, compelled by my compliment. As he walked toward me, I mused on the mortal ego, wondering if such fragile creatures knew how often it was their Achilles heel. '*Should have stayed with your initial assessment,*' I admonished within my thoughts. He folded his arms in front of his chest, failing to notice my smirk as his eyes surveyed his wares. "The knives and other weapons are shipped in from Japan, but these –" He nodded at the display. "– I made myself."

"You are truly gifted." I followed his gaze to the wall. Once more, the siren song of steel held me hostage and I plucked a sword from the first shelf. My eyes ran along its exterior once before I spared the craftsman a quick glance. "I trust you do not mind."

"Not at all," he said, but my attention had already returned to the weapon I cradled in my hands. My gaze strayed to a set of kanji which had been painted in gold under the picture of a dragon.

"What does it say?" I asked.

"It is a blessing to the warrior who uses it."

"Fascinating." Taking hold of the sword's hilt, I tugged the sheath off with all the reverence of an acolyte handling a sacred text. It slid free with perfect resistance and its steel shimmered in the light once exposed to view. My voice lowered in awe. "Masterful, indeed." I placed the lacquered wood onto an adjacent counter and flicked a finger across its edge to test its sharpness. Raising the sword, I shut one eye and peered down the length of its blade. "Who taught you your craft?"

"I learned from a master. He made me his apprentice because he believed it was my calling." In my periphery, I saw him nod. "For many years, I studied, until I was told where The Fates wanted me to go."

"And The Fates wished you to grace Philadelphia with your talent?" I looked at him and perked an eyebrow.

He smiled. "They have mysterious ways."

"Apparently." Sheathing the sword, I placed it back on the shelf and continued to the next one. While I did not reach for it, I paused to admire it and gave the other pieces a proper amount of deference before progressing up the shelves. I did not pull any of them down, though. Not until I saw the one destined to be mine.

My hands reached for it slowly, as if afraid to do my new friend harm. "This one is... astonishing," I said, breaking a brief quiet which had settled between us. Wonder painted itself across my countenance. I studied the piece, eyes fixed first on the red and black weaving which adorned the hilt. The sheath itself was fully black, save but for a red braid tied close to a polished brass tsuba. The hand guard was etched with the two halves of a yin-yang. I slid the sheath off with more than a trifle amount of haste, eager to examine the blade. "And just as I thought I owned the finest pieces of steel ever crafted, I come upon this sword."

The man hesitated. I held the weapon out in front of me to peer down its sharpened edge, ignoring him. It was as though it had been made for me – the hilt rested perfectly in the palm of my hand, with just the right balance, and the blade length could not have been more tailored to my height. When I swung it to the side, I felt it cut through the air as though it could rend the very atoms of the wind.

"I wish to procure this one," I said, my eyes shifting back to the shop owner.

He swallowed hard. The amount of pause between my question and his response was enough to ignite the beginning embers of my impatience. "I can't sell it," he said, his voice demur.

"I beg your pardon?"

His gaze shot first to the sword, then back to me. Clearing his throat, the shop owner spoke again, this time with more confidence; even if he knew his words would displease me. "This... is part of my personal collection. It was made to be given to the right person, and I don't think you are that person."

Our eyes met in a seconds-long stalemate before a laugh bubbled up from my throat at the incredulousness of his comment. It warred with the fire I felt churning in my chest. "You do not think I am that person? Well, is that not precious? Please, explain how I am not worthy of this weapon, sir."

He sighed. "There are elements in this sword I haven't used in any other. The Fates themselves... commissioned it. They gave me the instructions for it in a dream. I saw its owner as somebody with a different heart, a warrior with a different spirit. You are not that warrior." ·

'*Oh, this simply is too delicious.*' My lips spread in a menacing smile, the gaze behind my dark sunglasses turning sinister as I allowed my fangs to slip from their slumber. Stalking forward, I moved like a cat inching toward its prey. "Not that warrior? And what sort of warrior did you have in mind? A champion or a savior, perhaps? Maybe one destined to save the world of evils such as me."

The man stumbled backward, fear written on his face as I swung his precious sword around with a capricious air. "I am a killer, but you already knew this, I am assuming, for you claimed to know the heart of he who stands before you. I drain the lives of you wretched beings and bathe in rivers of blood Elizabeth Bathory could not have imagined in her most twisted fantasies. I am the devil himself. Then again, you knew this, too."

"Yes." The word floated past his lips weakly, which only served to excite me more. "Fates, it is you. I have seen you in my dreams, you are the demon who –"

With a quick thrust of the sword, I impaled him through the stomach, the momentum of the weapon continuing until it severed his spinal column. I smirked. "The one who shall end your life?" I asked. Twisting the blade, I laughed in a much more sadistic manner, watching his eyes widen, knowing his knees would fail him soon. Crimson trickled from the wound I inflicted, which whetted my desire to see more. "Consider your dreams prophetic and me your angel of death."

Extracting the blade, I flicked it to the side and watched him crumple to the ground.

The sight of his blood splattered across the wall provoked a gasp from another being's lips, drawing my eyes to its source. My tongue slid across my fangs as I lowered my sword, drinking in the sight of a frightened Asian woman I assumed was kith and kin to the swordsmith. Tears brimmed in her eyes. Her small hands rose to cover her gaping mouth. "Madame, allow me to make your acquaintance," I said, bowing with a flourish and keeping my eyes fixed on her. "My name is Flynn, and you have the honor of being my second victim for the evening."

Whether or not she understood what I said, she heard the tone of my voice clear enough to interpret my intent. Her black hair swept around her shoulder as she turned, dashing for a room in the back of the shop while leaving the door ajar. I leaped over the counter separating us, moving far faster. Before she was able to reach the exit, I had an arm wrapped around her torso and her back pressed against my body. She let out a surprised yelp.

I drew in a deep breath. Her exotic scent overwhelmed me, teasing me with the temptation to make her more than a meal. My fangs ached for purchase on her skin, though, and could not be ignored. Lips grazing her ear, I hummed and whispered, "Relax, my dear, and embrace death." I plunged my fangs into her neck and drank deeply, savoring her with each mouthful I imbibed.

Her blood was warm and her taste just as tantalizing as her scent. Within moments, her heart ceased beating and she fell to my feet, just another notch on an already long belt. I shut my eyes while wiping her remnant from my mouth and savored the afterglow. "Of all the mortals I have consumed, you were one of the more delightful ones." Opening my eyes, I peered down at her. "Join your husband in the afterlife."

As I turned around, I clutched my new companion in one hand, feeling a connection form between man and weapon. The swordsmith's words resonated in my thoughts, provoking a scoff at his insistence I was not meant to own it. I had it now, did I not? And I intended to put it to good use.

Some days later, I became ensnared in my own date with destiny. Even as I confronted my vampire nature and my mortal side rose once more to claim its fate, the sword remained by my side. The bloody coincidences of The Fates; I had only begun walking the path, but even then I knew I would never understand them.

Especially when they nearly took my watcher from me.

CHAPTER ONE

"Don't do this, Richard!" she yelled. Her voice reverberated from the walls of the meeting hall, seemingly preventing the elders from issuing a response. I sensed frustration overwhelming her and frowned. Now was not the time for Monica to become indignant.

"Get the devil out of there, woman," I muttered from where I stood, outside the abandoned church whose sanctuary was being used as a place of reckoning. The perfect guise for a covert organization, if I had to be honest. The grounds were surrounded by an ivy-choked wrought iron fence, the area poorly lit to discourage passersby from trespassing. I felt an undercurrent running through the very earth itself, as though spirits could pass through dirt and mark an area sacred. Incantations, no doubt. It made me the sole irreverent creature digging my feet into hallowed ground.

Indulging in a deep, steadying breath, I stopped myself from projecting the thought of caution to my watcher. Instead, I shut my eyes. My powers skipped between us, linking my mind to hers and making her eyes available to witness that which my vampire hearing was already eavesdropping on. A Council of the Supernatural Order sat before her, six elders who had already made their ruling.

"It is the decision of this Council that you be arrested and stripped of your abilities. We further rule that the vampire named Flynn, formerly known as Peter Dawes, is to be turned in to the Order and executed. We make this decision in accordance with our solemn oaths, and for the protection of the human race.

"May The Fates have mercy on his soul."

Such is why I wished her to flee to safety. She had been cordial, if a bit flustered, up to this point, but now it seemed she had been incited past courtesy. I could almost see her green eyes blazing fury, a deliberate stare settling on each narrow-minded man and woman seated before her while her gloved hands balled into fists. Petite – nearly to the point of emaciation – and yet weak from being drained of blood a few days prior, the girl dressed in black possessed enough attitude to make her a force with which to be reckoned.

Put another way, she was a rather pissed off sorceress.

"When I came to this Council four years ago," she said, her attention fixed on the middle-aged man who had issued my condemnation, "I concealed my intentions for exactly this reason. The minute I came clean about what I've been doing, I've encountered nothing but resistance and I'm beginning to think Flynn's past has nothing to do with this."

Richard scowled, his gaze that of a schoolmaster beholding a recalcitrant student. "It has everything to do with his past. Watch your tongue with me, Miss Alexander. You've lost sight of your place and we're not going to tolerate it, regardless of who your parents are."

"Bullshit. I've told you this all happened for a reason, Richard. I told you that while it was a gross oversight of this Council to allow a seer to slip through the cracks in the first place, we can't pretend it didn't happen. You told me if I could prove The Fates intended for a vampire-seer to go on living, you'd hear me out."

"So far, we've yet to hear any such proof," one of the female elders said. Monica's eyes darted to the speaker – Beverly – entering the discussion again.

Monica laughed. "You were the one that told me the day we got Peter Dawes back would be the day hell froze over.

"And as far as we're concerned, that has yet to happen." Beverly raised an eyebrow. "All we have is an unstable vampire on the loose and this time, he's a supernaturally-gifted one, thanks to you."

Monica shook her head. I heard the response she wished to administer clamoring in her mind, but she bridled her tongue. "Lydia said he has other duties to fulfill."

"Duties?" asked another elder – a blonde-haired man who looked to be Richard's junior by several years. "What's this about Lydia?"

Her attention shifted to the new speaker. Reading her thoughts, I could just imagine the smirk Monica forced herself to suppress straining at the corners of her mouth. As such, I grinned for her sake while raising my cigarette to my lips. I drew deeply, exhaling a puff of smoke through my nose as I mused on the card she had yet to play, a final plea I knew might be our last hand in reasoning with these daft creatures. I interrupted this time, sending a message through the telepathic channel we shared.

'*If this does not work, get the bloody hell out of there. I do not give a shit what we discussed last night.*'

I sensed her brush aside my words. Last night's admonition lay implied between the lines, provoking me to frown.

Her focus returned to the man. "Lewis, a few nights ago Flynn received a communication from The Fates through Lydia. She said he has more trials ahead of him." Monica paused to sigh, her next words grave. "You can't forget the fact his powers were identified before he even realized them. Consider Lydia's warning on top of it and your decision leaves us with a huge paradox. Everything has a balance. If there's a seer like Flynn, then there's something just as formidable out there waiting for him."

I perked an eyebrow, wondering what she meant by that, but seemed to be the only one intrigued by her statement. Everyone else gazed back at her in a stoic manner. Not wanting the silence to linger, Monica moved to continue. "And with a little official training, he'll be ready for –"

Richard cut her off. "Are you finished yet?"

I could nearly feel the weight depositing itself upon her shoulders. "You haven't been listening to a word –"

"If the guards could please escort Miss Alexander to the holding room? I think we've had enough."

Monica gasped. Her voice rushed into my head, panic-stricken. '*Get away from here, Flynn!*' The sound of a door opening produced an eerie echo inside the hall and Monica forced me from her perceptions as though shoving me away.

I scowled. '*Oh no,*' I said. '*No, no, we shall not be having this. Not so long as I can do something about it, witch.*' I blinked twice, adjusting to using my own sight once more, and flicked my cigarette away. My thoughts spiraled, trying to form a coherent plan in the midst of so much chaos. I peered at the converted church before me and one notion finally broke through, an idea which presented the best impromptu plan I could conjure.

"And to think I used to pride myself on this sort of thing," I muttered, running my fingers through my hair. "Fucking humans, forcing my hand." Indulging in a steadying breath, I paused to clear my mind. A distinct portion of me knew I deserved the Council's pronouncement; indeed, heaven itself would have crushed me under the weight of my sins if I tried to deny it. The truth of things became apparent to me, however, as I surveyed the building I was about to vandalize.

I was not merely being condemned for my transgressions. The Supernatural Order despised me most because I was a vampire, plain and simple. I could have ascertained as such from a quick scan of their thoughts, but their arguments spoke volumes in their own right. It was not that I had been a murderous bastard, or that I had done the bidding of a power-hungry vampiress, both accusations toward which I would have to plead guilty. They despised that an immortal possessed their coveted secrets. Wore the mantle of a seer. Had used his talents to slay mortals for the sake of sating his bloodlust before repenting of his actions. Everything said in my defense fell on deaf ears, just as Monica had feared.

I was not about to continue forward without the one being on this mortal coil I could call a friend.

My eyes narrowed, sight fixed on a stained glass window. Images of serpents in the Garden of Eden stared back at me, not issuing any protest. I nodded, resolute, and paused to tighten the katana fastened at my side while putting distance between me and the church. With a final adjustment to the dark sunglasses protecting my sensitive vision, I crouched low. "Here goes nothing," I said to myself. The night fell to a hush for a split second before I launched forward, dashing for my target.

Reckless abandon marked every extension of my legs, each pump of my arms until I leaped into the air. With my vampire strength behind the follow-through, I kicked the window with such force it exploded into a thousand colorful and crystalline pieces. They descended with me in a glorious baptism of glass that landed on the jacket of my black suit when my feet hit the floor. Dusting the shards from my shoulders in apathetic manner, I glanced upward at the panel of mortals I had previously beheld through borrowed eyes.

They all stared back. Loathe emanated from their eyes once they realized who I was. I detected a hint of fear as well, which curled the corner of my mouth into a wicked grin. '*Good,*' I thought. '*Let them be uneasy at seeing the condemned present before them.*' Strolling forward, I stole a moment to admire the polished wood floor and lingered on the ornate remnants of the church this had been before turning my attention back to them.

'*Little more than scared humans. Which hardly makes you so high above me.*'

"My apologies for the sudden entrance," I said, well aware they might have been reading my thoughts and caring little if they did, "I hardly thought it fitting for there to be a trial without the defendant, though. If I have breached some form of etiquette, I trust you shall inform me."

"Damn it, Flynn, I told you to get away from here."

My gaze drifted toward Monica, spying two men standing behind her and blocking the closest exit. While they did not have her in their clutches, I could tell I entered just before she had been manhandled. "Now, my dear —" I paused halfway through the room to smile at her, despite the figurative flames of wrath shooting from her eyes. "— Surely it is bad luck to damn the damned. Besides, I am certain they wished me here inevitably, do you not agree?"

Monica had no chance to respond. I turned to regard the others before she could so much as open her mouth. "Good evening, ladies and gentlemen. I understand I have vexed you all in some manner or another."

Richard straightened in his chair, his posture turning rigid. "The Vampire Flynn," he said. His voice took on an authoritative tone. "I must say, I'm surprised. I figured you'd be far away from here by now."

"I am certain cowards such as you think the rest of the world acts in kind, but such is not the case." Advancing again, I closed the distance between me and the elders, stopping a few yards away from where they sat. I adjusted my tailored suit jacket, prompting some of the lingering glass shards to fall to the ground, and allowed my hands to drop to my sides. "A person wiser and fairer than me cautioned me to avoid these proceedings. I fear I have disappointed her."

My eyes found Monica once more. Time seemed to halt for half a second, long enough for me to remember our conversation from the night before. "*If they threaten action against us,*" she had said, "*I want you to get as far away from here as possible, with whatever you can carry on your back. Don't come for me, just go.*"

"My apologies," I said with a frown, "But I could not have them condemn you in my stead. If I am to fulfill my destiny, I shall not do so without your oversight."

She mirrored my frown, but did not answer. My attention shifted back to Richard while I squared my shoulders and stared intently at the Council elder. "So tell me, Richard, why is it that a death warrant has been issued against me? I wish to know what limited imagination you humans possess."

Richard glared, but held fast to his composure. "I doubt I have to remind you of your sins, Mr. Dawes. You are condemned by the —"

I held up a hand, stopping Richard. "You would do well to place that name back on the shelf. I might not be an assassin any longer, but I am no Peter Dawes. Flynn is the one you should be prosecuting."

"Very well." Richard cleared his throat and visibly regrouped. "Vampire Flynn, you are condemned by the Supernatural Order for multiple offenses. For murdering a watcher and a Council elder while you were still a human. For slaughtering hundreds of souls within the space of five short years. And for using the gifts of a seer – gifts to be taken with gravity and decorum – for your wanton gain."

"And if this was where the story ended, I would save you the trouble and throw myself upon my sword as retribution." I perked an eyebrow at him. "I have reformed my ways, though. Miss Alexander attempted to explain this and informed you I have been commissioned by The Fates to continue walking this path. Besides, the murder of Lydia Davies and her advisor was coerced from me by my former mistress."

"So you claim."

"No, I assert. My actions were my own when I murdered as a vampire, however. You see, this is what I find amusing." I paused to chuckle, knitting my hands pensively behind my back while my feet commenced to pacing. I looked first toward the ground, then back to the human council. "The lot of you only imagines my atrocities while I relive them each time I pause to consider what brought me here. I orchestrated things you dared not even fathom. Embodied sadism your underdeveloped creativity could not grasp. If you truly knew the monster I am you would not be looking down upon me with such smugness."

"This is supposed to change our minds about you?" Beverly asked, interjecting.

I flashed my most disarming grin. "Not in the slightest, my dear." The curl of my lips evened to a more sober expression. "What should affect your decision, however, is the fact that a killer such as I has proven capable of reform. If my repentance has not been enough to convince you otherwise, then you are still left with the charge given to me by Miss Davies. I failed her once. I do not wish to fail her again."

Richard scoffed. "It doesn't matter and, quite frankly, I don't believe it. You're to be put to death and your watcher punished for setting loose this whole circus in the first place."

"She only brought out that which would have emerged naturally. And because she did, I had not yet passed the point of no return. Your qualm is with me, not Monica."

"It's with both of you."

"Come now, Richard." I smiled with no small amount of teeth being presented in the action. "Surely even Neanderthals such as you can recognize an innocent when presented one."

Richard clenched his jaw. "You'll do well not to smile in my presence, demon."

I blurted out a hearty chuckle before it could be suppressed. "Ah, you see? There it is." Spreading my arms out to my sides, I bowed slightly at the waist. "What is it, Richard? Do you see my fangs? Do you grow loathe to consider this 'demon' is in possession of such great power? Well, these gifts are mine, as is my mission, and I shall not be deterred."

My arms lowered to my sides. I straightened my posture and pivoted to face Monica. "Our business with them is through," I said. "Let us be on our way."

"You'll do no such thing."

I ignored Richard and began a tempered walk toward Monica. She motioned forward, but so did the men standing behind her. They closed the distance and apprehended her before I could reach where she stood. She tensed at the sudden feeling of two sets of hands taking hold of her and gave a spirited buck against their grip. "Let me go, damn it."

I stopped when our eyes met. Their hold on her tightened. "Now, gentlemen," I said, pushing back the fabric of my jacket and brushing my fingers across the hilt of my sword. "I suggest you do as she says before I become fidgety. I can assure you an angry and armed vampire is not a positive combination."

"Don't listen to him," Richard said, commanding the room's attention once again. He stood, looking first at the bodyguards before casting his sights on me. "Your weapons are useless here."

"We shall see how bloody useless they are in a moment." My gaze shifted back to the guards. "Come now, or have you forgotten already? Angry and armed vampire? Release her so we can be on our way."

"Flynn, just get out of here," Monica said, her eyes projecting an urgency bordering on panic. "Hurry."

"Nonsense. If they wish a confrontation, I shall be more than happy to obl–"

My words ceased at once, interrupted by a peculiar sound which echoed throughout the meeting hall with an ominous overtone. My already-tepid blood turned cold as I looked back toward the source of the noise. Richard's eyes were fixed upon me, his hands steepled and wrists bent as if he had just finished cracking his knuckles.

The implication of this action barely registered before every other Council member stood and did the same. Their gazes all took on the same severe look and a shiver afflicted me from head to toe. Magic. It filled the air like quicksand with me sinking in the epicenter. Richard raised a hand and pointed his palm in my direction. Unintelligible words spilled from his lips, droning with the cadence of an incantation. The room closed in around me; I had been struck dumb while a flurry of anxiety passed through my bones.

It brought out a sneer of self-disgust. "Oh fuck your magical bullshit, Richard."

I pushed aside the fledgling intimidation they had inspired. With one swift, practiced motion, I drew my sword. Richard's eyes widened as I ran for him, my pace too fast for any of the others to come to his aid. I leaped for him when close enough, cutting off his spell with a soundly-placed kick aimed square for his chest that laid him out on the floor. Turning to face the other members, my adversaries glared back at me; two women and three men.

"Ladies and gentlemen," I said through gritted teeth. "I shall offer you a mercy I would have never offered a human when I was yet an assassin. This is your final chance to back down and allow me and my watcher to leave without your interference. I promise you I shall inflict grave injury upon you otherwise."

One of the women – one I recalled being called Joan – snickered. I shifted my focus toward her, but her hands flew up before I could do anything. An invisible force impacted me and sent me flying onto the ground. My back hit first, followed by my head bouncing from the unforgiving floor. I groaned involuntarily when a jolt of pain sent my vision to swimming for a brief moment.

"I'd like to see you try," she said.

"Bloody fucking hell." Quickly, I stood, ignoring the ache which radiated from head to back in favor of readying myself for their next onslaught. '*Ah, but I am hardly one for being on the defensive,*' I thought, a smirk accompanying the slow descent of my fangs. '*No, I much prefer dominating these sorts of games.*'

A growl rumbled from my throat. I dashed for Joan, who lifted her hands again, but fumbled for words as I closed in on her. I drove my hand into her windpipe, and then crouched as she fought against a temporary impediment to her breathing. The dull edge of my katana impacted her knees from behind as I swept around her, all one fluid motion which ended with her landing on the floor and me springing back into a stand.

I sneered. "You best be fucking grateful you are not dealing with my former self."

One of the other elders – a tall man with jet black hair – stepped forward as Joan fell, drawing my focus over to him. I raised an arm to block an attempted punch, and answered with a kick to his chest. As he toppled, I turned and countered another advance from another elder who had remained quiet up to this point. He fell when I swept his legs out from under him. My mental tally ticked to four, with one final male elder – the blond-haired Lewis – the last man standing between me and Monica. I managed one step forward before a harrowing premonition overwhelmed me, compelling me to spin around and glance at the ground behind me.

Richard stumbled to his feet some distance away. I watched his lips move and knew what he meant to continue.

'*Flynn, stop him!*'

"Damn it to hell," I muttered. Monica's voice still reverberated in my thoughts as I floundered for what to do. The lost moment cost me dearly. The ignored-Lewis spoke and in the time it took for me to begin to turn, he lifted his hands and ceased my attempt to face him. Whatever mental ability he used to place a lock on me kept me tethered in position, giving him the advantage.

My katana involuntarily dropped from my grip. My knees began buckling, threatening to drive me to the floor, but I struggled against it, clenching my jaw in concentration while indulging in a steadying breath. My thoughts spun wild with potential solutions, panic threatening to paralyze me. Monica telepathically spoke to me again. '*Fight against it, Flynn,*' she said. '*Remember, you're just as powerful as they are. This is just textbook telekinesis and I bet you can break free of it.*'

'*Telekinesis?*' I wrestled with the urge to ask what sort of textbook contained such a lesson and opened my eyes, not realizing I had closed them in the first place. '*How? You make it sound so bloody simple.*'

'*'Cause it is. Now hurry up, we're running out of time.*'

'*Oh yes, Mistress. At once.*' I filled my lungs again and exhaled the breath slowly, calming my nerves while tapping into that part of me which read minds and sifted through intentions. '*You are a seer,*' I told myself. '*About bloody time you started acting like one.*'

Immediately, it was as though a switch flicked on inside of me. A sinister grin crept across my mouth as I felt the lock upon me relent, the influence of my adversary buckling the harder I focused on my gifts. Directing the assault back onto Lewis, I thrust myself into his thoughts and forced him away from mine with increasing – albeit surprising – success. I could almost see him pale when I freed my limbs and made certain he knew how vexed he had made me when I turned to face him. "Lewis, Lewis, Lewis," I said, wagging my finger at him. "I might be ignorant, but I am a quick study."

I left him no time to counter. Raising my hand as I had seen the others do, I felt a bolt of energy run through me and watched the same invisible force which had previously laid me prone shove Lewis onto the floor. When he failed to stand again, I shifted my attention to Richard, realizing belatedly that the cadence of his words had intensified.

Pivoting, I plucked my katana from where it lay and slid it into its sheath while sprinting for the stubborn, judgmental elder. One of the downed women stumbled to her feet, but I sent her crashing back to the floor using my newly-explored telekinesis, not skipping a beat in the action. Continuing my run with all the determination I could muster, I closed the distance between us. But Richard did something first which disconcerted me.

He ceased speaking. And, at once, I knew why.

Richard's spell enclosed me. My running halted to an abrupt stop. This time, the lock enveloping me was far sounder than Lewis's had been, subduing me from head to foot as though my shoes had been nailed to the ground; my arms tied tight against my body. A feeling of helplessness rushed through me, something I attempted hiding as my antagonist advanced on me, murder in his gaze.

'*Shit. Now what, Monica?*

"I'm sure you think you're special," Richard said, adjusting his wool blazer as though it had been violated. "A regular god among men because you've figured out you have a few new handy tricks."

"Well, any assassin shall tell you it never hurts to have an extra dagger up his sleeve." Monica failed to respond. I attempted not to become more troubled.

Richard scowled. "Well, you're not special, Flynn. All you are is evil, and around here, we exterminate your kind."

I stole a glance toward my partner in crime, seeing her struggle against her guards while staring intently at me. Her lips moved, however, and, I realized, not with a covert message. Something about their cadence rang familiar. My eyes shot back to Richard before he realized the same thing I did, and I fought against a grin as I formulated a plot. "Tell me something," I said, "Before you send me to my second death. Would you humor a convicted criminal, Richard?"

He stopped a few feet shy of me and looked up at me skeptically. "Why on Earth would I do that?"

"I want to know how beings such as you think." I tilted my chin, able to do that and nothing else. "You presume yourselves higher than The Fates if you think you can ignore a direct communique from them. You did not put it to the test or evoke whatever fucking charlatan witchcraft you bastards wield to see if we were lying. You automatically discounted us in favor of your own agenda."

"Because I know your kind." With one hand, he unbuttoned his coat, and with the other, he reached inside. "Vampires are devious and incapable of reform."

Something about the motion of his hand unnerved me, but I suppressed the urge to react. "Devious? I suppose so. The duplicity of vampires is rather infamous, but this does not make me a liar by default."

"True or untrue, we're still left with what you are – a killer. I don't care if you think you're reformed now, eventually you'll slip and we'd be right back to where we are." As he pulled his hand out from beneath the veil of fabric, he revealed a wooden stake etched with strange symbols, each bearing an arcane – almost Celtic – quality to it. His fingers tightened around the base. "Your sentence is to be carried out before that happens."

"And here, I thought I was the only one who liked to conceal weapons." I grinned as Richard reared back to administer the death blow. He paused when he caught sight of my fanged smile.

"Look at you, a devil who would smirk all the way to the grave."

My grin broadened. "What good is death without a dance? Though I am hardly the one *you* should be interested in right now."

"Oh really?" Richard laughed. "And who would that be?"

My eyes flicked toward Monica. "Her."

He turned to look at Monica as I heard her say, '*Now, Flynn,*' in my thoughts. My focus divided between the guards, necessity forcing me to the next stage of my lessons. Teeth gritted, I shoved the bodyguards away from Monica so her gloved hands could rise. As everyone floundered to regroup, she finished her spell.

"Be freed!" she said.

Richard's incantation surrendered its hold. I fell to the ground, knees buckling from the sudden need for self-support. Richard spun back around as I stood. Our eyes locked and I felt anger surge. My fingers clenched into a fist and, before I could stop to consider the action, impacted Richard's jaw with the force of my vampire strength behind an untempered blow. Lifting my foot, I kicked his knee with the same amount of vehemence and ignored his wails of agony as he toppled to the floor. I brushed the dust from my suit jacket as I strolled forward. If not for the fact that Monica ran for me, I might have been tempted to drain the elder councilman.

She took hold of my hand and tugged me forward. "Let's get the hell out of here," she said, "Before I completely lose my faith in humanity."

"My sentiments precisely." Together, we walked swiftly toward the opposite end of the meeting hall. We made it halfway to the double doors standing between us and freedom when a voice compelled my watcher to pause. "Don't do it, Monica," Richard said, his speech labored.

Monica's hand tightened around mine as she turned to look at him. Richard met her gaze from his position on the ground. "You leave with him and that's the end of any leniency," he continued. "You'll be hunted right alongside the vampire."

I frowned, trapped in the awkward position of holding hands with a statue. She narrowed her eyes at Richard. "If that's how it has to be, I refuse to leave Flynn."

"And throw your life away? Why? For some pledge you made to your sister?"

"Sister?" I asked, interjecting.

Ignoring me, Monica let go of my hand and marched a few paces toward Richard. "Why should I abandon him? So I can create a self-fulfilling prophecy for you? You'd love to be right, but I'm not going to give you that satisfaction. You do whatever the hell you want."

Monica continued raining curses down on Richard, but something tickled at my subconscious, forcing my attention away. A chilling omen drowned out my watcher's words of condemnation as the air began feeling fifty fathoms deep. I turned my head and perked an eyebrow, trying to discern its source.

The hair on the back of my neck stood aloft. Warning sirens blared inside my mind, frustratingly unspecific in their message. I studied the Council members, seeing them still laid out on the ground as they had been before. All four, besides Richard.

Four. My eyes widened. There had been five others, and I realized this just as the premonition turned more urgent. I swung around and received the largest shock of my immortal life at the sight before me.

"Flynn! Look out!"

Monica's command only froze me in position, rendering me the proverbial deer gazing stupidly into a pair of headlights. Lewis was the one I failed to take into account and, as he dashed toward me, murder clouded his thoughts. In his hand, he held Richard's stake.

'*Fates be damned, I am about to become a pile of dust on the floor.*'

Made in the USA
Charleston, SC
14 July 2012